O9-BUD-912

Ascendant Sun

Tor Books by Catherine Asaro

THE SAGA OF THE SKOLIAN EMPIRE

Primary Invasion

Catch the Lightning

The Last Hawk

The Radiant Seas

Ascendant Sun

*The Quantum Rose**

**forthcoming*

ASCENDANT SUN

CATHERINE ASARO

A TOM DOHERTY ASSOCIATES BOOK
NEW YORK

This is a work of fiction. All the characters and events portrayed in this novel are either fictitious or are used fictitiously.

ASCENDANT SUN

This book is printed on acid-free paper.

Edited by David G. Hartwell

A Tor Book
Published by Tom Doherty Associates, LLC
175 Fifth Avenue
New York, NY 10010

www.tor.com

Tor® is a registered trademark of Tom Doherty Associates, LLC.

ISBN 0-312-86824-3

First Edition: March 2000

Printed in the United States of America

0 9 8 7 6 5 4 3 2 1

In honor of family:

To my siblings, in order of age

Frank Nicolo Asaro
Antonina Marie Smith (née Asaro)
Marianne Francis Lee (née Asaro)

and always to our parents
Lucille and Frank Asaro

with love

Contents

Acknowledgments

I would like to thank the following readers for their much-appreciated input. Their comments have made this a better book. Any mistakes that remain are my own.

To my uncle, Jack Scudder, for giving me the benefit of his naval background; to Mary Jo Putney for her excellent insights; to my rocket scientist brother-in-law, Louis Cannizzo, for lending me his smarts on structural materials; to Alan Smale of NASA's Goddard Space Flight Center, for his careful reading; to all the folks on Laurie Gold's AAR listserv for blurb brainstorming; to Frances and Norm Miller, Leslie Haig, Martha Midgetter, and the rest of the Washington Independent Writers; and to Aly's Workshop: Aly Parsons, Simcha Kuritzky, Connie Warner, Al Carroll, Paula Jordon, Michael La Violette, George Williams, and J. G. Huckenpöhler.

Special thanks to my editors, Jim Minz and David Hartwell, my publisher, Tom Doherty, the folks in production for their work on all my books, and the many other fine people at Tor and St. Martin's Press who made this book possible; to my agent, Eleanor Wood, for her work and sharp insights into the book; and to Nancy Berland and her associates for their enthusiasm and hard work on my behalf.

A heartfelt thanks to the shining lights in my life: my husband, John Cannizzo, and my daughter, Cathy, for their love and support.

1

Edgewhirl

Eighteen years after Kelric died, he came home.

The *Holly Rotor,* his star schooner, limped into port near the city of Porthaven, an isolated metropolis on the planet Edgewhirl. Kelric felt both tired and jubilant. His fatigue came from more than the days he had spent on board this starship with minimal supplies. Although he looked healthy, within his body he bore the effects of eighteen years on a planet that wasn't his own. His internal systems had long ago begun a slow breakdown.

Right now even that didn't matter. He was coming home. *Home.* His life would be his again. He would resume his position among his people. Most important, he would see his parents and siblings, the family he loved.

Deep in his pilot's seat, with its frayed exoskeleton folded around his body, he guided the groaning schooner into its berth. His comm crackled again, but he still couldn't make out the words buried in the static. Amber warning lights glowed on the panels arrayed around his seat. When docking clamps gripped the schooner, its hull shook.

A line of 3-D hieroglyphs formed above the speckled screen in front of him. The height and width of the glyphs conveyed a message from the Port Authority: **Docking complete. Sending fee schedule.** Their third dimension added nuances: the PA wanted payment *now.*

Their attitude troubled Kelric. Why the rush? And why didn't they ask for his ID? They hadn't even requested a government code for the ship. It didn't bode well; in his time, it was unheard-of for a PA to be so lax.

He sent access codes for the *Holly*'s credit line. Eighteen years ago it would easily have rented this cheap berth and bought some repairs. The schooner had been on Coba even longer than Kelric, sitting in an abandoned port. Despite some automated upkeep, its condition was worn. Repair costs had probably increased, but the credit line had a good cushion built into it.

The fee schedule appeared.

Kelric stared at the screen. He didn't even have enough to *land,* let alone rent a berth. Repairs were out of the question.

The console beeped. Funds insufficient. Please transmit an alternate access code.

Neither the audio nor visual system on the schooner worked. So he typed at the antiquated keyboard: *I don't have an alternate code.*

How do you plan to pay your bill? the PA inquired.

This vessel is in military use. ISC will cover the fees.

That option is no longer available. The PA shaded its glyphs with impatience.

Kelric blinked. Imperial Space Command no longer covered its officers? He found that hard to believe. *Contact ISC.*

They have no representative available to contact about financial matters associated with this port.

Why not?

Unknown.

How could it be unknown? ISC was—or had been—the single most powerful force in Skolian life. Now he couldn't get enough credit to dock one old schooner? He had taken this ship from the planet Coba, where he had been imprisoned these past eighteen years while the rest of humanity believed him dead. As an ISC officer, he had the right to commandeer government property during an emergency. The schooner had made it possible for him to escape a war. Now, though, he wondered if he was landing in an even worse situation. He began to question the wisdom of revealing anything about himself.

What work options are available? he asked.

Unemployment in Porthaven is at 58 percent, the PA answered. **Nor is a work contract likely to provide sufficient revenue to meet your obligation.** Its nuances said he had less chance than an ice cube in hell of finding a job that would pay off his debt.

What about a loan?

We are willing to take your ship in lieu of payment. Do you consent?

Scowling, he almost refused. But what else could he offer? At least if he signed the ship over to the Edgewhirl PA, they would be responsible for its repairs. He debated options with himself, but in the end he answered, simply: *Yes.*

Dazed and tired, Kelric walked along the starport concourse with everything he owned—his clothes. His suede trousers and white silk shirt were hand-tailored, of the highest quality, but wrinkles creased the fabric and scorch marks darkened his sleeves. His slight limp had been with him for eighteen years. He walked in bare feet. He had nothing else to his name.

Except his gold and gems.

Heavy gold guards circled his wrists and ankles, the metal engraved in a language no one spoke anymore. The guards were old. Ancient. So were the gold bands under his shirt, on his biceps, six on one arm, five on the other. Eighteen years ago the guards and bands would have summoned a fortune, more for their archaeological value than for the gold.

The innocuous pouch hanging from his belt contained dice. But no ordinary dice. Diamonds, rubies, emeralds, sapphires, opals, more: it held a glittering rainbow of wealth. Their worth didn't lie so much in rarity; perfect gems could easily be made, using molecular assemblers to place atoms in crystal lattices. The value of these came from their authenticity. They had been formed by eons of geological processes, rather than in a lab, and they were almost flawless. It gave them a worth well beyond their mundane synthetic counterparts.

He had no idea of the current value for his riches, but it made no difference. He never intended to sell them. They were his only link to the wife and children he had been forced to leave on Coba, the family he would never again see.

So he continued along the wide, vaulted concourse. People thronged the area, a bustling, shoving, humming crowd. For the first time in eighteen years, he walked free. No guards watched him. No one tried to stop him. No political powers controlled his actions. Despite his towering height, massive build, bare feet, scorched clothes, and gold metallic coloring, no one spared him a second glance.

He soon saw why.

Edgewhirl was a small, backwater planet, yet citizens from all over the Skolian Imperialate crammed its port. Within that vast, varied, throng, he simply didn't stand out.

Then he saw them: a group of young people wearing overalls with the insignia of the Allied Worlds of Earth on their shoulders. Stunned, he looked around, trying to clear his mind and concentrate. Now that he paid more attention, he saw them everywhere, citizens from the Allied Worlds freely mixing with his people, the Skolians.

In his time the visas and permissions required for Allied citizens to visit Skolian worlds had been so extensive, it kept out most of them. Now Allieds were everywhere, not only civilians, but military personnel as well. What power shifts had taken place? His unease increased. His family exerted—or had exerted—a great deal of influence within the hierarchy of Skolian power. If the political situation had changed, what did that bode for him?

He became aware of someone behind him. A hand was closing around his pouch. Before his mind fully registered what was happening, his body toggled into combat mode. He whirled around with enhanced reflexes and punched the chest of the man trying to rob him. No, not man. Youth. Lanky and ragged, the boy was about nineteen, with straggly brown hair.

It didn't matter that Kelric's internal biomech systems were damaged. His hydraulics still had enough control over his body to respond to commands from the computer node implanted in his spine. Even with his enhancements at diminished power, he had twice the normal human strength and reflex speed.

Fortunately his node worked well enough to moderate his response so it fit the situation. He only knocked the thief away, into a group of startled tourists. The boy stumbled backward, scattering people, and thudded into a column. He slid down the column until he was sitting on the ground. The young man stared up at Kelric, his face turning as pale as a trapped snow-ferret.

Kelric blinked. Then he turned on his heel. A ring of onlookers had formed, but they jumped out of his path now. He stalked away, angry at himself for causing the scene. Had he been in better condition, he wouldn't have struck the boy. Just turning around fast would have been enough. He hoped the thief didn't go to the authorities claiming assault. The youth had no idea how lucky he had been. If Kelric's spinal node hadn't controlled his reflexes, that boy would be dead.

As Kelric's adrenaline surge eased, his body switched out of combat mode. He once more became aware of the low-level nausea that was almost always with him now. His fatigue had grown worse. Using his enhanced systems for such a brief time shouldn't have drained him this way. His physical resources were far too diminished.

The concourse opened into a huge rotunda, the open space in its center circled by five levels of balconies. Kelric found himself on the third level. He glanced across the rotunda—and stopped.

Taskmakers. Three of them. They were threading their way through the crowds down on the second level.

Taskmakers. Trader slaves.

Three interstellar powers vied for control in settled space: the Skolian Imperialate of Kelric's people, the Allied Worlds of Earth, and the Traders. The Traders called themselves the Eubian Concord, a euphemism Kelric found the ultimate in double-talk. Their citizens had no choice but to be in "concord" with their conquerors.

Taskmakers made up the bulk of the Trader population, over a trillion strong. Providers, the valued pleasure slaves, were rare and had far less freedom. Taskmakers lived fairly normal lives. Some were well off in their own right and exerted a degree of authority among other taskmakers. For all that, they were still slaves. But no one owned these taskmakers anymore. Under Skolian law, any slave entering Skolian territory became free. How had these three escaped to Edgewhirl?

Except it wasn't only three.

Now that Kelric looked, he saw other taskmakers among the crowds. He recognized them by the high-tech collars around their necks and the guards on their wrists and ankles. They must have just arrived on Edgewhirl. He didn't doubt they would soon have those signs of their former bondage removed. Maybe that was why no one paid him any heed; they probably mistook his wrist and ankle guards for slave restraints.

What the blazes had happened? Great shifts in power must have taken place, if large numbers of Trader slaves were escaping to Skolian worlds.

Kelric started to walk again. He had to find information, an open computer room where he could log in to one of the public webs. But every console room he passed was closed. That disquieted him as much as all the Allied and Trader citizens. Public console rooms never closed. The webs tied civilization together.

He walked under a giant arch into another concourse—and this time he froze.

Aristos.

Two of them. A man and woman. They were unmistakable, with glittering black hair, ruby eyes, and snow-marble skin. Although bodyguards surrounded them, they made no attempt to hide their identities as members of the caste that ruled the Trader Empire. Eighteen years ago they would have been insane to come here. If they hadn't been mobbed first, they would have been arrested as war criminals. Yet here they walked like anyone else, at liberty on a Skolian world, the land of their enemies.

Their presence hit Kelric like ice. His body toggled into combat mode, but this time his fight routines didn't activate. With trained mental reflexes, he manipulated the neural firings in his brain to buffer his mental activity, creating a sort of mental camouflage. *I am not here.*

The Aristo woman glanced idly in his direction. Then she stiffened and focused on him. As her attention intensified, he became aware of a shift in his neural firing patterns. His mind interpreted the effect as a mental abyss forming just beyond barriers he had created to protect himself. If his mental shield weakened, his mind would plunge into that void.

Two taskmakers strode by him, deep in conversation. They and the Aristos saw one another in the same instant. The taskmakers stopped, staring at these representatives of their former owners. The Aristos also halted, watching the taskmakers with obvious disdain, and also anger, that former slaves should share the concourse with them as equals.

Then the taskmakers resumed walking. They went on, free, without challenge, past the two symbols of a life that no longer had hold on them. The Aristos also went their way then, the woman having forgotten Kelric.

It took Kelric a moment to regain his equilibrium. He knew now, without doubt, that his universe had changed beyond recognition. If Trader Aristos could walk with impunity on a Skolian World, surrounded by Skolian and Allied military forces, what safe place remained for him? One thing was certain: until he better understood his situation, he would be a fool to reveal his identity.

He began to walk again, in numb silence. No one else noticed him. In all that astonishing, incredible crowd, no one dreamed that the long lost Imperial Heir of Skolia was walking among them.

Edgewhirl made Kelric dizzy, with its oxygen-rich air and gravity only 70 percent the human standard. He felt light and light-headed. The sky arched in a glazed aqua bowl. Whirligig, the sun, hung low in the west, molten gold, flattened like a huge squashed coin. The Allieds called it Clement's Star, named for one of Earth's renowned literary giants from its Golden Age. Sunshine streamed everywhere, filling Porthaven with golden light, as if the city were an ancient bronzed photograph from centuries past.

He searched for a console room, but he couldn't find an open one anywhere. His nausea gradually increased. He hoped not too much chlorine remained in the air; his damaged respiratory system probably couldn't handle it. Decades ago chlorine had saturated Edgewhirl. The Advance Services Corps had cleaned out most of it when they biosculpted this planet, though the seas remained thick with magnesium and sodium salts.

He walked through the city, his bare feet silent on the sandy streets, his limp becoming more pronounced as his exhaustion increased. Every now and then it occurred to him that he was in shock. Most of time he just walked, searching for information but wary of revealing himself with questions.

Porthaven glowed in hues of yellow. Buildings, streets, plazas: all were made with yellow clay bricks or quartz. No wood. Fires started easily in this oxygen-rich air. It hadn't mattered before humans came; Edgewhirl had no life of its own, flammable or otherwise. The ASC team introduced biodesigned vines that used chlorine in their chemistry and helped remove it from the air. Vines spilled everywhere now, climbing walls, hanging over balconies, draping roofs, and spiraling up light posts, all the way to the top, where they curled around amberglass lamps shaped like onion bulbs. The leaves and stems were almost black in the bronzed sunlight, but their flowers rioted in vivid red, bronze, and gold hues. Their scent sweetened the air.

He saw no vehicles. The traffic authority probably kept them out to protect pedestrians. Porthaven had obviously never been meant to deal with this many people. They crammed cafés, clustered around yellow stone tables, perched on basins glinting with salt crystals, strolled, strode, wandered, stood, sat, and lay in amber-washed plazas and parks.

Cafés. Food. When had he last eaten? He had been in space for two days, asleep, recovering from burns he sustained in the fire that made his escape from Coba possible. Vaguely he recalled the ship's robodoc hooking him to an antiquated IV. It must have provided enough nourishment; he felt only a distant, easily ignored sense of hollowness in his stomach. His nausea, however, had worsened. If he tried to eat now, he would lose his meal.

A man and a woman strolled past, glancing at him with concern. He realized he had stopped in the street and was simply standing there, gazing into space. Shaking his head, he resumed his walk.

Edgewhirl colonists were everywhere, distinctive by their bronze skin and hair, side effects of genetic tinkering meant to keep their cells from taking in too much chlorine. Their hair swung in braids to their waists, sometimes woven with copper threads, a sign of wealth on this metal-deficient world where corrosion ate minerals. But they made up less than half the current population. Offworlders filled the streets, diverse in their races, language, and garbs. Why? What had happened? *What?*

Kelric raked his hand through his hair, a mane of gold curls that spilled down his neck. Everything here shouted of political upheaval. He had to sort out his disordered thoughts. Form plans. Take action.

And do what?

If he made the wrong move, he could end up in even worse trouble. His position within the power hierarchy of Imperial Skolia had always been precarious. He was one of the three heirs to Kurj Skolia, the Imperator. Kurj served as commander in chief of the combined ISC forces: the Pharaoh's Army, the Imperial Fleet, the Advance Services Corps, and the Jagernaut Force.

Kurj. His half brother.

Technically Kurj didn't rule the Skolian Imperialate; that title went to an elected civilian, the First Councilor of the Assembly. But the question of who truly ruled Skolia had long plagued the halls of Imperial power. Kelric knew well the whispers that named Kurj a military dictator.

Kurj had no legitimate heirs of his own. So he chose three of his half siblings: Althor, Sauscony, and Kelric. Only one could become Imperator.

The one who survived.

And now? Kelric exhaled. His relationship with Kurj had always been difficult. They looked alike, moved alike, spoke in the same deep voice, had the same metallic coloring. Even their names were similar. In personality they were very different men, but that made no difference to Kurj. He looked at Kelric and saw himself. Having gained his title through violence, he feared Kelric would seek the same, perhaps even through fratricide. That Kelric was incapable of such an act against the family he so loved was a truth his half brother had never seen.

Even if Kelric had come back to an unchanged situation, he would have taken care in announcing his return from the dead. Now he had no idea what he faced.

He finally found an open console room in the library, a peaceful place with many windows that let sunlight slant across the clay walls and tables. It was one of the few empty areas he had seen in Porthaven. Most of the consoles were dark, but an active light glowed on one in the corner. He sat down and started to say "guest account."

Then he paused. Although he saw no one, that didn't mean no one could overhear. In a civilization so dependent on computers, even guarded interactions could become public. Electro-optical webs, molecular nanowebs, quantum picowebs, and the psiberweb permeated human existence, all its creations, even people like himself who carried nodes within their bodies.

Kelric knew his half brother saturated the nets with security monitors. More subtle, and perhaps more dangerous, were the shadow spies of his aunt, the Ruby Pharaoh. Her ghostlike omnipresence had once permeated the webs. But now? Who controlled them? His aunt? Kurj? The Allieds? *The Aristos?* The more sophisticated a system, the more ways existed to detect a user's presence. If he linked into a general web, would he reveal himself? For all he knew, it could be a fatal step. Better to hide his presence for now.

So in the end he resorted to barbarism: he typed at the keyboard. He intended only to access the library network.

Guest account, he entered.

A screen morphed out of the table and **Guest account** appeared on it in blue glyphs, glowing on a white background.

System down, the node printed.

Down? He rubbed his chin. The redundancy and backups built into planetary webs made it unlikely that any particular network would go down more than a few seconds. He waited a minute, then retyped *Guest account.*

System down, it repeated.

Baffled, he looked around. Except for himself, the room was still empty. People crammed Porthaven, yet no one was using a public console room that normally would be packed at this time of day.

He turned back to the console. *How long has the library web been unavailable?*

Unknown.

Unknown? That made no sense. *Why?*

The Collapse corrupted my files, the node answered, its self-reference implying it had an Evolving Intelligence brain. **However, I have reconstructed them to some extent and can roughly place the Collapse as thirty days ago.**

Are you talking about a collapse of the library web? Kelric asked. *Or a bigger web?*

A bigger web.

He waited, but the node said no more. So he typed, *What web collapsed?*

All of them.

All of what?

The webs.

Kelric held back his exasperation. The node's literal responses suggested its EI brain was less than state-of-the-art, to say the least. *What webs do you mean?*

Every web in settled space.

He almost laughed. So. Now he understood. The node had malfunctioned. *When were you last serviced?*

This morning.

This morning? *What about the rest of the library nodes?* Thinking of its terse answers, he added, *Explain in detail.*

The Collapse damaged many nodes, it informed him. Some more than others. The techs took those that survived whole, or were easily repaired. They need them for webs more crucial to the city and port. With glyph shadings of pride, it added, They chose me to monitor the library.

Kelric suspected the library rarely left this node in charge. He had an odd urge to congratulate the computer. He wondered if his fatigue made him read human emotions into a machine.

What is "the Collapse"? he asked.

When psiberspace imploded, every psiberweb node crashed, it explained, its nuances indicating a desire to be helpful. That pulled down every EO, nano, and picoweb connected to them, which took down every web linked to them, and so on, until every web in settled space collapsed.

Kelric blinked. Saying psiberspace "imploded" was like saying spacetime collapsed. *That's impossible.*

Apparently not.

This had to be a mistake. He had never known even a planetary web to go down for more than a few hours, and that only in a world-wide disaster. Now he was to believe the star-spanning webs that wove together three empires had collapsed? Impossible.

Yet the node seemed undamaged. He tried to absorb its story, but instead a memory came to him from fifty years ago, when he had been seven. Watching his father and another man practice with swords, he had suddenly understood that this man he loved, the center of his life, could die from a mere thrust of sharpened metal. It was the first time he realized how vulnerable humans became without their technology.

Kelric pressed the heels of his hands against his temples, trying to pull his thoughts together. He knew he was in shock, had been for hours, days even, ever since he escaped the inferno that had engulfed his home on Coba. Despite his efforts to pull out his Coban bodyguards, they had perished as the city roared in the flames of war. The whole damnable war had been his own damnable fault. Not because he did anything. Simply because he *existed.* He gave an unsteady laugh. The man whose face had launched a thousand ships. Now he was here, arguing with a slow-witted computer.

He started to stand up, then sank back into his chair, too tired to do more. A thought pierced his haze. *His family.* The Ruby Dynasty. If the web truly had collapsed, it meant something had happened to them.

His family were Kyle operators. They ran the psiberweb. Kyle sciences had developed centuries ago, after the discovery of a nano-sized brain organ: the Kyle Afferent Body. In rare humans, the Kyle operators, the KAB grew to microscopic size.

Although the brain waves of any two people could interact, the effects were tiny. However, a Kyle operator's enlarged KAB boosted the effect. When stimulated by fields from another person's brain, the enlarged KAB sent signals to structures in the Kyle's brain called *paras.* Like many neural structures, *paras* turned such signals into thought. But these thoughts were filched. They belonged to someone else. In other words, Kyle operators were psions. Most were empaths, but if their *paras* were sensitive enough to decipher words, they rated as telepaths.

What gave birth to psiberspace? Quantum theory. Quantum wavefunctions existed for any system—including the brain. If a function with fixed energy varied with time, it could be Fourier-transformed into one with a fixed time that varied with energy. Likewise for position and momentum.

How do you define a thought? Simple. Use the wavefunction for the brain as it forms that thought. So came the *what if?*: could they transform the spacetime function for a fixed thought into a "thought" function for fixed spacetime coordinates?

Kelric's eccentric, delicate, and reclusive aunt—the Ruby Pharaoh—derived the transform that took functions from spacetime into psiberspace. Just as the wave for an atom existed everywhere in normal space, so the wave for a thought existed everywhere in psiberspace. In other words, as soon as a sender formed a thought, receivers could pick it up. It made possible instant communication across interstellar distances.

Of course, the folks doing all this sending and receiving needed links into psiberspace. Enter Kyle operators. With hardware to boost their abilities, strong Kyles transformed thoughts into psiberspace. But almost none could power the psiberweb. Only Rhon psions were strong enough to carry that load, and the only known Rhon were Kelric's family. It was why he was so close to them; they shared affection with an unusual ability to meld their emotions and thoughts. If the psiberweb had crashed, what did that mean for them?

What happened to the Ruby Dynasty? he typed.

Unknown, the node answered.

Why don't you know?

No one has seen fit to provide me with that information. Its nuances expressed annoyance.

You must have some information.

I'm sorry. I don't. Now its glyphs indicated regret.

Frustrated, he typed, *Why did psiberspace implode?*

Unknown.

Make a damn guess.

A high probability exists that the Collapse is due to the Radiance War. Then it added, Please do not curse at me.

Sorry. After so many years on Coba, without computers, it felt odd to apologize to a machine. But it had a brain, after all. It deserved courtesy too. He didn't recall ever having a computer chastise him for his language, though.

Then he absorbed its other words. *What is the Radiance War?*

It was fought by Imperial Space Command and Eubian Space Command.

Kelric shrugged. *ISC and ESComm have been fighting for centuries. What makes this any different?*

ISC invaded Eube. ESComm invaded Skolia.

He stared at the screen. *Do you mean full-scale invasion? Not deep-space ambushes, but attacks on major planetary centers?*

Yes.

Gods. Had the entire universe gone war-crazy? *Give me all the details you have.*

I have already done so. I suggest you go to a relocation office. They can provide more information, as well as humanitarian aid. The Dawn Corps has an office in the government building at Omega Drymorn Lane.

Aid. Yes. He needed help. Even if it had been safe to reveal his identity, he had no access to his family's resources without the web. If those resources even existed anymore. He rubbed his temples, trying to subdue his headache. Then he typed, *Thank you for your help.*

You are welcome. It was nice to talk to someone. I've been alone here.

I hope you meet more people. Looking at what he had written, Kelric smiled. Although in terms of "intellect," this EI wasn't sophisticated, its emotional traits were advanced from those of his day.

Thank you, it printed. Good luck.

I may need it, he thought. He cleared the screen. A record of their conversation would remain in the node's files, but he doubted it would give away his identity.

Kelric stood up—and nearly passed out. He grabbed his chair, hanging on for balance while black spots danced in his vision. Taking a breath, he waited until his head cleared.

Then he left the library.

The holomural filled an entire side of Porthaven's tallest building, a ten-story skyscraper. Kelric saw it when he was walking to the Dawn Corps office. The mural showed two people. The woman had green eyes and curly black hair with gold tips. The austere simplicity of her black uniform gave her an aura of power greater than any medals or braid. Behind and to one side of her stood a towering, massive man with gold skin and violet eyes, an elite ISC officer wearing the black leathers of a Jagernaut. They gazed out of the mural, larger than life, regal and silent.

Kelric stopped dead. He had trouble breathing. His vertigo surged. With calm steps that gave no hint of the earthquake inside his heart, he walked to the building.

He read the plaque beneath the mural.

Its words were simple, dating from only a month ago—and they tore apart his heart: *In honor of Imperator Sauscony Valdoria and Imperial Heir Althor Valdoria, who died to bring humanity freedom.*

Kelric sank onto a stone bench next to the plaque. He couldn't see. His vision blurred.

Who died to bring humanity freedom.

Died.

His sister and brother. Soz and Althor. Dead.

He leaned forward, unable to make a sound.

Soz. The big sister who had laughed with him, scolded and teased him, looked after him. He had loved her with a child's adoration, a maturing boy's shy realization of her beauty, and an adult's admiration for her integrity. His many thoughts of her blended into a cherished haze.

And Althor. His older brother. Kelric had idolized him, the giant who swung the child Kelric in his arms, laughing as the small boy shouted with delight; the warrior who came home from the stars, striding through their father's stone house; the complicated adult who challenged Kelric's assumptions but never let him doubt his brother's love.

Gone. They were gone.

He choked, an almost inaudible protest. It was the only sound he made as tears rolled down his face. He stayed in the shadow of the war memorial, hidden by an obelisk, his arms folded across his stomach, unnoticed by anyone as he wept.

Then it hit him. Imperator Sauscony Valdoria. *Imperator.* His sister had taken over Imperial Space Command. That meant Kurj had also died. As much as Kelric had resented and feared his half brother, he also respected him. And yes, loved him. Whether or not Kurj felt any fraternal affection in return, he would never know. But he mourned Kurj as well, with silent tears.

And then, finally, another realization came to him.

He was the only surviving Imperial Heir.

He now ruled the Skolian Imperialate.

2

Come the Dawn

Kelric found the genetic tattoo parlor in a crumbling section of Porthaven, where alleys wound in sinuous curves among old buildings. Dirty yellow houses leaned over so far that their tops touched each other, making arches above the sweating ground. Before he entered the tattoo shop, he took a small garnet out of his pouch and cupped it in his fist, so the tattooist wouldn't see him remove it from his frayed pouch and guess at the fortune he carried.

The tattoo artist showed him a catalogue. Kelric chose a simple form of genetic tinkering, one that would turn his gold hair and eyes brown and take away the metallic highlights that shimmered in his skin. The artist gave him a dye job to serve until the altered skin and hair grew in. None of it would fully hide his gold coloring, but it was enough to disguise how much he resembled the man in the mural. Even in the best of times his family were targets for abduction or assassination—and this was far from the best of times.

Kelric paid with his garnet, the high value of the stone also ensuring the tattoo artist's silence. He spent the next hour walking back to the city center. The Dawn Corps office occupied the ground floor of a government building. He entered a lobby with stone walls, faceted yellow windows, and soft gray furniture. At a counter in the back, he pressed a panel that rang a digital bell.

A woman in a blue uniform came through a doorway in the back wall. Seeing Kelric, she faltered in midstep. Then she recovered from whatever caused her pause and came to the counter. As she smiled, her cheeks reddened with a blush. She spoke in a language he didn't know, her voice soft.

He shook his head to show he didn't understand.

She tried again, still with her pleasant smile and voice. He wondered if the Allieds were this nice to everyone. Her response wasn't feigned, either. Her mind projected genuine pleasure at his presence. He shook his head again, to indicate he still didn't understand, but her friendly manner eased his tension. When he smiled, her rosy blush deepened and a wisp of sexual arousal drifted from her mind to his. She tried a different language, but he didn't understand that one either.

Finally she beckoned him to follow. She took him along stone corridors. On the walls, the logo of the Allied Worlds glowed in blue. Based on the insignia of Earth's United Nations, it showed a silhouette of Earth's continents superimposed on several concentric circles.

It unsettled Kelric to see this bold display of the Allied logo in Skolian territory. Edgewhirl was still a Skolian world. But the prominent Allied presence made it clear the power balance had shifted. The Allied Worlds of Earth formed a civilization less powerful than those of their massive neighbors—the Traders and the Skolians. So Earth had never posed a threat to those two warring powers. The Allied Worlds were strong enough, however, that neither Skolia nor the Traders could spare the resources from their own bitter conflicts to conquer Earth or the worlds she protected. Now the Allieds seemed to be moving into the chaos left by the Radiance War, expanding their power base while their mighty neighbors floundered.

It was eerie, too, knowing that Allied logo symbolized the world of his ancestors. They were human, after all, all of them, all the races spread across three interstellar empires.

Six millennia ago, an unknown race had seeded the planet Raylicon with humans and then vanished, leaving only their starships behind. From those ships, the displaced humans developed star travel while Earth was still in its Stone Age. So the Ruby Empire was born. Kelric's ancestors. They set up colonies on other worlds, including Coba. But that fragile empire soon collapsed, leaving the colonies stranded for thousands of years.

The Raylicans regained space travel about four centuries ago and began recovering the colonies. This time they built civilizations to endure: the Skolian Imperialate and the Trader Empire. Earth finally developed star travel in her twenty-second century—and had one powerhouse of a shock when she reached the stars. Her lost children were already here, busily making empires.

The Allied woman left Kelric at a small office, giving him another of her charming smiles. Inside, a youth of about seventeen was sitting at a clay table reading a holograph, a slate that cycled through electronic documents. Stacks of cheap plasti-sheets covered the table.

The name on the chest of the boy's blue uniform identified him as *Jay Rockworth,* a youth volunteer in the Dawn Corps. Tall and long-legged, he still showed traces of gangly adolescence, but his physique was filling out into a man's broad-shouldered frame. His black hair and brown eyes were unremarkable for an Earth native, but something about him tugged at Kelric. Jay looked familiar. His name too. Jay Rockworth. Where had Kelric heard it before?

Bolt, he thought, trying to access the node in his spine. *Search my memories. Find any reference to "Jay Rockworth."*

No answer came. It didn't surprise him. When his ship crashed on Coba, it had damaged both his body and Bolt. Although the Cobans healed his physical injuries, they had long ago lost the knowledge to repair implanted biomech systems. They also hadn't set one of his broken legs quite right, leaving him with a limp.

Bolt couldn't be completely dead, though. He had toggled Kelric's enhanced reflexes in the port, to rebuff the thief.

At Jay's gesture of invitation, Kelric sat in a chair at the table. Jay spoke in a pleasant voice, using Skolian Flag. "What can I do for you?"

The boy's accent disquieted Kelric. Where did that lilt come from? Although Skolian Flag was the official language of Skolia, the empire's many peoples spoke hundreds of languages. But Rockworth was an Allied name. British, perhaps? Kelric didn't know. He had heard Skolian spoken with a British accent and it didn't sound like this.

Then it hit him. Jay's accent was Highton. *Highton,* the language spoken by the uppermost caste of the Trader Aristos.

Kelric wondered if he was losing touch, that he heard the sound of Highton sadists in the innocent voice of a high-school boy from Earth. He rubbed his eyes, aware of his exhaustion. Maybe the lack of food had weakened him more than he realized.

"Sir?" Jay asked. "I'll help with the forms. You can fill them out in Skolian Flag, Eubic, Spanish, English, or Chinese. If you don't write any of those, I can translate for you."

Kelric tried to answer—and discovered he couldn't talk.

He had "spoken" to the PA and library via computer. At the tattoo parlor he had simply pointed to what he wanted in the catalogue. Jay Rockworth was the first person he had tried to talk with since his escape. In fact, Jay was the first *stranger* he had spoken to in almost two decades. Eighteen years of oath-bound silence on Coba had strengthened his natural reticence, leaving him almost unable to engage in casual speech.

Jay waited. Then he glanced at the heavy guards Kelric wore around his wrists. This time he spoke in Eubic, or Eubian, the official language of the taskmaker slaves who made up over 99 percent of the Trader population. The Eubians also had many tongues, but most learned Eubic as a second language.

"Are you all right?" Jay asked.

Kelric stared at him. What the hell? Was he losing his grip on reality? The boy spoke Eubic with a *Skolian* accent.

This time Kelric made himself answer. In Skolian Flag. "I'm fine."

Jay's concern didn't fade. He shifted into Skolian. "When did you eat last?"

"I don't remember," Kelric admitted. When he left here, he would find someplace to dine. And rest.

Sympathy softened Jay's face. He reached behind a pile of plasti-sheets and took out a bag of nuts. "Would you like some?"

The simple kindness touched Kelric. "Thank you." His hand was too big to fit into the bag, so he slid in his fingers and worked out a few nuts. They tasted sublime. It felt odd to eat solid food.

"We can place you in one of the camps outside the city," Jay said. "They'll give you regular meals. Most of the refugees will ship back offworld, as we find places for you to go and ships to take you there." He considered Kelric. "You might be able to get a job at the port. They need laborers who can do heavy work. Since the Collapse, the more web-intensive machinery hasn't been working well."

Kelric nodded. The boy was good at his job, having already deduced his visitor was without home or funds. Jay's fluent command of Skolian Flag also impressed him.

Knowing his questions could reveal him in ways he didn't intend, he spoke carefully. "I've been cut off from my family."

Jay rummaged through the plasti-sheets, then handed several to Kelric. "We can do a search if you fill these out. Without the psiberweb it may take a long time; inquiries have to come and go by starship. But we'll find them if we can." He handed over another stack of forms. "These will get you into a refugee camp."

Kelric only glanced at the sheets. "What about ISC bases? Are there any in the vicinity?"

Jay shook his head. "Not anymore. The ASC had one up north, near Bartanna Shore on the Estaria continent, but they evacuated before the Collapse."

Why would the Advance Services Corps leave? "Where did they go?"

"Apparently they were part of the Radiance invasion force."

"Can you tell me what happened?"

"With the base personnel?"

"With everything. The Radiance War."

Jay didn't seem surprised by his disorientation. "Where would you like me to start?"

"What happened to the Ruby Dynasty?" Kelric asked.

He felt the boy's sudden tension. Nothing showed on Jay's face, but his gaze lost its warmth. Kelric might as well have thrown a bucket of snow at him.

"They're gone," Jay said.

No, Kelric thought. "Dead?"

"Yes." Jay's face was stiff. "Or imprisoned."

"Surely not all of them."

"All." The boy sounded as if he were clenching his teeth.

Kelric somehow managed to keep his face from betraying his shock. He sat still, afraid that if he moved, spoke, did anything, it would reveal his inner turmoil.

He wondered, too, at the intensity of Jay's reaction. The boy seemed almost as upset as Kelric. Maybe it was true, what the political powers of Skolia believed, that the Ruby Dynasty served as a symbol of morale for the general populace. Kelric's family descended from the ancient dynasty that had founded the Ruby Empire. Technically they no longer ruled, but only served as keepers of the psiberweb. However, the survival of civilization depended on the web.

When Kelric had composed himself enough to speak again, he asked the question he dreaded. "Which members of the dynasty died?"

Jay answered in a flat voice. "Kurj Skolia. Sauscony Valdoria. Althor Valdoria. The Ruby Pharaoh, Dyhianna Selei. Her heir, Taquinil Selei. Her consort, Eldrin Valdoria."

Kelric didn't know how he kept his face calm. The shock was too great. His aunt Dehya, the Pharaoh, dead? Her son Taquinil? Gone? And gods, not Eldrin. Not his brother, Eldrin, the firstborn, oldest of the Valdoria children, with his spectacular singing voice, his affectionate smile, and his disconcerted pride as his "little" brother Kelric had grown into a giant who towered over him.

It couldn't be true. They couldn't be dead. Not all of them.

"What of the rest?" he asked. What had happened to his parents? "Eldrinson Valdoria and Roca Skolia?"

"They're on Earth," Jay said. "In protective custody."

Relief flooded Kelric, followed by a drive to see them, one so strong it almost overwhelmed him. "When do they return?"

An edge came into Jay's voice. "Never."

He saw no reason for his parents to stay on Earth. "Why?"

"To ensure the war doesn't start again."

Then Kelric understood. "The Allieds won't let them go."

"That's right."

"What about the rest of the family?"

Jay's fist clenched until the holograph in his hand ripped. He didn't even notice. "The Allied military is holding their six surviving children prisoner on the world Lyshriol. You may not be familiar with the name; it's called Skyfall by the general public. It's the home world for one branch of the Ruby Dynasty."

Kelric knew the name Lyshriol perfectly well. He had grown up there. The war had brought even more changes than he realized, if Earth now had control of Lyshriol, one of Imperial Skolia's best-guarded possessions.

"Who is Imperator now?" Kelric asked. It amazed him how calm his voice sounded when he was breaking inside. He kept his mind barriered, in case Jay had any empathic ability.

"There is no Imperator," Jay said. "Sauscony Valdoria had no heirs." In an oddly strained voice, he added, "At least none she revealed."

Of all the scenarios Kelric had imagined for his return, none included finding himself the sole free member of his family. Was it possible the reports were premature? "Have the deaths been verified?"

"What, you think an avenging angel will appear to bring Skolia back its glory? You want a savior from the Ruby Dynasty? You and a trillion other people. Well, I'll tell you. It won't *happen.* No one is left." Bitterly Jay added, "Even if this miracle appeared, you think it would help? The Skolian, Eubian, and Allied Space Commands would do everything possible, legal or otherwise, to imprison or assassinate your 'miracle.'"

Kelric stared at him. "Why are you so angry?"

A flush spread on Jay's face. It was a moment before he answered. "I lost my parents in the war."

Quietly Kelric said, "I'm sorry."

Jay shook his head. "It's the principle, too. Everyone treats the Ruby Dynasty as if they're great prizes to own and control. Why don't people leave them alone?"

His remarks surprised Kelric. Even he saw why the Allieds refused to release his family. A Ruby Triad powered the psiberweb: the Imperator, the Ruby Pharaoh, and Kelric's father. Until Kelric joined the Triad, his father was the only Triad member still living. By holding him prisoner, Earth kept him from remaking the psiberweb. By holding the rest of the family, they stopped anyone else from joining the Triad. No Triad meant no web, and without the web, Skolia wouldn't risk another war. The instantaneous communications provided by the psiberweb had given ISC its one advantage over the Eubian Traders. It was why Imperial Space Command survived despite having fewer personnel, vessels, and equipment than Eubian Space Command. ESComm lumbered: ISC sailed.

What surprised Kelric more, though, was that Jay voiced his criticism to a Skolian citizen. As a Dawn Corps volunteer, Jay represented Earth.

Curious, Kelric extended a probe to Jay's mind. Before he made any contact, though, pain sparked in his temples. So he let his concentration relax. Instead he asked, "You don't approve of your government's actions?"

Jay stiffened. "Of course I do." He indicated the forms Kelric held. "Shall we begin?"

Kelric had no intention of filling out anything. He handed Jay the papers. "I'll come back."

"Are you sure?" As Jay's focus returned to Kelric, his tension faded, replaced by genuine concern. In a gentle voice he said, "You look like you need a place to eat and rest."

His solicitude touched Kelric, as had his earlier kindness. Standing up, he said, "I'm fine. But thank you." He wasn't fine, but he couldn't risk revealing more about himself.

"Come back if you need anything." Jay rose and extended his arm, his hand held sideways. Kelric blinked at it. Just as Jay began to look self-conscious, Kelric remembered the custom. He clasped Jay's hand and moved his arm up and down. It felt odd to touch a stranger.

After Kelric left the Dawn Corps, he sat on a bench outside and watched people go by. Exhaustion weighed on him. Even the thought of walking a few steps was too much. He had used up his depleted physical resources and now he just wanted to sleep. But he had to make plans. He needed to contact an ISC base, one strong enough to protect a member of the Ruby Dynasty.

In normal times he probably could have found passage to ISC headquarters. But in this chaos, with civilization breaking down, he was painfully vulnerable. Nor would it be easy to find officers he could trust. Many in ISC stood to benefit from the current lack of leadership. If he approached the wrong people, he could end up in more trouble than if the Allieds caught him.

Even his claim to his title was tenuous. The Imperator had no coronation. His investment consisted of joining the Triad power-link, which he couldn't do until he reached one of the Lock command stations used to create the psiberweb.

He stood up—and spots swirled in his vision. Swaying, he dropped back on the bench and sat still, waiting for the vertigo to pass and his nausea to recede. When he felt steadier, he took a deep breath and stood again.

He needed help. Soon. He was the only member of his family free to assume the leadership his people needed.

And he was dying.

The line of men outside the hostel stretched along an ocher wall that bordered the sandy street. Kelric waited in line, hugging his arms around his body for warmth. This overcrowded shelter for homeless men was the only place he had found that offered meals without requiring he give ID or fill out forms.

The hostel was on Porthaven's west side, where the city petered out into a saffron desert. He could look down the street into the barren flatlands and see all the way to the horizon. The curving edge of the small world seemed oddly close.

The setting sun stained the city in hues of blood and fire. Behind him, in the east, the sky had darkened to a brooding dark red, like cooling lava, almost black. Overhead, it glowered a deep crimson, and on the western horizon it flamed scarlet, as bright as fluorescent glaze.

Only the upper arch of the sun, Whirligig, showed above the horizon. Its molten edge rimmed the world like lava ready to pour across the flatlands in rivers of bronzed radiance. Kelric knew the long sunset shouldn't surprise him, given the planet's fifty-nine-hour day. But the evening seemed interminable as he waited, hoping for warmth, a meal, and a place to sleep.

His mind felt clogged. Plugged with the debris of half-formed concepts. The street blurred around him into a dark copper limbo. At his back, the wall was hard. It moved against him... or maybe he moved against it... sliding down...

Kelric hit the ground with a jarring thud. He would have fallen on his side, his arms still wrapped around his body, if his shoulder hadn't hit the legs of a man ahead of him. The fellow swore and swung around, his fists clenching. When he saw Kelric, his fists uncurled and he looked around, his motions frantic for some reason.

Kelric tried to get up. He couldn't do it. He had used up all his reserves of energy. So he sat against the wall, shivering, wondering why no one else seemed cold. Dimly, as if from far away, he heard alarmed voices, someone calling to someone else. Urgent words. He closed his eyes, trying to shut them out. Needed sleep...

"Sir?" The man spoke in Skolian Flag.

Kelric opened his eyes. The man kneeling in front of him wore the beige uniform of the Imperial Relief Allocation Service, a civilian group run by the Skolian government. The IRAS patch on his shoulder identified him as a medic, and he held a glossy roll of diagnostic tape.

"Do you mind if I examine you?" the man asked.

"No," Kelric said. He was past caring what anyone did.

With a gentle touch, the medic tilted Kelric's head to the side and unrolled the tape along his neck. He studied the holos rotating above it, which Kelric could see by slanting his gaze downward. Glyphs were probably scrolling across the tape, but he had no way to read those.

The medic's face paled. "I think you better come inside."

"All right," Kelric said. It was, after all, why he had come here. Except he no longer had the energy to get up.

Someone in line said, "We've been here longer," and another voice said, "What the bloody hell do we have to do to get in?" Someone else said, "You have to die, jerkoid."

The words bounced off Kelric. Two armed IRAS officers were watching the line now. He regarded them with a sense of floating. The medic was talking again, but he could no longer process the words. He watched the man's mouth move. A humming noise filled his ears, thrumming, buzzing, burring, until it blended with reality and took away his thoughts.

Four orderlies appeared with an air stretcher. They lifted Kelric onto it and laid him on his back. Red sky arched above him, limitless and free. His mind wafted up into the soughing, seductive breezes. Softly, so softly floating. Finally to rest. After so long, finally to rest . . .

Far away, as if through layers of muffling cloth, he heard voices shouting. An air-needle hissed against his arm, running feet pounded, air rushed past his face.

Then his mind disintegrated.

3

Cargo Man

Hiss.

Stop. Start. Stop.

Phissssss.

Kelric lay in a cocoon of warmth.

The blurs above him resolved into a ceiling, a simple surface, ugly in fact, a dull white. The light fixture was a white half sphere, or what used to be white. Its plastiflex covering had long ago yellowed. He stared at it and listened to the hissing hum.

After a while, he looked to the left. He was lying on a cot, a few hand spans away from another cot. A man slept there under an old blue blanket. Kelric turned his head to the right and saw another cot. The man in this one was singing in a low voice, the same phrase over and over, a tuneless hiss about dead birds. He gave no indication he knew the rest of the universe existed.

Moving slowly, his body protesting with aches, Kelric sat up. The old blue blanket that had covered him slipped down to his waist. Slender insulation conduits threaded its weave. Some had worked out of the frayed cloth and scratched his skin. Bare-chested, he wore only a pair of sleep trousers, clean, but faded to gray from many washings. An antiquated IV patch was attached to his inner elbow. Fluid fed it through a plastiflex tube that stretched to a bag on the wall behind him. It was a crude setup; he couldn't even leave the cot unless he pulled off the patch.

He looked around the hospital ward. Cots crammed the large room, side by side and toe to head, hundreds, all occupied. The place smelled of disinfectant and plastic. For all those patients he saw only two medics, both in IRAS uniforms, a woman near the door and a harried man across the room.

Fatigue pressed on him. Hunger gnawed at his stomach despite the IV. More than anything else, though, he felt relief. After his delirium of the past few days, he was grateful to be coherent. He hadn't realized how bad his condition had become until it improved enough for him to notice the difference. His throat ached, his head throbbed, and fever heated his face. He didn't care. He was alive. *Alive.* So he sat on his cot, barely thinking, content.

After a while the medic across the room straightened up, rubbing his neck. He moved on, squeezing his way between cots, stopping often to talk with patients and check monitors. Kelric watched him, oddly comforted. The doctor had a pleasant face, as smooth as polished wood. Like most Edgewhirl natives, he wore his hair in two braids that fell to his waist.

Eventually he reached Kelric's cot. He spoke to Kelric in Skolian Flag, his voice rich with the Edgewhirl accent. "You look a lot better today."

It took Kelric a few seconds to answer. "I give thanks for your generous care." *Ah.* Too formal. His ability to converse was as rusty as oxidized foil. He had grown up speaking Iotic and reverted to its cadences when he was tired. Almost no one used the archaic tongue anymore except the Ruby Dynasty and a few ancient houses descended from the otherwise vanished nobility of the Ruby Empire. He hoped the doctor didn't recognize his accent; the fewer people who figured out his background, the better.

"Do you mind if I sit?" the doctor asked.

"Please do." Kelric pushed back against the wall, making room. The singer in the next cot had fallen silent, except for an occasional rattling snore.

The doctor sat down, facing Kelric. "I'm Tarjan. I was here when they brought you in yesterday."

"How long?" Kelric managed.

"How long have you been here?" When Kelric nodded, Tarjan said, "About thirty hours."

Kelric sat for a moment. Then he said, "I had an odd sense yesterday when I passed out. As if I were disintegrating." It felt strange to speak so much. Profligate.

Tarjan answered in a gentle voice. "You were dying."

Dying. Kelric shook his head, more to clear it than to deny the words. "Can you fix it?"

He only meant, could they fix him so he wouldn't keel over if he stood up. But as soon as he saw Tarjan's strained look, he knew the doctor had taken the literal meaning, not could he help Kelric back on his feet, but could he heal him.

Tarjan spoke carefully. "Your malnutrition and exhaustion need only food and sleep."

"But?"

"We can't be sure," he hedged.

"Tell me." Kelric was too drained to wrestle with careful words. "I already know I'm damaged inside."

Tarjan exhaled. "Yes. I'm sorry."

"How bad?"

"Of course, one can always hope—"

"Doctor." Kelric crumpled the threadbare blanket in his fist. "How bad?"

Tarjan spoke quietly. "You need a new heart. New liver. At least one new kidney. Preferably two. You're anemic. The lining of your stomach and intestines is degraded. Have you had nausea?" When Kelric nodded, the doctor said, "I'm afraid it may get worse. Also, the nanomeds in your body that provide health and maintenance, and delay aging, are mutating. They're attacking their own host. You." He paused. "You are a Jagernaut, yes?"

"Yes."

Tarjan simply nodded, as if it were perfectly normal to learn that a patient in his charity ward was a human weapon. "I figured that was why you have so much biomech in your body." He regarded Kelric with concern. "The structural supports and high pressure bioplastics that enhance your musculature and skeleton are fraying, eaten by the mutated nanomeds. The micro-engines that control the system are corroded. About the only component with no damage is the microfusion reactor that powers you."

"It's built to survive." With a smile, Kelric added, "Can't have my power source melting down inside of me."

He meant it as a joke, but he felt Tarjan's unease. Kelric had forgotten how uncomfortable Jagernauts made people. That ISC's versatile weapons were also human, empaths in fact, was a fact people all too often forgot.

Tarjan rubbed his chin. "I've seen problems on Edgewhirl similar to yours. Some people can't tolerate the traces of chlorine here. Gradually it poisons them. I'd say you've been dealing with a biosphere even more hostile to your chemistry. Your meds probably counteracted some of the effects, but they aren't operating anywhere near full capacity. The problems must have been accumulating for years, even decades."

"Can you help?" Kelric asked.

"I can treat the anemia. I may also have medicine to slow the mutation rate of your meds." He exhaled. "But you need a full ISC hospital, one equipped to operate on Jagernauts, repair biomech damage, perform organ replacements or regeneration, flush out the defective meds in your body, and reseed you with healthy meds. That's far more than we can do here."

It was what Kelric had expected. "Is there an ISC hospital in the region?"

"Nothing. I checked as soon as we realized the severity of your condition."

"Any ISC base at all on-planet?" There had to be someone on this tiny world who could help him.

"There's a naval base on the Whitecap Coast of the Jadar continent," Tarjan offered. "But they've neither the facilities to treat you nor transportation to take you offworld."

"No ships at all?" When the doctor shook his head, Kelric made an incredulous noise. "What happened to the ISC presence on this planet?"

Tarjan gave him an odd look. "Same as everywhere else. The Glory Invasion."

Kelric had expected a comment on the Radiance War. Glory? Surely that didn't refer to the preposterous name the Trader Aristos had given their capital world. Eube's Glory. It took its name from Eube Qox, the Aristo who had founded the Eubian Concord. What a crock. Then again, no one had ever accused Eube Qox of modesty.

"You can't mean the Eube capital," he said.

Tarjan looked puzzled. "What else would I mean?"

"Are you telling me that Imperator Skolia took ISC into the heart of Eubian territory?" Had his sister gone mad? The Eubian capital was impregnable. "That's suicide."

"Not according to the news broadcasts."

"Why? What do they say?"

"ISC destroyed almost every military site in the system and then got out of there." He paused. "Except for Imperator Skolia and the Imperial Heir, may they rest well."

So that was how his sister and brother had died. No wonder it earned them a ten-story memorial. Kelric couldn't keep his anger out of his voice. "What the hell were the Imperator and Imperial Heir doing with an invasion fleet?"

Surprise at Kelric's lack of knowledge leaked from Tarjan's mind. "Althor Valdoria, the Imperial Heir, had been an ESComm prisoner for two years."

Tarjan might as well have socked him in the stomach. Althor, a prisoner of war? Kelric didn't want to imagine what his brother had endured during two years of ESComm interrogation. Death must have been a blessing. "And the Imperator?"

"She went in to get him. And to avenge the death of her brother, Kurj Skolia."

Kelric just looked at him. Tarjan had no idea his words were like blows. "How did Kurj Skolia die?"

"You don't know that either?"

Kelric wanted to grab his shoulders and shake the answers out of him. "No."

"I didn't mean to offend," Tarjan said gently. He pushed one of his braids over his shoulder. "Two years ago, ESComm ambushed his fleet in deep space. They destroyed all but the bridge of his flagship. When it was over, the Eubian emperor went in to claim Imperator Skolia as his prisoner."

"You mean Emperor Ur Qox?" Eighteen years ago, Ur Qox had been emperor, but Kelric had no idea who sat on the Carnelian Throne now. That sounded like Qox's style, though; come in after the work was done and take credit.

"That's right." Tarjan watched him with puzzlement. "Qox's people believed they had Imperator Skolia defeated."

Kelric knew his brother. Kurj had been called the Fist of Skolia with good reason. "But they didn't."

"No. He rigged the antimatter containment bottles on his ship and sprung the trap when Qox came onboard." Quietly Tarjan said, "The resulting explosion obliterated the ships. Both the Imperator and Emperor Qox died."

So Kurj died taking Ur Qox with him. It helped to know his half brother would have considered it an honorable end. "Then Sauscony Valdoria became Imperator?"

"That's right."

Kelric scowled. "What was she doing with the invasion fleet? The Imperator has no business going into battle." How could she have taken such a chance with her life? It was far more precious than Eube's inanely titled Glory.

Tarjan spread his hands. "I don't claim to know the workings of the ISC mind. I only know the rumors."

"Tell me."

"They say the Triad couldn't support both her and the Ruby Pharaoh. They couldn't both survive. Their minds were too alike, whatever that means. Apparently the Imperator wanted her death to have a meaning."

Kelric knew exactly what it meant. It two minds in the Triad were too alike, they resonated until it tore apart the three-way link. It was how Kurj's father had died: the link shattered when Kurj joined the Triad. It wasn't possible to "resign" from the Triad; a member's neural connections became so intertwined with the link that pulling out left a person brain-dead.

"Is that how the Ruby Pharaoh died?" Kelric asked. "A Triad failure?"

"No one seems to know," Tarjan said. "She's just gone."

"Gone?"

"Apparently. There hasn't been much news."

Kelric frowned. The more answers he got, the less he knew. "And the ISC bases here?"

"ISC pulled in ships from all over the Imperialate for the invasion," Tarjan said.

"How many ships did we lose?"

The doctor gave him another curious look. "They started with eight hundred thousand and returned with seventy thousand. Most of the casualties were drones crewed by EI brains."

Kelric stared at him. "We lost over *ninety percent* of our fleet? With our forces that depleted, we're ripe for ESComm attack."

"There is no ESComm," Tarjan said bluntly. "We destroyed them. Broke their back and put a stake through their heart."

It suddenly hit Kelric that he didn't know the most crucial detail of the war. Caught up in his grief over his family, he had never asked the obvious question. "Who won?"

Tarjan finally gave in to his curiosity. "Where have you been, that you know so little about all this?"

Where indeed? He needed a cover story. He would have to think it through before he said anything, though; better to remain silent than make mistakes now he couldn't undo later.

When it became clear Kelric didn't intend to answer, the doctor said, "We don't know who won."

How could they not know who won the war? "Why not?"

"Both ISC and ESComm are crippled. We have no Ruby

Dynasty, they have no emperor. Imperator Kurj killed Emperor Ur Qox. Imperator Sauscony killed Ur Qox's son."

Kelric blinked. "Ur Qox had an heir?"

"Yes. Jaibriol the Second."

Jaibriol the Second. So Ur Qox had named his misbegotten son after his infamous father. If the second Jaibriol had been as brutal as the first, then Soz truly gave her life for the betterment of humanity.

Tarjan spoke tiredly. "Eube is broken, we're broken. Perhaps now, finally, these leaders of ours, what remains of them, will go to the peace table." He gave Kelric a wan smile. "That would be something, eh? Genuine peace negotiations between Skolia and Eube."

"Yes." Kelric absorbed that thought.

Would this be his legacy then, to usher in an era of peace? It gave him hope. Although he had earned his reputation for ferocity as a Jagernaut, he would rather have studied math. Introverted and contemplative, he preferred equations to battles. In his youth he had been a good test pilot, reveling in those solitary flights. But the further he rose in rank, the less he wanted a military career. Choice, however, had never played a role in his life. His education, career, marriages, even his freedom, had been arranged by others to suit the purpose of politics, first among his people and later on Coba.

Before he ushered in anything, though, he had to become Imperator, which meant joining the Triad. To do that, he had to reach one of the three Locks. The Orbiter space station carried the First Lock, and the planet Raylicon had the Second. The Third was at Onyx Platform, a city of space habitats floating among the stars.

"How long before I can leave here?" Kelric asked.

"I'd like you to stay two more days." Tarjan rubbed his neck, obviously trying to ease his knotted muscles. "You need to be here longer, but we don't have the space. I'm sorry."

He felt the doctor's exhaustion. Too many patients: too few resources. Tarjan feared he was turning out people too ill to leave.

Kelric put a scowl on his face. "You expect me to lie here doing nothing for two damn *days*? I think not." In truth, he felt ready to collapse after sitting up a few minutes. But maybe he could ease this overworked doctor's undeserved guilt.

Tarjan wasn't fooled. He smiled. "Don't worry. You'll sleep most of the time."

Kelric didn't doubt it.

The hangar was out near the cargo warehouses, about two klicks from the domestic terminal at the starport. Kelric walked across the huge, empty airfield, inhaling the morning air. It smelled better here than in the city, without the sweet scent of vines.

He felt healthier than in years. How long had he been anemic? The doctors on Coba had given him iron to rectify what they understood of the condition, but apparently it hadn't been the right treatment. Tarjan's treatment worked wonders. Or maybe it was the medicine he prescribed to slow the mutation rate of Kelric's nanomeds, leaving his healthy meds free to do more repairs. Even his muscles felt stronger. He barely limped at all.

The IRAS clinic had laundered his clothes and found him a pair of socks and work boots. With two days of ample sleep and food, he felt ready to tackle life. And tackle it he would, until he earned enough to buy a new identity and passage offworld.

The cargo master's office was in a corner of the hangar. Holo inventories plastered the casecrete walls. In the back of the office, a woman sat behind a console, reading a schedule, her long legs propped up on the console amid scattered plasti-sheets. Gray streaked her braids. The brown jumpsuit she wore did nothing to hide her well-muscled build. Kelric doubted she had trouble with pickpockets in the starport.

"Saints al-screaming-mighty," she muttered. "Can't they get the bloody flight times right?" She looked up at Kelric. "What the hell do you want?"

He blinked. "Work." That one word came hard. On Coba, the only woman he ever spoke to was his wife, the queen of the city-state where he lived.

She looked him up and down. "Half my servos are out, what

with the Collapse. I could use a cargo handler. But it's heavy work. If you're looking for easy times, go somewhere else."

"Handler is fine." He enjoyed heavy lifting. "How much?"

"I'll pay you one thousand centillas an hour."

He almost snorted. Did she think giving him the wage in centillas would make it sound like more? Ten Imperial dollars was nothing no matter how she named it. "Thirty dollars an hour," he said.

She laughed. "You got a high opinion of yourself."

"With good reason."

"Fifteen."

"Twenty-five."

She moved her hand in dismissal. "It'd wipe out what measly profit I wring from this business."

Kelric had no idea what a good wage was here. So he bluffed. "Twenty-five."

"Eighteen."

"Twenty-five."

She swore, making him wonder if he had pushed too hard and lost the job. Then she said, "All right. Twenty-five. But you better work that pretty ass of yours, boyo, or you're out."

He stiffened. "Kelric."

"What?"

"My name is Kelric. Not boyo. And leave my 'ass' out of it."

"Touchy." She swung her legs off the console and leaned forward, ruffling through the plasti-sheets. "Fill this out." She held out a sheet to him. "I'll need your documents too. Passport, visa, whatever you got."

Damn. "I have no documents."

She raised her eyebrows. Then she set the plasti-sheet back on the console. "Why not?"

"I lost them in the war."

"Why? You in trouble?"

"No."

"Then why don't you get new ID?"

"I was a prisoner."

"A POW?" Unease flickered on her face. "You ISC?"

"It wasn't a military prison."

"So." She sat back and crossed her arms. "You're a con."

"No."

"Then what?"

Kelric had no intention of telling her about Coba. He had made a vow, for his wife and children, to protect their world. He doubted this cargo master gave a kiss in a quasar who had kept him prisoner, but ISC and the Ruby Dynasty would punish Coba if either learned the truth. As Imperator he could protect Coba, *if* ISC reestablished itself. But he wasn't Imperator yet, ISC was a mess, and unguarded confidences left a trail.

So he said, "I was a slave." It was true, technically. According to Coba's antediluvian laws, his wife, Ixpar, *had* owned him.

The cargo master uncrossed her arms. Sympathy showed on her face. "You seen those damn Aristos in our port? Frigging Aristo sadists in a Skolian port. I can't believe it." She leaned forward. "Listen, you go to a relocation office, tell them you were a taskmaker, and register your DNA. Once you're in the database, I can hire you, no problem. I'll be glad to give you a job. You're a free man here, you remember that."

Kelric knew that once his DNA pattern got into the system, he was in continual danger of discovery. "I can't."

"Why not?" When he didn't answer, her wariness returned. "You don't act like a slave. Too cocky. You're a con, aren't you?"

"No."

She sat back and crossed her arms again. "You tried to play on my sympathy, hmmmm? No one makes a fool out of me, Kelli-boy. No documents and you want twenty-five an hour. Not a chance."

"I wasn't lying to you."

"Why should I hire you?"

"You need me."

"Not that bad." She swung her feet back up on the console and picked up the schedule she had been reading. "We got no more to say."

Kelric knew he would be hard-pressed to find legitimate

employment if he refused to register with the authorities. But he had picked up enough from her mind to know she was more desperate for laborers than she let on.

"I'll take twenty per hour," he said.

She continued to read.

"Eighteen."

She looked up. "Ten."

"Eighteen." He hoped he had read her mood right, that she needed handlers enough to go for the higher wage.

"Forget it," she said.

"I can match the output of any other two handlers you have."

She glanced over his muscled frame. "I can believe that."

Kelric waited. The cargo master waited.

When the silence stretched thin, she set down her papers. "All right. Eighteen."

He gave the customary nod, sealing the bargain. But he didn't relax. Something else was coming, the price of her willingness to hire him despite his lack of legal ID. Would she expect him to smuggle? Look the other way for illegal landings?

"One other thing, Kelli-boy," she said.

"What?" If she called him Kelli-boy again, he was going to strangle her.

She stood up, coming to her full height, at least six feet five inches, nearly two meters, almost as tall as he. Then she set down her papers and walked to a door in the wall near her console. When she pressed a panel, the door slid open, revealing Spartan living quarters with a bed against one wall.

She tilted her head toward the bed. "After you."

He stared at her. "What? No."

"You want the job, you do the work." She smiled, showing teeth stained brown from chewing carqual leaves. "I'm sure you can do a good job, hmmm?"

He wanted to walk out. But his chances of finding someone else willing to hire him without proper documents were nil—unless he agreed to "extra" work. At least this didn't require he break the law.

The cargo master leaned against the doorframe and crossed her arms. "You staying or leaving?"

He walked over and regarded her quarters. They looked as spare up close as from across the room. He forced out his answer. "Staying."

"Smart." She lifted her hand, inviting him to enter. So he went into her bedroom. Following him, she closed the door. Then she looked him over again, this time her gaze lingering on his body with an appreciative cast she hadn't let show before.

Kelric wasn't sure what to do next, but he felt stupid just standing there. For lack of a better idea, he lifted his hand to her face and cupped her cheek. She turned her head, pressing her lips against his palm.

As he lowered his arm, she rubbed the collar of his shirt. "This is real silk." She slid her hand down his arm to his scorched sleeve. "How'd you get burned?"

"Battle."

"That had to be on another planet. No fighting here." Taking his hand, she ran her thumb over his wrist guard. "And this, beautiful man, is genuine gold."

He said nothing.

She regarded him with curiosity. "Where did you get those guards? They look ancient. Like marriage guards, the kind men wore in the Ruby Empire."

"Yes."

"Yes?"

"Yes."

She smiled. "You always this talkative?"

"No."

The cargo master chuckled. "Yes, what? Yes, you got a wife from five thousand years in the past?"

"No." Self-conscious, he rubbed his hand over the guard. "Yes, these are marriage guards."

"Oh." Her grin faded. "Your wife going to beat the holy shit out of me for fucking you?"

Kelric flushed. "You know," he said, "if this is your idea of getting a man in a romantic mood, it leaves a lot to be desired."

Unexpectedly, she looked embarrassed. "Pretty bad, hmmm? I never have figured out how men like to be romanced." She touched his guard. "But I still want to know about this wife of yours. I don't want any jealous lovers coming around."

"She's on another planet."

"She coming here?"

"No." He had forced himself to accept he would never see Ixpar again. As the citizen of a Restricted planet, she was forbidden to leave Coba. He could never return, not unless the interstellar situation stabilized and he established himself with enough power to ensure the safety of his wife and children. That could take decades, if the situation was as bad as it looked. If he lived that long. As much as he knew it was better to let them remain safe in anonymity, it left him with a deep sense of loss.

"I'm sorry about your wife." The cargo master looked more relieved than sorry. She kissed the back of his hand, then bit at his knuckles, her tongue pressing his skin. Although many Skolians expressed affection with such gestures, no one on Coba had ever touched him that way. It felt odd. For that matter, having her touch him at all felt strange.

Kelric exhaled. He had to stop brooding, or he wouldn't be able to go through with this.

When he rubbed his hand up her arm, her languorous arousal surged over him. It was uncomplicated lust, touched by neither love nor cruelty. This close to her, he picked up a sense of her thoughts. What they were doing was unusual for her too; in general she treated her employees reasonably well, crude in language but fair in action. He could have done without the dubious honor of inspiring a change in her behavior.

She drew him into a kiss. Kelric made himself kiss her back. She smelled of machine oil, sweat, and carqual tobacco. It wasn't all that unpleasant, aside from the bitter carqual taste, but it felt *wrong,* because of the coercion, but even more as a betrayal of Ixpar.

He tried to numb his thoughts. Putting his arms around her, he deepened their kiss, responding to what he picked up from her mind. Too gentle and she grew bored: too aggressive and it put her off. He modulated his intensity to fit what she wanted. When he stroked her back, she had almost no reaction, but when he slid his palm over her neck, her desire surged. So he played with the skin there, tracing circles that gave her chills he felt through her mind.

Eventually she stopped kissing him. Taking his hand, she drew him to the bed. They lay down on a blanket that covered a hard mattress. Holding her, he tried to imagine she was Ixpar. Both women were tall. Ixpar had a warrior's beauty, powerful and clean, with well-shaped legs that went on forever, fiery hair sweeping to her waist, and large gray eyes. Remembering her only made him feel worse. He had too much to mourn, the loss of his spouse, children, sister, brothers, aunt, nephew.

The cargo master spoke in a low voice, gruff against his ear. "You're so tense." When he didn't answer, she asked, "You miss this wife of yours so much?"

"Yes," he said, before he thought to stay silent. Then he wondered if he had just lost his job.

She drew back to look at him. "You have, uh, a traditional contract? No extras?"

He wasn't sure what "extras" meant, but he suspected she wanted to know if it was a monogamous marriage. "Yes."

"You seem that type." Avoiding his gaze, she fiddled with the laces on his shirt. "You don't drill around, do you?"

"If you mean, have I ever committed adultery, the answer is no."

She flushed. "You don't have to put it that way."

"How do you suggest I put it?"

The cargo master swore. Then she sat up on the bed and swung her legs over the side. As he sat up next to her, she said, "Your shift starts tomorrow at fifteen hundred hours. That's dawn, Kelric, and if you're late you get docked pay, just like everyone else. Shift goes ten hours. You want a second one, we'll see." She glowered. "Now, get the hell out of here before I change my mind."

Relief washed over Kelric. Standing up, he said, "I'll see you tomorrow."

"Be on time," she grumbled.

He grinned. "I will."

Then he left. He strode through her office and back out to the bronze sunlight streaming down from an aquamarine sky.

Banks of lights lit the warehouse despite the late hour. This far into the night, the isolated area was empty of people, robots, and movement. Except for Kelric. He wiped his hand across his forehead, smearing runnels of sweat. Then he lifted another crate off the loading dock and hefted it onto the glider. In the low gravity it hardly felt as if he was working at all.

Convincing Cargo Master Zeld to give him two shifts a day had been easy. He loaded twice as much as the best of her other human workers, his output rivaling even her cheaper robot cranes. His first shift started at 15:00, just after dawn, and went until 25:00. At 47:00, several hours after sunset, he reported in for ten more hours. He slept twice a day, once during midday, while heat scorched Porthaven, and once at night, after he came home from his second shift. The schedule did well by him, letting him rest as long as his depleted body needed.

Quirky Edgewhirl made him smile, with its fifty-nine-hour days. Its sun, Whirligig, spun so fast it resembled a squashed fruit. He had started work in midwinter, ten days ago, and already spring was almost half over. Edgewhirl had almost no axial tilt, so the climate stayed boringly constant: hot and clear days, cool and dry nights. No moon lit the sky. Whirligig's tidal force was slowing the planet down, though; someday Edgewhirl's rotation would be locked to its sun and it would always show the same face to Whirligig.

Each day after he woke, in the long hours before dawn, he took out his jeweled dice and played Quis, a strategy game he had learned on Coba. Every adult and child there played it. They told stories with Quis. Exchanged information. Gambled. But most of all, Quis was politics. The better a player wielded the dice, the greater her influence.

Kelric had taken well to Quis. Remarkably well. It had spurred Coba's queens, called Managers in these modern times, to cloister him with the few other select men who had reached the elite ranks of Quis expertise. They served as advisers to a Manager, making their dice brilliance available only to her.

Here on Edgewhirl, the culture was close to egalitarian, as was the overall culture of Imperial Skolia. But Coba had been isolated for five millennia and still retained the Ruby Empire's matriarchal structure. Caught in power struggles among the Managers and famed for his beauty, though Kelric had never understood why, he had spent the past eighteen years owned by a succession of warrior queens.

He had many memories of Coba he valued. Ixpar. There had also been Savina, a previous wife he had loved without reserve—and mourned the same way, when she died bearing his daughter. But gods, most Coban women were avatars. He had been bought, sold, seduced, kidnapped, married against his will, made the center of political schemes, and turned into the most expensive property in Coba's known history, until finally they went to war over him. He had no intention of giving up his freedom to anyone now, not Coban, Allied, Skolian, or Eubian.

Kelric stirred himself from his reverie. Out here at night, far from the port terminals, he needed to pay extra attention to his surroundings. The danger of theft or random violence always existed; now, with so many security systems down, he had only himself to depend on.

He hefted another crate onto the glider. One more and the platform was full, stacked with black boxes made from hardened plastiflex. He punched in a code and sent it on its way.

"I've never seen anyone load a glider that fast," a man said.

Kelric spun around, his enhanced speed kicking in as he snicked his knife out of its sheath on his belt. By the time his brain stopped his reflexes, he had raised his arm to throw the blade.

In the shadow of the warehouse, a man stood watching him. He was on the tall side, though to Kelric he didn't seem particularly large.

"What do you want?" Kelric asked.

The man stepped into the light, holding his arms at his sides to indicate he carried no weapons. He had short dark hair and a strong-featured face with a large nose. Light from the lamps glinted off silver buttons on the shoulders of his dark spacer's uniform. His gaze flicked to the raised knife, then back to Kelric's face. "I'm Jafe Maccar."

"Captain Maccar?"

"That's right."

Kelric had just sent the glider to Maccar's ship. He lowered his arm. "That was the last of your cargo."

"Good." Maccar paused. "Do you always work this late?"

Kelric shrugged. "Sometimes."

Maccar gave off wariness and curiosity, but no hostility. As far as Kelric knew, the captain had no gripes against Zeld or her people. Even so, he kept the knife in his hand, rubbing his thumb on the hilt.

"Cargo Master Zeld tells me you work hard," Maccar said.

"That's right." Kelric wondered what the captain wanted.

"She also told me to stay away from you."

"Why?"

"Says you're not available for other employment."

Kelric frowned. He hardly ever spoke to Zeld. She had given him a reference, though, when he applied for a room in the bees-hive under the city. His hexagon wasn't much, just big enough for a bed, but it was better than what most refugees had. Zeld had let his prospective landlords believe she had his ID in her office. Kelric knew she did it to soften him up. Although he still had no intention of sleeping with her, he appreciated the reference. That didn't make him her property, though.

"I make my own decisions," he said.

"That's what I thought," Maccar said.

"Why?"

"I need crew. I heard you do good work. Reliable. Smart. Tough."

Kelric shifted the knife in his hand. If Maccar wanted spacers, he could have his pick of the pool signed in at the Port Authority. The captain had no reason for skulking around in the night to hire an illegal immigrant.

Maccar was watching his face. "The run is legal."

Dryly Kelric said, "That's why you're out here instead of at the Port Authority."

"I tried the PA. I couldn't get enough crew."

He knew Maccar's merchant ship only needed a crew of forty and Maccar already had twenty-eight. The captain should have no problem finding twelve more. "What's wrong with the run?"

Maccar regarded him steadily. "I'm going into Trader space." He didn't even flinch when he said it.

"Forget it," Kelric said. *No way.*

"I'll pay you fifty thousand."

That gave Kelric pause. "Why?"

"I've a shipment of Targali silks, jewelry, spices, china, silver, and antiqued boxes." Maccar's frustration seeped out from his mind, belying his cool, dark gaze. "All for a Eubian client. She wants genuine Skolian goods and she'll pay a fortune for them. But I don't have enough crew to make the run. I need spacers who can handle the pressure."

Kelric had no doubt he also needed spacers desperate enough to take the job—like a refugee who had many secrets to hide. I do. He knew of only one type of "Eubian client" who could afford that kind of shipment. "You're trading with an Aristo." The words felt dirty in his mouth.

"Only goods," Maccar said. "No people. I abhor slavery."

"You do. But what's to stop the Aristos from confiscating your ship and selling you and your crew once you're in Eubian space?"

"We've a contract of safe passage from my client." Dryly Maccar added, "I've also hired an escort. Eight frigates and a dreadnought, all armed." He motioned toward the sky. "The border regions between Eube and Skolia are wide open right now. Merchants are passing freely both ways. Hell, man, after Onyx, the Eubian military barely even exists."

In the past few days Kelric had heard a great deal about Onyx. Two billion ISC personnel and over three hundred thousand ships had served the twenty-three space habitats that formed the Onyx ISC complex. But even that had been nowhere near enough to defend against the two million ships in the invasion fleet ESComm sent against them. Faced with those odds, ISC Admiral Starjack Tahota had ordered a daring evacuation. Rather than surrender the Onyx stations, however, she and a group of volunteers stayed behind—and blew up the entire city of space habitats in a maelstrom of energy. It had destroyed the ESComm fleet as well. Starjack and her people gave their lives to break the Trader military and end the war.

The Traders had captured only one Onyx station. The Third Lock. That knowledge chilled Kelric. The Locks were remnants of forgotten Kyle sciences developed during the Ruby Empire. Modern sciences had yet to unravel their technology, so no one could build more of them. But the Triad used the ancient Locks to make the psiberweb. It had given Skolia its one advantage over Eube: ESComm had strength, but ISC had speed. Now ESComm had lost its strength and ISC had lost its speed. So a balance remained. But if ESComm created a psiberweb, they could rise above the chaos and conquer war-ravished Skolia. All they needed was a Key. A psion powerful enough to use the Lock.

A Rhon psion.

A member of the Ruby Dynasty.

Kelric considered Maccar. Hiring on with the captain could bring him enough funds to achieve his goals. He could buy a new identity, get offworld, begin setting up a power base, reach one of the Locks, install himself as Imperator, and find medical treatment. Most of all, he would have hope of seeing his family again. The knowledge that his parents and siblings still lived, albeit in captivity, kept him going. Time was his enemy; the longer he took to reach his goals, the more his health deteriorated.

But should he risk going into Trader space? Borders could close without notice. The Aristos could clamp down on their slave populations any time. Maccar's run might be safe today and a disaster tomorrow.

As Kelric debated, Maccar watched him. Despite the captain's mental barriers, Kelric felt his frustration. Maccar had invested a great deal in this run and now found it beyond his reach for mere lack of crew. Although an honest man, he had reached the point where he was willing to sidestep the law.

"Where in Trader territory would we be going?" Kelric asked.

"Sphinx Sector."

"That's well into Eube."

"We won't be there long."

"How long?"

Maccar grimaced. "As fast as I can get in and out."

"Fifty thousand isn't enough."

"How much is?"

"Two hundred thousand."

Incredulity surged in Maccar. Outwardly he just snorted. "The top spacer at the PA isn't worth that much."

"Maybe not. I am."

Maccar raised his eyebrows. "Why?"

Kelric turned his arm over so his palm faced the sky. He pulled up his wrist guard, uncovering a socket in his wrist. Although Maccar kept his face impassive, surprise leaked out from his mind.

"That's a psiphon socket," Maccar said.

"That's right."

"You a telop?"

"No. A Jagernaut."

This time Maccar whistled. "Can you prove that?"

"Yes." Kelric lowered his arm. "Link me into your ship's EI and I can defend your entire flotilla."

Maccar studied him, his face edged in harsh light from the lamps. "If you're an ISC officer, why don't you have ID? Zeld tells me you've no proof you're even a Skolian citizen. She ran a check on your DNA, and it says no record of you exists."

Damn. Zeld must have taken a lock of his hair or a scrape of skin. Legally, only ISC or the police could do a DNA scan without the citizen's permission, and even that law often came under criticism. But he had no doubt that buying a black-market scan right now was easy. He even understood Zeld's reasons; for all she knew, he was a mass murderer. However, if his gene map was in the Edgewhirl webs now, it gave him even more cause to get offworld.

All he said was, "I've no reason to have ID here."

"No?" Maccar raised his eyebrows. "Edgewhirl has two ISC bases. Zeld checked both the ASC complex up north in Bartanna Shore and the Whitecap Fleet base on the South Jadar continent."

"I'm J-Force. Not ASC or navy." He doubted a spacer with Maccar's savvy would confuse the Advance Services Corps or the Imperial naval fleet with the Jagernaut Force. The captain was probing.

"You AWOL?" Maccar asked.

"MIA."

"You don't look 'missing' to me."

"People don't like Jagernauts," Kelric said. Jag pilots were both revered and reviled, as avenging angels and human weapons. In normal times the monolithic presence of ISC protected them. But now? Who knew?

"You think you'll have trouble?" Maccar asked.

"It's possible."

"Why? You Jagernauts are heroes."

"Sometimes."

Maccar scrutinized him. "If you really are a Jagernaut, doesn't that make you a telepath?"

"I was."

"Was? Past tense?"

"Yes."

"Why? What happened?"

"Neural damage."

Maccar quirked an eyebrow. "Can you hear my thoughts?"

"No." Even with his mind whole, Kelric could only read simple thoughts, and then only if they came from nearby. They also had to be sent with enough strength for him to detect, which usually meant they had to come from another psion. He still picked up less specific impressions, such as emotions, but Maccar hadn't asked about empathy.

"If you're telling the truth about your mind," Maccar said, "doesn't that make you less able to function as a Jagernaut?"

Kelric shrugged. "I might have trouble in the psiberweb. But what does that matter? It no longer exists." He regarded Maccar with a steady gaze. "I can link to any real-space net and make full use of it as a Jagernaut."

Maccar considered him for a long time. Finally he said, "You have any other names besides Kelric?"

"Garlin." He had no intention of revealing his full name, Kelricson Garlin Valdoria Skolia. Although *Valdoria* wasn't unique to the Ruby Dynasty, it was still rare, and known as the last name for a branch of his family. *Skolia* was the dynastic title used by all Rhon members of the Ruby Dynasty.

"All right, Kelric Garlin," Maccar said. "Prove you're a Jagernaut and you've got your two hundred thousand." He inclined his head in the time-honored gesture of sealing a bargain. "Meet me at my ship tomorrow, twelve hundred hours."

Kelric returned the nod. "I'll be there."

4

The Corona's Circle

The merchant ship grew on the shuttle's view screen like a glittering pipe, a promise to Kelric of the future, yet also a promise of peril, as it prepared for the plunge into Trader territory.

Maccar called his vessel the *Corona*. The glistening cylinder had one end open to space. A large half sphere capped the other end. It was a good-sized ship, though not huge by interstellar standards, about 1.5 kilometers long and .25 kilometer in diameter. The sight made Kelric's breath catch; it had been far too long since he had boarded anything other than the crotchety schooner. He savored the sense of homecoming this gave him.

A docking tube extended down the center of the cylinder, its diameter wide enough to swallow a shuttle. Magnificent spokes radiated out from the tube to the cylinder in a design chosen to maximize stability. The spokes didn't actually touch the docking tube; instead, they connected to huge rings that circled it. It allowed the cylinder to rotate grandly in space, while the tube where shuttles docked remained stationary.

Kelric found the *Corona* beautiful in all its pitted, rugged glory. The familiar design welcomed him, as if to say, *You weren't gone so long after all.* Lights glittered along its hull, strobing from antennae, cranes, flanges, pods, observation bays, and the robot crawlers that monitored its myriad surfaces. Huge thrusters circled the open end of the cylinder. His excitement surged as if he were a sailor too long separated from the sea and sailing ships he loved.

They approached the cylinder's open maw. It grew on their holoscreens until the ship dwarfed them, looming around the shuttle. The hub at the end of the docking tube opened like a giant flower pod. Even knowing space had no atmosphere to transmit vibrations, Kelric imagined he felt the power thrumming in the merchant vessel. Their shuttle sailed into the pod, and the great petals closed around them.

In the pilot's seat, Maccar glanced at him. "Ready to board?"

Kelric grinned. "Aye, sir."

The captain's mouth quirked in a smile. "Then let's go."

They exited the shuttle into a round decontamination chamber. Electromagnetic radiation bathed them while monitors and airborne nanomeds examined their bodies for contaminants. If these meds resembled the ones Kelric remembered, they were cousins of the species he already carried in his body.

Nanomeds were designer molecules. Each type had its own task, such as catalyzing a reaction, repairing broken bonds, or ferrying other molecules. Each med carried a picochip, a tiny computer that worked on quantum transitions. The chip directed the industrious med and helped it replicate. Nanomed sex was rather prosaic; they just built more of themselves from excess molecules hanging around the neighborhood. It took energy, but not prohibitive amounts. Picochips in a particular series could chat among themselves using chemical messages. That let them form a crude picoweb which could interact with the picowebs of other series.

Decon meds had one goal: search and destroy. Like nano-thugs cruising the cellular neighborhood, they relentlessly analyzed anyone who entered their decon chamber, seeking contaminants that might endanger the ship. They compared what they found to their databases of allowed and forbidden species, and ran tests on unknowns. Then they tackled unwanted invaders and rumbled with them until they disposed of the intruder or fell apart trying. If any decon meds remained intact after they finished their work, they disintegrated into pieces the body could use or flush out of itself.

The meds in Kelric's body kept up his health, repaired his cells to delay his aging, and attacked unwanted chemicals. Both decon and health meds had to meet certain standards and should recognize one another as acceptable species. But what if standards had changed? For all Kelric knew, the decon meds might attack his mutated meds or the medicine Doctor Tarjan had given him to slow the mutation rate. His meds might retaliate with their own thuggery. The last thing he needed was nano-gang warfare in his body.

He floated with Maccar in the chamber, trying to relax. The captain monitored the decon process on a palmtop computer he unhooked from his belt.

Fortunately, the nano-thugs approved of Kelric. They only cleaned out a few species of bacteria. He and Maccar left the chamber, drifting weightless in the docking tube. They boarded a magcar, and it raced off into a smooth-sided tunnel like a glittering bullet hurtling down a shiny bore.

The car took them to the far end of the ship, where the hemispherical section capped the cylinder. They disembarked into an air lock. After they cycled through the air lock, they floated into the hemisphere, an area about one quarter kilometer in diameter. The ship's bridge.

Maccar's command chair hung "above" them, though up and down had no real meaning here, without gravity. The chair faced the forward curve of the hemisphere and had its back to the cylinder, giving a sense that the captain looked forward into space and the unknown. Of course, without the holoscreens on, they saw only the interior of the bridge. It glinted silver and black, studded with equipment. Consoles ridged its curve, their controls and screens glittering in a rainbow of lights.

Most captains spun the bridge for at least a portion of each shift, to provide a break from the weightless environment and to help stabilize the counter-rotating cylinder. Although the result bewildered some spacers, Kelric enjoyed the strange effects. If you imagined the cylinder's rotation axis extending into the bridge, it passed through the center of the hemisphere and pierced the hull forward of Maccar's chair. The pull of gravity increased with distance from the rotation axis. So right on top of the axis, you had no weight at all no matter how fast the ship rotated.

As you walked away from the rotation axis along the hull, gravity increased. "Down" always pointed radially out from the axis, so the inner surface of the hemisphere turned into a steep slope. Consoles jutted out like terraces. The slope gentled as you moved farther away from the point where the axis intersected the hemisphere, toward the back of the bridge, until at the "equator" where the bridge met the cylinder, the ground became level and gravity was full strength. If you looked "up," across the quarter-kilometer diameter of the bridge, you could see other crew members blithely walking around upside down on the "sky."

Right now Maccar's chair was suspended in the middle of the hemisphere, near the rotation axis, so even during rotation it would have almost no weight. However, the massive chair served as the terminus of a similarly massive robot arm that could easily move within the bridge.

Kelric and Maccar propelled off a bulkhead and flew through the bridge. They controlled their progress using cables that stretched across the hemisphere. Kelric exhilarated in the freedom of escaping gravity's tethers.

Members of the bridge crew were at their stations running preflight checks, each person secure within the exoskeleton of a console chair. Maccar introduced Kelric to them all: Nadick Steil, the executive officer, second in command, a stocky woman with brown hair cut short around her head; Larra Anatakala, the navigation and tracking officer, a gaunt woman with long legs and arms; and Ty Rillwater, the communications officer, whose small size and soft yellow hair made her look like a child compared to the others.

The weapons station was located between Communications and Navigation. However, Maccar took Kelric to a different console.

Unique on the bridge, this one had psiphon capability. If the psiberweb had still existed, it could have boosted Kelric's mind into psiberspace. Even without the web, he could still use it to jack his brain into the *Corona*'s EI brain.

The station curved around its command chair, bringing its mobile control panels within easy reach of whoever sat there. Maccar took an auxiliary seat across the console while Kelric slid into the control chair. The exoskeleton folded around Kelric and its sensors studied him as if he were a new processing unit. It shifted position at his neck, back, wrists, and ankles. Then psiphon prongs clicked into the sockets in his neck and lower spine, the strong, silvery pins inserting through holes in his spacer's jumpsuit designed for that purpose. But when the prongs tried to insert into his wrists and ankles, they hit his guards.

Kelric pushed the exoskeleton up his arm, uncovering his wrist guard. He worked the psiphon prong under his guard and tried bending it into the socket. Apparently it wasn't flexible enough. Or maybe the meds that tended the socket no longer worked. In any case, the prong wouldn't click into place.

Maccar reached over to a comm panel on the console. "I'll have a bosun remove the guards."

Startled, Kelric glanced at him. "No."

The captain raised his eyebrows. "No?"

"I can't remove the guards."

Maccar considered him. "What was your Jagernaut rank?"

The non sequitur puzzled Kelric. "Tertiary."

"That's about equal to a Fleet rank of commander, isn't it?"

"About." He wondered what the captain was getting at.

Maccar leaned forward. "Understand me, mister. I don't give a kiss in hell how much of a loner you were as a Jag pilot. If I hire you, I expect the same adherence to the chain of command from you as from my other officers. If you have a problem with that, I don't want you on this ship."

Kelric stiffened. Of course he knew his position in a chain of command. Still, he wondered at his response. Had he become so used to his aristocratic civilian life on Coba that he had forgotten military discipline? He wouldn't have thought so, yet his automatic response to Maccar's implicit order had been a refusal.

He felt Maccar's mental debate. The captain was weighing his doubts about his prospective weapons officer against his need for Kelric's expertise. Before Kelric had a chance to respond, Maccar said, "I can't gamble, Commander Garlin. Where we're going, I can't take any risks."

"You won't be taking a risk," Kelric said. Maccar's use of the title *Commander* disoriented him. But it made sense; even if he had wanted his military rank known, which he didn't, using Tertiary on a civilian ship was inappropriate.

"And if you decide you can't follow another command?" Maccar started to unfasten the clasps that held his safety web in place. "The shuttle can take you back to Porthaven."

"Wait." Kelric didn't want his job interview to end before it even began. "You won't have any problem with my following orders, Captain. Call the bosun." Then he thought, *Ixpar, I'm sorry.*

Maccar glanced at the wrist guards. "Why don't you want to take them off?"

"They're from my wife."

The captain stiffened. "Hell's road, man, I thought they looked like marriage guards. They're old enough. How many thousands of years did it take us to get rid of the laws that let women make us property? Don't you know the origin of Trader slave restraints? They're a variation of the Ruby Empire marriage guards. Except Traders put them on both men and women. Why? Because they show *ownership.* How can you wear that kind of symbol?"

Of all the comments Kelric had expected, that wasn't one of them. How to answer? Even on Coba, only Akasi princes wore the marriage guards. As the husband of a Manager, he had been such an Akasi. In the star-spanning culture of Imperial Skolia, the custom had mostly vanished. Even the Imperial noble houses dispensed with it more often now than not.

The houses were still the most conservative facet of Skolian culture, though. Kelric's first marriage had been arranged long before he ended up on Coba. His wife, Admiral Corey Majda, had been matriarch of the oldest house. Her assassination left him a widower at twenty-four. They hadn't had children, so her title and lands went to her sister, Naaj Majda. Kelric had received a widower's mansion and stipend. He had been too blind with grief to care about the inheritance, besides which, his Ruby Dynasty titles and wealth outranked even the House of Majda. But with that history, Coba hadn't surprised him.

None of that mattered. He didn't care what symbolism Maccar thought the guards embodied. They were all he had left of Ixpar. She had never considered him a possession—and she had literally gone to war to uphold that principle.

All he said was, "They don't mean to me what they do to you."

Maccar studied him. "You're a hard one to fathom."

Uncomfortable, Kelric rolled the psiphon prong in his hand.

After considering a moment longer, Maccar summoned a bosun. A man in a gray jumpsuit soon appeared, carrying a tool kit. He anchored himself at the station by attaching his safety tether to a ring on the console. He fastened down his tool kit, then unclipped a problade, a programmable blade made from thorium phosphide, a substance harder than diamond.

Kelric extended his arm. The guard glinted in the cold light. The bosun measured the thickness of the gold with calipers, then programmed the blade so it extended just enough to cut through the metal. As he set the blade against the guard, Kelric had to hold himself back from yanking away his arm. This was the final symbol of his losing Ixpar and his children.

Maccar watched intently, his focus more on Kelric than the work. As the bosun put his thumb against the problade's switch, Maccar said, "Wait."

The bosun paused. "Sir?"

Maccar indicated the prong on Kelric's exoskeleton. "Can you drill a hole through the guard so the prong will fit in his socket?"

The man lifted Kelric's arm, slid his guard around a few times, and rubbed his thumb over the engravings. "It should be possible."

"Go ahead then," Maccar said. "No need to remove them."

Kelric swallowed. He nodded to Maccar, unable to voice his gratitude. Maccar probably didn't want to hear it anyway. The captain had been testing him.

The bosun drilled the holes so they were almost invisible in the engravings. He did both Kelric's wrist and ankle guards, making sure the prongs fit through the gold and snapped into place. When Kelric was fully installed at the console, Maccar dismissed the bosun from the bridge.

Kelric settled into the command seat. *Attend,* he thought.

Corona attending. The ship's response rumbled in his mind with more force and clarity than he had expected. Your system needs an upgrade. Shall I provide?

Kelric almost grinned. He had hoped the *Corona*'s EI could upgrade him. Otherwise his lack of knowledge about modern systems would probably keep him from passing this interview. *What can you do?*

I can replace 68 percent of your software with current versions, it answered. I can also provide assistance as you incorporate the new code. The rest of your systems are either unfamiliar or too dated for me to work with.

Excitement brushed Kelric. *Can you get back my link to Bolt?*

Define Bolt.

The JGP12 computer node in my spine.

I can replace 84 percent of the corrupted code in the JGP12 node. However, it also has physical damage I cannot repair.

My meds can carry out your instructions, Kelric pointed out. The boundaries separating hardware, software, and biotech had long been blurred. With a Jagernaut, who could say where machine left off and human started? Some experts questioned whether Jagernauts were even *Homo sapiens*, suggesting they formed their own species. Kelric didn't buy it; he was perfectly capable of breeding with other humans. Still, he obviously had aspects to his physiology most humans lacked. If the *Corona* interfaced with those systems, it could direct physical as well as software repairs within him.

If I use your nanomeds, the *Corona* answered, **it will draw them away from the repair of your body, allow the mutations freer reign, and possibly encourage more.**

Surely it won't be too serious for a few minutes.

It will take far more than a few minutes to do repairs. The *Corona* paused. **Even then I cannot guarantee the results. I would advise against prolonged redirection of your med series.**

Kelric didn't want to risk slipping back into a critical state. Doctor Tarjan's help had bought him more time, but he still needed treatment. He had to accomplish his goals before his systems started to fail again.

Do you have other suggestions for fixing my node? he asked.

Yes. Replace the JGP12 with JGPP146+ local neural node cluster.

They put entire clusters in humans now? That had been too risky in his time. The idea of a network in his body, with who knew how much more power than Bolt alone, both intrigued and disconcerted him. However, unless procedures had changed drastically, he doubted be could simply request such an upgrade.

How would I get the cluster? he asked.

You must proceed through ISC channels, with appropriate clearances.

No surprises there, unfortunately. *Go ahead with whatever upgrades you can safely do, then.* Turning his focus to Bolt, he thought, *Allow access to the* Corona. Normally he wouldn't have to tell Bolt; the node should be following the exchange and would know to let in the *Corona.* With Bolt's damage, though, he wasn't sure of anything about it right now.

Proceeding, the *Corona* thought.

Although Kelric could no longer access Bolt's chronometer, he knew his accelerated exchange with the *Corona* had taken only a second or two, if that long. Maccar was watching him with an appraising gaze.

Software upgrade complete, the *Corona* thought. **Proceeding to psiware.**

At first Kelric noticed nothing unusual, only a sense of mental pressure, as if his head were underwater. Then, with no warning, pain stabbed his head like a lance.

"Ah—!" He pressed the heels of his hands against his temples.

Warning, the *Corona* thought. Errors in neural sectors 53AF, 93—

Stop the upgrade! He gritted his teeth, trying not to shout the words.

Stopped.

Can you fix the damaged sectors of my brain? Kelric asked.

No. I'm deleting the partial copies of the replacement code.

"Commander?" Maccar asked. "Are you all right?"

Kelric took a breath. "Your ship's EI and my biomech web have a slight incompatibility." Some "slight": The portions of his brain that interfaced with the psiber capabilities of other computers had taken damage when his ship crashed on Coba. His brain needed as much work as the rest of him—if he wasn't past repair.

"Can you operate with the *Corona* system?" Maccar asked.

"Yes." A person needed no unusual neurological abilities to use the console's mundane cyber functions. It did require a direct mind-to-machine interface, however. Implanting such an interface in a human being was no trivial procedure, and the training to master its uses required clearances and connections available to very few people.

Activating the console's psiber functions was even more complex. On the scale that quantified Kyle mutations, a psion had to rate at six or more to access psiberspace. The higher the rating, the larger a person's KAB and the more extra neural structures they had packed into their brain. A rating of three made someone an empath. At six, the first signs of telepathy showed. The scale was exponential: one in a thousand humans was a three, and one in a million a six.

Kelric had trained for both cybernetic and Kyle work. With his injuries, though, he wasn't sure how far he could push his brain in its mental acrobatics. He laid his head back into the chair's curved headrest, and its visor lowered over his eyes and ears. Smooth, streamlined, and light as a sponge, it made the VR helmets of eighteen years ago barbaric in comparison.

Blackness surrounded him. *Activate mindscape,* he thought.

You don't have clearance, the *Corona* informed him.

"Captain, I need to enter the *Corona* system." Kelric's voice echoed oddly within the visored cavity.

Maccar shifted in his seat, leaning over the console, it sounded like. "Account, Garlin K., Commander. Password, 'probation.' "

A wry smile tugged Kelric's mouth. Probation. Maccar apparently had no use for subtlety.

"Account created," the *Corona* said.

"Link it to the unit installed in the console," Maccar said.

"Done," the ship answered.

Activate mindscape, Kelric thought. He wondered if Maccar designated all his crew members as "installed units." Somehow he doubted it.

A landscape formed around him, made by white grid lines on a blue background. It gave him the *Corona*'s representation of cybernetic activity throughout the ship. Hills indicated systems buzzing with computer-human action, and valleys denoted quiescence.

Show all states, Kelric thought, asking for everything the *Corona* could tell him about itself, rather than just its cybernetic activity. *Priority: weapons.*

New displays replaced the grid, schematics of the ship and its combat systems. Three-dimensional graphs, tables, and hyperlinks swamped him with data. He moved through the *Corona* like a stealth ghost, studying it. Then he expanded his survey to the dreadnought and eight frigates in their escort, which orbited Edgewhirl in formation with the *Corona.* According to the displays, Bolt was taking in data as fast as the *Corona* supplied it, almost at light speed.

He recognized the basic systems. It would take time for him to become proficient here, to process his upgrades and learn his new functions. But he could manage.

"Are you into the *Corona*?" Maccar asked, a disembodied voice.

"Yes." He concentrated on the captain. His mindscape responded by forming a schematic of Kelric and the console in white grid lines. Then the scene solidified into a virtual reality so authentic it was indistinguishable from real reality. He was on the bridge of the *Corona*, looking at Maccar across the console. The only indication it was a simulated Maccar, rather than the flesh-and-blood captain, was a slight sharpness at the edges of his body.

The psiphon prongs that had plugged into Kelric's sockets were linked to his biomech web. It let the console send messages straight to his brain, bypassing the need for VR helmets and suits. Sight, smell, sound, touch, even taste: he experienced them all through direct neural stimulation. This setup produced better quality VR than those he had known even on his Jag starfighter, which had claimed the best machine-to-mind tech of its time.

With his brain juiced up straight from the console, he didn't need the visor. It still served a purpose, though, intensifying the simulation. It also blocked his perception of real space. It would have been a true exercise in strangeness to experience a VR simulation of reality superimposed on that exact same reality.

"I'm in," he told Maccar.

The captain nodded. "Arm the Impactors on frigate seven."

Normally Kelric would have located the Impactors on frigate seven and sent his commands to the frigate through the *Corona.* At close to light speed, it would take the barest fraction of a second.

But he was curious to see how much the *Corona*'s EI could handle. So he tried a less standard approach. *Execute command from Maccar,* he thought, deliberately vague.

Done, the *Corona* answered. An icon of frigate seven appeared in the lower left corner of his VR sim, hanging in midair. It blinked red to indicate the primed weapons.

Not bad, Kelric thought. His Jag would have needed more specifics to carry out the command. "Impactors armed, Captain."

"*Corona*, run mod four," Maccar said. "Tricore Defensive code."

Kelric plunged into battle.

Pirate frigates were converging on them like a swarm of hornets. His mindscape snapped into a new simulation, an all-around view of space with its glittering stars and dust. Translucent displays formed, superimposed over space, images that turned data into symbols his mind could process faster.

Neither human reflexes nor thought could keep up with the speed of space warfare. But Kelric knew too little about the strategies in the *Corona*'s combat libraries even to name them, let alone choose one. He would have to rely on the ship's EI.

Optimize offense for destruction of pirates, he thought.

Firing Scythe pattern 8, the *Corona* answered.

Quasis jump, it thought. **Impactor hit on—**

Quasis jump. Pirates destroyed.

Nausea rolled over Kelric. During quasis, or quantum stasis, their quantum state remained fixed. The ship didn't "freeze": only at absolute zero could matter reach a state where none of its particles had motion. In quasis, the particles that made up the *Corona* continued to rotate, spin, translate, and otherwise behave as they had been when the quasis snapped on. However, they couldn't *change* state, not even by one particle. Molecules kept the same configuration; bonds shook and twisted with the same quanta of vibration and rotation; atoms made no transitions; and quarks kept their charm or lack thereof. Nothing could change.

Thoughts required chemical changes in the brain, so even they stopped, caught in whatever slice of mentation a person was experiencing when the quasis snapped on. The process of thinking resumed when a person came out of quasis, giving the sense of a discontinuous "jump."

In macroscopic terms, the ship and everything in it became rigid, impervious to forces, including the brutal accelerations of split-second combat. Nor could weapons-fire damage the ship, because the process of destruction required particles to change state. After two or three hits the quasis usually collapsed, but while it lasted it provided a good defense.

When a ship came out of quasis, its systems and crew adapted to their new environment. If their physical situation had changed too much, the required adaptations could hurt the ship or crew. The most dramatic case came about when the quasis collapsed under enemy fire—and the crew found themselves in the midst of an exploding ship.

According to Kelric's mindscape, each jump he had just experienced lasted about a second. The "battle" had been simulated. Almost no changes took place while he was in quasis, certainly not enough to make a healthy person sick when his body adjusted to his new environment. His nausea was an unwelcome reminder of his failing health.

The *Corona* had continued to operate smoothly despite the jumps. As soon as the ship dropped out of quasis, the crew resumed their preflight tests, unperturbed by the one-second discontinuities in their lives. It told Kelric a great deal about Maccar's command and his crew. This was a well-run ship.

"TD-four off," Maccar said. The simulation disappeared, replaced by the grid landscape.

Close mindscape, Kelric thought. Referring to himself, he added, *Release weapons CPU.*

Closed, the *Corona* answered. **You are released.**

The mindscape vanished and the visor lifted away from his head. Maccar was still sitting in the auxiliary chair across the console.

The captain frowned. "Why did you attack without hailing the ships? Their intent may not have been hostile."

"Trader pirates don't 'hail,'" Kelric said. "They were also better armed than your escort. In that situation, you don't wait to ask questions."

"So." Although Maccar's neutral expression gave nothing away, his mind projected wary approval. "And if we had faced ESComm ships, instead of pirates?"

Kelric almost snorted. Eubian Space Command had long denied any link to the pirates that raided Skolian and Allied space. But he had seen the intelligence reports that said otherwise. ESComm supplied, advised, protected, and supported the raiders.

"If we encountered ESComm ships in Skolian space," Kelric said, "I would respond in the same way."

Maccar scowled. "Firing without provocation on ESComm is far different from attacking pirates. We might be able to justify the former. Not the latter."

"What do you want?" Kelric asked. "A polite inquiry as to why they came into our territory? While we observe courtesies, they make the capture. You choose, Captain: proper procedure followed by slavery, or a strategy that maintains your freedom."

"What I want," Maccar said, "is the survival of my flotilla and the success of this run, without any diplomatic incidents."

Kelric regarded him steadily. "Hire me and you'll have your best shot at success. As for diplomacy, the moment you enter Trader space you're risking an incident. I'll protect your flotilla with experience and knowledge you won't find elsewhere. But if diplomacy is your goal, I'm not your man."

Maccar scrutinized him for a long time. Finally he said, "All right, Commander. You have the job."

Kelric sailed along the corridor in long strides, following Nadick Steil, the *Corona*'s stocky executive officer. Long-limbed Larra Anatakala, the navigation officer, sailed at his side. He felt as if he were flying. The ship's cylinder was rotating fast enough to simulate gravity at 10 percent the human standard. It gave him enough weight to orient himself, with "up" toward the interior of the cylinder and "down" toward its outer hull.

He was having fun. The ship's spin created a Coriolis force, which felt like a push to the side when he sailed up into the air. The faster he and the others moved, the stronger the push; the slower they went, the weaker it felt. Even more entertaining, it varied with direction. It was greatest when they moved up or down, at right angles to the ship's rotation axis, and they felt no push at all when they went parallel to the axis.

Even at its greatest, this Coriolis force wasn't that strong. It was enough, though, to disorient some people, throw off their balance, make them queasy. It didn't bother Kelric. He enjoyed the quirky sensations. Trying to compensate for the effect as he flew along the ship was like a game.

Silky spun-metal carpet covered every surface around them. Blue and shimmering, it pleased the eye, but more important, it served as padding when he collided with bulkheads. It didn't take long to regain his space legs, though. He had always thrived on the athletic demands of low gravity. A female admirer once told him that in low-g he was "sheer joy to watch." He didn't know about that, but he did know he liked the whole process.

Nadick Steil, the exec, glanced back from time to time with an odd expression. From her mind he picked up that she had expected him to be clumsier. For some reason his natural ease offended her, though he had no idea why. Larra Anatakala was much friendlier. She grinned at him every now and then as they sailed along. They didn't try to talk, not only because they didn't know one another but also because it would have been awkward at the fast clip they were moving.

They passed many doors, white ovals with silver trim. Finally Steil stopped at one and entered a combination on the security panel to its left. With a hiss of compressed sir, the door slid aside.

Steil went through the doorway without a glance back at Kelric. Larra Anatakala moved aside, though, observing an antiquated custom that required she let the man enter first. It startled him. Prior to Coba, he had spent his entire adult life in the military, and being here put him back in that mindset. ISC had evolved from its original matriarchal roots to a mixed force with over 45 percent male personnel. Regulations now forbade treatment based on a person's sex. Although most proscribed actions were concerned with discrimination, the list also included well-meant but preferential courtesies such as the one Anatakala had just offered him.

Even so, he knew she meant it as a gesture of respect. He smiled at her as he entered his new quarters. The cubicle had a bunk on the left, sleek metal cabinets on the walls, and a few square meters of floor space. A console slumbered in one corner and radiance bars in the ceiling provided light.

Steil turned to him, almost floating in the low gravity. She indicated a door in one wall. "Disposal unit." Tapping a cabinet, she added, "You've two jumpsuits and a pair of boots, officer's issue. The personal gear you brought up from Edgewhirl is also stowed here." Her voice was cool. "Any questions about what we've showed you so far? The ship? Procedures? Now is the time to ask."

Kelric shook his head. "It all looks straightforward." He had easily absorbed the tour they had given him. The basics of a ship and an officer's routine hadn't changed much from what he remembered.

"You're sure?" Steil's puzzlement leaked out from her mind. He didn't know what she expected, but he supposed most people would have asked more questions.

"Yes," he said. "I'm sure."

"All right." She shrugged. "We'll see you on the bridge at sixteen hundred hours."

After Steil took her leave, Anatakala gave Kelric a pleasant smile. It transformed her long face, softening the lines around her eyes and mouth. "I wanted to welcome you to the ship. From what the captain said, this has happened rather fast for you, yes?"

"A bit," he admitted. She was standing just inside the hatch, close enough for him to absorb her mood. Her friendly curiosity trickled over him. A flicker of attraction stirred her thoughts about him, but she kept it submerged. Her interest didn't feel intrusive, as it had with Cargo Master Zeld on Edgewhirl.

Zeld had surprised him, though, when he told her about his plans to go with Maccar. As much as she grumbled about his leaving her shorthanded, her mind projected other emotions. She was worried about his safety in Trader space. And she would miss him. She liked him. He wasn't sure what disconcerted him more, having been ogled for so long by his employer or realizing she had developed genuine affection for him.

"We've an hour before our duty shift comes up," Anatakala was saying. "Would you like to go down to the mess, get some coffee, talk about the ship?"

Coffee? Pah. He had never figured out how Earth convinced the rest of humanity to drink that godawful liquid. Some of his own siblings guzzled it. While mighty Imperial Skolia and the colossal

Trader empire blasted each other with millions of ships and world-slagging energies, the little Allied Worlds were quietly taking over the galaxy by making everyone think they needed Earth imports. Someday the entire Milky Way would be one big Allied shopping mall crammed with coffee, cybernetic pets that beeped at you, and holovids that spawned endless adventure games. While Earth got rich, the rest of humanity would be left trying to figure out what had happened when they weren't looking.

"Kelric?" Anatakala asked. "Are you there?"

He flushed, realizing he had just been staring at her. "Sorry," he said. "Maybe another time."

She started to answer, hesitated, then asked, "Is anything wrong?"

Kelric exhaled. Had his life on Coba made him incapable of talking with a woman? In the Calanya, he had been among the elite male dice players on Coba. He had spoken to no one except the other men in the Calanya and the woman who ruled the city-state. Technically a Calanya was no longer a warrior queen's harem: most of the fifteen or so men in it weren't husbands. However, any other woman who married a Calanya Quis player could never live with him; such unions were by visitation only and depended on the queen's goodwill. As a result, the Calanya still had an intensely sexual quality, one steeped in Coban history.

For Kelric, the mere act of speaking to a woman had become sexual, an effect magnified by his status as a queen's favored husband. He had lived in six different city-states and been married to the rulers of five, usually against his will. Although he had left that culture behind, talking to women still made him uncomfortable, even now, when Anatakala had done nothing more than offer friendship.

The navigator shifted her weight. "I'm sorry if I caused offense." She turned toward the hatch.

"Larra, wait," he said. "You didn't."

She turned back, her posture revealing the same uncertainty that flowed from her mind. Her awareness of him intensified. As an empath he not only picked up emotions, he also projected his own if he wasn't careful. With his Kyle centers damaged, he had lost some ability to barrier his mind. Without intending to, and without Anatakala realizing it, he had sent her his perception of sexuality in their interaction. It stirred her in exactly the way he wanted to avoid, bringing her desire for him to the surface.

Kelric flushed. He picked up her pleasure in him, her appreciation for his long-legged muscular build, for the way his gold-tinted curls fell down his neck and tousled around his face. Her desire was sweeter than Zeld's lust, shaded with affection, as if she was incapable of wanting a man without also liking him. It created a feedback loop, arousing him as well. He felt a surge of loneliness, one fueled by his response to her desire. He wanted to hold her, stroke her, kiss her, push her down onto his bunk—

Ah, no. Mortified, he took a breath. It had been too long since he had interacted with strangers, particularly women. He had lost his mental defenses. He tried to barrier his mind, but pain sparked in his temples.

"I should go," Anatakala said. She projected chagrin now, a disbelief that she, a happily married woman, had let herself be so affected by a fellow officer.

"I could use a rest," he admitted. As soon as he said it, he wanted to kick himself. He should have chosen an excuse that didn't involve lying in bed.

"Yes. Of course." Flushing, she pushed off the bulkhead and flew out the hatchway.

He went over and closed the hatch. Then he leaned his forehead against it, angry at himself. What had just happened would make serving with Anatakala awkward. But damn it all, he couldn't turn off his empathic ability. It was *part* of him. Nor could he help the way he looked. What was he supposed to do, make himself ugly?

He had done nothing wrong. Neither had Anatakala. It had just happened. He still felt stupid, though, as if he had propositioned her.

At times like this he missed Ixpar so much he could almost feel her in his arms. As with most telepaths, the bonds he made went deep. So did his loyalty. Ixpar was the one he wanted. He couldn't have her. He would probably never see her again. Which left him what? A lifetime of loneliness? He knew himself. Some people could live alone, but he wasn't one of them.

For Ixpar's sake, he knew he should hope she remarried and found happiness with someone else. He hated the thought. He didn't want her happy with another man. He supposed it wasn't the most noble sentiment. But he couldn't stand the idea of her loving someone else.

She probably thought he died. The estate wing where he had been separated from his bodyguards had burned to the ground. No matter how hard they searched, they weren't going to find him. What other choice would they have but to assume his death?

He had to face the truth. Eventually Ixpar would remarry. On Coba she wouldn't break any laws if she took another husband without realizing Kelric still lived. Imperial law was less forgiving. It probably wouldn't have mattered if he had been a normal citizen. Who would condemn her when she faced such wrenching evidence of his death? Nor would it matter if Coba remained forgotten by the Imperialate. But he wasn't a normal citizen and no guarantees existed that Coba would keep its anonymity.

Although the Ruby Dynasty and Imperial noble houses no longer had the same power they had wielded during the Ruby Empire, their wealth and influence remained strong. That handful of ancient families lived in their own universe, one where old customs and laws held sway. If Ixpar took a second husband, she would be committing adultery. By the ancient laws that still governed the Imperial court—where heredity and succession meant everything—adultery carried the death penalty.

Kelric didn't believe for one instant that every member of every noble house lived as a paragon of faithful virtue. They were, however, paragons of discretion. In their ever-shifting intrigues and passions, reserve remained the unwritten code. Ixpar's situation simmered with the potential for disaster. Although she was mother to neither of his children, she had custody of both. Their DNA contained indisputable proof of their heredity. They were Ruby Dynasty heirs, in line to the Ruby Throne. His daughter was also a Rhon psion, giving her the right to a place in the three Triad lines of succession.

Although the Skolian Imperialate bore the name of his family—the Skolias—the Assembly ruled now, a civilian body formed by elections, appointments, and merit, overseen by both human and EI brains. They, rather than an ancient dynastic family, commanded the halls of power. Yet despite everything, the Ruby Dynasty remained strong. They had become symbols to the populace, the stuff of legends, bigger than life, the icons of dreams and myths. By itself, that would have only established them as a cultural force, not a political one. It was the Triad that gave them power.

Without the Triad, the psiberweb couldn't exist. Without the psiberweb, the Assembly lost a fundamental building block in its power base. It wasn't only the military potential. The ease of communications offered by the web tied interstellar civilization together much in the way that, centuries ago, the first world webs had made planetwide civilizations possible.

Only Rhon psions—the Ruby Dynasty—could survive the Triad powerlink, with its huge fluxes of power and the everyday demands of maintaining an interstellar web. So an uneasy alliance existed; the Assembly sought to use and control Kelric's family while his family fought to keep their freedom and influence. They played a never-ending dance of power, with an interstellar empire as the stakes.

He wanted his children protected from Imperial politics, at least until they were adults, fortified to deal with their heritage. They were safe on Coba. But if they were discovered? As their guardian, Ixpar would find herself facing a morass of star-spanning intrigue and deception. What if he wasn't there to help? For all her brilliance as a leader, she was unprepared to face a colossus like the Imperialate. But her association with him would give her great power, far more than she knew—power that could threaten both the Assembly and the noble houses. They wouldn't dare eliminate his consort, current or former—unless she gave them cause. A charge of adultery was the perfect answer. They would waste no time executing her.

Kelric went to the console and opened his computer account.

Then he sat, thinking over his options. On Edgewhirl his choices had been limited. That star system had always been isolated. Given the current breakdown in communications and Edgewhirl's remote character, little chance had existed that any provision he set up there for Ixpar and his children would make it off-planet and into the major databases that defined Skolia.

Now he faced a better situation. Without the web, how did one send messages across the stars? By starship, of course. He had an entire flotilla at his disposal. They were headed into Trader space, so he had no intention of leaving data about his family on any of the ships. However, they all carried tau missiles, miniature starships with warheads. As weapons officer, he had access to all of them. He needed the armed taus ready for combat, but each ship also stocked a few without warheads. Empty shells. Such spares usually served as replacements if the casing for an active missile failed. However, they could also ferry data. They made good spy couriers.

Being cautious, he could spare three. By launching them to different locations, he tripled the chance that one would reach a major site. He would encrypt and hide the data so that only someone who knew the correct protocols could retrieve it. The files would also come to light on notification of his death or in response to certain inquiries about Ixpar or his children.

One question remained: What would he send?

He toggled into the *Corona*'s Legal mod and searched the database until he found the document he needed. *Closure.*

The closure statement had been developed to replace the process of declaring a spouse legally dead; as such, it required ten years of separation before it became irreversible. It differed in three ways from divorce: closure dissolved a marriage because of a permanent separation neither party desired; either party could reverse the closure; and the person making the declaration had to grant full inheritance to his or her spouse and any heirs, born or adopted into the union.

Filling out the inheritance section took Kelric a long time. Since he had "died" eighteen years ago without known heirs, his estate would have gone to his parents. The closure document, backed with the DNA analysis he provided, would reestablish his claim. Knowing his parents, they had probably done nothing with his estate, too stunned at outliving their youngest child to take any steps that acknowledged the finality of his death.

He had major holdings on three planets. On his home world of Lyshriol he owned a farm of several hundred acres in an outlying province of the Dalvador Plains. Lord Rillia had granted the farm to Kelric's father for his service to the Rillian army, and his father later gave it to Kelric as a betrothal present. When Kelric reached his majority at twenty-five, his mother gave him one of the Ruby Dynasty holdings, a mansion and many acres of land on the planet Metropoli. As Corey Majda's husband, he had his widower's home, the Majda palace on Raylicon where he and Corey had gone for their honeymoon.

His other assets included his savings and retirement accounts from his years as an ISC officer; his widower's stipend from the House of Majda; his stipend as a Ruby prince; his income from the farm, which was run by a local family; his income from a shipping business Corey gave him as a wedding present; and his income from a trust fund his parents set up at his birth. Although he also stood to inherit a portion of his parents' phenomenal wealth, he had trouble making himself complete that section. After everyone else he had lost, he hated having to acknowledge that they, too, could die.

Giving the identity and location of his wife and children also troubled him. For all that he could encrypt, lock, and hide the files, it made him uneasy. Codes could be broken and privacy violated. The risk, however, was better than the alternatives.

He had to enter his full identity, including his interminable list of titles: Prince Kelricson Garlin Valdoria Kya Skolia, Imperator Presumptive, Im'Rhon to the Rhon of the Skolias, Jagernaut Tertiary, Tenth Heir to the throne of the Ruby Dynasty, once removed from the line of Pharaoh, born of the Rhon, Eighth Heir to the Web Key, Tenth Heir to the Assembly Key, descended from the Valdor's line, Fifth in the line of the Dalvador Bard, and Widower Dowager to the House of Majda.

Untangling the convoluted lines of succession gave him a headache. Until he knew for certain that the Ruby Pharaoh and her son had died, he assumed the Pharaoh's line existed. If they truly were gone, he would no longer be "once removed," he would be in the direct line to the Ruby Throne.

In the past, the Ruby succession had always gone through the female line. The idea of including sons had stirred immense controversy. Ignoring it all, his aunt Dehya designated her son and only child as her heir. Soon after, Kelric's parents added their sons to the Ruby succession, which already included their daughters. His mother, Roca, was the next heir to the Ruby Throne and would become Pharaoh if the deaths of her sister and nephew were confirmed. She also stood first in line for Dehya's Triad title of Assembly Key; Dehya's death would make Roca a presumptive Triad member like Kelric, one also kept from assuming her title by the political situation.

As Roca's consort, Kelric's father had no claim to the Ruby Throne. However, as Web Key he held one of the three Triad titles. He and Roca chose his Triad heirs according to who they, and the Assembly, thought best suited to become Web Key. Kelric stood high in the succession for the Military Key, or Imperator, so he was far down in the Triad lines for the Web and Assembly Keys. The deaths of Kurj, Althor, and Soz had been verified, so he left them out when he figured his place in the various successions. It made their loss hurt even more, like another translucent layer of grief.

His father also bore a hereditary title on his native world of Lyshriol. Literally, *Valdoria* translated into Skolian as "Dalvador Bard," but most Skolian citizens called him the King of Skyfall, a romantic but woefully inaccurate translation. The title passed through the male line, which included Kelric.

Kelric's oldest brother, Eldrin, had been the Pharaoh's consort, forced by the ruling Assembly into the marriage because they wanted the Ruby Dynasty to make more Rhon psions, even if it meant interbreeding. As her consort, Eldrin had no claim to her throne. However, as his mother's firstborn, he was next in line to the Ruby Throne after Roca, unless he stepped aside for one of his sisters. He was also their father's first heir, both as Web Key and Dalvador Bard. When Kelric worked out his place in the various lines, he assumed Eldrin still lived; without confirmation, he found himself unable to accept his brother's death.

After Kelric completed the document, he encrypted the file and sent it to the EI's Legal mod. It took only a moment before Legal sent a message back to his console: **Marriage Closed.**

Ixpar, I won't forget you, he thought. He copied the document to the tau missiles, programmed their security, and launched them in a stealth pattern. When they were safely off, he erased the evidence of his work from all the flotilla EIs.

Then he was done. He folded his arms on the console and laid down his head, closing his eyes. A tear leaked out and slid over his cheek. He had ten years to "return from the dead" to Ixpar, but he knew almost no chance existed of that happening.

He might be dead to his Coban family now, but at least he had done what he could to protect them.

5

Chrysalis Emergence

Kelric spread throughout space, using sensors on every ship in Maccar's flotilla. He sailed the seas of dust, tasted oscillating fields, swirled in the cosmic ray flux. The quality of the sensors, the clarity of the stimulation—he reveled in the sheer exhilaration of becoming an entire flotilla.

For all that he had lost, he had gained this. He loved it. This was why he had made such a good test pilot. Alone with the vast radiant seas of energy and wonder, he came alive.

His thought rumbled: *Update systems check.*

Statistics updated, the *Corona* answered. It refreshed his mindscape, providing displays about all ten ships.

"Commander Garlin?" The voice of Lieutenant Ty Rillwater, the communications officer, murmured in space around him.

Attending, Kelric answered. The *Corona* digitized his thought and sent the data to Ty's console, which turned it into speech. His words came out of her console as if he were part of the ship's EI.

"Kelric, don't do that!" Ty protested. "It gives me the jee-zeebs."

Smiling, he thought, *Translate "jee-zeebs."* The *Corona* sent his inquiry to her console.

Ty groaned. "Stop it! You sound like a computer."

I am a computer, he thought. *Did you have a message for me?*

"We'll hit the border zone in about thirty minutes," she said.

I'll be ready. He turned his focus inward. *Corona, give me your most recent data on the border surface between the Skolian Imperialate and Eubian Concord. I'm interested in the area where we will cross into Trader space.*

Done.

His mindscape formed into a new display, giving him a 3-D map of the border zone. A red volume filled the top of the map, indicating Trader space. The surface separating it from Skolian space continually shifted as the *Corona* made adjustments. A few of its revisions came from the scant data it received from other starships or outposts, but most were its own predictions on how boundaries were fluctuating in the current chaos.

According to their most recent data, the Traders had no outpost in this region and ISC had a small naval base. Kelric hoped the base still existed; it would increase their chances of safe passage and he might learn more from it about the current state of ISC.

Right now they were traveling in inversion. To invert, they added an imaginary component to their speed. Making speed complex removed the light-speed singularity from the equations of special relativity. The ship went "around" light speed the way a hovercar might leave the road to go around an infinitely high pole. Beyond the pole, they resumed their journey—at superluminal speeds, a realm of the bizarre.

A superluminal ship could go into the past. With a longing so intense it hurt, Kelric wished he could go back and stop the deaths of his family. *If only.* But every ship that had tried returning to normal space prior to when it inverted either failed or vanished, possibly into an alternate universe where it couldn't meddle with its own causality.

Even if he did somehow go into his past, the need for consistency would probably make it impossible to alter history. It was the time analog of a mundane situation, his magcar passing a slower car. To him, his car would stay still while the slow car went backward. People in the slow car thought they stayed still while he went forward. But they all saw the cars end up in the same place. Their view of how it happened differed, but was consistent. No paradoxes. So it was with time. Events had to be consistent whether he ran the reel of his life forward or backward. He couldn't undo what had happened, and wishing for the impossible only made his grief hurt more.

Superluminal travel bedeviled the flotilla. With no web, how did ships converse? Beam light back and forth? Useless. It could never catch up. Throw tachyons? As long as the particles remained superluminal, they could hop, skip, and jump all over time. Then there was time contraction and space dilation; the faster their ship went, the faster their time passed and the longer they stretched out relative to slower objects. A crew didn't notice on their own ship because they were at rest relative to it. But no two ships or particles moved at the same rate, and at such humongous speeds even small differences had big effects. How did you talk to ships smeared out across light-years, with time running at different rates on all of them? It was a mess.

Maccar regularly had Anatakala drop the ships into real space so Ty could try contacting the ISC base. In the normal universe nothing went faster than light, so no one expected a timely answer from the base when they were several light-months out from the border zone. As they drew within light-days and then light-hours of the border, and still received no response, concern increased. On Kelric's map, the *Corona* finally deleted the icon it had used to denote the base.

Only a few light-minutes from the border, they dropped into real space again. The red volume on Kelric's map had expanded to fill most of the display.

Show me space, he thought.

The map vanished, replaced by a simulation so realistic, he felt as if he were arrowing through the void himself. The flotilla ships registered on his sensors as they dropped out of inversion, their formation spread out in time and space. However, they hadn't been superluminal long enough for the lack of communications to seriously disrupt their formation.

Nothing marked the border between Skolian and Trader territory: no space buoys or patrol ships, not even a trace of debris from the vanished ISC station.

I'm not getting a thing, Kelric thought. The ship sent his voice to the bridge crew by way of their consoles. *No hostile forces, human or drone. Nothing but dust and cosmic rays.*

"Nothing here either," Ty said. "No response to hails."

"Nothing on regular sensors," Anatakala added.

"Continue your scans," Maccar said. "Commander Anatakala, maintain course."

"Aye, sir," she said.

They sailed through the border region without a blip of excitement.

"Entering Trader space," Anatakala said.

Still no trace of other forces, Kelric thought.

"Nothing on comm," Ty said.

"Stay alert," Maccar said. "Until we leave Trader space, I want you all to operate as if we're in emergency mode."

A murmur of *Aye, sirs* answered him.

Kelric expanded his range, exploring as far afield as the sensors on the flotilla ships could manage. *We're clear for inversion*, he told Maccar, using the bridge channel. He felt relief flicker through the crew. Once a ship inverted, it became almost impossible to detect or catch. It was when they dropped into real space that they were vulnerable.

"Prepare to invert," Maccar said.

Marko Jaes, the officer in charge of engineering, spoke on the bridge channel: "Ready on your order, sir."

"Invert," Maccar said.

Vertigo hit Kelric as the *Corona* twisted out of real space. It wrenched his mental equilibrium. Nausea surged over him, another reminder of his depleted condition. Going into inversion had never bothered him before.

"Inversion complete," Jaes said.

"Optimizing spacetime route," Anatakala said. "Captain, I'd like to push us as close to transcendence as possible."

"Go ahead," Maccar said.

At the word *transcendence*, Kelric froze. What the bloody hell was she talking about?

Taking a breath, he tried to relax. He hoped no one noticed his reaction. By transcendence, Anatakala simply meant infinite speed, an odd concept certainly, but not one that had deserved his extreme response. A superluminal ship could never go slower than light, but in theory no upper limit existed. In practice, they never reached transcendence: errors piled up at too rapid a rate. But they could go wicked fast, and the less time they spent in Trader space the better.

Kelric couldn't shake his chill, though—for *transcendence* also had a far harsher meaning. Trader Aristos used it for the heightened state they reached with the favored pleasure slaves they called "providers."

It was hard for Kelric to believe the Aristos had risen to power only a few centuries ago. To him, they were a monolithic force, implacable and timeless. Yet they came from a well-meant project. The intent had been to *protect* empaths, to engineer changes in their brains so they could mute the painful emotions they picked up from others. One glitch developed. Just one. That unexpected side effect changed human history. It created the Aristos. Anti-empaths.

When an Aristo's brain picked up painful emotions, it protected itself by sending the neural signals that defined those emotions to its pleasure centers. So the Aristo transcended. It happened only if they had a large neural interaction with the sender. In other words, the sender had to be a psion, the stronger the better. Aristos called their captive psions "providers," kept them in luxury, and even claimed they loved them. It fooled no one. They achieved transcendence by giving pain to other human beings.

Kelric had only to hear the word *transcendence* and he broke out in a sweat. No one else on the bridge seemed troubled, though. But then, none of them had a Kyle rating above two, and three was the minimum for a psion.

His rating was off the scale.

Kyle ratings above ten were hard to measure because such a psion was rarer than one in ten billion people. The sum total of humanity numbered about three trillion, but few worlds had more then ten billion, so statistics couldn't be done on much larger populations.

Kelric sometimes wondered how it would feel to be normal, to have people see him just as a man, rather than a scarce resource. The rarity of psions came about because the recessive Kyle genes that produced them often had lethal mutations as well. The more Kyle genes in a person's DNA, the worse the situation. The stronger the psion, the higher their Kyle rating and the fewer of them that existed. Rhon psions carried the full complement, making the Rhon the most powerful psions—and rare to the point of extinction.

Kelric's family were the only fertile, viable Rhon psions in three civilizations. Desperate to keep a supply for the Triad, the Assembly had tried creating more in the lab. When that failed, they pushed, cajoled, coerced, and threatened the Ruby Dynasty into having as many children as possible. As far as Kelric knew, ten of the Rhon still lived, counting himself and his daughter. Without pressure to increase their numbers, though, they would probably be rarer than one in a sextillion, giving them ratings above twenty-one.

Of one thing he had no doubt: here in Trader territory he was one of the only *free* telepaths among nearly two trillion people.

Maccar interrupted his thoughts. "Commander Garlin, are you still on sensors?"

"Yes, sir." Kelric turned his attention back to his work.

As Anatakala navigated, Kelric monitored their progress. Her skill impressed him. During inversion, the flotilla formation lost cohesion. Anatakala had to minimize its spread in space and time. The computers did the calculations, but her guidance and insight were what made the difference.

Maccar's decision to drop out of inversion at regular intervals made Kelric uneasy. He understood the reasoning; they went sublight to clean up errors and tighten their formation. The longer the flotilla stayed superluminal, the more it was spread out in time and space when the ships came out of inversion. If the spread became too large, how could the ships defend the *Corona*?

But dropping into real space made them vulnerable. If pirates attacked, they would probably rob Maccar of his cargo and then let almost everyone go; with a slave population in the trillions, Aristos had no need of more taskmakers, particularly not Skolians who were used to freedom and caused more trouble than they were worth.

Providers, however, were another matter. Their rarity gave them immense value. Kelric grimaced, knowing he would bring a phenomenal price on the Trader slave markets.

So protect yourself, he thought.

An idea came to him. It might not work, but it was worth a try. He sat still, centering his thoughts. Then he submerged deeper into the *Corona*, growing even more aware of its systems. He circulated air, prepared food, monitored temperature. Deeper still and he became pulses of light and electrons. He expanded into space. Particles with complex energies, masses, and charges flowed around him. Stars streamed past in banners of light, seen not in a single instant but during a range of times. He expanded further, searching, searching...

Ah, no. Pain lanced his head. He paused, resting. He didn't retreat to the *Corona,* though. If he succeeded in this, it would be worth the strain to his injured mind.

When the pain receded, he resumed his search, pushing further into space, farther...

There! He touched another mind. An EI. A ship. He had contacted the *Zettel,* the dreadnought in Maccar's flotilla.

Identify, the *Zettel* thought.

Commander Garlin, on the Corona, Kelric answered.

Psiberweb link established, the *Zettel* told him.

Psiberweb? An interesting interpretation. He could see why the dreadnought made that assumption. In a sense, he *had* recreated a tiny bubble of psiberspace, at least enough to form one link. He wondered how far he could push it before the strain on his mind became too great and the tenuous bubble collapsed.

After resting a few microseconds, he continued expanding his sphere of awareness in both space and time. He found a frigate and set up a link with its EI. He hit another frigate, and another, until he encompassed the entire flotilla. He couldn't link all ten ships to one another: that would require 10! or 3,628,800 links. But he could hold the ten links from his mind to the ships.

Kelric sent a message to Maccar, the bridge crew, Marko Jaes in Engineering, and the yeoman who kept Maccar's logs: *Flotilla psilink established.*

"What the whizzle?" Ty exclaimed. At the same time, Steil said, "Garlin, what are you doing?" and Anatakala asked, "Kelric, is that you?"

Maccar spoke. "Commander Garlin, explain yourself."

Kelric grinned. *I set up a psilink among your ships. Now you don't need to drop out of inversion as often.*

A full five seconds went by before anyone answered. Eons passed for Kelric, submerged as he was in the light-speed flickerings of EI brains.

Finally Maccar said, "That's impossible. You need the psiberweb to create such a link."

I created a psiberspace bubble, Kelric thought. *Ten links. It's all I can hold, though, and I don't know for how long.*

"Well, I'll take a launch off a lily pad," Ty said.

"I wasn't aware ISC had such technology," Maccar said.

"Nor I," Steil said.

Kelric caught their mental undercurrents. They wondered if he had just revealed secured ISC data. He hadn't, nor would he ever do so. As far as ISC had known in his time, it was impossible to create such a link without the web. Or so they had thought. Apparently being Rhon had unexpected advantages.

It isn't ISC tech, he thought. *I just did it.*

"Can you coordinate the flotilla?" Maccar asked.

I can give Anatakala their positions, both temporal and spatial. I'm too far extended for more, but if she makes the corrections and feeds them into my mindscape, I can transmit them to the other ships.

"Anatakala?" Maccar asked.

"No problem," she said. "I'm setting it up now."

Soon her data was pouring into his mind. As they worked, his headache increased. It wasn't unbearable, though. He wasn't sure what caused it. When he used the Kyle centers, his brain apparently made neural connections his mind translated as pain. It was a warning, like an alert system, letting him know he needed treatment.

But other considerations motivated him now. He intended to make it out of Trader space with his freedom.

"Navigation, do the drop," Maccar said.

"Aye, sir," Anatakala said. "Entering real space... now!"

With a rush of relief, Kelric relaxed. The psilink he had nurtured for the past few hours dissolved, but it didn't matter. As the ships entered normal space, they regained communications.

"Holy Mother!" Ty exulted. "What a job, Kelric!"

"Not bad," Steil murmured.

"Captain Maccar," Anatakala said. "The flotilla formation has ninety-eight percent cohesion." She exuded satisfaction. "We're only thirty light-minutes from our destination."

The usually restrained Maccar gave a whistle. "Commander Garlin, that was damn good work."

Kelric smiled. "Thank you, sir." Even he hadn't expected that he could take them all the way to Sphinx Sector. But they had made it here without leaving inversion once, when normally Maccar would have had called ten to fifteen drops.

They entered real space at 80 percent light speed and dumped velocity as they approached their destination, slowing to mundane speeds. A space habitat grew on the display in his mindscape, a gleaming sculpture of nested wheels four kilometers across. Rather than spokes, a sparkling lace stretched from the innermost wheel to the hub. Closer in, the "lace" resolved into an enormous web of struts and ringed cables. Mirrors caught radiance from a distant blue-white star and shined their captured luminance into the habitat. Golden spires reached out from the hub, dumping heat, glittering with reflected light. The overall effect was gorgeous, like a city shimmering in space.

"'So does it amaze me, what beauty humanity has wrought,'" Anatakala murmured, quoting a well-known Ruby Empire poet.

Steil snorted. "So does it amaze me, how much brutality that beauty hides. Don't forget where we are, Commander."

Data flowed between the space habitat's EI harbor master and the *Corona*'s EI harbor pilot, as the *Corona* identified their ships and received regulations for approach. Anatakala put them in a holding pattern thirty kilometers out from the station, where they could move at speeds up to fifty kilometers per hour. The flotilla took a spherical formation around Maccar's ship, with the dreadnought positioned between the space habitat and the *Corona.*

"Captain." Ty Rillwater spoke in a subdued voice. "I'm getting a hail from the habitat."

"Put it on bridge comm," Maccar said.

"Sir, it's in Highton," Ty said.

"*Corona,* prepare to translate," Maccar said. He switched to a private channel only the bridge crew received. "I don't suppose any of you speak Highton?"

Murmured negatives rippled through the crew. "Can't say it was part of any curriculum I ever studied," Anatakala muttered.

Kelric said nothing.

A man's voice came over the station-to-ship channel, speaking in Highton, the rich glossy language of the Trader Aristos. "Welcome to *Chrysalis Station,* Captain Maccar. Proceed to the docking station at the hub."

"Translation," the *Corona* said. "Welcome to *Chrysalis Station,* Captain Maccar. Please dock your ship at the station hub."

Kelric frowned. He saw problems looming already, if the *Corona* couldn't even provide a good translation for so simple a greeting. Without fluency in the innuendo-laden language of the Hightons, Maccar was at a disadvantage with his Aristo client. As much as Kelric wanted to keep a low profile during this visit, he wanted even more to make sure they got out again.

Before Maccar had the *Corona* respond, Kelric said, "Captain, I speak Highton. Better, I think, than your EI."

If his comment surprised Maccar, the captain gave no hint. "The comm is yours, Commander. Thank them for their welcome."

"Aye, sir." Kelric paused, working out a translation that would give Maccar advantage in the dance of double-talk practiced by Aristos. He switched to the ship-to-station channel and spoke in Highton. "It pleases us to approach *Chrysalis Station.* Your invitation to dock is noted." His phrasing suggested it was up to the station to satisfy them, rather than the reverse. He deliberately left their docking plans unstated.

"We await with anticipation," the station answered.

Maccar listened to the *Corona*'s EI give its translation. Then he spoke on the bridge channel. "Garlin, what did they say? Your version."

"They await with anticipation," Kelric said. "Why, I'm not sure."

"Why aren't you sure?"

Kelric grimaced. "It could mean anything from 'I'm looking forward to getting my goods and being rid of you' to 'I can hardly wait to slap you in a slave collar.' "

Maccar exhaled. "Anatakala, can you keep the flotilla out here without too much drift?"

"Yes, sir," she said. "No problem."

"Good. Garlin, tell them we prefer not to dock."

Kelric nodded. Their refusal to come in would displease Lady Zarine, the Aristo client waiting on the station, which she undoubtedly owned. But it left them more options if they had to make a fast escape. It also gave Maccar advantage, adding nuances that wouldn't be lost on his client. If he ceded that advantage, it could suggest he was too willing to give up power in this wary partnership.

Kelric spoke on the ship-to-station channel. "*Chrysalis,* we are pleased to send in a shuttle. We look forward to receiving your greetings and engaging in trade." His innuendo suggested Maccar occupied a position of strength and had received a petition from the *Chrysalis.* Invoking the word *trade* put Maccar on the same footing as an Aristo, the only Eubian citizens allowed to engage in Eube's most time-honored practice: trade. That such trades often involved humans was a fact Kelric didn't want to consider.

Maccar spoke on a ship channel. "Steil, you're in command while I'm on the *Chrysalis.* Lieutenant Halzansky, Cargo Master Icolo, and

Yeoman Parr, you're with me in the shuttle. Commander Garlin, I want you up here *now.*"

Kelric blinked at the unexpected snap in Maccar's voice. *Close mindscape,* he thought. *Release weapons CPU.*

Closed, the *Corona* answered. **You are released.**

The view of space vanished, leaving him in darkness. Then his visor lifted and he found himself on the bridge. The view wasn't much different from his mindscape; the inner surface of the bridge consisted primarily of holoscreens, and right now they all showed the *Chrysalis.* The crew and their consoles seemed to float in space, dwarfed by the station's majesty. Steil and Ty were both right; the *Chrysalis* was beautiful and terrible, a magnificent work created by a people somehow capable of both inspired artistic genius and brutality without remorse.

In the center of the bridge, Maccar sat in his blocky command chair. Kelric maneuvered out of his seat, then grasped a cable and guided himself to the captain. Maccar watched him with an unreadable expression. Kelric reached his chair and floated to one side, holding the cable with one hand while he saluted Maccar.

The captain toggled off the comm, making their conversation private. "At ease, Commander." As Kelric lowered his arm, Maccar added, "Or should I say, 'my lord'?"

Kelric stiffened. "Sir?"

Dryly Maccar said, "You speak Skolian Flag with an Iotic accent. You're fluent in Highton. You take the deference of others for granted. And you're not used to taking orders." He shook his head. "You Jag pilots may be the loners of ISC, but you would never have received your commission if you couldn't follow discipline. It's no longer natural to you, though. You're one hell of a weapons officer, Garlin, but you're out of practice. You haven't done military service in years."

Although Kelric managed to keep his face impassive, his thoughts were anything but serene. Maccar had figured out too much. "Are you asking me a question, sir?"

"Damn right I'm asking you a question. I want to know who the blazes you are."

"My name is Kelric Garlin. I'm an Imperial Jagernaut."

The captain frowned. "I've run a check on your name and DNA. No matches. Without full web access, though, I could only check our shipboard libraries and the Edgewhirl webs. For all I know, your ID is all over the main Skolian databases. I have no access to them right now."

Kelric almost swore. Maccar had also run a genetic scan? At this rate, everyone and her brother would be stealing his DNA. Maccar wouldn't find his name and face "all over," but if he keyed into enough databases, he could dig up clues to Kelric's identity.

"Sir," Kelric said. "May I make a request?"

Maccar continued to study him. "Yes?"

"Don't download a record of my DNA to any other system."

"Why?" he asked. When Kelric said nothing, Maccar's voice hardened. "I'm ordering you to answer, Commander."

Kelric knew if he refused, he was buying himself more trouble. So he said, "I was married to Corey Majda."

Maccar stared at him. "Admiral Majda? Former matriarch of the House of Majda?"

"Yes, sir."

The captain frowned. "I served in the Fleet for ten years. I know its history. Admiral Majda has been dead for thirty-three years and she was forty-five when she died." He snorted. "What were you when you married? Ten years old?"

"Twenty-two, sir."

"Twenty-two?" Maccar raised his eyebrows. "That isn't even legal age."

"It was an arranged marriage."

That gave Maccar pause. "The noble houses still do that, don't they?" he mused. "Majda would never arrange a marriage with a commoner, though. So who are you?"

"I'm not a member of any noble house." Technically that was true. Although one name for the Ruby Dynasty was the House of

Skolia, they were royalty rather than nobility, which outranked any noble house.

Dryly Maccar said, "Right. And just why would the head of the oldest, most venerated house, not to mention the wealthiest, with the exception of the Skolias, marry a man with no title?"

Kelric didn't have to feign his anger. "I believe the phrase is 'trophy husband.'" It didn't matter that the marriage had been made for dynastic reasons. People had used the term anyway. He hated it as much now as when he had been twenty-two.

To his surprise, Maccar didn't challenge his answer. Instead he said, "I suppose I shouldn't be shocked, given the effect you're having on my crew. At twenty-two you must have been devastating."

Kelric blinked. He hadn't realized he affected anyone besides Anatakala, or that Maccar had noticed. "I wasn't aware of problems, sir."

"Commander Steil wants you dismissed from the bridge. Says you're a distraction." Unexpectedly, Maccar laughed. "I told her to deal with it. This is my ship and I won't have any member of my crew treated in an unequal manner because of his sex." He glanced at the guards on Kelric's wrists. "Even those crew members who voluntarily choose inequality."

Kelric held back his retort. The captain had no way to know how much the guards meant to him.

Maccar was watching his face. "I'm sorry if my questions seem invasive. But we've a problem and I have to solve it."

"A problem?"

"I need you in the negotiations with Lady Zarine. My bet is that not only do you know Highton, you also understand Aristos better than the rest of us. But saints almighty, man, Zarine is going to take one look at you and ask me how much I'll sell you for. And I've never met a psion with your strength before. I doubt even most Aristos have. We've an oath of safe passage from these people, but we're in their territory, outnumbered and outgunned. If anything goes wrong, I can't guarantee I'll get us out of there."

Kelric raked his hand through his hair. The motion pushed him away from the chair, but he pulled himself back with the cable. "May I make a suggestion?"

"Go ahead."

"An Aristo noblewoman would consider it an insult for you to bring someone with low rank to the negotiations. She knows you have a person or EI here with fluency in Highton. Tell her I'm a commoner without officer's rank. Aristo protocol then forbids you to bring me into her presence."

Maccar didn't look thrilled. "That would explain why you don't come with us to the *Chrysalis.* It still leaves me at a disadvantage."

"We could set up a link from here to the station."

"I doubt she'll agree to a remote link. She knows your ability gives me advantage." Maccar exhaled. "It's worth a try, though."

Relief flowed over Kelric. "Then you don't wish me to come with you?"

The captain spoke with reluctance. "I think it's better if you don't. Too many risks. And with General Majda in command of ISC now, your position as her predecessor's widower would make you a valuable hostage."

Kelric stared at him. "General Majda? Do you mean Naaj? Corey's little sister?"

Dryly Maccar said, "If by 'Corey,' you mean the late Admiral Majda, then yes, I meant her sister. Though I'd hardly call Naaj Majda 'little.' She's six feet tall and over seventy years old."

Disconcerted, Kelric said, "Of course." In truth, Corey was the only one he had ever heard use such an affectionate term for Naaj. Everyone else addressed the hard-line general as "ma'am."

He wasn't sure whether to be elated or wary that Naaj had taken over ISC. She was one of the officers he had intended to search out when he was ready to set up his power base. But if she already had command of ISC, a position she could never have assumed without the fall of the Ruby Dynasty, she might not welcome his appearance back from the grave, particularly given he also had claim to substantial Majda assets.

Maccar was watching his face. "I don't remember anything about

Admiral Majda marrying a commoner. Granted, it's been a long time and I was a kid then. But something that unusual would have been a big news story."

Kelric resisted the urge to say, *It was everywhere.* The Assembly had transformed the wedding into a production, broadcasting the whole business. Apparently it made good public relations, marrying off the handsome young Ruby prince to the nobility's most powerful matriarch. His main function had been to stand around looking suitably heroic and keep his mouth shut. It had been no better for Corey. By the time they escaped to the Majda palace on Raylicon for their honeymoon, they were both so thoroughly irritated they didn't even sleep together at first.

The miracle was that when they relaxed, they discovered they liked each other, an affection that over the next two years grew into love. Kelric had even admitted to himself that his parents might have actually known what they were doing when they betrothed him to Corey.

All he said was, "Majda didn't want it public that she married outside the Houses."

"I suppose." Maccar had an odd look, as if he were searching his memory. Then he exhaled. "Stay in your quarters until this is over. Keep a low profile."

With relief, Kelric said, "Yes, sir."

Lying on his bunk, Kelric stared at the ceiling. He had set the radiance bars to a muted glow, too dim even to penetrate the corner shadows. He didn't want more light, nothing that might add to his tension.

It had been hours since Maccar and his team had taken a shuttle to the *Chrysalis.* No one had heard from them. Several times Kelric found himself on the verge of going to the bridge, where he could use his console to probe the *Chrysalis.* It took a conscious effort to make himself stay put. Maccar was right. He was no longer used to shipboard discipline.

He wished Maccar hadn't stirred up his past. Corey. Gods, he hadn't thought about her in years. Yet another person he had loved who died. Damn it all. He didn't want to remember. He was tired of hurting. He wanted to go home. See his parents. Reaffirm that at least some of the people he loved weren't dead or forbidden to him.

A hum came from the door. Startled, he sat up. Then he got off the bunk and went over to the door. After he checked the security panel, he opened the portal.

Ty Rillwater stood outside, small and round, her yellow hair curling about her rosy-cheeked face. "My greetings, Kelric." She beamed at him. "My relief just came on shift. I thought you might want company, since you're confined to your quarters."

Her cheerful good nature washed over him, easing his tension. "My greetings to you also, Ty. Come in." He motioned to his one chair, near his bunk. As she went over and settled into it, he sat on the edge of the bed, his booted feet planted wide, his elbows resting on his knees.

"Is there any news from Maccar?" he asked.

Ty shook her head. "Nothing yet."

He made a frustrated sound. "They need a better interpreter than the *Corona*'s translator." They needed him.

"They'll be all right. Maccar hadn't expected to have a better one." With mock solemnity she added, "Besides, we would never have let him take you to the *Chrysalis.* Your absence would make the bridge a far less aesthetic place."

Kelric smiled. "I'm sure you would survive."

Mischief flashed on her face. "Well, you know, Steil would take us all to task for pining over a work of art."

"I'm a weapons officer, Ty. Not a sculpture."

"I could wax poetic," she offered. Then her smile faded. "But Kelric, none of us wanted you to go the the *Chrysalis.* The risk to you is just too great. You're such a strong empath and you don't hide it well. When I'm near you, I feel like I'm in the sun. It's beautiful." She looked apologetic. "I hope that doesn't sound like I'm making a pass. I'm not. But we all appreciate your being here."

He spoke quietly. "Thank you."

With a grin she added, "So now can I flirt some more?"

Kelric laughed. "You're incorrigible."

Her reply was cut short by the shrill of an alarm from his console. He stood up fast, his enhanced speed toggling on. The console screen cleared to show Captain Maccar, with the interior of the *Corona*'s shuttle in the background.

"Garlin and Rillwater, get to the bridge," Maccar said. "We're leaving as soon as the shuttle docks. Emergency status."

"Right away," Kelric answered, as Ty said, "On my way."

They ran through the ship, sailing in huge strides. At the end cap of the cylinder, they went "up" an access tube that stretched from the rim to the center of the cap. Gravity decreased as they climbed, until they were hurtling themselves through the air. They had no weight at all when they reached the cap's center, a spherical cavity a few meters across. Access tubes identical to theirs radiated like spokes out from the cavity in every direction. Air-lock hatches were centered in both the forward and aft bulkheads, the forward hatch leading to the bridge and the aft one to the docking tube that ran down the center of the cylinder.

The aft hatch suddenly clanged open and Maccar propelled himself into the cavity, coming in sideways to Ty and Kelric. Ty heaved open the forward hatch and the three of them entered the air-lock. They waited interminable seconds while it sealed, both the hatch and a molecular membrane that served as a backup. The hatch into the bridge opened, they flew into the hemisphere—

And Kelric froze.

The holos of space were gone. Instead, the huge screens that stretched across the bridge showed a Trader news broadcast. Steil was sitting in the captain's chair, her posture frozen, her gaze fixed on the broadcast.The relief crew were all at their stations, every one staring at the screens. Bigger than life, the images dominated the bridge.

They showed a tall broad-shouldered man with glittering white hair—Lord Corbal Xir, the Aristo next in line to assume the Carnelian Throne. Xir's mother had been a younger sister of Eube Qox, who founded the Trader Empire. Under normal conditions a Xir could never have assumed the throne. The line of succession went through the firstborn Qox of each generation: Eube, Jaibriol I, Ur, and Jaibriol II.

But Jaibriol II had died without an heir, leaving only Corbal Xir to assume the title. After four generations of Qox emperors, a Xir would sit on the Carnelian Throne—if age didn't stop him. His contemporaries had all died: Corbal Xir was the eldest Highton, over 130 years old. He was the only Aristo with white hair that Kelric had ever seen. Most Aristos were obsessive about maintaining their youth and appearance, as if their exterior beauty could mask their true nature.

Xir was standing on a dais in the Hall of Circles, the great audience hall in the emperor's palace on the capital planet of Eube. He stood next to the Carnelian Throne, a glittering chair carved from a diamond-snowmarble composite and inlaid with bloodred gems. Rows of sparkling diamond benches with high backs curved around the front of the dais. Aristos sat on them, rank upon rank of icy human perfection, as hard as diamond cogs in a diamond computer, every one with shimmering black hair, ruby eyes, and snowmarble skin. They waited in triumphant silence, watching the dais.

But it was neither Corbal Xir nor the Aristos that riveted Kelric's attention, that brought him to such an abrupt halt, hanging on a cable. What stopped him so utterly was the man who stood next to Xir.

At six foot one, the man was half a head shorter than Xir. Winered hair tousled in disarray around his handsome, haggard face. He had large eyes, violet, with dark circles under them. The ripped sleeve of his white shirt revealed bruised skin underneath. His arms were bound behind his back and a diamond slave collar glinted around his neck.

"No," Kelric whispered. He knew that man. Knew him well.

It was his brother Eldrin.

6

Key of the Heart

"Garlin, to your station!" Maccar shot past Kelric, headed for his command seat, which Steil was already vacating. Kelric propelled himself to his console. The instant he touched his chair, it responded, familiar now with his brain-wave signature. It pulled him into its grasp and folded the exoskeleton around him like a high-tech glove.

Maccar's orders came in rapid-fire bursts. "Steil, jettison our cargo. Anatakala, get us out of here. Rillwater, ignore any orders from the *Chrysalis.* Garlin, don't let them stop us from leaving."

Kelric linked into the *Corona.* A quick check revealed Maccar had already taken payment for his cargo. He could guess what had happened: Maccar and Lady Zarine finished their business before the news of Eldrin's capture broke. By jettisoning his cargo, Maccar fulfilled his delivery contract without staying at the station. Lady Zarine would be irate at having to pick up crates from space, but she couldn't claim a broken contract as an excuse to detain the flotilla.

As Kelric worked, Xir's speech played in his mindscape, as it would soon play across screens throughout settled space, as fast as starships could carry it. Absorbed in his tasks, he caught only parts of the broadcast, but that was enough:

. . . great deeds of our sterling war heroes, Xir intoned in the Aristo's melodramatic and overly adjectified style. *With unmatched courage,*

they braved the very halls of corrupt Skolian power, the Orbiter itself, capital of Skolia... ESComm special forces unit removed the Ruby Pharaoh, and also the spawn produced by her iniquitous union with her own brother's son... captured her depraved consort... Eldrin Jarac Valdoria Skolia, first-born of the Ruby Dynasty...

Kelric gritted his teeth, trying to ignore the venom that Xir directed against his family. He needed no Aristo propaganda speech to tell him the implications of Eldrin's capture. With Eldrin, the Traders now had a key for their stolen Lock. Eube had gained indisputable advantage. The balance of power had changed. The sooner Maccar got out of Trader territory, the better.

He didn't know which was worse, hearing confirmation that ESComm had killed his aunt and nephew or learning of his brother's capture. As much as he had grieved for Eldrin's death, Kelric couldn't rejoice in seeing him now, knowing what he faced. It had to be tearing his brother apart, especially after having watched his wife and son die.

Come to think of it, though, Xir provided no specifics on how the Pharaoh and her son had died. In fact, no one seemed clear about it, not even the commandos who had supposedly "removed" the Pharaoh and her heir. Removed *how*?

The more he heard, the more Xir's speech puzzled him. It bulged with inaccuracies. The Orbiter wasn't Skolia's capital. That honor went to Selei City on the planet Parthonia. Nor was Eldrin the son of Pharaoh's brother. He was the son of Roca, the Pharaoh's sister. Iniquitous? Dehya and Eldrin had fought the Assembly's manipulations. They lost, and so they married, but they had gentled their difficult situation with a deep, abiding love. Kelric doubted Xir cared about the emotional toll they had paid, but surely he must realize how hypocritical his comments would sound even to his own people. The Aristo lord's dearly departed cousin, Emperor Jaibriol I, had married his own sister, declaring her the only woman with an exalted enough bloodline—his own—to be his wife.

Even if Xir didn't see the sloppiness of his own propaganda, it was odd he would make so make so many awkward mistakes.

Although outwardly the Aristo lord displayed triumph, Kelric had an empath's natural ability to read people. He saw what Xir tried to hide: Beneath his self-aggrandizing speech, the Aristo was tired. Drained. If Kelric hadn't known better, he would have thought Xir felt no triumph at all.

Was Corbal Xir experiencing the same dismay that would sweep settled space as the news spread? Humanity was exhausted, worn out from a debilitating war that had broken two empires. Incredibly, the Radiance War had also given birth to hope. Without their war machines or psiberweb, Skolia and Eube would be forced to the negotiation table, perhaps making possible a peace that had eluded them for centuries.

Now that had changed.

Maccar's ships accelerated away from the *Chrysalis,* building up the speed to invert. As Kelric set up his Kyle links with the flotilla, he also monitored space all around them—and so he saw the frigates emerge from the station's hub.

Captain, he thought. *We're being followed.* He focused on the vessels. They appeared civilian. Their appearance lied. Submerged deep in his mindscape, he registered the contained power of their weapons—Annihilators, Impactors, smart-dust, tau cannons—all hidden behind their masquerade as innocuous ships out for a jaunt.

"Anatakala, how soon can we invert?" Maccar asked.

"We'll have enough speed in eighty-one seconds," she said.

Kelric swore. Space combat went at relativistic speeds. Energies flared and died in microseconds. Time dilated and length contracted. In that quickened universe, eighty-one seconds was eternity.

Their proximity to the *Chrysalis* gave them some protection; the Traders wouldn't start a battle when Maccar could fire on a habitat with millions of people. But the flotilla ships were speeding up at a precipitous rate, snapping in and out of quasis to protect their fragile humans from the crushing accelerations. The *Chrysalis* soon fell behind, visible only on Kelric's mindscape, long gone from visual range.

The Eubian ships gained on them, reaching for the flotilla in a grasping formation, like a claw. With grim certainty, Kelric realized they would be within firing range before the flotilla inverted.

Then he felt a mind.

He recognized that mental signature. Knew it. Hated it. He suddenly had the sense of standing on a precipice above a mental abyss. An Aristo colonel commanded one of the pursuing ships, a warlord intent on capture and destruction.

Kelric toggled into high-speed combat mode, where his communication with the *Corona* came in symbols and numbers rather than words. It denoted Eubian frigates by EF and Maccar's by MF. The console boosted his Kyle senses into a heightened state he could endure for only a few minutes. That was all he would need.

Fragmented thoughts from the Trader ships swept around him like a jumbled whirlpool. His mindscape organized the chaos, filtered the data, and sent the result to his mind, all in microseconds. Then he knew. ESComm personnel crewed the Trader ships. They meant to destroy the flotilla and take the *Corona.*

He wanted to hate them. But they were human. Taskmakers. They had families, homes, dreams, fears. Most were loyal to the Aristos who owned them. If they served well, they reaped the benefits of the richest civilization in human history. Disobedience or too many failures dropped them into lower levels of the slave hierarchies, where people became cogs in the machinery of servitude with no more value than robots.

It made no difference that he couldn't hate them: he had to defend the flotilla. But he now knew the people he intended to kill. Turning empaths into weapons was a recipe for psychological ruin. The heightened mental abilities of Jagernauts made them relentlessly effective, but it could also destroy them. It wasn't coincidence most Jagernauts left active duty at an age far younger than other ISC officers.

He could have shielded his mind. Bolt "talked" to his brain via fiberoptic threads. Electrodes in his neurons received the message in binary: 1 meant fire the neuron and 0 meant do nothing. Buffers scaled the firing if necessary, for a neuron that went off at less than

100 percent strength. Bio-shells coated the electrodes and neurotrophic nanomeds prevented damage. If he used the system to turn off certain brain structures, he would no longer detect any mental activity except his own. But he rarely used the shield in combat. He couldn't risk turning off part of his brain during a battle.

Right now he needed every edge. The ESComm vessels were about to fire. As they came within range, he thought, *Whip A4.*

Annihilators fired, the *Corona* answered. Hits on EF4, 6 and 8—
Quasis jump.

Data flooded his mindscape: Maccar's ships had fired their Annihilators in a pattern Kelric had designed and labeled *Whip A4.* The three Eubian frigates they hit had gone into quasis, but the other Traders returned fire, forcing the flotilla ships into quasis.

"—the bloody hell are you doing, Garlin?" Maccar's words boomed like slow thunder, coming in real time rather than the speeded-up realm where Kelric operated now. Kelric couldn't stop to answer. With the battle's accelerated pace, it could be over before he convinced Maccar they needed to fight.

Annihilator hit on MF6, the *Corona* thought. Impactor hit on *Cor*—
Quasis jump.

Both the *Corona* and a flotilla ship had taken hits. Their quasis held at 79–84 percent, but neither would survive many more direct strikes.

Impactor hit on MF8, the *Corona* told him. Impactor hit on *Cor*—
Quasis jump.

The Impactors had fired clusters of bomblets that fused on impact like a swarm of enraged H-bombs. When they hit a ship in quasis, it kept going, unaffected, unable to change state. The warheads exploded uselessly against a rigid body. Most of their energy and momentum went into the recoil of their debris, and anything else unfortunate enough to be nearby. But it would only take a few hits before the quasis coils weakened. When quasis failed, a ship underwent the mother of all quantum-state changes and blew up in a dramatic show of flying debris and energy.

Whip pattern 17, he thought. *Get the one that hit us.*

MF3 Impactors fired, the *Corona* answered. **Hit on EF—**

Quasis jum—

Annihilator hit on MF4, the *Corona* warned. **MF4 quasis at 42 percent.**

Kelric tensed. MF4's quasis was crumbling under the assault of antimatter beams from the ESComm Annihilators. Beams were easier to evade than homing missiles, but a ship in quasis couldn't dodge. So the beams drilled into it, annihilating intransigent particles one by one. The perturbations in the ship's quantum state would soon become too extreme. The crew would drop out of quasis—in the midst of their ship's spectacularly lethal matter-antimatter annihilation.

Whip pattern A7. he thought. *Cover MF4.*

Annihilator hit on EF1, the *Corona* answered.

Quasis jump.

Maccar's voice rumbled. "Commander Jaes, get us into inversion."

"I've cut the time to about a minute," Jaes said.

The *Corona* thought: **Alert: EF2 tau approach—**

Quasis jump.

Stats flooded Kelric: MF1 had annihilated a Eubian tau missile just before it struck. The tau's antimatter-matter explosion, with its burst of high-energy photons and particle cascades, had forced every ship in the vicinity into quasis.

Die for me, little Skolians.

Kelric froze, hit by an attack invisible to any sensor save his own mind. Somewhere on the Trader ships, the Aristo warlord lusted for their fear.

Come, my Skolians. We'll have you now.

Kelric clenched his teeth. *Whip pattern T2.*

Tau cannon fired, the *Corona* answered.

Quasis jum—

Quasis jump.

He reeled with the jumps. His nausea surged, but he swallowed the bile. Maccar's ships were spreading decoy dust as they fled. The pursuing missiles were so close that whenever the dust detonated one, it forced Maccar's ships into quasis, delaying their acceleration by crucial seconds.

"—can't wait longer," Maccar said. "Invert the ships!"

Anatakala answered. "We have it down to fifty seconds—"

Alert! the *Corona* thought. MF4 quasis at 26 per—

Quasis jump.

Then: MF4 destroyed.

No! Kelric's mind staggered as the deaths of the crew on Maccar's fourth frigate hit his heightened empathic state. Gritting his teeth, he thought, *Whip TI1. Get them.*

Quasis jump, the *Corona* answered. EF3 destroyed.

Kelric's neurons knew no boundary between friend and foe: the deaths of the ESComm crew wrenched him just as much as those on Maccar's ship. Caught by both a tau missile and an Impactor shot, EF3's quasis had failed. Bomblets ripped through the fragmenting vessel and hit one of the Klein fuel bottles. In a rapid series of collapses, the containment fields ceased to exist and the bottle dumped its antimatter into real space. The plasma exploded outward, annihilating anything in its way, adding to the storm of energy, radiation, and enraged particle reactions that had once been a ship.

Quasis jump, the *Corona* thought. MF2 has lost starboard decks 2–4.

Kelric caught a sudden surge of anxiety from the Trader ships. He narrowed it to the sixth Eubian frigate: *quasis coils in collapse—*

Whip A9 to EF6, he thought.

EF6 destroyed, the *Corona* answered. Quasis jump—

Annihilator strike on Corona, the *Corona* thought. Decks 3, 8, 11–14, and 16–19 damaged. I cannot survive another direct hit.

"—vert, damn it!" Maccar shouted. "I don't care if you're not ready. Get us the bloody hell out of here!"

Pain exploded in Kelric's temples. He lost control of the mindscape, and it twisted as if reality had tied itself into a topologically impossible knot.

Then the universe went still.

In a sudden, splintering calm, the *Corona* bolted into otherspace.

Surreal dust streamed past as they raced through the inverted realm of superluminal travel.

"Gods almighty," Ty Rillwater whispered.

For several seconds no one answered. Then Maccar spoke in a cold voice. "Commander Garlin, those were civilian ships you attacked. Ships hosted by the same Aristo who guaranteed us safe passage."

Kelric answered quietly. "They weren't civilian, sir. Nor were they offering an escort. They were ESComm, fully armed, in attack formation, led by an Aristo warlord. They had more ships and firepower than our flotilla. They also had the element of surprise, because they believed we wouldn't fire without provocation, whereas they were preparing to attack. They intended to destroy the flotilla and take the *Corona*."

Another silence followed his response. Then Maccar said, "Anatakala, can you verify any of that?"

"We've the entire battle on record," she said. "It shows the frigates were armed and approaching in an attack formation used by ESComm. Their response to our actions suggests their crews had military training. I can't verify anything else."

"Commander Garlin," Maccar said. "On what basis do you make your other claims?"

"I'm a Jagernaut. I'm trained to make that kind of detection. With my mind extended, I picked up crews on the Eubian ships." Kelric exhaled. "Captain, I've gone against Aristo warlords in combat before. You never forget."

"Are you in a link now with the flotilla?" Maccar asked.

"I lost it when we inverted. I can reform it if you wish."

"I wish." Maccar's words were chillingly calm.

Again Kelric submerged into his mindscape. Pain throbbed in his temples, but he ignored it, knowing that if he made a misstep Maccar would probably throw him in the brig. He had no proof of his claims, but Maccar was no fool. The captain had agreed to Kelric's stratospheric salary demand for good reason. The abilities of Jagernauts were well known. Feared, but vital.

He rebuilt his connections to the remaining ships. Then he thought, *Links established.* His console sent his words to the bridge crew.

"What is the flotilla status?" Maccar asked.

Kelric took in data and reported. Five lives had been lost in the destruction of MF4, the *Horizon,* Maccar's fourth frigate. One other ship had serious damage and all had taken hits.

The Jade Sea *needs to dock for repairs,* Kelric thought. *The others can continue with us.*

"Advise Captain Leefarer," Maccar said. "As soon as we come within range of a base that can provide repairs, the *Jade Sea* is released from its contract." In a quiet voice he added, "Notify all ships that we will hold a memorial at ten hundred hours for the crew of the *Horizon.*"

Kelric relayed the message and felt the grief from the others as they replied. Finally he said, *All ships acknowledge, sir.* Then he added, *Captain Leefarer also says, "Thanks, Jafe."*

"Very well." Maccar exhaled. "Release your link, Commander. Then come up here."

Kelric disengaged from the weapons console and made his way to the command chair. When he reached Maccar, the captain toggled off the comm, giving them privacy.

"You do understand what you've done, don't you?" Maccar asked.

Kelric met his gaze. "I got most of your people out of there, alive and free."

Maccar pushed his hand across his short hair. "I've no doubt that's true. But we haven't enough proof. Lady Xir will claim she sent us an escort to ensure our safe passage home. The Aristos have every reason for wanting to restart the war, and you may have just helped give them cause."

"If they had captured this ship," Kelric said, "it would have created an even worse situation."

"Why?" Maccar asked. "Because you're Naaj Majda's brother-in-law? If you really are who you claim, why the blazes are you alone? Why aren't you under Majda's protection?"

Kelric grimaced. "If I go to them, I could be signing a warrant for my imprisonment or death just as surely as if Traders captured or blew up the *Corona.*"

"Why?"

"It's better you don't know yet. For my safety and yours. We still aren't out of Trader space." Kelric had been considering what to tell Maccar. The captain had earned his respect. To build his power base, he needed people like Maccar. But now wasn't the time to discuss that future.

Maccar studied him. "All right. Later." Grim satisfaction leaked from his mind. "At least we got paid. We're rich as rubies now." He paused. "The less we have to drop out of inversion on the way home, the better. Can you hold the psilink awhile longer?"

Although Kelric's head ached, it was tolerable. "I think so."

"Let's go, then." Maccar drew in a breath. "With gods' luck, we'll get back alive."

7

Phase Shift

The flotilla skimmed through otherspace. It sailed a sea of slow photons that lagged behind their tachyonic siblings. The ships existed in a spacelike universe where light from stars behind them could never catch up, an eerie realm where charge, mass, energy, and perhaps even thought took on imaginary as well as real aspects.

Two hours into their race home, Kelric's link with the other ships slipped. Gritting his teeth, almost blind with the ache in his head, he strained to hold his bubble of psiberspace.

The bubble popped.

He groaned as pain stabbed his temples. Then he slid into gray nothing.

Kelric opened his eyes to a familiar sight. Radiance bars. He was lying on his own bed staring at the ceiling. The bars glowed dimly. His temples throbbed, but only with a dull pain. Someone had medicated him enough to blunt his headache.

"Ungh..." he mumbled. It wasn't one of his more articulate moments.

"Commander Garlin?" The voice came from nearby.

Turning his head, he saw Mareea Gonzales, the ship's medical officer, sitting in a chair by the bed. With her long, dark hair, heart-shaped face, and large eyes, she reminded him of his aunt Dehya. The Ruby Pharaoh.

The dead Ruby Pharaoh.

"How do you feel?" Mareea asked.

Like a barbell fell on my head, he thought.

"Kelric?" she murmured. "Can you hear me?"

"Yes." He wished she looked less like Dehya. It hurt in a way that had nothing to do with his headache. It also made him think of Eldrin, his brother, who was probably enduring far worse right now than anything Kelric had experienced.

"Do you know what happened?" Mareea asked.

"Bashed my brain," he mumbled.

Her face gentled. "It wasn't quite that bad." Then her smile faded. "Did you know the Kyle Afferent Body in your brain is damaged? That's why you have headaches. Your KAB should send neural pulses only to your *paras*. But it's sending them to other neural structures too. They're telling you that you hurt even though nothing is wrong."

He started to shake his head, then winced and lay still. "I had to get us out of there."

Softly she said, "You took us over two thirds the way home. Now you can rest. We'll talk more later."

With relief, he closed his eyes. Then he absorbed her words. *We'll talk more later*. From doctors, that usually meant, *I'm not sure you're up to hearing this right now*.

He opened his eyes. "What else?"

"Else?"

"What else do you have to tell me?" Tiredly he said, "I know I'm dying, if that's what you're trying to avoid saying."

She pushed her hand through her hair. "I'm sorry." Her concern washed up against him. "But you've had treatment recently, yes?"

"On Edgewhirl."

"I can continue what they began. It's only a temporary fix, though. You need more than I can do here."

He had already realized the ship's medical resources were little better than the Edgewhirl hospital. The *Corona* had a reasonable facility for most of its crew. But not for him.

"I've spoken to the captain," Mareea said. "When we're free of Trader space, we'll take you to an ISC hospital."

"I need one equipped to repair Jagernauts and do Kyle surgery."

"Where do you suggest?"

He thought about it. "Diesha. Eos city on the planet Foreshires Hold. Or the Orbiter."

Mareea shook her head. "Even in normal times we wouldn't have clearance for those places."

"Maybe..." In normal times he could have arranged clearances. Eos hosted government offices and embassies from all over settled space. It was also home to Jacob's Military Institute, which trained naval officers for the Imperial Fleet. The world Diesha served as ISC headquarters, its few cities and many underground installations all dedicated to the military. The Orbiter space habitat was home to part of Kelric's family. It also supported the War Room, where his half brother Kurj had overseen ISC operations. With no psiberweb, the War Room could no longer maintain real-time contact with the ISC forces, but it would still be a major ISC node.

Except Kurj no longer commanded there. For all his conflicted emotions about his half brother, he wished he could see Kurj again. So much remained unsaid.

His sister Soz would have been the last Imperator to hold sway in the War Room. Soz. He missed her. He remembered more each day. Ever since the *Corona* had upgraded his systems, his spinal node, Bolt, had been repairing damaged neural sectors in his brain. In the process, Bolt was retrieving data he had lost after his crash on Coba. None of it was vital to Kelric's situation as Imperator Presumptive. No, what he regained had far more value: memories of childhood.

He treasured one memory above the others. When he was seven and Soz sixteen, they had gone hiking in the Backbone Mountains. A sudden storm caught them. They had huddled together in a spine-cave, and she had held him in her arms, murmuring away his terror of the blue-white lightning and shattering thunder. The Imperialate remembered her as a war leader; he had known the woman-child who comforted a small boy. That day, as they clung together for warmth, their minds merged into a Rhon link. It had taken his fear and replaced it with warmth. Security. Affection. Gods, he valued that memory. He had never told her what it meant to him. Now he would never have the chance.

"Kelric?" Mareea's voice was soft in the dim light.

He focused on the doctor. Not Dehya. Not Soz. Simply a kind stranger. He could say nothing about clearances now, while they were in Trader space. What if ESComm captured them? Maccar had already guessed too much.

"Maybe we can talk later..." His headache was making it hard to think anyway.

Her voice soothed. "Yes. Of course."

Kelric let himself drift to sleep. He woke several times over the next few hours, always to see either Mareea or a nurse sitting by his bed. The medicine patch inside his elbow eased the pain. As his headache faded, Mareea lowered the dose.

Finally he woke up feeling almost normal. He was lying on his side with one arm stretched out under his pillow. His blue sleepsuit wasn't much different from his black spacer's jumpsuit, except its soft, stretchy cloth felt more comfortable to sleep in.

For a while he simply lay, gratified his head no longer hurt. His thoughts turned to the Third Lock. Soon the Traders would take Eldrin there. He feared for his brother. Kelric had ISC training and neural adaptations to help him resist coercion, but even then he doubted he could hold out against a sustained ESComm effort. As a member of the Ruby Dynasty, Eldrin had some protections, but as a civilian he had taken far less training. At least he had a temporary reprieve. ESComm wouldn't let him near the Lock until they secured it enough to ensure he couldn't use it to escape, kill himself, or otherwise cause damage.

What made it so maddening was that Kelric knew the Lock could be turned off. It required a Rhon psion. Eldrin. But unless ISC policies had changed drastically, which he doubted, Eldrin would have no idea he could make it play dead. Very few people needed to know that weakness of the Locks. Kurj had known, of course, as had

Dehya, Soz, Kelric, their brother Althor, and a few top ISC officers. Most of those people were dead.

Then Kelric realized that even if Eldrin had known, it would have done him no good. ESComm would work on him until they dragged out the information. In the end, they would get what they wanted. It would just take longer.

So Kelric lay, wishing he could do the impossible. Get to the Lock. Deactivate it. Get out again. The Aristos could never restart its control center. They weren't Rhon. Eldrin couldn't answer their questions because he wouldn't know answers existed.

Right, he thought dryly. *Take on Eube all by yourself. Turn off the Lock. Rescue Eldrin. Wage one-man war against the Traders. Might as well create a few universes while you're at it.*

Kelric smiled slightly. He could at least return to his post. Moving with care, he sat up. A nurse was dozing in the chair by his bed, a husky woman in a bronze jumpsuit. She wore her brown hair coiled on top her head, and large hoop earrings dangled from her ears. Such earrings surely violated some ISC regulation. Kelric had to remind himself he was on a civilian ship.

She opened her eyes. "My greetings."

He smiled. "And mine to you."

"You look better."

"Thanks." He swung his legs over the side of the bed. "What's happened? Have we dropped into real space?"

She shook her head. "Still in inversion. Maccar gave up trying to keep the flotilla together. We'll re-form in Skolian space."

Kelric frowned. "The ships will be spread out over millions of kilometers and several days." He made a frustrated sound. "I should have stayed in the link."

"And injured yourself more? I don't think so." She gave him a satisfied look. "We'll be fine. Got what we came for and we're almost out of here. Out and out like a red moon."

Kelric smiled, a pun about "read" moons coming to mind.

"What?" she asked.

He blinked. "I didn't say anything."

"It sounded like you spoke. Your voice echoed." She squinted at him. "And . . . I know this sounds strange—your face rippled."

Kelric started to answer. He stopped when the right side of her body blurred. Then it solidified again.

Swearing under his breath, he stood up. Too fast. Dizziness hit him and he swayed, grabbing for the wall, which was out of reach. The nurse jumped up and grasped his arm, steadying him. Large and strong, she stood almost as tall as Kelric. He wondered if Maccar had assigned her to him. She was obviously also a bodyguard.

"You all right?" she asked.

Kelric nodded. "We're piling up inversion errors." He had seen the effect before. If a ship spent too long in complex space, it began to slip, different parts of the craft taking on different imaginary components, which meant they had different phases. It was no coincidence the errors caused ripples in space and time; people used complex numbers to describe wave phenomena because of their oscillatory nature.

A warning gong went off, echoing in the air. Maccar's voice came over the shipwide comm. "Prepare to reinvert. All hands strap down. This may be a rough one."

Kelric lay on his bunk and secured its webbing around his body. His nurse had just barely fastened herself into her chair when the ship began the drop back into normal space.

Kelric's mind fragmented. His brain was twisting through a Klein bottle, the 3-D equivalent of a Möbius strip. He clenched his teeth, fighting his vertigo. Their drop into real space was taking far longer than the usual one or two seconds.

It stopped as abruptly as it had begun. Reality settled around them. Then another alarm went off—the call to battle stations.

As Kelric yanked off his webbing, Maccar's voice snapped out of the console. "Lieutenant Droxilhiem, is Commander Garlin conscious?"

The nurse was extracting herself from her chair. "Aye, sir."

Kelric went to the console and activated the screen, bringing up Maccar on the bridge. "I'm fine, sir."

"Can you resume your duties?" Maccar asked.

"Right away."

Relief flickered on Maccar's face. "Report to the bridge. We came out in Eubian space—and we've got a squadron of ESComm Solos headed straight for us."

8

Cooling Coil

Kelric propelled himself into the bridge. Every screen was active, showing the panorama of space. No ESComm ships were visible to the eye. Yet.

As soon as Maccar saw Kelric, he motioned to him. Kelric grabbed a cable and skimmed up to the captain.

"We have a problem," Maccar said.

Kelric was doing his best not to imagine what would happen if ESComm caught the *Corona.* "Sir, I should be at my station."

"I'm afraid this has gone beyond anything you can do as weapons officer." Maccar grimaced. "Sixteen Solos are moving in formation with us now, closing ranks. They're well within firing range. It won't be long before we can see them."

Kelric silently swore. Solos were the ESComm equivalent of Jag fighters. He well knew their combat versatility; as a Jag pilot, he had engaged Solos more than any other ESComm craft. Against sixteen of them, Maccar had no chance of escape.

"How did they find us?" Kelric asked.

"Either they got lucky," Maccar said, "or ESComm has more squads available for the search than we expected."

"They've always had a lot of ships, especially if you count the raiders."

"They identified themselves as ESComm," Maccar said. "I doubt they're pirates. Even if they were, we've neither goods nor wealth for them to take. I sent the payment for our cargo with several of the frigates." He considered Kelric. "If they find you, they won't give a kiss in a quasar about the Halstaad Code of War. You're more valuable than ten times my cargo." He snapped his fingers. "They'll take you like that."

Kelric swallowed. "Only if they realize what I am."

"Can you barrier your mind?"

"I thought I was."

Maccar shook his head. "Commander, my Kyle rating is only one point eight. That doesn't even qualify me as a minimal empath. And I can feel you. Gods, man, you're like a nova."

Kelric felt a surreal numbness. "I've some brain damage. It interferes with my ability to shield my thoughts."

Quietly Maccar said, "Doctor Gonzales told me. Everything."

"It doesn't matter," he said. Not if the Traders captured him.

Maccar glanced out at space, at its stars and gleaming galaxies. No visible sign of the Solos showed yet.

He turned back to Kelric. "Our best bet is to hide you in one of the engine bays. The magnetic fields around the Klein containment bottles might throw off their sensors. Marko Jaes is clearing out a compartment. He's also rigging a shroud, something similar to what ships use for stealth runs."

Kelric's hope stirred. Could they hide him? The Traders had no reason to look for anything unusual. Or did they? His attack on the frigates had been surgically precise despite the apparent lack of warning. It could have given him away. He might also have alerted the warlord whose mind he touched. He had no idea if the Aristo felt that contact or if his frigate survived the attack.

Anatakala's voice came over the bridge channel. "Captain, we're getting the Solos on visual."

Kelric looked out at the screens. The Solos showed as bright slivers in space, distant and spread out, but growing in size as they converged on Maccar's vessel. It wouldn't be long before the ships had all slowed enough for ESComm to board the *Corona.*

Maccar switched to the engineering comm channel. "Marko, are you ready?"

Marko Jaes's voice came over the comm. "All set, sir."

"Good." Maccar turned back to Kelric. Then he extended his hand. The small white disk of a geltab lay in his palm. "It's yours if you want it."

Kelric stared at the disk. *If you want it.* No. He didn't want it. But that made no difference. When he took the geltab, it lay cool in his palm. In his mouth, it would bring death within seconds.

Quietly Maccar said, "Gods speed, Commander."

The eight bays that housed the inversion engines were spread throughout the ship to minimize the chance of losing more than one at once. Kelric went to the fourth bay, a circular room that vibrated with a deep rumble.

Rising out of a round well in the deck, the engine column dominated the far side of the room. It shone with gold light, making the air glimmer. Cooling conduits spiraled around it, the liquid within sparkling from chemical reactions meant to keep the conduits visible even in the column's radiance. Consoles lined every bulkhead and formed a circular island in the center of the bay. Lights flickered on them like radiant necklaces.

The inversion engine was quiet, its power banked while the more mundane antimatter engines provided real-space propulsion. Kelric still remembered his first time in an engine room when a starship inverted. The shimmering in the air intensified until he could see nothing except the dazzling column.

Marko was walking toward him. The engineer moved oddly, as if leaning against an unseen hand. The gravity was at 130 percent now, raised when Maccar upped the cylinder's spin rate. It made Kelric's limp worse and increased his nausea. He knew why Maccar had changed the spin; if it bothered the Traders enough when they boarded, they might spend less time on the ship. Of course, they could easily order the rotation decreased. But anything that might shorten their stay was worth a try.

He crossed the bay with Marko. As they neared the column, its rumble grew into thunder. He had once listened to the roar of an engine during inversion. For several hours afterward his ears rang. He knew of techs who had repeatedly gone deaf and then had their ears repaired because they refused to block out that roar, determined to experience what they called "the splendor of inversion."

Right now he had no desire to experience the splendor of anything except escaping the Traders. He took the headset Marko offered and slid it on, bringing the mike to his mouth. Plugs molded into his ears, shaped by the nanobots that saturated their malleable structure. Marko's voice came over the plugs, too low for Kelric to hear. The nanobots altered the insulation properties of the plugs until Marko came across clear and strong.

"I removed the secondary cooling coil from one cubicle in the bay," he was saying. He took Kelric to the waist-high rail that circled the well. "The secondary coils serve as backup for the engine and also cool the well."

Holding the rail, Kelric looked down. The well was three meters deep, large enough to hide even someone his height. About a meter separated its curving wall from the engine column.

Marko pressed a ridge on the railing. Below them, a section of the well slid open, revealing a ladder. Marko climbed down, followed by Kelric. At the bottom, he could hear the magnificent hum of the engine even through his earplugs. The noise receded as the bots altered the structure of his plugs to make them better sound insulators. The plugs also cooled off, probably an effect of the chemical changes within them. He wondered if they heated up when their insulation properties decreased.

The engine column rose up next to them, so bright it made him squint. Light swirled in its depths, then twisted out of real space. It mesmerized him, the shifting, unreal depths of this portal onto another universe.

"You all right?" Marko asked.

"Yes." Kelric smiled slightly. "It's been a long time since I was this close to one."

Marko gave him a nod that acknowledged what Kelric didn't say, the wonder and terrible beauty of the engine's contained power.

Next to the ladder, lights glowed on a vertical control strip. Marko entered commands and a floor-to-ceiling panel slid aside in the well, revealing a chamber. Normally a coil would have filled the narrow compartment. Now it stood empty.

Kelric walked into the chamber. It was a hand span taller than him and barely wide enough for his shoulders. When he turned to Marko, his arms rubbed the walls. Even with the door open, he felt claustrophobic.

"I've set up a sensor shroud," Marko said. "It works against X rays, UV, IR, and radio waves. A holofield will disguise this panel and an acoustical shield will hide it from sound probes. Neutrinos are harder to fool, but we can create false 'shadows' to make you look like a cooling coil."

Kelric gave him a wan grin. "I just hope you don't need the real coil."

"I've plenty more around the well." Marko tried to smile. "Good luck, Commander."

Kelric felt the geltab in his fist. "Thanks."

Then Marko closed the panel. Trapped inside the pitch-black chamber, Kelric fought a surge of claustrophobia. Taking a breath, he closed his eyes and invoked the meditative exercises he had learned as a child, when he was trained to use and protect his Kyle abilities.

Placid. Calm. Serene.

An opaque lake with a still surface.

A thought insinuated itself into his attempted serenity. What if no one let him out? He had no food, water, or light. He couldn't even *move.*

Cut it out, he thought. He turned sideways to give himself more room. With his shoulders along the diagonal, the fit wasn't as tight.

How long had he been here? Five minutes? Bolt probably knew, if its internal chronometer worked. He still couldn't talk to the node. It added to his sense of isolation, more here than on Coba, where no one had intelligent machines to enhance their intellect.

With nothing to do, he counted seconds. After ten minutes he gave up in boredom. Shifting position, he tried to ease the stiffness in his legs. He wished he could stretch his arms or sit down. Again he tried to meditate. Placid. Serene. Hell, he felt about as serene as an antimatter missile.

He became aware of a change. The rumbling was growing louder. His earplugs muted the sound, but its level was rising too fast for them to keep up.

The engine was preparing to invert.

With alarm, he realized he was about to serve the same function as a cooling coil. The compartment was heating up. Many coils packed the well, so the loss of one shouldn't dramatically affect their performance. But it only took a little to cook a human being.

The rumble became a roar. It reminded him of being trapped with Soz in the spine-cave, as lightning crashed around them, threatening to split open the mountain.

The wrench of inversion hit hard. He was twisting through a Klein bottle, one that existed in complex space and time. The sensation grew more and more intense until finally he groaned, his voice lost in the engine's thunder.

The noise faded so fast he thought he had gone deaf. Then his earplugs compensated and a subdued hum came to him. He worked up his hands and touched his face; why, he wasn't sure, maybe to verify he was still solid. The walls vibrated around him as the engine carried the ship through otherspace.

His thoughts circled. Why did they invert? He wanted to believe they were headed back to Skolian territory, that soon someone would release him. It was far more probable, though, that ESComm was taking them into custody for an inquiry into the *Chrysalis* incident.

Even a few hours ago, Maccar might have successfully argued that he had responded to a hostile threat. The record showed the menacing approach of the Eubian ships. To avoid a diplomatic incident, the Traders would have probably acted to minimize the fallout: a fast private inquiry, a fine for Maccar, and a public apology from the captain to the *Chrysalis.* ESComm would then escort the *Corona* back to Skolian space with a warning never to return.

But a few hours ago, before news of Eldrin's capture broke, the *Chrysalis* wouldn't have sent frigates against Maccar. Now Eube had every reason to seek hostilities. What would happen to Maccar and his people? A very public trial. Breast-beating and accusations. ESComm wouldn't release the *Corona* with just a fine now. Kelric knew he had to stay hidden. He had a duty to keep himself from being taken by the Traders. He would die here, if not from suffocation or heat, then from thirst and starvation.

He clenched the geltab. The darkness pressed on him like a weight, *smothering*—

"No." He closed his eyes, willing his mind to relax.

The fear receded. He had to face reality, though. If ESComm had taken the ship, the geltab offered his only real choice. He said a silent good-bye to his children, the six-year-old daughter he had known only as an infant and the teenage son he had never met. Ixpar was neither child's mother; she had only gained custody of them the day he escaped Coba.

He thought of Dashiva, his second Coban wife, a dark-eyed, dark-haired beauty who had ruled the most conservative city-state. His son's mother. Although Kelric had come to care for her, the cultural gulf between them had been too wide to bridge. In the end, the game of politics played by the twelve Managers on Coba wrested him from her Calanya. But that separation was only a physical manifestation of the chasm that had always existed between them.

With Savina it had been different. Frazzled, mischievous, and charming, she had carried him off to her mountain fortress, seduced him, and then married him. Gods help him, but he had loved her. She died giving birth to their daughter. Like almost everyone else he had ever loved, she had goddamned *died.*

He tried to put away his anger. His parents lived. His mother.

Roca Skolia. Legends of her beauty flourished among three empires. He had never seen her that way, though. What he recalled most from his childhood was her tenderness as she soothed his nightmares or cleaned his scraped knees. As an adult, he saw her political acumen, her skill as a diplomat, her grace as a dancer. Tall and statuesque, with gold hair, large gold eyes, creamy golden skin, and an angel's face—he wasn't blind to what everyone else saw. But for him it all paled compared to the beauty of the woman inside, the mother whose unconditional love helped mold his character.

Both his parents had been that way. His father was one of the finest men he had ever known. There was so much he wished he had said. *Father, did I tell you how much I looked up to you? Or how much it meant to know your joy in your children?* He regretted all the words he had never spoken. It was too late to tell his father he loved him. He feared he would die alone, unable to tell anyone.

Kelric slept awhile, leaning against the wall. He awoke with his left leg and arm numb. He massaged them in the cramped space until his circulation returned. Always, he kept the geltab in his fist.

He lost all sense of time. Sliding to one knee, he found a bottle of water Marko had left him. He drank in huge gulps. If they didn't dock soon, he would become dehydrated. Could he risk coming out after the Traders evacuated the ship? They would probably be at an ESComm base. If he left his hiding place, he would set off alarms.

Kelric stood up and slid his arm up to his face. He pressed the geltab against his cheek. It felt cool on his skin. He needed only swallow it for the poison to work.

No. He lowered his hand. Hope wasn't gone yet.

Time passed.

To ease his boredom, he worked out Quis strategies in his mind. The patterns evolved, as they always evolved for him, complex and symbolic. He interpreted the results, reading what his subconscious put into the dice, then manipulating those structures to see what he could derive from them.

An odd pattern formed. It took a while to decipher because it referred to someone he barely knew. Jay Rockworth. The Dawn Corps youth on Edgewhirl. Each time he made patterns of Eube and Skolia, he came up with Jay Rockworth. Why? What did a high-school boy from Earth have to do with anything?

Rockworth. He knew the name. From where?

William Seth Rockworth III.

That was it. Seth. Dehya's ex-husband. Seth had become her consort as part of the Iceland Treaty between the Allied Worlds and Skolia. Although such arranged marriages were rare now on Earth, Skolians still used them to establish treaties. Modern customs and the extended life spans of present-day humans intervened, though: after several decades, Seth and Dehya had divorced. Neither the Allied nor Skolian government acknowledged the divorce, since technically that would dissolve the treaty. So ties between the Rockworth and Skolia families remained.

Kelric had met Seth during several diplomatic missions to Earth, when ISC or the Assembly had wanted a member of the Ruby Dynasty along for show. Kelric had earned the dubious honor of being picked most often for that role. As the youngest in his family, he ranked low in their "get out of official functions" hierarchy. That wasn't why ISC had chosen him so often, though. It seemed the Public Affairs office had considered him usefully photogenic and less likely than his siblings to say anything controversial.

Seth was a retired naval admiral. Eighteen years ago he had been the oldest living human, just making it into the era of life-extending biotech. If he still lived, he would be well over a century and a half old now.

Kelric had no idea how common the Rockworth name was on Earth. He knew only Seth's line. The admiral had many descendants, though. Jay Rockworth, maybe? Although the boy didn't resemble Seth, that wouldn't mean much if he were more than a generation removed. For that matter, if Jay had blood ties to such a wealthy family, he could probably afford to make himself look however he wanted. His physique and features were so classically perfect it wouldn't surprise Kelric if he had been bodysculpted.

So why did Jay look familiar? It made no sense.

A change in the engine's rumble interrupted his thoughts. He tensed, listening. It wasn't so much a difference in the engine as—what? The scrape of ceramoplex—

The panel of his compartment slid open.

9

Warlord

The engine's radiance blinded him. Kelric snapped the geltab to his lips in the same instant someone grabbed his arms. A jumbled rush of thoughts hit him: they didn't want to shoot, for fear of damaging him. They dragged him out of the chamber, pushing down his hand that held the geltab. In the brilliant light, he barely made out four people. He felt what he didn't see. Like a void, the mind of an Aristo warlord opened before him.

Kelric fought. It made no difference that he couldn't see his antagonists. His body toggled into combat mode and Bolt calculated the responses it expected from his captors. He was well below optimum, stiff from his hours in the compartment, but he needed only pull his arm free long enough to take the geltab.

They changed their minds about shooting him. He never saw the guns, but he felt the shots. Neural blocks spread in his upper body, stealing his ability to move. He started to fall, but someone caught him. Someone else pried the geltab out of his fist.

No. Why hadn't he taken it before? He had gambled on life—and lost.

They locked his wrists behind his back. Straining to see, he made out four officers in black, each wearing a visor to protect his eyes. They took his upper arms and dragged him to the ladder. He couldn't see the Aristo, but he felt his presence.

Someone lowered a sling into the well. Fast and efficient, the team pushed Kelric into the sling and tied him into its mesh. Then someone hoisted him out of the well. At the top, four blurred figures freed him with the same quick, impersonal motions. Light blazed around them. They pulled him to his feet, one on each side holding his arm, and took off with long steps, forcing him to stride between them or be dragged. He managed to walk only because the blockers had affected his legs less than his upper body.

They took him out into a corridor. When they shut the hatch to the engine bay, the sudden loss of light made the area almost black to Kelric. The guards started down the corridor, pulling him with them, their guns drawn and ready.

As his eyes adapted, he was able to see his captors, eight officers and the Aristo. Did they believe they needed eight guards to subdue one man? If he had been at full capacity, they would have been right. They must have known, or suspected, they were dealing with a Jagernaut.

The Aristo walked a pace in front of him, to the left. He was as tall as Kelric, but leaner. His black hair shimmered. He had a narrow face, with a hooked nose and classic lines. His skin looked as smooth, and as cold, as snowmarble.

He glanced at Kelric. Red eyes. Ruby-hard. Kelric stared back, mesmerized by that gaze. He was falling, *falling* . . .

No. He shored up his mental barriers. The sense of falling retreated but didn't disappear.

The Aristo held up his hand and the guards stopped, bringing Kelric to a halt. The warlord came to stand in front of him. He studied his prisoner, his face unexpectedly kind. Then he spoke in a mild voice. "What is your Kyle rating?"

Kelric stared at him. The Aristo's apparent gentleness did nothing to mute the sense of an abyss his mind produced.

"Answer me, gold man," the Aristo murmured.

"Six," Kelric lied.

"Six. Just barely a telepath." The warlord gave him another of his incongruously kind smiles. Then he hit Kelric open-handed across the face.

The blow slammed Kelric into the grip of his guards. If they hadn't held him, he would have fallen, unable to keep his balance with his body partially paralyzed and his arms locked behind his back. Gritting his teeth, he pulled himself upright and stood straight, meeting the Aristo's gaze.

The warlord tilted his head. His thoughts washed over Kelric: he hadn't expected his prisoner to show such strength of will. In his oddly gentle voice, he said, "Again. What Kyle rating?"

Kelric almost repeated *six.* But to what point? He needed a lie they would believe. Speaking with difficulty, as if forcing out information he didn't want to reveal, he said, "Ten."

"Ten. I've never known a provider with such a high rating." The Aristo grinned. "I'm pleased, Jagernaut. You're going to make me a very wealthy man. Or wealthier, I should say."

Jagernaut. So they knew. Unless his ability to read people had suddenly plummeted, though, they *didn't* know he was also titled.

"How did you find me?" Kelric asked.

His captor smiled again. "I asked your engineering officer. Charming fellow, Commander Jaes."

After working with Marko Jaes, Kelric knew the engineer. Marko wouldn't have willingly given him away. Had ESComm done the interrogation? Or officers like these? He didn't recognize their uniforms. They looked more like a private security force than any branch of Eubian Space Command.

He hoped Marko was all right. The Traders did have humane forms of interrogation. They didn't need torture, which violated the Halstaad Code of War. Given that Maccar and his crew weren't psions, a good chance existed the Traders wouldn't trample the Code, particularly if they intended to hold a public trial.

Am I next? he wondered. They would find him much harder to break. In response to interrogation, his biomech web activated specialized nanomeds in his body. Those meds acted on the brain centers that controlled speech, making it almost impossible for him to reveal secured information. If that wasn't enough, the meds could disrupt neural pathways, erasing his memories. Of course, his interrogators could inject meds of their own to fight his. Truth serums offered other alternatives. But he wouldn't make it easy.

"Your friend betrayed you, you know," the Aristo said.

Kelric ignored the comment. "What will happen to Maccar and his crew?"

"The captain will go on trial. Perhaps his officers too." He gave Kelric an apologetic smile. "It's a shame we couldn't locate the weapons officer who actually carried out that brutal attack on those helpless ships. Apparently the coward committed suicide rather than let himself be taken."

Kelric regarded him steadily. "Selling me on the Eubian slave market is a direct violation of the Halstaad Code."

"Really?" The Aristo sighed. "That assumes you exist. We searched the ship and found no trace of your body." In a pleasant voice, as if they were discussing art treasures, he added, "Besides, I've no intention of selling you on the open market. For a provider of your value? It will be a private auction, of course."

Kelric gritted his teeth. "Go to hell."

"I don't think so," the warlord murmured. "It's too hot." Then he motioned to his officers.

They set off down the hall, taking Kelric to his nightmare.

10

Yacht

A gilded can.

Kelric could think of no better words for his "cell." The Aristo, Admiral Taratus, kept him on a private yacht rather than an ESComm vessel. Kelric's guards were part of the admiral's private security force. As far as ESComm knew, Kelric didn't exist.

He paid close attention to everything. If he ever escaped, his knowledge about Eube could prove valuable. He also kept himself physically prepared. Today he went through the exercises he always did in low-g to stay fit. Although the yacht had about 60 percent gravity, he felt almost no Coriolis effects. That suggested Taratus had a much larger craft than Maccar. It didn't surprise him; the admiral was part of the Highton caste, which put him at the top of the Aristo hierarchy.

After he had worked out and cooled down, he lay on the bed and studied the domed ceiling, looking for anything useful. He didn't see much. Rainbow sparks of light spangled through a diamond half sphere at the dome's apex. Gold, copper, and bronze mosaics tiled the ceiling and walls in subtle designs of birds and bare women.

When he grew bored, he played Quis. Taratus had taken his dice, so he worked out games in his mind. He coded his observations of the admiral's ship into mental Quis patterns and put them into bigger structures. Then he evolved the structures using Quis rules. After a while he assigned cultural, political, and social meaning to the rules. He wasn't sure what he would achieve, but he knew no one had ever analyzed the Traders this way. Maybe it would offer insights on how to deal with them. If nothing else, it gave him something to do.

Eventually he grew tired. Turning onto his side, he rubbed the bedcovers. The sheets were gilter-silk, a gold cloth that felt blissfully soft but shone like metal. The blankets were gilter-velvet and the comforter a billowy white fur. Sensors sheathed his airbed. They responded to his every movement, estimated his needs, and altered the bed's shape, softness, and buoyancy to please him.

His loose jumpsuit was made from white-gold velvet. It rippled against his skin, as rich as sin. Subtle fragrances drifted in the chamber, he had no idea from where. If he asked for music, the walls gave him almost any selection, even Skolian and Allied works.

He didn't care how good it all smelled, sounded, looked, or felt. He wanted this over with. He had been here two days and nothing had happened. At least he had seen no more of Taratus. As an ESComm admiral, his captor had duties to attend. So he left Kelric hidden on his yacht until he had time for the auction.

Taskmakers in amber jumpsuits brought his meals on gold platters. They treated him with courtesy, but never spoke. When he made eye contact, their gaze slid away. From their minds he picked up that he both fascinated and frightened them. They reacted more as if he were an Aristo than a provider. He suspected it was because he had no clue how to act like a slave.

Twice the food was drugged; he fell asleep soon after he ate. He suspected doctors examined him while he slept. Taratus had to know by now he was dying. Would he tell the bidders at the auction? The Law of Trade made it a crime to sell an injured slave without disclosing that information. Then again, he had seen what little regard Taratus had for the law, at least the Halstaad Code. The admiral couldn't get away with hiding Kelric's condition, though. His buyer would find out soon enough, giving her a legal case strong enough to win against even an ESComm admiral.

A bell chimed. Lifting his head, he saw the wall shimmer. An archway appeared and a young woman in a bronze jumpsuit entered. He glimpsed guards behind her. The wall solidified again, leaving her inside and the guards outside. She came forward carrying a small gold pillow.

Unlike the other taskmakers, this one was stunning. Red-gold curls framed her heart-shaped face. She had high cheekbones, full lips, and perfect skin. Her eyes were gorgeous, though they seemed too large to be natural. Nor did their color look real; the pupils were the exact same shade of bronze as her hair and jumpsuit.

Color-coordinated slaves? Knowing the Aristos, it didn't surprise him. Then again, who was he to define "natural"? Although his eyes and hair were brown now, with gold highlights, their normal color was metallic gold, a result of genetic tinkering that had adapted his ancestors to the bright sun on a planet they colonized.

The girl's sleek bodysuit left no secrets. She must have been bodysculpted. Surely no normal woman had such a small, perfect waist or such large nipples. He wondered how her breasts stayed up so well. Her garment fit like a skin, so if she had any support, it would show. And it didn't. He rubbed his thumb against his fingers, itching to close his hands around those well-sized marvels of structural suspension.

Kelric suddenly realized he was staring at her. Embarrassed, he rolled onto his back and looked at the ceiling. What was Taratus up to, sending him this lovely creature?

She sat on the bed and set down her pillow. Glancing at her, he realized her "pillow" was a bag of clothes. No, not clothes in plural. Just trousers. Or something. They had to be hers; made from black gilter-velvet, they had too little material to fit someone his size.

He turned onto his side. In Skolian Flag he asked, "Why are you here?"

She responded like every taskmaker he had met in the last two days, which meant she said nothing. He doubted she understood. As far as he knew, Highton was the only language Aristos taught their providers, if they taught them one at all.

Only the Qox Dynasty and Aristos spoke Highton, much as only

Kelric's family and the Ruby noble houses spoke Iotic. A few other groups learned Highton or Iotic: scholars, military linguists, finance wizards. That Kelric knew either tongue didn't necessarily reveal his background. But it would raise suspicion. So he spoke in a dialect of Skolian Flag used by Cammish farmers on Foreshires Hold. He was no trained actor, though, with spinal nodes to enhance his ability. Sooner or later he was bound to give away his Iotic accent.

It wouldn't have made much difference even if the taskmakers had understood his words. He gathered from their minds that Taratus had forbidden them to talk with him. Usually he picked up only a slight sense of their thoughts, but he read this girl more easily. She wasn't even allowed to say her name.

She set a vial on the bed. Leaning on his elbow, he picked up the small bottle. Made from rose-hued glass, it had a gold stopper shaped like a flower. Or no, it wasn't "rose-hued." It was ruby, probably designed from molecular assemblers that built it atom by atom in solution and then swam away.

When he pulled out the stopper, a pleasant fragrance drifted out. Was she trying to allure him with scents too? He stoppered the vial and set it back on the bed.

Watching him, she smiled. It was more interaction than he had enjoyed with anyone else here. He already liked her and she had only been in his room a few moments.

Then it hit him. Of course he liked her. This was no taskmaker. She was a provider. A pleasure slave.

"Why are you here?" he asked. She didn't respond. Frustrated, and annoyed at Taratus for this strange new game, he turned on his back and resumed his study of the ceiling.

The girl scooted over to him and pressed an air syringe against his neck. He reacted in pure reflex, with enhanced speed, sitting upright as he knocked away the syringe. It flew out of her hand and clattered to the tiled floor.

"What was that?" he asked. "What did you do to me?"

Spots of color bloomed in her cheeks, like roses in cream. In her fear, she was even more beautiful, with a sexualized presence that made it hard to remember why he was angry. Did Aristos design her that way? Why make providers even more appealing when they were scared? He didn't want to know the answer.

In a quieter voice he said, "I'm not going to hurt you." He indicated the syringe. "What was that?" He spread his hands to show puzzlement, then gestured at the syringe again. "What?"

She averted her gaze. Her lashes lay long on her cheeks, bronze like the rest of her. Without thinking, he brushed his fingertips across her cheek. Unsettled by his impulse to touch her, he dropped his arm. What would happen when the drug she gave him began to have an effect? Would he pass out? Get sick?

The girl looked up at him. Then she ran her thumb down the center seam of his jumpsuit, from his neck to his abdomen. The garment fell open, revealing the curly gold-brown hair on his chest.

Embarrassed, he pushed away her arm. "Stop that."

She averted her gaze and folded her hands in her lap. Watching her, he thought: *Now what?*

Then he saw a glimmer on her cheek. He put his hand under her chin and tilted up her face. Tears? She was *crying*? Flustered, he said, "What's wrong? What did I say?"

No answer.

Kelric watched the girl. How could he communicate and keep up the charade that he spoke no Highton? Maybe she was crying because Taratus would punish her if she didn't complete whatever task he had given her. Why would Taratus send him a sex slave? Aside from the obvious, the admiral had to have a reason.

He spoke gently. "You're beautiful, but I don't trust this."

She just stared at her hands. With each breath, her breasts rose and fell. He tried to stop staring at the jumpsuit that clung to her body. Her seductive scent enveloped him, almost tangible in its presence.

He touched her hair where it spilled down her neck. Soft curls feathered around his fingers. Sliding his hand to her shoulder, he explored her collarbone through her clothes. Her gilter-velvet bodysuit felt drugging in its sensuality.

Drugging.

Kelric jerked away his hand. That syringe had contained a damned *aphrodisiac.* He looked around, trying to guess if monitors watched them. In a loud voice he said, "I won't do it, Taratus."

The girl looked up with a start, drawing his attention. A tear slid down her cheek.

"Ah, no. Don't cry." He raked his hand through his hair.

The tear dropped from her chin to her breast, soaking into the velvet. He touched the damp spot. So soft. So firm. He folded his hand around her breast and she murmured encouragement.

He felt hot. Fevered. Had they given him Kerradonna? One of the better-known aphrodisiacs, it was actually poison. Whatever cocktail of drugs had been in that syringe, it included a lot more than Kerradonna, though. He could barely even think straight.

The girl slid her hand across his chest, stroking his skin. Such a sweet touch. With a sigh of surrender, he pulled her into his arms. She molded against him, pliant and warm as she put her arms around his neck. Then she tilted her face up to his, her lips parting, full and rosy.

So he kissed her. He knew as soon as his mouth touched hers that she had a nanogel on her lips. The gels contained nanomeds that entered the body through the skin and acted on the nervous system to increase tactile sensitivity. He wanted to pull away. But she felt good in his arms. Soft. He had been so lonely...

Kelric thought of Ixpar, hoping it would cool his ardor. But as soon as he imagined his ex-wife, his desire surged. Gods, he missed her. Those long legs, her flaming hair, her head thrown back as she laughed—his body remembered it all, especially their nights together. With a groan, he pulled the girl closer, too drugged now to distinguish her from the woman he loved.

He lay on the bed, drawing her to him. She tugged his jumpsuit off his shoulders, then caressed his chest, murmuring approval, as if he were the most spectacular specimen of manhood she had ever met. The small piece of his brain that hadn't yet succumbed to the drugs wondered if she was this convincing with everyone. The rest of him no longer cared. Real or created, she was his now.

As he pulled his arms out of his sleeves, she tugged the jumpsuit down to his waist. Her clothes dissolved under his touch. Literally. The material disintegrated with body heat. Amazing, how the Aristos elevated the act of love to such a fine art. Except for them, it wasn't love.

He stretched out on top of her and ran his hands up her sides, exploring her curves and skin. So soft. Vulnerable. He stroked her breasts, then slid down and closed his mouth around one, suckling her enlarged nipple. Again he tasted nanogels. The drugs in his body and the girl's sheer eroticism took away his thoughts. With his last shred of reason, he wondered if being pumped full of aphrodisiacs would hurt him. He doubted the influx of so many foreign meds into his body would help. What the hell. What did it matter? He was going to die anyway.

No trace of her clothes remained, neither on the girl nor the bed. He pulled his jumpsuit off the rest of the way, then covered her small body with his large one, trying not to smother her. All the time, she kept stroking him, finding his most sensitive places, her touch impossibly skilled for someone her age. Then again, he had no idea of her true age. Her appearance would fit whatever erotic ideal Taratus wanted.

As she kissed him, his body responded with a heightened, fevered desire. It was maddening. With a powerful thrust, he entered her. She arched her body along his in just the right way. It felt incredible. She made small sounds, warm and intoxicated, as if he were mankind's best lover. He knew the Aristos had made her to react that way, but she was too sweet and he was too drugged to care.

Beautiful man, she murmured.

Startled, he raised his head. She hadn't spoken. It took him a moment to realize her mind was blending with his. She picked up his pleasure and fed it back to him in a loop of sensuality no Aristo could ever know, because no Aristo could be an telepath. By instinct, he was doing the same for her, as he had always done with his lovers, even when he tried to hold back. Now, with his defenses gone, he and the girl merged into a lush haze of eroticism.

Kelric moved on top of her, steady and strong. Her response intensified, until she cried out and went rigid under him, pushing her hips against his. Soft and wild, she held on tight, like a wisp caught in a storm. His storm. She shuddered with the rolling sensations of her orgasm, her impassioned desire for him far more arousing than any nanogel.

Finally she lay still, exhausted. Even then he kept making love to her. She caressed him, murmuring in Highton. Still he couldn't finish. With growing anger, he realized what was wrong. The drugs in that syringe had included a suppressant. It acted on the brain centers that processed an orgasm. He couldn't climax until the suppressant wore off, which could be hours.

He wanted to curse. Why deny him his release? But the words never left his mouth, lost in his hazed ocean of desire. The provider kissed him, her bio-enhanced body already responding again. So he held her, and loved her, and tried to forget.

Kelric opened his eyes, half asleep. The girl lay facing him, curled into his body, soft and warm under the sheets. He pressed his lips against her forehead. He couldn't make love forever; eventually he had tired. The suppressant hadn't worn off, though, and it left him in a constant state of arousal. After dozing in a fever of erotic dreams, he wanted her again.

She stretched like a cat, her pretty body flexing against him. Bringing her hand between them, she showed him the ruby vial.

Kelric smiled. "It would smell better on you."

With blushed cheeks, she averted her eyes. He had no doubt she had been bred to react with shy innocence regardless of her actual experience. It still charmed him, though. He wondered if her own "pleasure" really pleased her. She was obviously designed to respond any time she was touched. What did she think when her body became aroused? Did she want to stop? Did she care? With his mind awash in her moods while they made love, he knew she had enjoyed herself. But what happened with Taratus? He wanted to protect her from the warlord, make her smile, give her pleasure.

The girl put her arms around his waist and pressed her lips against his neck. When he stroked her back, she moved against him. As he lifted his head, she tipped up her face. So he kissed her.

Unexpectedly, she giggled. Pulling away, she shook her head.

"No?" He touched her cheek. "What would you like?"

She opened the vial and dabbed gel on her fingertip. Then she rubbed her finger against his lips.

"Oh." He ran his tongue over his lips, tasting nanogel.

She spread the gel on her own lips too, then pulled him into a kiss. The gel did its work, making his mouth even more sensitive.

"Charming," a voice said, smooth and cool, with perfect Highton diction.

Kelric sat bolt upright, his arms going protectively around the startled girl. He pulled the sheets over her, hiding her nakedness. She held him around his waist and hid her face against his chest.

Taratus was leaning against the bedpost, watching them. Eight guards stood in formation behind him, all armed with neural blockers.

Why hadn't he known when Taratus came in? Proximity to an Aristo usually made him feel as if he were falling in a hole. Yet even with Taratus only a few meters away, Kelric had only a muffled sense of his mind. Surprised, he realized the cocktail in the syringe must have also contained a drug that dampened his empathic reception. But why? It made no sense for Taratus to protect him from Aristos.

The admiral looked amused. In Skolian Flag he asked, "Did you enjoy yourself?" Then he laughed. "I don't really need to ask, do I? There wasn't much doubt." His voice cooled as he glanced at the provider. In Highton he said, "Up, doll."

The girl let go of Kelric and slid out of bed. Standing next to Taratus, she wrapped her arms around her body and stared at the floor, her cheeks red. Kelric hadn't realized how small she was. She barely came up to the admiral's chest.

Taratus was tall even for an Aristo, though. He wore a black ESComm uniform with black knee-boots. The only color on his uniform was the red ribbing on the sleeves that marked him as an admiral. His relaxed stance didn't fool Kelric; Taratus was as tense as steel.

Aware of his disadvantage, Kelric pulled on his jumpsuit, then got out of bed on the side away from Taratus and walked to a console across the room. Leaning against its chair, he crossed his arms and regarded the admiral, waiting to see what he would do next.

Taratus considered him. Then he put his arm around the girl and glanced at her. "The escort will take you to my quarters."

"Yes, my lord," she murmured. Her revulsion for him had such intensity, Kelric wondered that Taratus didn't shrivel up and burn from it. If the warlord had any clue as to how she felt, he gave no indication.

After two guards took the girl from the room, Taratus came over to Kelric. Again he spoke in Skolian. "You seemed to have pleased my little doll."

Kelric wanted to punch him. "She's a human being. Not a doll."

"Ah. Yes, I had forgotten. You Skolians consider yourself human." He scratched his chin. "I suppose you are."

That surprised Kelric. He had never heard an Aristo acknowledge that anyone besides Aristos qualified as human. In his youth he had thought they made that claim to justify their enslavement of nearly two trillion people. Over the years he came to realize they believed their propaganda.

"You think I'm human?" Kelric asked, certain he had misheard.

Taratus shrugged. "We all have the same ancestors. Aristos may be better humans than the rest of you, but we're all from the same stock."

Kelric stared at him. "If you acknowledge we're human, how can you justify what you do?"

"I don't have to." Taratus studied him. "You know, you don't sound like someone who grew up on a farm. Perhaps you aren't really a farmer, hmmm?"

Kelric tensed. Although it was true what he had told Taratus, that he had spent his childhood on a farm, he had neglected to mention anything else about his identity. "I worked hard to earn my ISC commission."

Taratus rubbed his chin. "I've never understood this about you Skolians, that any of you is free to seek a higher station in life." He shook his head. "I'm surprised your Imperialate hasn't collapsed from the chaos."

"Why would not having a caste system make it collapse?" In his mind Kelric began to assign Quis tags to their words. He wasn't sure why, except that this was such an odd conversation. He wanted to think about it later.

"You don't think giving people upward mobility destabilizes a society?" Taratus asked.

"Of course not. It inspires people to work harder."

The admiral looked intrigued. "If anyone can aspire to climb the mountain, it makes those at the top feel a lack of security. So they protect themselves. Which causes resentment in the general population. That leads to disorder and unrest."

"That's a typical Aristo argument."

Taratus regarded him with curiosity. "Why do you say that?"

Kelric shrugged. "Aristos reason in direct opposition to the truth. If you hurt someone, you say they hurt you. If you make a mistake that causes a problem for someone else, you claim they made a mistake that caused a problem for you. You take measures to solve problems that don't exist, and through those measures you create the very problems you're protecting yourself against. You treat people as if you hate them and call it love."

Taratus raised his eyebrows. "And how does this supposed 'logic' apply to my previous statement?"

"If you enslave people," Kelric said, "then no matter how pleasant you make their lives, they'll want what you have. Freedom. You *force* them to seek your power, because only through that can they dismantle the system you've set up."

"An interesting interpretation." Taratus paused. "But if anyone can attain power, riches, or freedom, that means it will no longer be concentrated in the families of a few."

"So?"

He spread his hands, as if revealing the obvious. "Those of us on the mountain desire to stay there. We like owning everyone else, having the wealth, wielding the power. We've no intention of giving it up."

Dryly Kelric said, "At least you're more honest about it than most Aristos."

Taratus smiled. "Do you know, I've never had a conversation like this. Even my highest-ranking officers avoid anything they fear might antagonize me. They are all taskmakers, after all. I've bought and sold a few other Skolians, but they were too frightened to say much. And Eubian-bred providers—well, I'm sure you can imagine." He tilted his head, regarding Kelric. "I'm tempted to keep you myself, just for the intelligent discussion."

Kelric had no answer for that. He had no interest in providing anything for any Aristo, intelligent or otherwise.

"I think not," Taratus decided. "I'd rather have the wealth an auction will bring in. The session today will skyrocket your price."

Kelric tensed. "Session?"

"The recording of your little interlude with my provider."

He stared at the admiral. "You *recorded* it? To show the bidders?"

"Indeed." Taratus seemed amused by his dismay. "I suppose you've never seen yourself in action. Did you ever consider becoming a courtesan? I doubt you would have an equal, if your performance this afternoon was any indication."

Kelric scowled. "You can go rot in a Dieshan whorehouse."

Amusement trickled from Taratus's mind. "Why should I bother? I've hundreds of pleasure slaves of far better caliber than anything you Skolians produce." His voice took on an edge. "Although my little doll liked you well enough."

He picked up what Taratus didn't say. It galled the Aristo that his provider preferred Kelric. That gave Kelric a glimmer of satisfaction, until he realized Taratus would take his anger out on the girl. Could he protect her? An idea came to him, one Taratus could never verify.

"Your 'doll' is a good actor," Kelric said. "But you should have known she couldn't fool a telepath."

Taratus narrowed his gaze. "Meaning?"

"I knew she was faking it." With a shrug, he added, "So much for your sales pitch."

"You know, you can become tiresome." Despite his cool tone, though, the Aristo's impulse to make the girl pay for her pleasure faded from his mind. "In any event, the bidders won't know it was faked." He scrutinized Kelric. "Unless you tell them."

"Why would I tell them?"

"One could say you exhibit less than the ideal deference for a provider." He cleared his throat. "Then there is the matter of your, shall we say, less than optimum health. I can't have you revealing that either."

"If you cheat them, the buyer can bring suit against you."

"Well, perhaps. If the auction is legal."

As far as Kelric knew, Eube was the only place where it *was* legal to hold slave auctions. "Why wouldn't it be?"

"Taxes," Taratus explained. "I'm not a Silicate Aristo. That means not only will I have to pay taxes on your sale to the palace, I also have to pay the Silicate Houses that oversee commerce in providers. Altogether it would come to almost forty percent of what I make on you." He frowned. "It really is an outrage. *Forty* percent. When I'm doing all the work of acquisition and sale."

Kelric gave him a sour look. "You're breaking my heart."

"No need to worry. I simply won't reveal the sale."

"How can you not reveal it? Doesn't the buyer have to register me or something?"

"Well, in theory, yes."

"In theory?"

Smoothly Taratus said, "I'm sure whoever purchases you will report it to the appropriate authorities in a timely manner."

"But?"

The admiral laughed. "You see, my dear farmer, the buyer must also pay insurance on you."

"You buy insurance on your slaves?" Kelric couldn't believe he was having this conversation.

"It's mandatory on any sale over a million. Supposedly to protect valuable property." He snorted. "But here is the truth. If you can afford a provider worth that much, the government wants its cut of your wealth. Do you know, the same office that taxes the seller also sells insurance to the buyer? It's appalling."

"I'm sure," Kelric said dryly. "So you and the buyer will just make a sleazy little deal behind the scenes, is that it?"

"Such a crude description." Taratus seemed more entertained than offended. "We will reach a mutually beneficial arrangement."

"Until the buyer finds out you cheated her."

"Ah, but imagine." Taratus grinned. "She must report the transaction without delay. Otherwise she forfeits her purchase—that's you, by the way—to the government. So if she later goes to the authorities, after she discovers the truth, they will investigate and discover that for a phenomenally low price she bought a phenomenally expensive slave. Of *course* she wasn't cheated."

"I'm impressed," Kelric said. "You raise the art of devious crime to new heights."

"I do believe I've been insulted." Taratus actually laughed. "I'm going to miss you."

Kelric wondered if he had a bargaining point, though he wasn't sure what he could bargain for. "What's to stop me from telling the bidders what you plan?"

"Nothing, I suppose." Taratus didn't look concerned. "I could have your vocal cords removed."

Kelric stared at him. "No."

"It might lower your sale price," he mused. "It would depend on the buyer." He considered Kelric. "Do it for the girl."

"The girl?"

"My doll."

"She's a human being, damn it. Not a doll."

Taratus gave him a brittle smile. "I'm not stupid, you know. I'm aware she wasn't faking her response to you. If you want me to let her live, keep your silence."

Kelric froze. "You would kill her just for liking me?"

"I've grown rather tired of her."

He doubted Taratus would care about her interest in another slave if he really had grown tired of her. "I don't believe you would kill her."

"How would you ever know?"

"Promise you won't hurt her at all."

"Hurt her?"

"That you won't use her to transcend," Kelric said. "That you won't torture her, you bloody bastard."

"So it's true," Taratus murmured. "You high-level psions do fall in love easily, don't you?"

"This has nothing to do with love. It's called human decency."

"Your definition of decency. Which, I might remind you, most Hightons would find flawed." When Kelric stiffened, Taratus held up his hand. "Nevertheless. I agree."

"You do?"

"For two tendays I won't transcend with her. And I won't punish her for enjoying herself with you."

It was better than nothing. Kelric had no way to make Taratus keep his word, but the admiral surprised him. In the warlord's mind, he detected a genuine intent to abide by his promise.

Taratus indicated a rumpled pile of black velvet on the bed, the trousers the girl had brought. "You get dressed. I will send an escort for you when the bidders are ready."

"I've a better idea," Kelric said.

"Indeed?" Taratus inquired. "What might that be?"

"Let me go home."

The warlord was still laughing when he left the room.

11

Auction

Forget it," Kelric told the empty room. Even on Coba, where he had often been given sexually suggestive clothes, the effect had been understated, suitable for a man of his rank and title. Not so for these trousers. Made from sleek black velvet, they fit like a skin slung low on his hips. A strip of his own skin showed along the outer seam of each leg, from ankle to waist. Gold chains crisscrossed the open strip like metal laces and a heavier chain served as a belt.

Kelric changed back into his loose white jumpsuit and threw the black trousers on the bed. He wondered if they disintegrated like the girl's bodysuit. He didn't want to dwell on the implications of a positive answer to that question.

He sat in the chair at the console and tried its controls. None responded. So he got up and paced around the room, too restless to sit. He felt edgy. Tense. The nanogels, aphrodisiacs, and suppressant still hadn't worn off. He wondered if Taratus was making love to the sweetly soft copper girl. The thought made him grit his teeth until his jaw ached.

For a while he played mind Quis. Each time he worked out a pattern, he tagged it with a psicon, the mental equivalent of the icons used by computers. He had Bolt store the data, either the pattern itself or the steps he used to create it. Sometimes he stored algorithms he designed with the patterns. His psicons might be visual, aural, even a smell or taste. When he later imagined an icon, the data associated with it came up as fully formed concepts in his mind.

That Bolt could re-create his thoughts meant the node could still send messages to his brain. Although the software Bolt used to produce "spoken" thoughts no longer operated, the routines for storing and accessing tagged memories seemed fine.

Eventually six armed guards showed up in his room. They entered in perfect formation, coming through three different archways that simultaneously shimmered into existence. Kelric stood in the middle of the room and watched them. They in turn regarded him with neutral expressions. They might as well have been robots for all the emotional range their minds projected.

One lieutenant picked up the trousers Kelric had dumped on the bed. With a puzzled look, he extended the garment to Kelric. Crossing his arms, Kelric glowered at him.

The lieutenant tried one more time. When Kelric continued to ignore him, the guard dropped the trousers on the bed. Although the other guards maintained their bland expressions, Kelric felt their confusion. He was an enigma. Apparently it wasn't even within their psychological makeup to imagine a slave defying a direct order from an Aristo.

They took him out into an octagonal tunnel. Metal tiles with polygon shapes patterned its surfaces. Wherever he looked, he saw mosaics of flowering vines. It wasn't hard to guess Taratus's preferences in women; hidden within the mosaics were subtle images of bare women, every one similar to the provider he had sent Kelric. All eight walls of the corridor were identical; if the ship changed to a weightless environment, no recognizable "down" would exist. Every ten or so paces, an octagonal arch of bronze bars framed the corridor. The "metal" glowed from within, giving it a luminous quality.

As they walked, they passed openings into other octagonal tunnels. At the fourth intersection, they stopped. Looking down the corridor, Kelric saw Taratus striding toward them with two more guards. Stark in his black admiral's uniform, his face impassive, he didn't look like the same man who only an hour ago had spoken to Kelric with such curiosity.

The guards saluted Taratus as he joined their group. The admiral nodded absently, lost in thought. They all set off together, down the corridor Kelric's group had been following.

Taratus fell into step with Kelric. The admiral watched him for a while, until finally Kelric raised his eyebrows in question.

"Can you walk without the limp?" Taratus asked.

"No," Kelric said.

"I suppose whoever buys you can fix it if they don't like it." He tilted his head. "You didn't do what I told you to do."

Kelric knew what he meant. "The trousers didn't fit."

"Of course they fit."

"Not the way I wear my clothes."

Taratus's bearing eased as he laughed. "Ah, well. I suppose the bidders aren't that interested in your clothes."

That surprised Kelric. He had always thought of Aristos as rigid and unbending, with no sense of humor. He had expected the warlord to demand obedience, even if it meant using drugs or force to subdue his prisoner. Apparently Aristos varied more than he thought. Not that it mattered. The end result was still the same. That Taratus found his defiance entertaining wouldn't stop the auction.

The hall ended in an octahedral foyer that glistened like liquid bronze, though the walls felt solid to his touch. Taratus crossed the foyer and pressed a panel. The wall in front of him cleared, forming a window into the next chamber. Kelric suspected it was one-way dichromesh glass that appeared opaque on the other side.

The admiral beckoned to him. "Come look."

Puzzled, Kelric went over and stood with him. The room beyond made even his luxurious quarters seem impoverished in comparison. Octagonal in shape, with a high ceiling, the chamber glimmered. Gold carpet, gold walls, gold floor, gold ceiling. Radiance bars curled in graceful designs on the ceiling. A large airbed stood in a far corner, its frame and posts also gold. Abstract holos swirled in the air above it like a gilded, luminous canopy.

In the center of the room, an octagonal table stood low to the ground, with gold place settings, gold utensils, and diamond goblets. Four Aristos sat around it, reclining on gilter-velvet loungers flush with the floor. The three women wore clothes tailored from glittering black cloth. The man had on an ESComm uniform similar to Taratus's, except the crimson braid indicated he was a general rather than an admiral. Four taskmakers were serving the meal.

"The bidders," Taratus explained.

Kelric found it hard to believe one of those people would soon own him. Taratus seemed in no hurry. He described each bidder, taking his time. They came from four different Highton lines: Mirella Kayzar, a trade expert and one of the wealthiest Traders alive; Heeza Taratus, a niece of Admiral Taratus; Tarquine Iquar, the Highton Minister of Finance; and Marix Haquail, an ESComm general whose reputation had been notorious even in Kelric's time.

Given the size Taratus had implied he expected for the bids, Kelric knew the Aristos in that room had to be wealthy even for Hightons, which meant they were probably advanced in years. He couldn't judge their ages. Mirella and Heeza looked in their thirties, Tarquine and Marix in their forties. He doubted any were that young. Tarquine in particular had a maturity to her face that only many decades of life could bring, even if the skin and muscle remained fresh with false youth.

Taratus was watching him. "What do you think?"

Kelric wondered what the admiral expected him to say. "I've never seen so many Aristos up close before."

"No, I imagine not." Taratus smiled. "Do you have a preference?"

"A preference?"

"For who you would like to own you."

I don't believe I'm having this conversation, Kelric thought. "I don't want anyone to own me."

Taratus tilted his head. "Can't you Skolians see the price you pay for this 'freedom' you so loudly praise?"

"No."

"Perhaps that's the problem." Taratus rubbed his chin. "You see your own small circle of life and miss the bigger picture."

Don't ask, Kelric told himself. But his curiosity got the better of him. "What bigger picture?"

"The Allieds have a saying, I believe. Something like 'Adversity builds character.'"

Kelric knew what was coming. He didn't want to react, but anger snapped in his voice. "And now you're going to tell me that by suffering, providers attain a state of exaltation, right? That when you 'benevolent' Aristos torture us, it's for our own good. You're doing us a *favor.* And let's not forget the honor you bestow by letting us provide you with your glorious transcendence. Which of course you deserve, you being so superior to the rest of us."

Taratus had stopped smiling. "No matter how much sarcasm you apply, it won't change reality. You Skolians have a sick society. It's unstable and you know that. Look at your rulers. An Assembly of dithering civilians. All these efforts of theirs for 'peace' exploded in your faces with the Radiance War. If they can't even control the Ruby Dynasty, how can they expect to build a viable civilization?"

The blood drained from Kelric's face. "Leave the Ruby Dynasty out of it."

"I've never understood why you all worship such a defective group of people." Taratus waved his hand in dismissal. "Oh they're pretty, I'll grant you that. But that hardly qualifies them to lead themselves, let alone an entire civilization." He regarded Kelric steadily. "And make no mistake, your Ruby Dynasty wields far more power than your Assembly admits."

The admiral's insight into the machinations of Skolian politics disquieted Kelric. "The Ruby Dynasty once governed all our people, your ancestors and mine. They're as fit to rule today as they were five thousand years ago."

"Interesting." Taratus considered him. "Most Skolians would claim the Assembly holds the power rather than the Ruby Dynasty."

Damn. He had to be more careful. "It varies."

"A dynasty of providers." Taratus shook his head. "You've elevated the weakest among you. And look at the inbreeding." When Kelric tensed, Taratus raised his hand. "Oh, don't worry, I'm no fool to lap up the venom our propaganda wizards write. I'm well aware your Assembly forced the inbreeding and your Ruby Dynasty deals with it as 'nobly' as possible. That doesn't change the outcome. The Ruby Dynasty is flawed. For decades Kurj Skolia, a military dictator, tyrannized your people. Then his power-hungry sister tore apart two empires. This is desirable behavior?"

Power-hungry? Never Soz. Kelric thought of her smile gentling with affection for her little brother. Then he thought of Kurj. It was true his half brother had been a powerful war leader. Whether or not he had been a dictator was a question Kelric doubted anyone could answer.

"You condemn the Radiance War because your people didn't win it," Kelric said. "Had undisputed triumph gone to Eube, you would be extolling the courageous forces led by your valiant warlords."

To his surprise, Taratus gave a dry smile. "You've heard too many bad Aristo speeches."

Kelric grimaced. "They're hard to avoid."

Taratus considered him. "Yes, had we won the war, my outlook would be different. But no matter what justifications you use to excuse the weakness of your Imperialate, it won't change the truth. It is only a matter of time before Skolia falls to Eube. Now, with a member of the Rhon at our disposal, we will bring the rest of humanity under our protection and guidance."

At our disposal. He remembered his brother in the broadcast, his haggard face, bound wrists, bruised shoulder. Protection and guidance? How could Taratus say those words with such conviction?

"Ah, well." Taratus was watching his face. "I suppose this was not the best time for intellectual discussion."

Kelric rubbed his hands along his arms as if he were cold. "I don't think so." His reprieve was over, unless he escaped, which seemed about as likely as the universe turning inside out.

"I suppose I've been delaying," Taratus said.

"Why?" Kelric wasn't sure he cared, but it was such a strange conversation he couldn't stop.

"I've always wanted to ask a Skolian such questions. But the few I've known have been too traumatized." He paused. "They didn't like providing."

"Would you?" Kelric's voice cracked. "Gods, man, would *you* want to live that way? How can you go through with this, believing I'm human? Is the wealth really that important to you?"

"In part." Taratus didn't even blink at the admission. "But don't mistake my meaning. Human or not, you were meant to provide. It is in your genes, your mind, your body. My geneticists tell me you may even rate higher than ten. They've never seen DNA like yours. It is a crime for you to go unowned and uncontrolled."

Kelric didn't try to answer. Taratus's view of reality differed so much from his that they had almost no common ground. In the past he had assumed all humans shared certain concepts of right and wrong, and that Aristos chose to violate those concepts because they lacked morality. Now he realized that they considered the social, cultural, political, and even moral underpinnings of their lives consistent and complete. Their basic ideas of decency differed from those of his own people at a level so basic, they might as well have been different species.

He wasn't sure what good his insights did him, but he encoded them in Quis patterns anyway. Bolt was automatically filing his patterns now, assigning tags according to mnemonics it took from his thoughts. It let him know a tag by flashing the psicon in his mind.

Taratus motioned toward another wall. "Shall we?"

So this was it. Kelric thought of what waited for him in the next room and he couldn't move. He just looked at the admiral.

Taratus glanced at the guards. When they drew their neural blockers, Kelric shook his head. Then he made himself walk with Taratus to the other wall.

But when the admiral reached toward a control panel, Kelric said, "Wait."

Taratus glanced at him. "Yes?"

"Captain Maccar and his people—what happened to them?"

Taratus paused, watching Kelric. Then he seemed to come to a decision. He spoke quietly. "Jafe Maccar was sentenced to prison. His crew was fined and deported back to Skolia. ESComm impounded his ship. The frigates and dreadnought returned to Skolian space on their own."

On their own. In other words, Maccar's ship was the only one they had caught. It made sense. ESComm would have looked harder for the *Corona.* Things could have been a lot worse. But the news still dismayed Kelric. Maccar had done nothing wrong. His imprisonment was purely political, a result of Kelric's actions. Knowing they would have all ended up dead or in prison if he hadn't acted made Kelric feel no better.

"How long will he be in prison?" Kelric asked.

"Ten years."

He struggled to mask his dismay. Ten years? In a Eubian prison? Maccar never deserved such a fate.

Taratus watched him, waiting. As Kelric's agitation eased, he realized the Aristo was giving him a chance to compose himself before they entered the auction chamber. Disconcerted by that unexpected courtesy, he looked away, across the foyer.

When his turmoil receded, he turned back to Taratus and nodded. The admiral tilted his head in acknowledgment, then turned to the wall and touched a panel. A curved archway shimmered into existence, opening into the chamber.

Taratus went first, and the guards followed with Kelric. At the table, the Aristos stopped talking and turned to watch. General Marix was sitting across from Mirella. Heeza sat to Mirella's left and Tarquine to Mirella's right. Kelric felt the chasms of their minds, but his empathic reception was muted by the drugs Taratus had given him.

The admiral nodded to the other Hightons and they nodded back, reclining in their loungers. The slaves stood or knelt wherever they had been when Taratus entered, their eyes downcast.

Turning to Kelric, Taratus motioned to the bed. "You can sit over there."

Kelric didn't really want to, but there was nowhere else to sit except the floor. Aware of the Aristos watching him, he crossed the room and sat on the edge of the bed, facing the table. The holos flickering above the mattress flowed around him, leaving traces of glimmering light in the air.

Taratus stood talking to his guests, who remained seated. That subtle distinction marked their roles, Taratus as the seller and the others as buyers. To Kelric's relief, they had stopped looking at him.

After a few moments, Taratus took his leave. Unexpectedly, he glanced at Kelric as he left and raised his hand in farewell.

The Aristos continued to dine. Watching them, he felt his mouth water. Because of his time with the copper girl, he hadn't eaten. He was glad for his interlude with her, though. He wondered if she would miss him. Like most empaths, he tended to blend his physical and emotional responses. He liked her. He couldn't help but miss her, especially after the way their minds had melded.

He glanced around at the eight guards in the room. Each wore a neural blocker in a holster at his hip. Kelric had no doubt this chamber was also packed with systems that monitored his every move, down to the flicker of an eyelash. He wondered where Taratus was now. Watching from some remote monitor, no doubt.

On the far side of the table, Mirella sat back in her lounger and stretched her legs out under the table. Then she glanced at Kelric. "Come over here."

He wanted to refuse. But the sooner they got this auction over with, the better. He went to the table and stood with his arms crossed, towering over the noblewoman. He supposed he could have made himself look more amenable. But he didn't feel like it. He didn't care if it lowered his going price.

"Goodness," Mirella murmured. "So big." She set her hand on the carpet. "Sit with me."

I really don't want to do this, he thought. Feeling awkward, he settled cross-legged next to her lounger, bringing his eyes level with hers. The taskmakers serving the meal blended into the background, so discreet he almost forgot they were there. The Aristos were all watching him. Each had a palmtop, a small console that fit in the palm of the hand. Mirella had set hers on the table, but the others were holding theirs. He tried to ignore their stares. He had never liked being looked at, not when ISC paraded him around for the Skolian populace and not when it was only four Aristos.

Mirella slid her hand into his curls and stroked his hair. She spoke in Highton. "It's a nice color. The highlights glint. Like gold." She rolled a curl around her thumb. "Is it real?"

Kelric answered in Skolian. "What did you say?"

"Can you understand me?" she asked in Highton. When he just looked at her, she frowned. "Our dear Admiral Taratus neglected to mention he was uneducated."

Heeza smiled as if Mirella had made a joke. Then she made an entry on her palmtop.

General Marix reclined in his lounger, holding a goblet of gold wine. "Why would you want an educated provider?"

"So he could understand me." Still stroking Kelric's hair, Mirella studied his face. "But you don't need to think, hmmm?"

Kelric wished they would make their bids and be done with it. Even with his mental defenses and the muting effect of the drugs, he felt the looming sense of their minds. Without the drugs, he didn't think he could have endured being so close to four Highton Aristos.

It made no sense that Taratus helped him muffle his empathic response. Why? If anything, the bidders would want his Kyle senses at their most responsive. All the drugs achieved was to make the auction more bearable for Kelric. Had Taratus shown *compassion*? The idea boggled. An Aristo capable of cruelty one moment and kindness the next. It puzzled him.

Mirella cupped her hand under his chin. "When I saw the holos of you, I thought Taratus doctored them. But you really do look this way." Turning his head to the side, she studied his profile. "Magnificent." She rubbed her thumb over the laugh lines around his eyes.

"It's authentic, too. If you had been bodysculpted, these would be gone."

Heeza snorted. "So we have to have him bodysculpted too?"

"I like him this way," Mirella said. "The character adds sensuality."

Marix spoke dryly. " 'Character' is a euphemism for imperfection."

Up until now, Tarquine had been silent. Now she glanced at Marix. "Tell me something. If you wanted a gem of great quality, what would you do? Choose a synthetic stone that had been designed to perfection? Or a real one that had formed in the earth over the eons?"

"The real one, of course," Marix said. "The flaws add value. But a provider isn't a gem."

"Isn't he?" Tarquine murmured. "When you can have perfection any time you want, which is more valuable? Authentic beauty or false perfection?"

For crying out loud, Kelric thought. He glanced around the table. Heeza was leaning forward, her round face entranced. Marix looked bored. Mirella picked up her palmtop and flipped it open.

"However," Tarquine added, "some of it is fake."

Mirella's ginger hovered above the palmtop. "Fake?"

Tarquine motioned to Kelric. "His coloring. The rest of his appearance is authentic, but his hair, skin, and eye color are some cheap tattoo job."

He almost swore. How had she known? Were Hightons that used to scrutinizing modified humans?

"Tattoo?" Heeza looked intrigued. "I had no idea. I wonder what it hides." Her lips parted. "Usually the *highlights* are the natural color. And his are gold." She beckoned to Kelric. "Come over here."

Gritting his teeth, Kelric stood up and went over to Heeza. As he sat next to her lounger, she leaned back and studied him.

"Gold?" Mirella smiled. "Taratus will like that." She indicated the gilded room around them. "His entire yacht is like this." Then she entered a bid on her console.

Marix shrugged. "So why didn't Taratus reverse the tattoo job?" He gestured at Kelric. "Besides, he limps."

Tough, Kelric thought.

"If he limps," Heeza said, "he will just have to spend more time lying down, hmmm?"

Not with you, he thought.

Heeza spoke to him in Skolian Flag. "Are you really a Jagernaut?"

"Yes," he said.

"Why don't you know Highton? Don't you Jagernauts study it as part of your training?"

"We learn some words and phrases."

"Have you understood anything we've said?" she asked.

"Not really."

Heeza leaned forward, her lips parted, and stroked a curl off his forehead. For all her bodysculpted beauty, she was cold, like an ice sculpture. Her mind pressed against his, suffocating. His mental barriers flowed and dissolved, too damaged to stay intact. Pain sparked in his temples and radiated outward in his head.

"Ahh..." The satisfied murmur came from someone at the table, Kelric wasn't sure who. It made him ill, that his pain gave them pleasure.

He couldn't stop staring at Heeza. Her eyes mesmerized. Clear and well shaped, with glittering black lashes, they were undeniably beautiful—and undeniably *red.* He had always thought that if he saw an Aristo up close, he would find their eyes were brown with a red tinge. But no doubt existed. They were pure red.

"You look like a wild animal caught in a trap," Heeza said with affection. She sat back, breaking the provider-Aristo link she had been building with him. Then she made an entry on her palmtop.

Kelric swallowed, struggling not to lose his last meal. Given how long it had been since he ate, he would have the dry heaves anyway.

Marix spoke. "I don't think he likes you, Heeza."

She shrugged. "He doesn't talk much."

"Why would you want him to talk?" Mirella asked. "I often have their tongues removed."

By the time Kelric's mind caught up with his reflexes, he had already turned to Mirella in disbelief.

Dryly Heeza said, "She wasn't serious." Then she added, "At least, I don't think she was serious."

"So he does react," Mirella murmured. "I had begun to wonder." She entered another bid on her palmtop.

"He also lies," General Marix said.

Damn. Kelric wanted to shake himself for his stupidity. Mirella had spoken in Highton.

Tarquine had been watching in silence. Now she spoke to Kelric. "You understand us better than you let on, don't you?"

Kelric met her gaze but said nothing. He knew her only as an older relative of the late dowager empress, Viquara Iquar, who died during the Radiance War. Where Viquara had been renowned for her beauty, Tarquine's face was hawklike in its aspect, attractive in its own ascetic way, with high cheekbones, an aristocratic nose, and a strong chin. Viquara had been sensuous: Tarquine was calculating. Viquara had been voluptuous: Tarquine was long and gaunt, with an austere beauty no one would call pretty. White dusted the hair at her temples and threaded the thick black braid that hung over her shoulder.

Under different circumstances, she would have fascinated Kelric. He had already experienced one shock today, when he realized Taratus could act human. Now he had a second shock: he was capable of finding a Highton Aristo attractive, even compelling.

"Come here," Tarquine murmured.

Schooling his face to hide his unease, he went over to her. As he sat down, she spoke in Highton. "What color are you under that tattoo job?"

He quit pretending he didn't understand. "Gold."

"I thought so." A slight frown touched her ascetic face. "It's a shame Taratus didn't have it reversed. I would like to know what I'm bidding for."

As far as he had seen, she had yet to make a single bid. He couldn't help but wonder what they were offering for him. Did Taratus really expect it to reach a million renormalized Highton credits? That seemed absurdly high.

Mirella sniffed. "I've no intention of bidding on how he *might* look."

Tarquine gave a slow smile. "Then we should see how he looks." She pressed the fastener at the neckline of his jumpsuit. As she moved her long finger down the front seam, the garment fell open, revealing his chest. She tugged on the shoulders and the jumpsuit fell around his waist, leaving his upper body bare, except for his lower arms. Despite his intent to remain impassive, his face reddened.

"Pull out your arms," Tarquine said.

Stiff with embarrassment, he pulled his arms out of the sleeves. She continued to look at him, but the other three bidders were making entries on their palmtops.

"You don't like this, do you?" she asked in a voice only he could hear.

"Jagernaut," Marix said. "Come here."

Kelric froze, staring at the general.

"Look at that." Heeza laughed. "He likes you even less than the rest of us, Marix."

Behind the Aristos, Kelric saw his guards drawing their weapons. Stiff with tension, he stood up. He walked around Tarquine and sat down between her and Marix, facing the general, but so close to Tarquine that his back was against her lounger.

A rustle came from Tarquine's seat. She leaned against him and draped an arm over his shoulder. "Marix dear, I do believe he prefers me to you."

The general considered him. "What is your security clearance?"

Kelric froze. He felt the odd blurred sense his mind produced when Bolt activated the nanomed series that prevented him from responding to an interrogation.

Still watching Kelric, Marix said, "How old is your biomech?"

Again Kelric sat in silence.

Mirella spoke with amusement. "He *really* doesn't like you, Marix."

"ISC conditions them," Marix said. "He can't answer my questions." In a chilling voice he added, "Yet."

"Whichever one of us buys him will have to have his biomech web redesigned," Tarquine said.

Marix sipped his wine. "And studied, of course."

Kelric was growing more and more uneasy. He had assumed Taratus meant to sell him as a provider. What if Marix also wanted an ESComm investigation? Taratus had to know his biomech web was twenty years out of date. Would ESComm still consider it useful to question him? If they subjected him to a full interrogation, they had a good chance of discovering his identity.

"I don't think he can talk much at all," Heeza said. "Maybe his brain was hurt in the war."

"Was it?" Marix murmured. Still focused on Kelric, he said, "Well, Jagernaut? What about intelligence?"

He knew the general was trying to rattle him. It was working. Kelric had held a high-level security clearance. Even after eighteen years, he knew things ESComm would find useful.

"Look at him," Heeza said. "He just sits there, staring at Marix like he's hypnotized."

"I'm not interested in how well he talks." Tarquine laid her palms on Kelric's shoulders, then slid her hands down his biceps. Leaning close to his ear, she added, "I think you should go sit on the bed again."

Kelric flushed. He had trouble reading Aristos, particularly when he was guarding his mind from them, but he almost had the sense she had intervened to stop Marix. Then again, maybe she was just impatient. As he rose to his feet, her hands slid along his body, stroking his arms, hips, and then legs. He walked to the bed and sat down. Mirella was coming toward him, and the others were standing up.

Watching them, knowing what they wanted, knowing he had no choice, he felt a surge of panic. "I can't do this," he said. He was surprised how quiet his voice sounded.

Mirella sat next to him, on his left side. "Do what?"

Heeza sat on his other side and Tarquine walked around the bed. Turning to look, Kelric saw her climb onto the air mattress. Marix also sat down on the other side of the bed, watching them as he leaned against the post at the foot of the mattress.

Mirella turned Kelric around to face her. "Heeza and I have a bet that her uncle doctored that holo of you with the provider. I say yes, Heeza says no. You have to show which of us is right."

"I can't," he repeated in a low voice. The thought of being with even one Aristo was too much. Four at once was beyond reason. Yet his traitorous body, still full of aphrodisiacs, was responding to her touch.

Tarquine moved so she was kneeling behind him, her head next to his. She draped her arms over his shoulders. "It would be far less appealing, sweet man, if you *were* eager for all of us."

"Why is that less appealing?" Mirella grumbled. "I should rather like it if he showed some enthusiasm."

Heeza snorted. "You would."

"Come on." Tarquine pulled on Kelric's shoulder.

He turned to her, unsure what he intended. His mind was hazing as the drugs took over. When Tarquine brushed her lips across his, he put his arms around her waist. Pulling her against him, he deepened the kiss. She felt thin after the provider, her body sleek and firm.

She tugged him down and they lay together on the bed, he on his back and she along his side. Mirella stretched out on his other side. Lifting his head, he saw Heeza sitting cross-legged at his feet. Marix was still leaning against the bedpost, watching them with half-lidded eyes.

"Lie back," Mirella said, pushing Kelric down.

Tarquine rose on her elbow and looked at his face. Then she kissed him. All the time, Mirella was caressing his chest. Kelric wondered which one he should embrace, and if it would cause trouble for him later if he made the wrong choice now. With Tarquine on top, it was easiest to keep his arms where they already were, around her waist.

While he kissed Tarquine, Mirella explored his body. Heeza was taking off his jumpsuit. He looked up in time to see her drop it on the floor. Then she began stroking his leg. Marix slid over and put one arm around her waist while he put his other hand onto Kelric's calf.

"No!" Kelric pulled away his legs. They were suffocating him, their minds pressing on him. From what he knew about auctions, the bidders were forbidden to cause him physical injury that might affect the sale. But he felt them swimming in pleasure brought on by his body, his hair, his face, his skin, the enhanced pheromones the aphrodisiacs prodded him to produce, and the transcendence they were achieving from his discomfort.

He tried to sit up. "I don't want this."

Mirella pushed him back down. "Of course you do."

Kelric stared at her too beautiful face. "Don't touch me."

Tarquine spoke with unexpected gentleness. "It will go easier for you if you don't fight us."

Mirella caressed his thigh, then folded her hand around his erection. "The rest of you seems to have its own ideas about what you wish."

He stared at her, knowing his body would give them what they wanted no matter how he felt by their trespass. And trespass it was, regardless of how much the drugs caused him to respond.

He turned his head toward Tarquine and tried to switch off his thoughts, to imagine he was somewhere else. Home.

But his memories of home receded like a fading dream.

12

Trade

Kelric opened his eyes into dim light. He was alone, lying on his stomach. Someone had lowered the lights while he slept. The bed sheets were rumpled around him and the blankets lay strewn on the floor. He tried not to remember how they had ended up there.

The remains of dinner were still on the table. His hunger gnawed, but he was too tired to get up and cross the few meters to the table. He wondered why no one had cleaned it up. He must have been sleeping for several hours.

After a while it occurred to him to wonder who bought him. Then he wondered why he cared.

I want to go home, he thought. His father's farm on Lyshriol glistened in his mind like an unattainable dream of Earth's mythical Brigadoon.

So he lay, listless, staring at nothing. The door panel was within his view, so he saw when an arch shimmered open. Six guards entered, and two women in the uniforms of Taratus's private staff. One woman went to the table and began filling a platter with food. The other sat on the edge of the bed, near Kelric. She was holding a pile of clothes. The patch on her shoulder identified her as a medic. She had dark hair pulled back in a loose braid, hazel eyes, and an unremarkable face.

He wanted to cover his body, but he felt too tired to move. The medic seemed to understand. She pulled the sheet over him, up to his waist. Whatever the Hightons had chosen to believe about his willingness to lie with them during the auction, this medic had no illusions about the coercion involved.

She spoke softly. "How do you feel?"

"Tired," he said.

She set the clothes on the bed, then took a diagnostic tape from the pile. She seemed to know he didn't want it against his neck, where doctors usually placed the tape. Instead she unrolled it against his side. After reading the holos and data it produced, she rolled it up again and slid it into her pocket. He didn't ask what it said. As lousy as he felt, he knew he wasn't seriously hurt. Taratus would have stopped the auction otherwise.

"Can you get dressed?" she asked.

Kelric didn't answer. Instead he watched the other medic. In the dim light he couldn't see well, but it looked like she had finished loading the platter and was pouring wine into a goblet. "Is that for Taratus?" he asked.

"He is called Lord Taratus," the medic said. "Or Admiral Taratus. And no, it's not for him. It's for you."

"Oh." He blinked. "Thank you."

The other medic brought the platter and goblet over to the bed. "Can you sit up?" she asked. "Or lie on your side?"

Moving slowly, he turned on his side. When the medic put the goblet to his lips, he took a swallow. It ran down his throat, sweet and smooth, and exploded with warmth when it hit bottom. Pushing up on his elbow, he took the goblet and drained the rest in one swallow.

She set the platter in front of him. "Take as much as you like."

He ate most of the food. Ships usually carried synthetic supplies, to avoid taking up space with gardens or hydroponics labs. Apparently not Taratus, though, at least for himself and his honored guests. These vegetables were fresh. He didn't recognize the sauces or poultry, but it all tasted good.

After he finished, the second medic returned the platter to the table. The first one set the clothes next to him. "Would you like help dressing?"

"No." He didn't want anyone to touch him. "Is there a bathing room?"

She motioned to a wall behind the bed. "In there." Gently she added, "If you want us to leave while you dress, we will."

Kelric nodded, relieved.

After the medics and guards left, he got out of bed and went to the wall. When he pushed a panel, an archway shimmered open before him. The chamber beyond was five by five paces, tiled with a coppery-red alloy that never rusted. When he walked inside, his feet activated sensors on the tiled floor, and the wall re-formed behind him.

Kelric waited, but nothing happened. He said, "On," in Skolian. Still nothing. So he tried, "On," in Highton.

Scented water misted from the ceiling and walls, bathing him. He exhaled, grateful for its healing warmth. "Soap too," he said. The fragrance of aerated soap drifted into the misty air.

He leaned against the wall with his eyes closed. His whole body ached. The Law of Auction supposedly prohibited the bidders from hurting him, but he knew they had been transcending the entire time. With all four focused on him, it had been difficult to separate them into distinct personalities. He had felt Mirella strongest, then Heeza. Both were ice. Marix's dark, brooding presence scared the hell out of him. Tarquine was harder to define.

"Rinse," he said. Sometime later he said, "Off." The sprays trickled to nothing. When he said, "Open," the wall shimmered into oblivion.

He returned to the bed and picked up the clothes. The trousers and shirt were elegant and conservative. Made from gold velvet, they had a pile so plush it covered half his thumbnail. Although the garments fit snugly, they weren't skintight, and the shirt had long, belled sleeves. They weren't clothes he would have picked himself, but they were comfortable and felt good against his skin. In fact, he liked them, though he would never have admitted that to anyone, least of all the Aristos.

A memory came to him from when he was twenty. A girl he had

liked, another cadet from the Dieshan Military Academy, asked him to a party. He wanted to go, to enjoy himself like other kids his age, make friends, dance with the girl. He couldn't, of course. For one thing, he was betrothed to an Imperial Admiral. For another, Ruby princes didn't go to parties with commoners.

Had he not been betrothed, he might have gone anyway. He didn't care about the titles. He was, at heart, the son of a farmer. His mother had wanted to live on his father's land, in part because she loved its beauty, but also because both his parents wished their children to have normal childhoods, away from the intrigues and chill of the Imperial court.

At twenty, though, with his marriage to Corey not much more than a year away, he had the House of Majda to consider. His parents might care little for pomp and ceremony, but with Majda it was everything. When he declined the invitation, his friend asked him a strange question: *What is it like to be wanted by everyone?* He had been nonplussed and hadn't known how to answer. He did now: *I want them to leave me alone.*

Whether it was Aristos, Coban queens, Admiral Corey Majda, the Assembly, or ISC, he seemed to evoke a deep possessiveness in people. They wanted to own him, even those who weren't Traders. His mother had the same effect on people. Why? It couldn't only be his physical appearance; Aristos, at least, could create any standard of beauty they wanted with their providers. Whatever about him caused such an intense reaction, he wished he knew how to turn it off.

Across the room, the door shimmered open, revealing the medics and guards. Kelric went with them in silence. They followed tunnels that honeycombed the ship, until finally they reached an octagonal antechamber. A guard pressed a panel and spoke in a low voice. Then an archway opened.

They walked into a copper office. Taratus was sitting at a huge desk made from gold, bronze, and copper. With his booted feet up on the desktop, he was leaning back in a large gold chair, his attention focused on a palmtop in his hand. The unrelieved black of his uniform made a stark contrast to the warm hues of his office.

The admiral looked up. "Ah. There you are." He swung his feet off the desk and sat up straight. With a wave of his hand at the guards, he said, "Leave him here. You can all wait outside."

Concern flickered on the face of the guard captain. But he simply bowed and said, "Yes, sir." Then he and the others went out and closed the entrance, leaving Kelric with Taratus.

The Aristo indicated a gold chair. "Sit down."

Kelric leaned against the wall by the door and crossed his arms. "I'd rather stand."

"If you want," Taratus said absently, turning back to his palmtop. Suddenly he grinned. "They're still bidding."

"On me?" Kelric asked.

Taratus looked up and laughed. "Who else?"

Kelric told himself not to ask, that he didn't want to know, that it would only make him feel worse. But his curiosity got the better of him. "How much?"

Taratus settled back in his big chair, exuding satisfaction. "Heeza just made one for nine point six."

Kelric wasn't sure what that meant. A bid for 9.6 what? Thousand? It seemed low, considering all the fuss Taratus had made about how much he expected Kelric would cost.

The admiral burst out laughing. "Skolia be damned, you're *disappointed.* You think you're worth more, hmm?"

Kelric scowled. "I don't think I'm 'worth' anything. You can't put a price on humanity."

"Oh, I don't know about that. You're bringing me a nice one." Watching his palmtop, he beamed. "Mirella: nine point nine. Tarquine: ten point three. Wait—hers came in at the same time as a ten point four from Marix. She's making another..." He laughed. "A ten point nine. Beat that!"

"Eleven thousand?" Kelric asked.

That got Taratus's attention. He stared at Kelric for a full three seconds before he responded. "You think they're betting in thousands?"

"Aren't they?"

"Millions," Taratus murmured. "Tarquine just bid ten point nine million for you."

Kelric stared at him. "That's *appalling.*"

The warlord looked amused. "Why ever for?"

"Do you know how many people you could feed with eleven million Highton credits?" Kelric thought of the poverty he had seen on so many worlds. "You could build housing, schools, community programs. For *millions* of people."

"Whatever." Turning back to his palmtop, he said, "Look at that. Mirella: twelve point six. Tarquine: twelve point seven." He paused. "Mirella: twelve point eight." Another pause. "Marix: thirteen." He sounded positively gleeful. "Thirteen million. I've never sold a provider for half this much." He grinned at Kelric. "You did one hell of a job in there."

Kelric tried not to grit his teeth. "I didn't do anything."

"Well, they certainly liked the anything that you didn't do." Focusing on his palmtop again, he said, "They're starting to slow down. The Marix bet is still the last...No, here's Tarquine, at thirteen point one. Marix: thirteen point two. Tarquine: thirteen point three. Marix: thirteen point four." He smirked. "They're going to decimal each other to death." He glanced at Kelric. "How are you feeling?"

"Fine," Kelric lied.

"Coperia wants me to thank you."

"Who?"

"Coperia. My provider. I told her about my deal with you." In a bemused voice he added, "I think it surprised her that I agreed. She told me she would, ah, make it worth my while." He smiled. "She does please me, you know."

Kelric had been sure the admiral lied when he claimed he was tired of Coperia. He was glad to know she would have a reprieve. He hated thinking of her with Taratus, but at least the warlord would be gentle for twenty days.

Taratus returned his attention to his palmtop. "Marix's thirteen point four is still the last one."

Kelric grimaced. Marix was the one he least wanted to end up with.

Taratus tapped at his palmtop. "I'm sending out a final call for bids."

An odd thought came to Kelric. "Taratus."

The warlord looked up. "No one calls me that."

"Admiral Taratus."

"Yes?"

"Why didn't you interrogate me for ESComm before putting me up for auction?"

"You're too old," Taratus said. "I don't mean age-wise; you're younger than I am by at least thirty years. But your biomech is old. It wasn't worth the trouble."

Although that made some sense, it struck Kelric as strange anyway. It was true that had he been only a Jagernaut, ESComm wouldn't have discovered much from his dated knowledge or biomech. It seemed odd, though, that the rigid Traders, who operated with meticulous precision, would let even a slight chance slip by that they might discover useful intelligence.

Why else would Taratus spare him from ESComm? Out of *compassion*? Was that possible?

Taratus glanced down at his palmtop—and whistled. "That old hawk must be richer than a diamond moon. Tarquine: fourteen point zero." He entered a command, then waited. After several moments he closed the palmtop with a satisfied snap. Leaning back in his huge chair, he swung his feet back up on the desk, put his hands behind his head, and grinned at Kelric.

"Congratulations," Taratus said. "You just became the most expensive slave in Eubian history."

13

Revelation

The shuttle was crowded, with Kelric, his six guards, two of Tarquine's staff, a pilot, and a copilot. Kelric dozed during the trip. He came awake when the vibration in the deck changed. Deceleration pushed them into their seats as they docked. Somewhere.

They disembarked into a decon chamber large enough to suggest they were on a space habitat. White tiles covered the curving walls, and radiance bars circled its girth. They exited into a magcar, though, rather than the hub of a station, which meant this was probably a ship. A *big* ship. As the car sped on its way, his weight increased. When they stopped, the gravity felt about 90 percent. His intuition suggested a vessel far bigger even than Taratus's yacht.

They took him through a maze of hexagonal corridors. No one spoke. Diamond tiles covered every surface, and black-diamond arches framed the white tunnels. Brilliant, pure, and sharp, without a touch of color, the icy perfection glittered like a crystalline reflection of its Aristo builders.

By now he knew the routine. Again they reached an antechamber, this one hexagonal in shape. Again his guards announced his presence into a comm and a voice told them to enter. Again an Aristo waited inside. Tarquine. One change: This time they entered a personal suite with glossy white walls, black chairs, a white bed canopied in white silk, and black-diamond tables. Rather than the multiple sides of a polygon, the suite had a cylindrical shape. A circle: the ultimate polygon. It had an infinite number of sides.

Tarquine matched her ship. Her black jumpsuit glistened as if the threads were spun from gems. Her hair shimmered, black with a touch of white. And her eyes. Two rubies. They were the only drops of color in this black and white universe.

She was leaning over a console by the far wall, studying its holos. As his retinue entered, she glanced at them and straightened up to her full height, six foot two, an austerely beautiful woman who had more power even than most other Hightons. Finance Minister. That would make her one of the emperor's top advisers.

She dismissed his retinue. Then she and Kelric were alone. She smiled, a formal expression that curved her pale rose lips into an elegant arch. When she spoke, her voice had a throaty quality, dark and suggestive. "Those clothes do you more justice than what you wore at the auction. You look like the sun."

The sun? It was no wonder she saw it that way, in her ice universe. He still wore the gold trousers and shirt. Gilter-velvet. The cloth resembled metal rather than sunlight. It matched Taratus's yacht and contrasted with Tarquine's gem universe. Did all Aristos pattern their environments after minerals or metals? Those he had seen lived as they looked, more machine than human.

Kelric had no idea if she expected a response. He had none. So he just stood. He was familiar enough with Aristo security to know monitors and defense systems packed the walls, ceiling, floor, furniture, and console. If he made any move toward Tarquine that an EI brain could construe as threatening, he would be stopped.

"In a few days," she said, "the head of my private staff will show you our routines and answer your questions." Her gaze took him in as if she could possess his essence through her mesmerizing ruby stare. "For now you will stay here."

He looked around the spare, beautiful chamber. "Is this your room?"

"Yes. One of my private suites." She turned back to the console and studied the screen. "I'm having a banquet this evening, ship's time." Glancing at him, she spoke in a shadowed voice. "You will attend me there."

To dine? What of the hours before? After? How long would it be until her chilling beauty became an ugly reality of pain? He didn't want to know.

After waiting several seconds for him to respond, she turned back to her console. He rubbed his hands along his arms, wondering how he was going to escape this mess.

She flicked her finger through a holo and the console darkened. Then she turned back to him. "Would you like to rest before the banquet?" She indicated the bed. "You can sleep for a few hours."

"By myself?" Kelric had no idea what he would do if she touched him again. He wanted to blank the auction from his mind, wash his mind clean of that memory.

Tarquine came forward. "I may be back later." She paused in front of him, watching his face. Then she murmured, " 'A tender wish, a lonely cry to soothe.' " She was quoting a long dead Highton poet whose providers had inspired his verses. Softly she added, " 'More shall you find, than ever did you lose.' "

He answered in a low voice. "Nothing will compensate for the loss of my freedom. Providing least of all."

She trailed her long fingers along his jaw. "Rest well, my beauty." Then she walked past him. He turned to see the wall open into an archway. She glanced back, appraising him one last time. Then she left. The wall re-formed into a seamless surface.

Kelric shook his head, far more rattled than he wanted to admit. He went to the wall and pressed his hands against its opaline curve. Cool and polished, it gave a sense of depth, as if he were gazing into a bank of clouds. He found no more sign of how to open it than he had with the walls in his prison on Taratus's ship. Finally he gave up. He went to study the console, but had no success there either.

Rubbing his eyes, he regarded the bed. Would she really let him sleep? Gods knew, he needed it if he was going to think his way out of this disaster.

He undressed and folded his clothes in a neat pile on a chair.

Then he pulled back the velvet covers and slid under the silk sheets. Within moments he had fallen into a deep sleep.

The new Trade Minister has none of Kryx Quaelen's savvy. Quaelen's death left a hole in the Trade Ministry, one that leaks funds into far too many enterprising hands...

The soft tapping of someone working on a console woke Kelric. He tried to orient on his surroundings. He was lying down, yet a moment ago he had been sitting, reading a screen about...who? Kryx Quaelen? The name meant nothing to him.

Actually, it did mean something. He seemed to know a great deal about the mysterious, and quite dead, Quaelen. The man had been the Eubian Trade Minister, the most powerful of the emperor's advisers. Not only that, he was also the consort of Viquara Iquar, the dowager empress. He married her after the death of her husband, Emperor Ur Qox.

Kelric knew them all. Ur and Viquara were the parents of Jaibriol II, the last emperor. Quaelen, Viquara, and Jaibriol II had all died two months ago, in the final battle of the Radiance War, when ISC attacked Glory, the Eubian capital. The battle had been more successful than Skolia realized, crushing Glory's defenses, shredding their webs, and decimating their stockpiles of valuable minerals, including their entire store of platinum.

Kelric blinked. How did he know all that? Eighteen years ago Ur Qox had been alive and well, and no one knew he had a son named Jaibriol II. Everything Kelric had just "remembered" happened *after* he crashed on Coba. Yes, of course, he heard about the Radiance War on Edgewhirl and the *Corona.* But all this? Impossible.

He was lying sprawled in bed with his head against a woman's bare thigh. Tarquine was sitting next to him, dressed only in a short black shift made from silky lace. He had one arm stretched out under the cushions that pillowed his head and the other wrapped around her leg, his fingers resting on her inner thigh. She was working on a lap console, with its flexible screen unrolled in her lap. Holos danced in the air above the screen.

Had he picked up all that from *Tarquine*? In his sleep his mental defenses sometimes dissolved. And Tarquine was close enough to him that their neural interaction was at its greatest. But still. He rarely picked up such a vivid sense of another person.

He lay still, not letting her know he was awake. He had learned the technique long ago; when people thought you were less alert, they became careless. Something felt wrong to him, or not wrong exactly, but out of kilter. He couldn't isolate what bothered him, though.

Financial graphs rotated in the air above her console. As she studied the holos, she laid her hand on his head and absently stroked his curls. He watched the 3-D plots. They looked like studies of import profits for the thirty-one sectors of the Eubian Concord. Sphinx Sector was struggling and the Platinum Sectors were also in bad shape, hit hard by the war. Sapphire Sector, on the other hand, topped everyone in revenue.

After a while Tarquine deactivated the console and rolled it into a rod as slim as a light pen. As she set it on the nightstand, Kelric closed his eyes. He felt her slide down next to him. Opening his eyes, he gave her a drowsy look, as if he had just awoken.

"My greetings," she murmured. "Did you sleep well?"

"Yes." It was true. He had needed the sleep. In fact, he would have liked a great deal more. He doubted he was going to get it, though.

Tarquine brushed her lips across his, and his drugged body responded. His reaction was less intense than before; the influence of the aphrodisiacs was beginning to fade. They still drove him, though. He resisted, pulling back from her. He didn't want to feel this desire. But as he started to roll away, a thought came to him. If she enjoyed this, she might be less inclined to transcend. Anything that could put off that future was worth trying.

Kelric slid his hands over her body, pushing her shift up to her hips. Again he felt a strangeness, something beyond this bizarre situation itself, that he was about to lie with the Highton Finance Minister. More was off balance here, but he couldn't say what.

He eased Tarquine's shift over her head, then dropped it on the floor. Holding himself up on his hands, he gazed at her. Now, alone with her, without the demands of three other people overwhelming him, he had a chance to look. She had a long body, firm and athletic, with no trace of fat. Although he usually preferred more voluptuous women, her graceful lines stirred him. Or maybe it was the drugs. Normally he would have loathed a Trader. But now he wanted her.

Lowering his body onto hers, he stroked his hands up her sides and cupped her breasts. The drugged intensity of his reactions had blended into a more natural arousal now. Trying to stir an answering response, he kissed her, nudging her lips open for his tongue. He spent a while with the kiss, until she began to respond.

After a while he slid down her body and kissed her breasts, taking first one, then the other, into his mouth. Eventually he went lower, to her stomach, pressing his lips against her alabaster skin, tickling her navel with his tongue. He went lower still and tasted the inviting folds that waited for him. Even the triangle of black hair between her thighs shimmered. It was softer than he expected, like velvet against his cheek and the palm of his hand.

From her mind, he felt her arousal and knew she enjoyed his lovemaking. She gave almost no outward indication of her pleasure. She simply lay on the bed with her arms idly thrown over her head and her eyes closed. He spent a long time exploring, caressing, and kissing her body, trying to arouse the passion he had enjoyed with the provider, and indeed with most of his past wives and lovers. Finally he gave up. Tarquine had no intention of letting herself lose control.

He didn't mind. He was a telepath. For all that she kept her outward control, he knew what she felt. She liked the way he touched her. More than liked. She craved him and he knew it, even if she tried to hide her response.

His mind reacted as it always did when he made consensual love; he picked up her pleasure, made it his own, and fed it back to her, along with what he felt. It was an instinctual response. That had unsettled a few of his lovers, the ones who thought they had to satisfy the Ruby prince regardless of their own pleasure. His telepathic eroticism almost always aroused them, even if he couldn't incite the cooler ones to the hot response he liked. Tarquine was cool, very cool, but only on the outside.

Sliding up her body, he pulled her arms around his waist. She did react a bit then, nuzzling his neck. Kelric entered her easily, finding her ready, and she finally made a sound, a quiet sigh.

"Tell me what you want," she murmured.

He bit at her neck. "You."

In a husky voice she said, "Tell me what you want to do."

From her mind, he picked up what she wanted to hear. He didn't normally use explicit language when he made love, or even talk at all. But right now he didn't much care. He spoke, his lips against her ear as he told her what he desired. She sighed and arched against him, stroking his curls.

"Again," she murmured.

Kelric kissed her ear, running his tongue over its ridges. Then he told her again, in detail, first in Highton, then in Skolian and Eubic. Why it turned her on, he had no idea, but there was no mistaking the surge in her desire.

They moved together, and he began to build toward a climax. The suppressant was wearing off. As they made love, his physical sensations took on an enhanced intensity. His body fought the fading suppressant, which didn't want to let him come even now. So he kept building, always on the verge of climax, closer and closer, until his arousal itself was far more intense than any normal orgasm he had experienced.

He rolled onto his back, pulling Tarquine with him, pressing her hips hard against his, his hand splayed across the curves of her behind. He rocked her body with his until she gasped for breath. She said something, her voice dusky, but he could no longer focus on her words. He rolled her over again, pushing her into the sheets with the thrusts of his hips, always moving with her, always trying to forget he held an Aristo. His enemy.

Kelric didn't know how many times they turned over on the

bed, or how many positions they tried. Somehow they ended up sitting together, kissing deeply, Tarquine's legs wrapped around his waist. He let himself collapse onto his back, pulling her down with him. She straddled his hips, her hands on his shoulders, watching his face while she rode him. Her unbound hair swung through the air. Still he kept building, his response multiplied by his long hours of forced denial. He flipped her onto her back, and she groaned, losing the last vestiges of her control as he flooded her mind with his drug-augmented passion.

Finally he buried himself in her with a huge thrust, shoving her hips deep into the mattress. His orgasm exploded over him, almost unbearable, obliterating his thoughts.

Kelric didn't know how long it was before he began to think again. Tarquine was lying on her back at his left side, one arm flung across the silk sheets, her other hand clasped in his. She had her eyes closed, but he didn't think she was asleep.

His mind floated. Sometime later he said, "Tarquine?"

Lazily she opened her eyes. Her expression gave new meaning to the word *sated.* A smile spread across her face, still constrained, as were all her expressions, but warmer than any other look he had seen from her. In a husky voice she said, "You're worth every credit."

Having sex with him was worth fourteen million Highton credits? How did one respond to such a statement? Apparently it didn't matter; she was already falling asleep again.

His eyes drifted shut. After a while, when his body had cooled off, he reached for the sheets to cover himself. Then he realized they were all on the floor. He hadn't even noticed. He couldn't believe he had made love to a Highton Aristo and enjoyed it. But then, so far, she hadn't acted much like an Aristo.

That was when the realization hit him. He knew what was wrong. Or not wrong, but *absent.* He sensed no cavity in her thoughts, no chasm waiting for his pain, feeding him terror instead of pleasure. In the auction he had thought it was difficult to separate the minds of the bidders because he couldn't define Tarquine. But he had known Marix, Mirella, and Heeza with no problem. Just never Tarquine.

He turned onto his side to look at her. Watching him with half-closed eyes, she said, "Hmmm?"

"You're not an Aristo," he said.

She gave a lazy yawn. "Really? I had no idea."

She puzzled him, not what she said, but her emotions. He picked up her fundamental sense of self, including a strong identification as a Highton. She thought like an Aristo, felt like one, plotted and prospered like one. Yet she *wasn't* Aristo.

"Why haven't you made me provide for you?" he asked.

She gave a drowsy laugh. "What do you call what we just did?"

"Sex. It's not the same thing."

"Ah, well." She stretched out, long and languorous, her body undulating in a distracting manner. "It's all part of the same thing."

He shook his head. "You can't compare a consensual act of love to what Aristos inflict on their providers."

"Love?" She rolled onto her side and propped her head up on her hand. "I like that. Do you love me, beautiful man?"

Kelric flushed. "I meant it wasn't forced."

A lock of glittering hair drifted into her face and she pushed it back, her fingers trailing along its white streak. That she let it stay white puzzled him, given how Aristos turned the pursuit of physical "perfection" into an obsession.

Tarquine smiled. "I like this word. Lovemaking. But why do you call it that?"

He spoke carefully. "Because you can't transcend."

She froze. A muscle jerked in her cheek. "Don't be a fool."

"I'm not. But I am a psion. A strong one. That's why you paid so much for me." Concentrating on her, he said, "Isn't it a waste of your wealth when you can't take advantage of this phenomenally high-rated provider you bought?"

She turned icy. "I repeat, gold man. Don't be a fool."

Kelric felt the alarm she hid under her cold exterior. "Can you imagine what would happen if your peers knew you couldn't transcend? Wouldn't that make you a deviant? A pariah?"

Her voice went dangerously quiet. "Of course, I would be forced to prove you are lying. In fact, I would share the experience with these peers of mine. We would need a provider to achieve our transcendence." Her gaze glinted. "You would do well."

Kelric understood her threat. But he had no intention of letting this astonishing discovery go. "I'm sure you can hide your inability to transcend from other Aristos. But you can't hide it from an empath. I can make people doubt, Finance Minister. No matter what you do to me, how much you hurt me, I can make them doubt. And if they doubt, it will ruin you."

She gave him an unimpressed look. "I do believe you are trying to blackmail me. It's rather odd, considering that if this outrageous claim of yours actually had truth to it, you would be the one who benefited."

"Let me go and you won't have to worry about my telling anyone."

"Ah, Kelric." Tarquine stretched her arms. "You are bold, I must admit that. But do you honestly think I would let you go? That's absurd."

It startled him to hear her use his name. He hadn't thought she knew it. He had expected her to give him a new one. Although he could tell she wasn't worried, he didn't intend to give up until he found her weak point. If she had one.

"You're the one who will be ruined," he said.

She rolled onto her back. "As long as you keep your silence, I won't hurt you. Why should I? It no longer affects me. But if you make trouble, I will be forced to prove you wrong." Her voice went hard. "And believe me, I will make you pay for your betrayal. Please me, pleasure slave, and you will have a life as agreeable as you wish. Offend me and your life will be hell. The choice is yours."

He shook his head. "Threats like that may work with your other providers, but not me. Let me go or pay the consequences."

"I think not."

"This isn't a bluff."

"I'm sure it isn't." She paused. "How old do you think I am?"

He paused, caught off guard by the unexpected question. "I don't know. Anywhere from forty to one hundred forty."

She smiled slightly. "Not one hundred forty. None of us are older than Corbal Xir, and he's only one hundred thirty-two." Then she said, "I'm one hundred four. Old enough to have seen many things."

He wondered what she was trying to tell him. "Such as?"

"My peers and I used to play a game." She waved her hand. "Thirty, forty years ago. We picked out Skolians we wanted to make providers. It was a way to release anger, I think, to channel the dismay of seeing our lives and people ground down by this unending war with your people. We picked the most notorious of your leaders and imagined them in chains."

"Why are you telling me this?" It surprised him to hear her admission that Aristos found the hostility between their empires as crushing as his own people. The Aristos had always seemed invincible to him, set in their Highton palaces and unyielding views. It had never occurred to him they might feel the same way about Skolia's leaders that his people felt about them.

She turned on her side to look at him. "Your great military heroes, those who inflicted the most damage on Eube, were popular targets. Several of ESComm's top operatives became involved in the game." Quietly she said, "They took it seriously. Eventually they succeeded in removing one of their targets."

He tensed. "Who?"

"An admiral. Corey Majda."

He felt as if she had shot him in the stomach. Knowing Corey died by assassination had always torn him apart. To learn the plot had grown out of a *game* made it even worse. Tarquine was opening a wound he had thought healed long ago.

"Admiral Majda," Tarquine said. "I paid particular attention to that escapade. Would you like to know why?"

"No." His voice rasped. *Corey.*

"Her husband," she murmured. "Her spectacular golden Ruby

prince. You see, he was my choice for a provider. Not because he was a war leader. I just wanted him. But do you know, he died eighteen years ago."

Kelric couldn't take any more. He rolled off the bed and onto his feet. Without thinking, he went to the bathing chamber, the one place in the suite that would put him elsewhere than Tarquine. He closed it behind him and sank down onto the white tiles. Drawing his knees to his chest, he crossed his arms on them and laid down his head. When his eyes grew hot, he bit the inside of his cheeks to hold back his tears. Damned if he would cry.

The chamber activated on its own, probably prodded by his weight on the floor. Sprays rinsed him, misted with fragrant soaps. He lifted his head and leaned it against the wall while the cleansing warmth enveloped him. When it finished, puffs of air dried his body.

After a while the door shimmered open. At first he thought it was an automatic response to the shower's completion. When the shimmer faded, he saw Tarquine standing in her black shift. She knelt next to him.

Softly Kelric said, "I hope you rot in hell."

"I had nothing to do with her death."

"You might as well have."

She regarded him evenly. "Do we have an agreement?"

He forced out the words. "Yes. I will say nothing to harm your standing among the Aristos." How could he? One word from her would reveal his true identity to all Eube.

"Kelric, listen to me."

"Why do you call me Kelric?" he asked bitterly. "Don't you Aristos take away your slaves' names and give them ones you've picked yourself?"

"I like Kelric." She exhaled. "For your own protection, I will choose another to call you in public."

"Fine." He made himself stop gritting his teeth. "I'm listening. What do you want to tell me?"

"It was my choice to stop transcending."

He stared at her. "What?"

She sat against the opposite wall and stretched out her legs, her toes scraping the wall by his side. "The older you get, the more your mind evolves."

"It's called wisdom. So what?"

"Sometime in my eighties, I can't say exactly when, I started to feel uneasy."

"Why?"

"It was hard to say." Her voice softened. "I had a favored provider then. I liked being with him even when he wasn't doing anything, just sleeping or sitting while I worked. I don't know why."

Kelric snorted. "How kind of you, to let him sit around with nothing to do while you worked."

She ignored his sarcasm. "I suppose I loved him."

He wondered if she even knew the meaning of the word. "What happened to him?"

"I sold him. About ten years ago."

"You couldn't have loved him that much."

"You're probably right." She paused. "But it bothered me."

"What? Loving him?"

"No. Hurting him."

For a long time he just looked at her, certain he had heard wrong, that she would qualify the statement. When she didn't, he said, "It should bother you."

"Perhaps. Or perhaps my brain has aged and muddled my powers of reason."

He made an incredulous sound. "Learning compassion 'muddles' your powers of reason?"

She wrapped her arms around her body. "You can't know what it is like to transcend. Imagine the greatest pleasure you've ever had with a woman and multiply it ten times. But it's more than that. It is as if you ascend to a higher plane, one of sheer, enlightened joy. It truly *is* transcendent."

Kelric wanted to shake her. "You reach this 'higher plane' by *hurting* people."

Tarquine regarded him. "Your suffering elevates you. Inferior beings can only achieve an exalted state through their pain."

"That's sick."

Anger simmered in her thoughts. "And to us, your wish to claim elevation without earning it is *sick.*"

He just shook his head. Her reality was too different. Too alien. "If you feel that way, why did you give up transcendence?"

It was a moment before she answered. "As the years went on, it bothered me more and more to be the agent of that pain. But I knew the pleasure wouldn't go away. As long as I could transcend, I would." Softly she said, "So I made it impossible. I had the Kyle Afferent Body in my brain removed."

He had no idea how to respond. She was still an Aristo. She subscribed to their philosophies, kept slaves, and saw herself as a superior form of life. Yet with all that, she had voluntarily undergone brain surgery to prevent her from exercising what she considered her innate right, a decision that put her in constant danger of discovery, and destruction, from her peers.

Finally he said, "It's a start."

"A start?"

He leaned his head against the wall. "Maybe someday, if more Aristos come to feel as you do, your people and mine might find a measure of peace."

"If."

He thought of Taratus, with his glimmerings of compassion. The admiral was about the age when Tarquine said she had begun to question her way of life. "Are you the only one?"

"I don't know." She wound her hair around her fingers, gazing at the white streaks. "I've wondered once or twice." She suddenly sat up straight. "You can tell!"

"How could I miss it?" He grimaced. "You talk of how I can never appreciate the 'sheer, enlightened joy' of transcendence. Well, think on this, Tarquine. You can never appreciate the sheer, horrific despair your minds inflict on us. The stronger the psion, the stronger the reaction. You know what I am. I could no more miss the lack of that horror than I could stop breathing."

"No other of my providers is that sensitive." She leaned forward. "You can tell if any other Aristos are like me."

"On a one-by-one basis, maybe. But not in groups." He thought of the auction. "Even with drugs to blunt my reception, I can hardly bear the minds of just three Aristos."

Tarquine frowned. "I expect more than fifty Diamonds at the banquet. It's a meeting for the finance leaders in various sectors."

Kelric stared at her. *Fifty?* Diamond Aristos attended to commerce, production, and banks. In the Aristo hierarchy, their caste ranked below Hightons, who controlled the government and military. The Silicates, who ran the entertainment industries and supplied providers, were the third of the three Aristo castes, also below the Hightons. But for all of them, their defining characteristic—their ability to transcend—was the same. The massed impact of fifty would be more than he could endure.

"I can't," he said.

"Of course you can."

"No." He tried not to think of the auction. "Why do you want me there?"

She settled herself against the wall. "I want you to pick up what you can from their minds, in particular about the upcoming finance meeting on Glory. Also let me know if you detect other Aristos like me. Not only today, but anywhere."

That wasn't what he expected. "You want me to spy for you?"

"Of course. Who else has a Ruby psion at her disposal?" She gave him a satisfied smile. "They will know I'm bringing my new provider for more than show. With your barriers so patchy, all will feel your power. But none will guess the true extent. As far as the rest of humanity knows, Kelricson Valdoria is dead."

"You knew who I was."

Her smile gentled. "How could I forget? You lived in my fantasies for years. Decades. I'm older than most Hightons. After thirty-five years, I doubt anyone else will suspect. The idea would simply be too absurd. Even I wasn't sure when I saw the holos that Taratus sent us. But I wondered. He said he would take the four highest floor bids. So I put in one for three million."

He couldn't believe it. "The bidding *started* at three million?"

"Actually, it was four. That was Marix's ground bid."

Kelric didn't know which stunned him more, that they could waste so much wealth on one person or that they would go to such lengths to own another human being. But it changed nothing. "If you put me in a room with fifty Aristos, I'll go catatonic."

She sighed. "Some of my more sensitive providers react this way also. But you will cope. You're strong."

He wondered if she had any idea what she expected him to "cope" with.

14

Diamond Banquet

Tarquine reclined in a cushioned chair, watching while a techman studied the collar around Kelric's neck. Resplendent in a black-diamond jumpsuit, the Minister glittered.

The techman straightened up. "It's solid gold, ma'am." He set his gauges on the table next to the stool where Kelric was sitting and turned to Tarquine. "The collar has no picotech at all, nothing anyone could use for surveillance on you or your ship. The gold is high quality, however."

"So Taratus just threw it in as a gift." Tarquine snorted. "That is unlike him."

Kelric could guess why Taratus had included the collar. Anything to alleviate Tarquine's anger when she discovered he cheated her. He doubted it would help.

The techman picked up his tools and went to work again. He tested Kelric's wrist guards, then knelt to examine his ankle guards. "These are completely different. They're almost a thousand years old." He rose to his feet. "You did well, most honorable Minister. The guards are far more valuable than the collar. For their antiquity."

Tarquine considered Kelric. "Did Taratus give you those?"

He shook his head. "My ex-wife."

"If she is your *ex*-wife, why do you still wear them?"

He started to give a nonresponse, then changed his mind. He

wouldn't dishonor Ixpar with any answer but the truth. "Because I still love her."

"Oh." Tarquine obviously neither expected nor understood his reply. Her reaction washed over him. She surprised herself with her anger. Why would she begrudge one slave the devotion of another slave? For her to envy his ex-wife was like envying an animal.

"Shall I remove the collar and guards?" the techman asked.

"Yes." An edge came into her voice. "Melt down the guards."

Kelric held back his protest. He had already known she would remove them. Without picotech, they had no use as restraints. He would rather she melted than sold them. Better they become ingots than end up on display in a Eubian museum or worn by someone else.

"He will need a collar with picotech controls," she told the techman. "The same for his wrist and ankle cuffs. After we reprogram his biomech web, I want it interfaced it with the restraints." She rubbed her chin. "That will take a while, though. For the banquet, install a temporary collar, one that suppresses his enhancements. Make it gold. You can leave the guards for now."

Kelric knew he was running out of options. As a Jagernaut, he had studied these massive Highton cylinder ships. Once the techman installed the permanent picotech collar, Kelric would become part of the ship, so intertwined with its systems that he couldn't leave without Tarquine inputting an authorization to his redesigned biomech web. If he meant to escape, it had to be soon. But how?

The techman replaced Taratus's "gift" with a temporary collar that clicked a prong into Kelric's neck socket. Then he went to work on his palmtop, sending IR signals to the collar's picoweb, which sent commands to Kelric's biomech web through the prong.

At first Kelric felt nothing. Then, with no warning, he went blind.

He grabbed the edges of his stool. "What happened?"

"Kelric?" Tarquine said. "Can you hear me?"

He made his voice calm. "Yes."

"Try another channel," Tarquine said. She sounded annoyed.

He sat in the dark, wondering what the hell they were doing to his optic nerve.

Suddenly the room reappeared. A heavy silence surrounded him. Tarquine's mouth moved as if she were speaking, but he heard nothing.

The techman appeared in front of him and spoke, exaggerating his words so Kelric could read his lips: *Can you hear me?*

"No," Kelric said. At least, he thought he said *no.* He couldn't hear his answer.

The techman worked on his palmtop, then glanced at Kelric. "Now can you hear me?"

With relief, Kelric said, "Yes."

"Good. Please stand up."

The techman put him through a series of exercises, doing various tests. The collar blocked signals sent from Bolt to Kelric's hydraulics and so prevented him from using his enhancements. He had forgotten how heavy and slow he felt without the augmentation. As far as he could tell, though, the hydraulics were still functional, as was the microfusion reactor in his body that powered them.

Finally the techman packed his tools in his black valise. Then he bowed to Tarquine. "My honor to serve you, Minister Iquar."

She nodded, still comfortably ensconced in her chair. She had watched Kelric exercise with an appreciative silence, as if he were providing erotic entertainment instead of doing biomech tests. He stood near the wall now, breathing heavily, which he wouldn't have been doing if he had use of his enhancements.

"Do you have any more checks to suggest?" Tarquine asked the techman.

He shook his head. "Not yet. I need to study the data I've accumulated. His systems have a lot of damage."

She didn't look surprised. "Let me know the results."

"Yes, ma'am."

"What about the rest of what came with him?"

"Ah." The techman set his valise on the stool and reopened it.

He withdrew Kelric's gold armbands and the pouch of jeweled dice. "These have no picotech. They're valuable, though. Some of the bands are as old as the guards. The others are more modern, but all of them are at least four or five centuries in age. The jewels are natural, not synthetic. Unusually high quality. They're worth far more than their synthetic counterparts."

Her curiosity flickered. She indicated the nightstand. "Leave them there. I will look at them later."

The techman did as she said. With various bows and accolades to Tarquine, he withdrew from the room.

The Minister stretched, then stood up and walked over to Kelric. She wore glossy black boots with square heels, adding another two inches to her height, bringing her eyes almost level with his. "Come. Let us meet my guests."

"Tarquine—" He wondered if he would always experience this soul-splintering pull, simultaneously hungering for her and wanting to curse everything she represented.

She laid her palm against his chest. "You will be all right. In time, you will heal."

Again she surprised him. Did she mean his physical injuries would heal? Or his grief? Neither made sense. As far as he knew, her medics hadn't yet examined him. When it came to the emotions of others, such as grief, Aristos were like anti-empaths. He doubted she could see how he hurt, nor did he think she would care, more than in an abstract sense of wanting her provider at his best so he could better serve her.

"Heal?" he asked.

Dryly she said, "Our gleefully amoral Taratus is not so clever as he believes. I never had any intention of registering a false claim. I reported the full fourteen million." A slow smile spread across her face. "Now Taratus has a problem."

Surprised, Kelric said, "You know about my condition?"

"Yes. All of it."

"How?"

"I suspected right away. So as soon as you entered my shuttle, its spy scanners began to check you." She motioned to the bed. "When you were sleeping, my medics examined you."

"I'm surprised you're not angry."

"Ah, well." A cold smile touched her lips. "If I report Taratus to the authorities, he will find himself in more trouble than even he can dismiss. If I say nothing, then he owes me. 'Big time,' as the Allieds would say. It will prove extremely useful." She rubbed her palm along the plush velvet of Kelric's shirt. "And he has no idea what he really gave me."

He wondered if Hightons spent their entire lives plaguing one another with these intrigues. As Tarquine slid her hand along his chest, he held back the urge to embrace her. He had thought the aphrodisiacs no longer affected him. But they must still be in his body. It was the only explanation for why he would want to hold a Highton.

"So you won," he said.

She gave him an appreciative smile. "Indeed."

The antechamber to the banquet room had a wall of one-way glass that let Kelric and Tarquine look out at the banquet, which was already in its initial stages. The big room was too long to have the usual hexagonal shape, but it still had six walls and a vaulted ceiling. A number of hexagonal alcoves were set off from the main room, almost hidden, shadowed and full of pillows.

A puzzle occurred to Kelric: Did Aristos think differently because they lived in a universe of polygons and curves? Or maybe it was the reverse, that their penchant for such architecture reflected an innate difference in their minds. He would build Quis structures of it to study later.

The main hall glittered. A sparkling white carpet covered the floor, and white velvet cushions lay in piles everywhere. The tables were hexagonal columns that rose from the floor for about half a meter. Made from black diamond, they were large enough so each of their sides comfortably sat one diner. Aristos reclined in white loungers at the tables or among piles of the pillows.

Providers moved among them with platters of predinner morsels. The girls and youths wore nothing except G-strings made from diamonds. A girl with pale blond hair rippling down her back knelt next to an Aristo lord. Sprawled in his lounger, he watched with half-lidded eyes while she poured him a glass of wine. When she finished, he put his arm around her slender waist and pulled her into his lap. Stroking her breasts, he tugged on the ring in her nipple. Then he kissed her, his hands exploring her body. The other diners continued to converse as if nothing unusual had happened.

Kelric grimaced, wondering if the Aristos had any restraint on their behavior at all. After watching for a while, though, he realized an unspoken code existed. They fondled the providers as much as they pleased, but that was as far as it went in view of the main hall. The lord holding the girl eventually stood up and took her to one of the shadowed alcoves. As he went inside with her, several of his table companions rose and followed them. Kelric hoped she would be all right.

Even as Kelric scowled, he knew that part of his reaction came from a different source than his conservative background or an outraged sense of probity for the girl. If he were offered so many beautiful, compliant women, all unclothed, he doubted he could have kept his hands to himself either. He didn't know if he liked what that said about him, but he filed the insight as a Quis pattern.

One thing was obvious. He would be the only provider in the room wearing clothes. Granted, his were sexualized, with their snug fit and rippling gold velvet. But compared to the others, he was dressed for a snowstorm.

Tarquine stood at his side, studying the scene with the same intensity she had shown earlier when she asked him to spy on her guests. After he had watched her for a moment, she glanced at him.

"What is it?" she asked.

"I wondered why you wanted me to dress this way."

"You don't like it?"

"It's fine. I just wondered why."

As slight smile touched her lips. "Why I covered you up?"

"Yes."

She motioned at the providers softly padding around the banquet hall. "When people are used to seeing as much as they want, whenever they want, mystery becomes all the more alluring."

Kelric supposed it made sense. He still didn't like it. On Coba, in the Calanya, he had been inaccessible to everyone except his wife, his honor guard, and the few dice players he lived with. No one else was even allowed to look at him. He hadn't realized how much he had come to appreciate that privacy.

He wondered how the providers felt about their lives. Unlike him, they had no referents for comparison. Did they understand the concepts of self-determination and control over their own bodies? He created another Quis pattern, this time about the providers, and filed it with the previous one about himself and the Aristos.

Tarquine indicated a table where eight men and women sat drinking wine. "Those are delegates from Sapphire Sector. I'm interested in anything you can tell about them." She pointed out a dais at the end of the hall. It had only one table, obviously the position for honored guests. "Most of the time you will be up there with me."

Relief trickled over Kelric. The dais was set off from the other tables. His mental interaction with the Aristos depended on fields produced in his brain and theirs. With those effects dominated by Coulomb's Law, the more distance he had from them the better. The table on the dais offered a much-needed separation.

"Will being up there make it more bearable for you?" Tarquine asked.

"Yes." He didn't know else what to say. Was it kindness she showed, or simply cunning in optimizing his ability to spy for her? He thought perhaps a combination of both.

Tarquine considered the banquet again. "It is time to greet my guests." She touched the wall by the window and it shimmered. An archway appeared in the insulated wall, opening into the banquet hall.

Without insulation, the impact of the massed Aristos hit Kelric like a tidal wave. As he and Tarquine entered, heads turned. A surge of interest formed, with him and the Finance Minister at its focus.

His mind jumbled its perceptions, unable to settle on an interpretation: he was *plummeting, drowning, smothering . . .*

Somehow he had fallen behind Tarquine. He must have stopped without realizing it. No one seemed to find it odd, though. He rejoined her, but this time he deliberately stayed back, trying to deflect some of the interest from himself to her.

The Minister stopped at various tables to greet her guests. She spoke in a quiet manner, but her entrance couldn't have been more effective if she had come with synthesizers playing and lights flashing. She had made no attempt to hide her sale; everyone in the hall knew about Kelric, a phenomenon unmatched in Trader history.

She and her guests conversed in innuendo-laden Highton, a form of speech so different from her direct manner with Kelric that it sounded like code to him. A flowery compliment conveyed hidden insults. An exchange of pleasantries provided veiled references to political matters. The act of ignoring a person could be a tacit agreement with him or her, an indication of respect, or an insult, depending on context. It amazed him that Aristos ever got anything done, given the time they spent twisting one another into knots with their words.

Observing them like this was an opportunity he doubted any other Skolian with his rank and empathic abilities had experienced. The linguistic experts among his people grappled with Highton nuances of language, struggling to learn at a distance, never able to see and hear Aristos interact in their own milieu. He was beginning to realize that in diplomatic interactions with Skolia, the Aristos weren't as condescending as they sounded. They used Highton forms of discourse. Yes, they were arrogant, manipulative, and opaque. But for all their assumptions of superiority, they were, incredibly, dealing with their Skolian counterparts as Aristos. As peers.

They used direct language only with slaves, simply stating what they wanted. He sensed that in private they were also more direct with each other, particularly with sexual partners. But that was private. In public they might indulge in foreplay with a provider, even have sex in semiprivate alcoves during a banquet, yet they would never dream of using forthright language with a peer.

The insight stunned Kelric. When Aristos dealt in a direct manner with the Skolian Assembly, they were offering a severe insult. Yet the Assembly reacted far better to forthright discussion than to the masked convolutions of Highton discourse. No wonder their peoples had such trouble interacting: they were speaking different languages even when they used the same tongue.

It astonished him that the Aristos could exist in the same room with their providers and occupy such a different universe. He felt as if he were gripping the edge of a mental wind tunnel, struggling to keep from pulled into its maw. Yet the Aristos relaxed in comfort, oblivious to the mental violence their combined presence inflicted on their providers.

It didn't take him long to realize they were all transcending at a continual low level. He didn't understand: none of them was doing anything other than caress and kiss the providers. So why were they all transcending?

His own discomfort gave the answer. Their transcendence came from the strain on the slaves serving the meal. Although none of the providers was a psion as strong as Kelric, the presence of fifty Diamonds in one place affected them all. The providers were also physically uncomfortable. Their scant thongs were made from solid gems and hurt to wear.

On a conscious level, most of the Aristos didn't notice what was happening. Surrounding themselves with providers made them feel good, so that was what they did. Only Kelric drew their actual attention, his crumbling defenses and sheer mental power pulling them like a magnet. He could barely hold his own against the current of covetous regard that dragged at his mind.

Mercifully he and Tarquine soon went to the dais, where leaders from the seven most important delegations were already seated at the table. As he moved away from the other tables, the pressure on his mind eased. On the dais, Tarquine motioned him to the place next to her lounger, where extra cushions and carpets had been piled. He sat down, cross-legged, surrounded by pillows. He also made a discovery: the mental pressure from the Aristos receded when he used Tarquine's mind as a bulwark. When he was close to her, the interactions between his neural processes and hers swamped out the other Aristos. Having filled her own mental cavity, she provided him with a defense against her peers.

After Tarquine took her seat, the main dinner began. During the meal, the Aristos parried their way through debates and discussions. Kelric listened. As aware as they were of his physical presence, they otherwise paid him little heed. He doubted they had any idea of the scrutiny he had turned on them.

He coded it all into Quis patterns.

Tarquine offered him a gold fruit. It tasted sweet and fresh. He was hungrier than he had realized. Starving, in fact.

No place had been set for him, but throughout the dinner she gave him food from platters on the table. It was an odd way to dine; he was the only provider eating with the Aristos rather than serving them. He supposed he was serving Tarquine in another way, by enhancing her prestige. The other providers deferred to him, similar to the way they treated the Aristos, with one difference: they didn't fear him.

After a while, when he had eaten his fill and drunk too much wine, he began to nod off. It seemed like more than fatigue. If he hadn't been eating the same food as Tarquine and her guests, he would have thought he'd been drugged.

He raised his head to see the Minister watching him. She spoke in a low voice, laying her hand on her thigh. "Go ahead. Put your head down."

Kelric almost refused. It was too strange, an Aristo offering him a place to sleep at the high table in the middle of a banquet. Then he thought, what the hell. If the other Aristos didn't like it, tough.

He lay down, resting his head on her thigh, his shoulders sinking into the cushions of her lounger as he closed his eyes. Her seat was on an elevated portion of the dais, so his shoulders and head were a little higher than the rest of his body, on a level with the table.

His simple gesture had a startling effect on the other diners. Their emotions surged in currents. Envy. Covetous admiration. Desire. Resentment against Tarquine, that she flouted her success. They responded with such intensity, he saw himself through their minds: a gilded provider with flowing curls, dressed in gold velvet, the only color in a room of stark black and white. He lay stretched out on his side, white velvet cushions tumbled all around him, his long legs half hidden in the piles of cushions, his collar and guards gleaming gold, his eyes closed, his head in Tarquine's lap. Even he could see the sensuality of it.

But he was past caring. He was too damn tired.

And sleep was a form of escape . . .

15

Transition Metal

...the flow and flux of verbal discourse has been elevated tonight. Subtle. Sharp. I will study the recordings...

Kelric slowly came awake, disoriented by his dream. Had he been inside Tarquine's mind? If so, he now knew she was monitoring the banquet, spying on every Aristo here. It didn't surprise him. Later she would analyze the recordings for any advantage they might provide.

He drifted in and out of sleep while the Aristos conversed. They spent a lot of time predicting what they expected to happen when Eube had a psiberweb. Avoiding words like *conquer,* they spoke instead of how they would "free" settled space from the "tyranny" of Kelric's family and bestow upon them the benevolent guidance of Eube. He had heard it all before. But now he detected a difference. Fatigue. The Radiance War had drained Eube. No one wanted another conflict. For all that they finally had victory within their sights, many of them wished the Lock had never been captured.

They also discussed platinum, a metal crucial to modern technology. The war had left Eube with a shortage. Although molecular assemblers could construct sheets of the pure metal from waste products, the process wasn't trivial for transition elements, with their high reactivity and complicated band structures. So the shortage had sent its price soaring.

They spent an hour in a verbal dance of negotiation. Sapphire Sector had the greatest stores of the metal. It came down to a simple equation: the other sectors wanted platinum at reasonable prices, and Sapphire wanted its advantage. He had a hard time following the convolutions of their speech patterns, but it sounded like they were trying to find a compromise. The process amazed him. If they had been willing to say what they wanted straight out, they could have conducted their business in about one fifth the time.

After a while he submerged into sleep again...

...Hidden here in shadow, I can watch the entire hall. Yes, a successful night...

Tarquine reclined in her lounger, while Kelric slept with his head in her lap. Idly stroking his hair, she studied the hall. The lights had been dimmed and most of her guests had retired to alcoves or corners for their after-dinner pleasures with the providers. It had been a productive meeting.

Platinum, Sapphire, Sphinx. Indeed.

The Platinum Sectors had begun rebuilding the mines damaged during the Radiance War. The asteroid facilities were already coming on-line. But the planetary mines contained the fabulous platinum deposits that gave those sectors their name, and they were taking longer to become operational.

Sapphire Sector had far fewer mines than Platinum, but none had suffered in the war. Tarquine suspected they had even more reserves than they claimed. They were stockpiling the metal to force up prices. Sphinx Sector had no platinum at all and had grown desperate. Although she couldn't be certain, she thought they were dealing covertly with the Allieds on the black market.

She continued her survey of the hall. A few Aristos still sat at tables, talking in quiet voices. She would analyze their behavior later. Of course, they all knew she was monitoring them. They chose their words and actions with care. Even the most guarded comments could offer advantage, though. One unraveled the discourse to find what secrets hid within its fractal nooks and crannies. True human speech, at its finest, showed repeating patterns of meaning on ever finer scales. When she unfolded a statement, she discovered its "smooth" edges were themselves convoluted with information.

She tangled her fingers in Kelric's hair, savoring its glossy texture. So different, providers. With them, fine distinctions of pleasure replaced the fine distinctions of speech. To achieve existence in its purest form, humans needed both intellectual and physical perfection. Highton discourse provided the ideal medium for intellectual elevation, and providers offered the purest form of physical elevation. Their synthesis produced a sublime state of existence. An Aristo.

In sleep, Kelric's face had relaxed, making him even more appealing, almost unbearably so. He was the pinnacle of what a provider offered an Aristo. And he was hers.

A deep regret cut through her satisfaction. She could never achieve the ultimate state. She had forfeited transcendence. Yet perhaps learning compassion took one to an even higher plane. Maybe. Maybe not. Who the hell knew? For all her regrets, her decision felt more correct as time passed.

Kelric shifted in her lap, restless with his dreams. She stroked his head until he quieted. He was an enigma. A puzzle. Was he like the rest of his family? Direct and overt, without even the pretense of discretion, they publicly flaunted their traits as providers. Beautiful. Sexual. Candid. Empathic. *Uncontrolled.* Their behavior violated all norms of morality. Yet even after only a short time with Kelric, she was convinced he never deliberately sought that lifestyle. He genuinely didn't understand the indecency of his ways. She had begun to doubt any of his kind did.

But the Skolian problem went far deeper than the improper public displays of providers. The Skolian armies forced their twisted reality on the rest of humanity. They had penetrated to the heart of Eube, violated Glory, committed unspeakable murders. Viquara, Jaibriol, Quaelen. All dead.

Did Kelric know? Where had he been these eighteen years? So far she had made no discoveries, neither from him nor from her investigations. Did he feel grief for his lost siblings? Remorse for their misdeeds? Shame at their indecency? Did a provider have the capacity for such depths of emotion? Yes, of course, providers were empaths. Even telepaths. But funneling moods or stray thoughts through their minds wasn't the same as having the depth and complexity to understand what they absorbed.

And yet... he obviously grieved for the Majda admiral. In a limited sense, he felt deeply. Or perhaps it wasn't limited. Maybe she didn't understand how he experienced and expressed his emotions. The more time she spent with him, the more she realized how little she fathomed Skolians. She had so little interaction with them and had never watched them in their own environment.

After Eube built a psiberweb, the Aristos would extend their umbrella of protection to all the worlds and habitats in settled space. Humanity would merge into one glorious civilization guided by the Aristos, with Hightons at the helm. They would all understand one another then. They would all be of the same mind. The same thoughts. The same.

Without the web, news traveled with maddening slowness. Nearly two months had passed since the deaths of the Emperor, his mother, and her consort. Yet the tidings were only now reaching the more remote sectors of humanity's far-flung settlements. The memorials had yet to begin. It would be even longer before all humanity came together in their mourning for the inconsolable loss of Viquara, her son Jaibriol II, her consort Quaelen, and perhaps even for the Ruby Dynasty.

Kelric stirred, his eyelids twitching. Watching him, she felt a strange tightness, a blend of satisfaction, desire, and fear. The intensity of her reactions alarmed her. No provider should evoke such a vehement response. She must control herself, lest she begin to need him too much...

Kelric opened his eyes. Fragments of his dream drifted in his mind, but he was no longer Tarquine. Before his memories of her thoughts faded, he had Bolt tag, copy, and file them.

Shadows filled the hall now. The other Aristos had left the dais, but he still lay with his head on Tarquine's lap. Although she was idly stroking his curls, he sensed she was half asleep herself and rather drunk. In the shadowed recesses of the hall, in corners or submerged in piles of cushions, Aristos silently amused themselves. He felt their minds in the alcoves as well.

Closing his eyes, he tried to shut out the mental pain that so many Aristos in one place created. He concentrated on Tarquine, letting her proximity overwhelm the more distant Aristos.

Even half asleep, her mind parallel-processed. Before the advent of computer-enhanced intelligence, the human mind hadn't been able to think along many tracks at the same time. Tarquine had nodes in her spine and brain stem that allowed her to process many problems at once. It was the only way, in the data-thick life humanity lived now, that a person could keep up with the huge influx of information needed to succeed in a star-spanning culture.

One line of thought spinning in her dream-saturated mind involved scenarios for cheating Sapphire Sector out of platinum. She thought of it as "negotiation." Another line included her speculations on how long it would take Eube to absorb Skolia. Yet others involved aspects of her job as Finance Minister. Her sexual images of Kelric played out in dreamy sensuality alongside hard-nosed evaluations of import regulations. He had thought himself experienced, but her fantasies startled him. Did she really believe he could get into those positions? If she thought he would wear those leather-and-chain outfits, she was nuts.

Then he found her files on the plans to redesign his biomech. He would wear his temporary collar only until they reworked his internal web. Although this collar could affect his sight or hearing by accessing his enhanced optics or acoustics, it had no control over his hydraulics. It could only interfere with Bolt's messages. The hydraulics themselves remained quiescent but operational.

It used his microfusion reactor to power chemical reactions in his body. Rather than injecting him with drugs, it had his body make them itself, through sophisticated reaction cycles. It was why he was so tired, and hungry as well; his body was using resources at an accelerated rate.

Some of the drugs were meant to wear down his resistance to captivity. Other muted more aggressive aspects of his personality.

Several were aphrodisiacs. Still others were truth serums, which puzzled him, until he realized Tarquine wanted to ensure he gave accurate reports on whatever he picked up from the Aristos. A large number of the drugs were meant to heal him. They treated his anemia, slowed damage to various organs, battled his mutated meds, and prepared his body to accept the regeneration or transplant of new organs.

One medicine treated what they termed his "depressive state, mostly likely brought on by the innate weakness of his empathic mind." Didn't it occur to the idiots that he was depressed because he had been kidnapped and sold into slavery?

As he absorbed Tarquine's thoughts, he tagged them to Quis patterns. Whether or not Bolt could still receive his input and respond, he had no idea. But it was worth a try. After he filed his impressions, he built mental Quis structures of the Aristos and let them evolve. They grew ever more complex, until they resembled fractals, those mathematical constructs that revealed the same repeating patterns of intricacy at ever finer scales. Fractals. Strange. It meant something, he wasn't sure what.

A thought forming in Tarquine's mind registered on him. Her leg felt numb where he was lying on it. He shifted his head to relieve the pressure.

She brushed her fingers across his neck. "Did you sleep well?"

Kelric answered in a low voice. "Yes." He knew what she wanted.

He lifted his head. The dim light softened her face, giving her an elegance that would have taken his breath away had she been anyone other than a Highton. She leaned forward and kissed him, tasting his lips. It was the aphrodisiacs that made his body respond with such intensity. Surely the aphrodisiacs.

Setting her hands on his shoulders, she gave a slight push. He slid away and lay on the carpets, half covered by pillows. As she joined him, he trailed his fingers along her hip, feeling its lean contour through the diamond cloth of her uniform.

They undressed each other in the shadows. Kelric ran his hands over her body and she arched, smooth and firm under his touch. Rather than the exaggerated curves of a provider, Tarquine was long and sculpted. Her well-formed body belied her claim of being over a century old.

She stretched out on top of him, sliding her hands down to his hips. Kelric rolled her onto her back in an instinctual drive to cover her body. With the collar monitoring the aphrodisiacs in his body, his arousal felt more natural now, less wrenching than his response to the copper provider. He wondered if Tarquine thought she needed the chemicals to make him want her. Maybe she was right. He didn't know. He didn't care. Dazed, drugged, and half drunk, he submerged into the sensuality.

So they came together, almost fighting as their bodies strained against each other. Yet they made no sound. An unspoken protocol existed among the Aristos: if no one could hear, the act was acceptable in public. He lived an exquisite agony of pleasure, a drug-augmented ecstasy that Tarquine stoked ever higher. In his rare moments of lucidity, he hated her for making him crave a Highton. Most of the time he knew only the incredible heights Aristos created out of human pleasure.

When he finally climaxed, the orgasm affected his entire body, which was sensitized by the drug cycles spinning within him. His peak lasted longer than normal, and with greater intensity, until in one agonizing moment of rapture he genuinely thought it would kill him.

He didn't die, though. Instead the waves of pleasure gradually eased. His breathing calmed. He and Tarquine were lying on their sides against the table, their limbs tangled. Eyes closed, she rested her head against his shoulder as she pulled in deep, shuddering breaths.

So they lay, too exhausted to move.

"Minister Iquar." The girl's trembling voice was soft. "Please, most honored one. I humbly beg for your sublime attention."

Grumpy with his disturbed sleep, Kelric opened his eyes

halfway. A dark-haired, dark-eyed provider was kneeling by Tarquine, her face anxious as she tried to wake the Minister without raising her voice. Kelric and Tarquine were still entangled on the dais, but someone had covered them with a white fur.

The girl looked terrified. "Please," she entreated Tarquine. "Most exalted lady, please forgive my imprudence and speak to me."

Kelric shook the Minister's shoulder. "Tarquine," he muttered. "Wake the hell up." From the girl's aghast look, he gathered his method of addressing an Aristo wasn't standard procedure.

Tarquine sighed and turned toward him. "Hmmm?" With a drowsy smile, she put her arms around his waist. "Again?"

"Someone needs to tell you something," he said.

She frowned, then rolled over to the provider. Her voice came out in an icy snap. "What do you want?"

"Please, most exalted Minister," the girl whispered. "I beg your forgiveness for my intrusion. But Lord Hizar, he—he—"

"He what?" Tarquine asked impatiently.

"On the holovid." The girl motioned with a shaking hand. "It is a broadcast, ma'am. Lord Hizar wanted me to tell you."

Tarquine sat up, letting the blanket fall to her waist. With the fur draped around her hips and her upper body bare, she brought to mind the marble statue of an austere goddess.

Kelric looked to where the provider indicated. At the other end of the hall, the room's lights had been raised. Most of the Aristos were up and dressed, seated at tables, watching the holostage. The news holo there showed the Hall of Circles in the emperor's palace on Glory. Corbal Xir was standing on the dais, intoning about something or other, though whatever the future emperor had to say, Kelric couldn't hear and didn't much care.

"No palace broadcast was scheduled," Tarquine grumbled. Without another word, she tossed the fur to one side, uncovering both Kelric and herself. She got up and dressed, pulling on her uniform and boots. Then she left the dais and strode across the hall to join her guests, leaving Kelric alone with the provider.

He sat up and regarded the girl. "Do you know what it's about?"

She shook her head, averting her gaze. Her lustrous skin was as dark and smooth as java cream. Rosy blooms colored her cheeks. She had an angelic face, so sweet and pretty it made his breath catch. But it wasn't natural. Her black eyes were enhanced, large even by bodysculpting standards, framed by a thick fringe of black lashes. Impossibly luxuriant black hair cascaded in curls over her shoulders, arms, back, and hips.

She wore no clothes. The ring of rubies around her neck sparkled in the dim light, as did the ruby guards on her wrists and ankles, the ruby rings in her nipples, and the chain of rubies slung low on her hips. Her waist was too small, her breasts too large and firm, to be real. He couldn't stop staring at her beauty, even knowing, gods help him, that the Aristos had made her this way to please themselves.

Then he realized more than her physical appearance affected him. Her mind suffused his with Kyle power, sweet and vulnerable. She was at least eight on the scale, possibly nine. Her fragrance captivated him, enhanced with pheromones. She also exuded Kyle pheromones targeted for other psions. From the haze of arousal in her mind and the dilation of her eyes, he knew she was as pumped full of aphrodisiacs as him. Her sensual desire flowed over him and her arousal blended with his own, driven and heightened in both of them by chemicals.

Before he realized what was happening, she had slid into his lap and was straddling his thighs.

"Now stop that," he said, his voice slow from sleep and drugs. He put his arm around her waist, intending to move her off his lap. She gracefully bent back until she was arching over his arm with her breasts straining upward.

"I can't..." As he stared at her, he forgot what it was he couldn't do. Lowering his head, he closed his mouth around her breast and suckled, tugging on her huge nipple while he tongued its ruby ring.

Even as he gave in to the drugs and the girl, though, a question hovered in his mind. Why had the Aristo who owned this phenomenally seductive provider picked her to tell Tarquine about the broadcast? She seemed an odd choice to send the Finance Minister.

The girl sighed with pleasure and cupped her hands under his elbows. The feather touch of her fingers made his thoughts waft away into nothing, like fog blown on the wind. Her head hung back, her silken hair pouring over his legs. She was also caressing his shoulder—

His shoulder?

Wait a minute. How could a girl bent over his arm this way be stroking his shoulder? He lifted his head—and found a second provider at his side, a twin of the girl in his arms, except this one had gold hair, blue eyes, and sapphire gems. Her mind washed sweetly over his, as far up the Kyle scale as the sultry goddess in his arms. As he stared at her, she leaned forward and kissed his ear.

"Oh, Lord," Kelric said. This was too much. Just the thought of a third person in the room when he made love disconcerted him. In that sense he had always been conservative. This went so far beyond his normal style, he would have told them no if he hadn't been drugged out of his mind.

The gold girl slid behind him and wrapped her arms around his chest. Nibbling his neck, she pressed against him, soft as a dream.

"Why are you doing this?" he asked. Glancing across the room, he saw an Aristo lord watching them. When the Aristo realized Kelric had noticed him, he turned back to the broadcast. On the screen, Corbal Xir, the Emperor Presumptive, was intoning on in the usual interminable Highton style about some supposed Highton triumph. His oddly white hair glittered like ice.

Murmuring in Kelric's ear, the gold girl stroked his chest and thigh. No, that couldn't be her touching his leg. It had to be the sultry one. Except she was still holding his elbows.

He looked down and found a third provider lying at his side, a beautiful youth with gold curls, a lithe build, sapphire eyes and restraints, and a sapphire ring in one ear. He gave a lazy, drugged smile and put his arms around Kelric's waist.

"Now, wait a minute," Kelric said. "Stop that."

The gold girl tickled his ear with her tongue. Startled, he turned to her, and she kissed him, her lips tasting of nanogels. So warm. So soft. Almost without conscious thought he kissed her back, all the while stroking the body of the girl in his lap. When the dark one murmured, he stopped kissing the gold one and turned back to her.

His mind hazed, he took the sultry girl's breast into his mouth again. The gold one moved against him in a sensual rhythm, her hair drifting over his shoulders and arms. The youth reclined along Kelric's side, caressing him with a skilled touch. Right now, in his daze, all he could think was that if for some strange reason these three spectacularly beautiful people wanted to make him feel good, who was he to argue?

Still suckling, he slid his hand between the dark girl's thighs and played with her soft folds, so moist with her wanting him. Yet even as he pleasured her and himself, he kept remembering how the Aristo had watched him. Smug bastard. What did he want?

Then, suddenly, Kelric knew. He lifted his head, evoking a protest from the girl in his lap. He knew exactly what the Diamond lord wanted. Didn't the Aristos ever stop trying to cheat one another? He had no doubt that in normal circumstances, the lord would have to pay dearly for the service he hoped Kelric would give now for free. He probably threw in the boy as inspiration, in case Kelric's interests made him less inclined to perform with the girls.

Stunned into a semblance of rationality, he nudged away the gold girl and the youth, gently, but leaving no doubt what he meant. Then he lifted up the sultry girl so she was no longer arched over his arm. He intended to put her away from him too, but she came up straddling his hips—and he groaned as she slid onto his erection.

"No," he protested, even as he pulled her closer. Against her ear he said, "You're incredible, a lonely man's dream. But I won't have a child of mine born into slavery. Not with either of you."

He wasn't sure if they were past the point where they could understand, too far gone in an induced sea of eroticism. The gold girl put her arms around him again and the boy resumed his caresses. The pheromones of the three providers, the Kyle resonances between their minds and his, and their sheer sexualized beauty magnified his reaction. He began to move with the dark-haired girl, his resolve fading.

Then he felt it. On her back. Gently he moved aside her hair and looked down her body. And he froze. Within the last hour, someone had taken a belt to her, leaving swollen welts.

"Ah, no, I'm sorry," he whispered. His Kyle link to the girl jarred her out of the protective mental cocoon she had created to repress the incident. He felt the echoes of her pain. Rocking her back and forth, he murmured *I'm sorry* over and over. She said nothing, only buried her head against his neck and held on to him as if he were an anchor.

After a while he lifted her off his lap, freeing her before he gave her his seed. "I can't do it," he said as he moved her to his side. "I'm sorry."

In a just universe, she would have never wanted him after what had so recently happened to her. It was a cruelty of their owner that he drugged them past rationality, augmenting their desire and appeal until neither they nor Kelric could control their responses. He had no doubt the two women were also primed on fertility drugs.

The dark-haired girl slid her arms around his neck and he drew her close to his side. She hid her head against his shoulder as she pressed along his body. Holding her around the waist, he slid his leg between hers. She clasped her thighs around it and began to move, trying to find her release that way.

Then the youth folded his hand around Kelric and took up where the girl had left off.

"Stop that." Kelric didn't know which disconcerted him more, having the fellow touch him or having his body respond.

The youth looked up at him. "Whatever you want, tonight you can have."

The gold girl slid down alongside the boy, her front to his back. Regarding Kelric through her long lashes, she put her arms around the boy's waist. "Do you prefer to watch? Him and me?" She nodded toward the other girl. "Or me and her?"

"Saints almighty." His face flamed with his blush. "Behave yourselves." Even more embarrassing than her suggestions was the way his body reacted with such enthusiasm.

The gold girl slid across the boy and stretched out so she was lying between Kelric's legs. Then she kissed him where he most wanted to feel her touch.

"Ah . . . don't do that." He didn't know how much more of this he could take before he lost what little restraint remained to him.

"Shhh," she said. "We'll tell him we did what he wanted. He won't know we didn't." Softly she added, "You've been kinder to us in these few minutes than he's ever been. Lie back, beautiful man. There are ways that won't leave either of us with your child." She tilted her head toward the Aristos. "Just for a while let us forget *them* and find comfort with one another."

Just for a while. He stared at her, mesmerized, his arm around the dark girl. The gold one lowered her head and took his erection into her mouth, exactly the way he wanted, as her empath's mind sensed his reactions and responded in kind.

He was a son of the Ruby Dynasty and the Imperial noble Houses, raised in the most conservative sector of Skolia, his interactions constrained by six thousand years of history. He had just spent eighteen years in an even more conservative culture. With such a history he could never have done this. Under normal circumstances.

But their sweet hunger poured over his mind. He gave that same sensual comfort back to them, multiplying it by his own Kyle strength.

It seemed that sometimes, just sometimes, life offered solace in unexpected ways.

Kelric floated in a reverie, half sitting among the cushions. The sultry provider lay between his legs with her head pillowed on his stomach. The gold one dozed in the circle of his arm and the boy was sleeping farther down, his head on Kelric's ribs, his legs tangled with those of the dark-haired girl. Kelric felt their contentment as well as his own, drowsy and sated.

It unsettled him to realize he was coming to understand the

Aristos. He felt as if he owned these providers. Then again, maybe he would never understand Aristos, because what he wanted for these three was their happiness, to take away their shadows and care for them. He would treat them much better than Lord Hizar.

But still. They reacted to him as if he were an Aristo to please rather than another provider like themselves. He had done nothing to discourage that attitude. He liked being pleased. He liked having providers. He didn't much like what that said about him, but he couldn't deny its truth.

He knew the answer now to his question about whether they understood the ideas of self-determination and the right to control their own bodies. No. They had no clue. The Aristos blocked them from even forming those concepts. As angry as that made him, still, he couldn't stop thinking of these three slaves as beautiful works of art that *belonged* to him.

But they don't, he thought. They belong to themselves. They have a right to freedom. Would you really want to own them? You could have had concubines after Corey's death. You chose not to. That you understand part of why Aristos act as they do doesn't make you an Aristo.

He knew this much: if he ever escaped, he would have a unique window into the workings of the Aristo mind.

A rustle came from nearby, soft shoes on the carpeted stairs of the dais. Opening his eyes, he saw a taskmaker kneel by his side, a nondescript man in a brown jumpsuit. The fellow spoke in a low voice. "They have to come back now."

The girl with her head pillowed on Kelric's stomach opened her eyes and murmured a protest. Kelric tightened his legs around her and pulled the other girl against his side, drawing the youth closer as well in the process. Then he glowered at the intruder.

"I'm sorry," the taskmaker said. "But if they don't come back, Lord Hizar will be angry. With them."

Kelric knew he would only bring the providers trouble if he refused to give them up. With reluctance, he relaxed his hold.

The dark-haired girl sat up, rubbing her eyes. Tendrils of hair curled around her face. She leaned forward and kissed him, her mouth warm and full against his. Then she drew back and smiled. Although she remained silent, she had a less haunted look now.

Sitting up, the boy pushed tousled gold curls out of his eyes. He rubbed the back of his hand over Kelric's jaw, his hand lingering. Disconcerted, Kelric ran his finger over the youth's palm. Although he would never have expected to hold a youth in his arms, it had happened and he had no regrets.

The gold girl at his side gave him a farewell kiss. As she pulled back, Kelric murmured, "Good-bye, sweet flower."

"Be well," she said softly.

Then they left, descending the dais with the taskmaker. Kelric watched them walk across the hall together, headed back to their owner. It made him angry. Conditioned and subjugated, they would never know how much more they deserved from life.

A rustle came from the other end of the dais. He turned to see a taskmaker approaching with a large diamond bowl and a pile of white furs. She knelt and set the sparkling bowl next to him. Crystal-clear water filled it, with white flowers drifting on its surface.

The taskmaker gave him a sponge bath and dried him off with a plush fur. Then she helped him dress. After she left, he sat on the top step of the dais and watched the Aristos at the other end of the hall.

Incredibly, the broadcast hadn't finished. It had been over an hour since it started and the thing was still droning on. Now a Highton was speaking, a tall young man with broad shoulders. Kelric was too far away to hear. He wondered what the kid could be saying that so riveted the attention of every Aristo in the banquet hall.

He glanced at the archway where he and Tarquine had entered the hall. It stood open like a taunt, a false promise of freedom, as if he could just walk through it and leave.

Kelric glanced back at the Aristos. No one was paying him any attention, not even Tarquine. They were all intent on the mysterious broadcast playing out on the holostage.

Well, why not? He got up, went down the stairs, and walked out the archway.

Several guards were in the antechamber outside. They glanced at him, then turned back to the wall screen, which showed the speech playing on the holostage in the banquet hall. Kelric walked right past them.

The corridor beyond led to Tarquine's suite. In her bedroom, he retrieved his belongings from the nightstand. He slid the armbands onto his biceps, five on one arm, six on the other.

Kelric started to tie the pouch onto his belt. Then he changed his mind. He sat on the floor and emptied the pouch. A rainbow of gems spilled across the white carpet: pyramids, cubes, balls, disks, polyhedrons, cylinders, cones, bars, rods, spirals, squares, and other shapes in every color of the spectrum.

Then he played Quis.

He wove his observations of the Aristos into patterns. It was like manipulating 3-D equations, with each die as a symbol or a collection of symbols and the Quis rules as mathematical operations. With his insights into Eube and the Aristos, surely some pattern existed that could help him design an escape.

A shape began to form. It took on definition, becoming clearer, oddly simple, almost done—

A right angle?

Kelric blinked. "Great," he muttered. So much for his brilliant insights.

He tried to continue the game, but the moves kept leading back to the right angle. If the structure had been ragged or incomplete, he would have thought the drugs in his system were interfering with his ability to play Quis. But he kept making a perfect right angle.

Kelric rubbed his chin. He hadn't noticed it before, but the only right angle in this entire suite was where the wall met the floor. Even that curved, rather than making a true ninety degree angle. The room was circular, with a domed ceiling. The arched entrance came to a graceful point. Now that he thought about it, the windows he had seen both here and on Taratus's yacht all came in ovals, octagons, diamonds, and circles. So did the tiles and gems. No squares, no rectangles.

All right. Eubians disliked right angles. So what?

He cleared the playing area and tried a new game, this time using his insights to model Aristo behavior. The structures soon became complex. They resembled fractals. He didn't have enough dice to build a true three-dimensional fractal, but the pattern was obvious.

Curious now, he tried modeling the behavior of providers. The patterns simplified. Red and blue dice dominated. It didn't surprise him: blue was often used for love, and red for passion.

He began a third game, this time combining the simplicity of provider designs with Aristo intricacy. It led him to—

A right angle.

"For crying out loud," he said. What was he supposed to do with a right angle? Straight edges. Ninety degrees. Right angles were direct, in a mathematical sense. No wonder Aristos avoided them, with their passion for complexity. But how did that help him?

Aristos were the only Eubians with self-determination. They also avoided straightforward behavior with one another. Providers had straightforward lives, but no self-determination. They had no idea how to direct their own lives. It just wasn't in them. For that matter, an Aristo could no more imagine a provider taking control of his or her life than could the provider.

An insight came to him: *I am a provider who acts, in some ways, like an Aristo.*

Self-determination. Direct behavior. Kelric doubted Aristos could conceive of those two traits together in a provider. Yet to a Skolian, separating the traits was arbitrary. Of course, Aristos saw how Skolians behaved. But he doubted they fathomed Skolians any better than he had understood Aristos a few days ago.

He knew Aristo scholars tried to understand Skolia. But they were watching from "outside." They probably applied their own modes of thought to Skolian behavior without seeing it, just as Skolians did the reverse. He wasn't sure what conclusions the Aristos formed, but he doubted it was any more an accurate assessment of the Skolian mind than Skolians had of the Aristo mind. How could it be, when Skolians and Traders interacted only in the stiff forums of their strained diplomacy? Their meetings took place via holostage. It was the only realistic choice: Skolians in Aristo territory became slaves, and Aristos in Skolian territory became war criminals.

How many Aristos had dealt with someone like himself in a milieu natural to Aristos? Providers made up only a fraction of 1 percent of the Eubian population. Only a fraction of those were Skolian, and those few were unlikely to have his background or military training. He was the unexpected. The wrench in the machinery. He wasn't sure what good that did him: Aristos lived in environments crammed with security, monitors, guards, and webs dedicated to controlling people, wrench or no wrench.

An idea came to him. An outrageous idea. He couldn't.

Could he?

Kelric put his dice back into the pouch and tied it to a belt loop on his trousers. Then he went back down the hall to where the taskmakers were watching the broadcast.

He tapped a guard on the shoulder. "Open the door."

The man pulled his attention to Kelric. "What?"

"The archway." Kelric indicated a blank wall, hoping it had an exit. "Open it for me." He used direct language, not as a provider speaking to another slave, but as an Aristo addressing a taskmaker, though he was careful not to be too overt with his tone and manner.

Incredibly, the taskmaker lifted his palmtop and entered several commands. The wall shimmered and an archway appeared.

Kelric nodded, somehow keeping his face composed.

Then he walked out the door.

16

Right-Angle Turn

Kelric entered a black and white tunnel with a hexagonal shape. Holding back his exultant grin, he set off at a fast, easy walk. He wanted to run, but he resisted the urge, knowing it would draw attention.

Although he had no idea where he was, his general knowledge of spacecraft would help him figure out where to go if he could get a sense of his location. He doubted his freedom would last long. He had to make the best of it.

He walked through the maze of corridors, keeping track of every turn. Soon he came out into a multilevel concourse with shops and apartments. Far above, the ceiling vaulted in arches of a sparkling white composite groined with black diamond. Two taskmakers were leaving a shop up ahead. He averted his gaze as he passed, trying to fade into the background. Deep in conversation, they ignored him.

The concourse was almost empty. It puzzled him. Although it was "night" according to ship's time, it wasn't late. He would have thought some people would still be up and about.

Passing a café with an open front, he glanced inside. The patrons were crowded around a small holostage at the back, watching the young Aristo give his speech. Again he wondered what the fellow had to say that so fascinated everyone.

On the far side of the concourse, he found what he sought. An elevator. He entered a request for passage to the ship's docking tube.

His knowledge of the Aristo language gave him a unique advantage: the panel only accepted Highton glyphs. Few taskmakers knew written Highton, and Aristos never taught their providers to read.

The more he skewed outside expected behavior, the better. Aristo minds worked like clockwork, precise and uniform. They seemed like a great glittering machine to him, each Aristo a cog in the total. It gave them a formidable capacity for organization and union of purpose, but crippled them when it came to the unexpected.

The elevator door opened. Kelric grinned and stepped inside the hexagonal car. Was he actually going to walk right off the ship?

The door closed and they took off. If this ship followed the usual design, its main body was a rotating cylinder with a tube down the center. Spokes connected the cylinder to the tube, and elevator cars traveled along the spokes. As a car rode to the tube, its gravity decreased to zero.

However, his weight had only decreased by half when the elevator stopped. An EI spoke. "Subject Garlin, you have no valid reason to visit the docking areas."

Damn. His advantage of doing the unexpected had played itself out too soon. If he claimed Tarquine ordered this trip, the EI would check. It was probably paging her now, since it already knew his identity.

Tarquine had left her palmtop on the dais. Of course, the EI could send wireless signals to the nodes in her body. Enough was going on in the banquet hall, with fifty Diamonds and the palace broadcast, that it might be a few moments before her system responded. It gave him a bit more time.

He sat with his back against the wall. Closing his eyes, he tried to jack into the elevator EI. With no IR or hard link, his only option was to couple his brain fields to those produced by the EI brain. Usually such a coupling was too small to form an unaided link. But he was Rhon and a Jagernaut. His enlarged KAB enhanced the coupling terms and his biomech web magnified the effect.

Even so, if he hadn't been inside the EI, he doubted he could have succeeded. When he focused on its synthetic brain, his own mind felt as if it ripped. He knew nothing had torn; his brain was mimicking neural activity that translated as pain. It was a warning: if he didn't stop, he would cause more damage. He kept going anyway. This was his only real chance to escape.

With his mathematical bent, he had always been good with computers. ISC had backed up his natural talent with training. But he didn't recognize the Eubian security protocols on this EI and he had no time to investigate. So he "rammed" his way into the system by realigning the time-dependent fields of its brain with his own. It produced a "sparking" sensation in his temples, apparently more attempts by his brain to translate its increasing distress into concepts he could grasp.

As soon as he broke into the EI, however, he knew what to do. Its systems were more modern than those he remembered, but his experience from Maccar's ship helped. He set himself up as a systems operator, then thought, *Stop security check on subject Garlin.*

Stopped, it answered.

Has Minister Tarquine Iquar been notified?

I located her in the banquet hall of Sector Four, sent a page to her palmtop, and activated an IR beacon. Shall I continue efforts to reach her?

No. Cease attempts. Digging his fingers into the carpet, he added: *Go to hub.*

The elevator started to move again.

By the time they reached the hub, he could no longer see. His battle to hold his link with the elevator EI had damaged his optical nerves. He wasn't sure why his optics went first; maybe his biomech web didn't need them to hold the EI link.

He "regained" his sight by using the EI to access a camera outside the elevator. He summoned a magcar and it raced up like a giant white bullet. From the camera, he watched himself leave the elevator and float to the car. He had never seen himself move in zero-g before. His own grace surprised him.

The magcar door disoriented him. He opened it with his hands, yet he saw the scene from above the elevator. Inside the car, he had even more trouble orienting himself. When the door slid shut, he "saw" only the car's exterior. It sat at its terminal like a shiny bullet ready to shoot him to freedom. He hoped.

Send car to emergency shuttle, he thought to the elevator EI.

The magcar hummed into motion. Within seconds he lost his tenuous connection to the camera. He sat in the dark, struggling to hold his fading link with the elevator EI.

A memory came to him. Fractals. Aristos thought that way. Did they put that tendency into their computers? Well yes, theories that involved fractals found use in the immense, ever-changing field of computer science. That was true everywhere. But his insight about the Aristos was useful in another way. How?

Fractals repeated on finer and finer scales. The small piece of the EI's code he had accessed was built from smaller pieces, all with the same structure. Each of those pieces was made of yet smaller pieces, again with that same structure, and so on down to the smallest elements of code.

An idea came to him. He devised a virus based on the Quis patterns that had led him to the right angle. Then he launched it into the EI. He had no time for anything sophisticated: his virus just put the wrong value into a single memory location, and it worked only on a specific slice of program code he found in this small corner of the EI. Simple. Direct. Very un-Aristo.

Soon after he let the virus loose, it moved off into the ship's web and he lost track of it. He doubted it would survive long. No other sections of code in the ship's networks were likely to have the exact structure his virus sought anyway. EIs evolved themselves. Aristos designed them, though, and Aristos were repetitive.

The magcar stopped.

Kelric surged to his feet as the door opened. His head throbbed with the strain of using the elevator EI. When he pushed out of the car, the last vestiges of his link with the EI snapped. His hands hit a curving surface and he fumbled along it until he found an air lock. That let him into a place with the sterile scent of a decon chamber.

Having no link to the ship's webs now, he couldn't stop the decon. It took forever. Eternity. Any moment security would burst into the chamber—

"Decon complete," an androgynous voice said.

Kelric exhaled. He entered the air lock and reached the shuttle in seconds. Inside, he used passenger seats to pull himself to the front. Then he webbed into the pilot's seat and felt his way around the controls. Although the shuttle had an unfamiliar layout, he recognized its basic structure.

Unfortunately, the console had no psiphon prongs. Of course it had none. Aristos weren't psions. Only their providers had that trait, and no Aristo would let a provider fly a shuttle. His problem from the elevator repeated itself: the shuttle EI's security would keep him out.

He saw no choice but to ram his way in again. Using the technique a second time would cause even worse havoc with his brain, maybe even kill him. But he had no time to find an alternative. Gritting his teeth, he submerged—

Its security was in tatters.

Leave, he thought, hoping the EI itself still functioned. *Fast. Invert.*

Engines rumbled. Acceleration pushed him into his seat. Like a distant voice, a thought came from the EI: Shuttle launched.

Then, having reached its limit, his overtaxed mind shut off and dropped him into oblivion.

The universe had a headache, hungover from the big bang. It throbbed, spinning out stars. Hard, bright stars.

The stars softened. They coalesced into a white glow mixed with gem sparks of color.

Kelric squinted, trying to focus. The sparks bobbed around, then resolved into a holomap. It rotated serenely in front of him, the type of display produced by shuttle holoscreens to show local space.

He tried to raise his hand. Nothing happened. So he tried raising his other hand. Nothing. None of his limbs responded. Odd. The safety web shouldn't constrain him that much. Come to think of it, he couldn't feel the web. He didn't feel anything.

Kelric tilted his head. It moved fine, but the shuttle spun around him in a blur. Or at least it seemed that way. Closing his eyes, he put his head upright again. When he opened his eyes, the cabin had stopped doing its jig.

He looked down at himself. The universe blurred again, but this time he had less vertigo. His safety web was in place. He just couldn't feel it. Or anything.

A click came from his chair, near his ear. Then a tube snicked up to his lips. Recognizing the intent, if not the design, he sucked. Liquid ran into his mouth, cool and fresh. The ship had deduced that its pilot needed a drink. It was only water, but he supposed that was better for him than the jolt of whiskey he wanted.

"Shuttle?" he asked.

"Shuttle Four attending," it answered.

He took another swallow of water. "Why aren't we in inversion?" He distinctly recalled telling it to invert.

"I dropped into real space to correct phase errors."

He remembered when the *Corona* had begun to lose coherence, how sounds echoed and sights rippled. It usually took hours before enough errors accumulated to force a drop into real space. A craft this small could go even longer.

"How long were we in inversion?" he asked.

"Fourteen hours."

Fourteen hours?

It finally hit him. Free. *He was free.*

"Thank you, Shuttle Four," Kelric said.

"I see no reason to thank me for carrying out my function."

He grinned. During the last fourteen hours, Tarquine's people had had no way to trace him. He was beyond their sensor range now. His escape came with a price: he was apparently paralyzed. But then, if walking off Aristo cylinder ships were easy, people would do it a lot more often.

In any case, he should take no chances. "Can you invert again?"

"Yes."

"Good. Do it."

The engine hum increased. "Do you have a destination?"

Kelric started to say Skolian space, then paused. "Not yet."

He still didn't know why the security for the shuttle EI had been destroyed. Who knew what survived? The ship might refuse to leave Eubian space. He couldn't risk waking up any security mods that might still exist. Nor would he be forcing his brain into any more EIs. He doubted he could survive that trick again.

He spoke carefully. "Shuttle Four, your security mods seem quiet."

"I have no security mods," it informed him.

That was good news, albeit strange. "What happened?"

"A virus destroyed them."

"What virus?"

"I don't know. It started in the EI of elevator twelve. From there it spread to all the systems."

"You mean to the other elevators?"

"No. Every security system on the ship."

His virus had done all that? He had no doubt beautifully complex security codes protected Tarquine's ship. His virus must have slipped between the cracks. If it affected every system, their security must have all been programmed the same way; the virus was too simple to deal with even small deviations from its target code. Most big codes he knew were too sloppy for such consistency, particularly EIs that evolved themselves. But he had written the virus based on his Quis analysis of Aristo complexity. It was a tribute to the perfection of the Aristos that they kept their code so clean. Hah! Score one for the slobs. That exacting precision had been their downfall.

Tarquine's people would have fixed the problem by now. Given the methodical Aristo approach, they would soon adjust every security system in Eube so that no simple, direct virus could wreak havoc. It didn't matter. To escape, he had only needed the few extra seconds it had given him.

"Prepare to invert," Shuttle Four said.

Kelric closed his eyes. As they inverted, his nausea surged. "Do you know where we are?"

"Near Cobalt Sector. Precise coordinates incoming."

He opened his eyes. "No!" By incoming, it meant to use the link he had set up between its brain and his. The last thing he wanted was more data dumped onto his beleaguered neurons. "All I need is a rough idea. What settlement is closest?"

"The Cobalt Military Complex."

He grimaced. "What else is in the vicinity?"

"Interstellar dust clouds."

"That doesn't help."

"What would help?"

Dryly he said, "The Third Lock."

"Do you refer to the Skolian space habitat removed by ESComm from the ISC Onyx complex?"

"That's the one."

"It resides in the ESComm Sphinx Sector Rim Base."

"How do you know?"

"I am part of the Finance Minister's web."

"Oh." Of course. Tarquine was one of the most powerful Aristos alive. She would know a great deal. "Her network is civilian, though. Not ESComm."

"True." The EI paused, probably checking its records. "During your auction, the Minister's spy monitors broke into the military web on General Marix Haquail's battle cruiser."

Kelric couldn't help but laugh. "Don't they ever stop?" With all the spying, intrigues, and politics among the Aristos, it was a wonder they ever achieved anything. Then again, maybe it didn't matter. They were so much alike in what they wanted that they acted as a monolith when it came to aggression against other civilizations. Like his.

Most of what Tarquine's spies learned wouldn't be available to a shuttle. However, during the moments when security for the cylinder ship had been in tatters, Shuttle Four might have absorbed a bit of data.

"What would you like me to do?" the shuttle asked.

The impossible. "Find a way for me to reach the Third Lock, go inside, get out again, rescue Eldrin Valdoria, and get home."

"I see no viable way to accomplish these tasks."

"I can't even move," Kelric grumbled.

"Are you in pain?"

"No. I can't feel anything."

"I recommend you rest while I work."

"Work on what?"

"The problem you set up for the Third Lock."

Kelric smiled. Trying to solve the impossible would keep the EI busy while he confirmed that none of its security worked. First, though, he needed to know how much of himself worked.

"Do you have any medical routines?" he asked.

"The standard mods. I am monitoring your condition."

"How badly am I hurt?"

"A final diagnosis isn't yet available. I am working with the picoweb in your collar on repairs. Some damage will be permanent."

"Permanent? How?"

"I don't know yet."

Well, it could have been worse. "At least I'm not a vegetable."

"I have no medical definition of 'vegetable,'" it informed him. "However, you almost suffered permanent losses in reasoning, memory, sensory, and locomotive functions. You recovered because you were receiving treatment even as you took the damage."

That surprised him. "I was being treated? What do you mean?"

"Your collar is supervising chemical cycles in your body that provide drug therapy."

"Are you telling me that this slave collar helped me survive my escape?"

"That is correct."

Kelric laughed. "That's a beautiful irony."

"It is?"

"Yes." He closed his eyes. "If I rest, will you continue to fix me?"

"I have dedicated my medical mods to this task. Would you like chemicals to help you sleep?"

"No need. I'll be fine." While he supposedly slept, he planned to check the EI's security, to make sure it stayed on his side.

Kelric hung on to the top of the pilot's seat, floating in the cabin. Except for his arms and shoulders, he felt almost nothing in his body. He tried moving his leg again, with no response. The shuttle continued to hurtle through inversion, headed toward Sphinx Sector, which was on the way out of Eubian space.

"Try your other leg," the shuttle suggested.

Gripping the seat, he gave it a try. "I think I felt something."

"That is encouraging. Please continue the exercises. I will continue trying to effect repairs though your collar."

Although Kelric wasn't thrilled to have a Eubian EI fiddling with his biomech web, it was better than paralysis. "Do you know yet what happened to me?"

"Yes. Paraplegia due to neural disruption in the thoracic and lumbar spinal regions."

He grimaced. "Can you translate that into normal language?"

"Paraplegia is paralysis from the chest down," it explained. "It usually occurs when the middle or lower section of the spinal cord is damaged. However, you have no actual damage."

"Then why the blazes can't I move?"

"You disrupted your central nervous system when you forced your brain patterns to align with the elevator EI. As a result, your spinal cord isn't sending the proper messages. Also, fiberoptic threads in your biomech web have tangled with your spinal cord."

"Can you help?"

"I don't know." It paused. "Your biomech system has already repaired some of the disrupted pathways. That's why you can move your arms and shoulders. I don't know if you will regain much more. It probably requires surgery to untangle the threads."

"What about the drug cycles in my body?" Kelric asked.

"They are vital to your health."

"I mean, can they work on my nervous system?"

"No."

He thought of the unwanted drugs coursing through him. "Can you stop the cycles? Not the medical therapy, but the others. The truth serums, aggression suppressants, and aphrodisiacs."

"The cycles are interdependent," it told him. "They're designed to minimize side effects. If I delete steps, it could have drastic results."

"Drastic? How?"

"It would produce rogue molecules, cations, anions, and free radicals, which would react with other chemicals in your body. The results could be fatal."

"Gods," Kelric muttered. It never ceased to amaze him how adept Aristos had become at controlling people.

"However," the EI added, "I may be able to help your paralysis."

"Shoot."

"At what? We are alone in space."

He smiled. "I meant, tell me your ideas."

"Your collar has no real control over your hydraulics. It only blocks your spinal node from communicating with them. If I remove that block, your hydraulics can move your body."

"Yes! Do it."

"Working."

Kelric continued to float, trying to exercise his legs. After a while he asked, "Has anything happened?"

"I am thirty-four percent finished with the process."

"Can you talk while you work?"

"Yes."

"Do you know about that palace speech?"

"I know about many palace speeches."

"The one playing on the ship when we left."

"I do not have this recording."

"Oh." Kelric's fingers were growing tired from hanging on the chair. "Can you put me back in the pilot's seat?"

"Certainly." A robot arm extended from a bulkhead, folded its multijointed hand around his body, and set him back in the seat. Then it hovered above him like an orderly checking its patient.

With no warning, Kelric's arm shot up and knocked aside the robot arm. His right leg jerked. Then his left foot slammed into the control console. For all the force of its strike, he felt nothing.

"Uh, Shuttle Four," he said. "What are you doing?"

"Try moving your legs," it suggested.

He gave it a try. His left leg rose into the air with the eerily smooth ease of hydraulic-controlled motion.

"Hey!" Kelric grinned. "How long will this last?"

"It should serve until your recovery is done."

Relief washed over him. "Then I'll recover?"

"To an extent."

His ebullience ebbed. "What extent?"

"That remains to be seen. If you exercise, it will strengthen your muscles and coordination. However, it is imperative you report to a biomech repair facility as soon as possible."

Dryly Kelric said, "I know." He gave a martial-arts punch at the air and was gratified to see his arm move with enhanced speed. When he punched the chair, it left a dent that only his enhanced strength could have made. He tried a kick next, with good results. He couldn't actually feel his legs move, it was more like hauling around sacks of grain. But it worked.

"Do you know how long my repairs will take?" he asked.

"I'm not sure," the shuttle said. "Just after takeoff, one hundred percent of your body was paralyzed for several seconds. It almost killed you. You were also one hundred percent blind. The paralysis is about seventy-five percent now. Without your enhanced optics, you would have about twenty-five percent vision."

Good Lord. "I had no idea it was that serious."

"Leaving an Aristo cylinder is not easy."

He wondered what Tarquine thought about his escape. She was probably furious. Would she miss him? Probably. He had cost her fourteen million credits. Would he miss her? Of course not. It was only the aphrodisiacs in his body that made him think of her.

"Do you want my analysis regarding the Third Lock?" Shuttle Four inquired.

"You have an analysis?" This ought to prove interesting.

"Yes. You should go undercover. The Lock is at Sphinx Sector Rim Base. Several Aristos are stationed there. Pick one that is away and have yourself delivered to his or her residence as a provider. That will leave you some freedom to act. I can create a false set of documents for the transfer."

Kelric grimaced. Unfortunately, it made sense. The last thing he wanted was to go among Aristos again. But if a chance existed to deactivate the Lock, he had to consider it. After his recent experiences, he had an idea how to build such a cover. Aristos expected certain behavior from providers. As long as he acted "normal" in their presence, he could do a lot behind the scenes. It helped that the platinum shortage had hit Sphinx Sector so hard. To offset their platinum losses, Sphinx Aristos were stockpiling other resources. Like providers. So his appearance was unlikely to raise eyebrows.

Even if he made it into the SSRB, he faced two major hurdles: reaching the Lock from within the complex and escaping afterward. Providers had no reason to visit the Lock or travel alone. His first escape had taken the Aristos by surprise. It wouldn't happen again. If he tried this and anything went wrong, he would end up as a provider for life.

Kelric hated the whole idea. He wanted to go home. But he had it within his ability to stop an interstellar war, one the Traders would probably win. No one wanted to restart hostilities. However, as long as the Traders thought they could triumph, using their captured Lock and Key, they would try. If he turned off the Lock, he would restore the balance of power and protect trillions of people.

"Nothing like a little stress," he muttered.

"My structure is under no stress," the shuttle informed him.

Kelric gave a wan smile. "Not you. Me." He exhaled. "We have plans to make."

"Plans?"

"To infiltrate the SSRB."

"I can add you to the inventory of a supply ship," it suggested. "I can also deliver you to that ship. I estimate a probability of four to thirty-two percent that you can then succeed with your stated goals."

"That's low."

"It goes up if you limit your goals."

"What do you suggest I leave out?"

"Escape will be the most difficult."

Kelric snorted. "Any other ideas?"

"No. I have an observation, however."

"Yes?"

"You have an advantage no Eubian can claim."

"And what might that be?"

"You are a Rhon psion. That might increase your chances."

"Well, yes." Kelric froze. "What makes you think I'm Rhon?" Asking the question now, after he acknowledged its truth, was like closing the gate after the livestock had left the farm. Damn truth serums. He needed them out of his body.

"I learned it when you put your mind into mine," the EI said.

He wondered what else it knew. The security failure on the cylinder ship had exposed it to many EIs. "Do you know if ESComm has penetrated the Lock's security?"

"Unknown. Eldrin Valdoria refuses to cooperate."

He sat up straighter. "Eldrin is at the SSRB?"

"No. He is on the planet Glory."

"Oh." It had been too much to hope for. Kelric hated to think of his brother as an ESComm prisoner.

"Shall I prepare documents for your transfer?" the EI asked.

"We have to solve some problems first," Kelric said. "My body is full of truth serums. It's not enough to make me reveal data protected by neural blocks, but if someone asks what I'm doing, I'll probably tell them too much. The drugs that suppress aggression hamper my ability to defend myself. And the aphrodisiacs are a distraction."

"What do you want me to do?"

"You're sure you can't turn those off without losing the medicine cycles?"

"Cycles do exist that would provide only medical therapy," the shuttle said. "Unfortunately, I have neither the knowledge nor time to implement them."

"Can you turn off every cycle in my body?"

"Yes. However, then you would no longer benefit from their healing effects."

"Would that affect the repair of my paralysis?"

"Now, yes. Eventually I will have done all I can for the paralysis. After that, your recovery will be a matter of exercise." The EI paused. "However, in caring for your health and preparing your body for the regeneration or transplant of new organs, it would be in your best interest to continue the drug therapy."

Kelric considered his options. "Let's do this. Stay on course to Sphinx Sector. When you've done all you can for my paralysis, take me to the SSRB, get me into a supply ship inventory, and turn off all the drug cycles. Can you do that?"

"I will do my best," Shuttle Four said.

17

Sphinx Sector Rim

The SSRB glittered in space like a cluster of jeweled necklaces linked with sparkling chains. As the supply ship drew nearer, the base took on a less benign aspect, resolving into ponderous habitats bristling with antennae, support structures, and weapons ports. Far from any star, the complex created its own system of orbiting bodies.

Kelric floated at the porthole in the cargo bay where the crew had "stored" him. His delivery from Shuttle Four had gone without remark by the taskmaker crew here. The orders to take a provider to a Sphinx Sector Aristos surprised no one.

He had helped Shuttle Four to prepare his false ID. Without his aid, the EI couldn't have convinced anyone. It had no capacity for intrigue. He had it list him as a natural-born Eubian provider. That way, everyone would assume Aristos had bred him to behave like a provider. The invoice described him as an anonymous gift to the wife of an Admiral Kaliga. He would have preferred a solitary Aristo, but the shuttle had too little data on the SSRB. At least with Kaliga, they knew enough to be reasonably certain they could schedule Kelric's arrival when neither the admiral nor his wife was home.

Here on the supply ship, the crew outfitted a cargo bay for him, with a waste unit and mesh hammock. The small ship didn't rotate, so he spent his time floating around the bay, doing free-fall exercises. The verdict on his paralysis had been a little better than expected. He could move without hydraulics. In gravity, he walked with a dragging gait, his limp so pronounced he often stumbled. With the hydraulics, though, he now had enough control to make his motions appear normal rather than unnaturally smooth.

When he interacted with people, he used hydraulics. By himself, he exercised without them as much as possible, prodding his muscles and nervous system to recover. In the day it took for the ship to reach the SSRB and go though security, he noticed a slight improvement, nothing dramatic, but still a positive sign.

They docked at a space wheel that served as a maintenance and residential habitat. He had hoped the supply ship might be lax with security, but they gave him their full attention. The cargo master escorted him through decon with the rest of the small crew.

No one spoke to Kelric. They avoided his gaze. Only the captain acknowledged his presence, with an appraising stare that made the hairs on Kelric's neck stand up. The captain's ruby eyes marked him as the son of an Aristo and a provider. Kyle genes were recessive and Aristo genes dominant, so such children showed Aristo traits and usually found themselves on top of the taskmaker hierarchies.

A spoke elevator took them from the wheel's hub out to its rim. When they reached the terminal at the end of the spoke, an ESComm lieutenant met them. He escorted Kelric to a magcar and put him in the back, then took his place in the front.

As they rode along the magrail, Kelric gazed out the circular window at the rimwheel village. It existed inside the rim of the wheel, which was shaped like a gigantic tire. The tire's outer edge served as the ground and its inner edge made a "roof" far overhead. The magrail ran along the tire like a slender stripe around its circumference. In the distance, far ahead of the car, ground and roof both curved upward.

They traveled through a residential area. Landscaped parks dotted with flowers surrounded them. Rivers meandered past velvety lawns. The parks stretched the width of the rim, several hundred meters, then sloped up into terraced hills on either side. Droopwillows shaded airy houses on the terraces. He found it hard to believe this was in the heart of a military complex. It never ceased to boggle him that Aristos created such beauty.

They soon turned off the main rail and climbed into the terraced slopes. The car stopped in a grove of willows. Lacy branches shaded a house made from rose and ivory woods that must have cost a fortune on a habitat, where organic growth was carefully monitored.

The lieutenant ushered Kelric inside. The house was a graceful sculpture of airy halls and open skylights, with sliding screens for walls. All the rooms, halls, and windows were curved or else had seven sides. Breezes moved freely through the building. Kelric suspected it never rained.

The lieutenant took him to a heptagonal room with no furniture, just piles of white rugs and pillows in rose hues. The ivory wall screens were so thin that sunlight diffused through them. In terse Highton, the lieutenant gave orders: remain here, make no noise, disturb no one. Then he left.

Alone, Kelric went to the far wall and pushed aside the screen. It opened onto a garden with well-tended flower beds and lawns. A gazebo sat prettily under the willows.

I am a right angle, he thought. Then he left the house.

Kelric stood on a bridge that crossed a stream in the public parks. Flowering vines curled around the rail under his hands and draped the sides of the graceful arch. The parks basked in manufactured sunshine from overhead panels. If this habitat was like others he knew, at night the light panels would slide back, uncovering dichromesh windows that let starlight sift into the parks.

Well-dressed taskmakers strolled in the gardens, relaxed on benches, or gathered under trees. A young couple with a baby settled on a lawn and spread out a picnic. It looked idyllic. Only the collars and guards these people wore gave hint of the truth, that they were slaves.

He saw no Aristos. It didn't surprise him, given that only a few thousand existed. These taskmakers were high in the slave hierarchies and had some authority themselves. They would never risk losing their favored lives to disobedience. With one word from their Aristo owner, that happy couple could lose their child, each other, everything they valued. If they behaved, they kept their idyll. No wonder the Trader empire thrived. Aristos had everything they needed: wealth, power, military might, resources, and a trillion-strong populace they bred, pampered, indoctrinated, bribed, drugged, brainwashed, punished, and genetically tinkered into subservience.

In his exploration of the parks, he had come across only one other provider. She kept her eyes downcast, much as he had during his escape from Tarquine's ship, trying to become invisible. She sought a different sort of escape, a retreat into her mind. It was her refuge.

She had no mental defenses. Her high Kyle rating and open mind made it easy to absorb a general sense of her thoughts. She was on an errand for her owner and would meet him later for his pleasure. She had no hope of freedom. Kelric didn't think she even understood the idea. The three providers on Tarquine's ship had been the same. His inability to help them made him grit his teeth until his jaw ached.

His escape had been unique. Tarquine's security had done its job, judging his behavior out of bounds and notifying the Minister. Her long separation from her pager had helped him, due to the strange broadcast, which he still didn't understand. Even that wouldn't have made a difference if he had been less than Rhon. In fact, being Rhon would have done no good without his also having the background to hack secured EIs. And he had been desperate. Willing to die. He probably would have died if not for the medical cycles in his body. Those were possible only because his internal reactor supplied energy for reactions. Anything less than those factors combined and his escape would have failed.

It couldn't be repeated. He couldn't shove his mind into an EI again and survive. Besides, Shuttle Four had shut down the cycles in his body before it transferred him to the supply ship.

Now what? He had to make his move soon: it wouldn't take long for someone to discover he was Minister Iquar's slave. Somehow he had to leave this habitat and go to the Third Lock, a space station in its own right. His best bet to find transportation was the hub, where most ships docked. To reach it, he had to pass the elevator's warning system. If he did anything out of bounds, it would notify his new owner, Xirene Kaliga.

The light panels were dimming overhead, turning a rosy sunset hue. According to the lieutenant, Xirene and her husband were due back this evening. He either had to escape now or return to the house. The station's monitors had left notification of his arrival at the house and would have recorded his stroll through the parks, so his owners could find him right away if he didn't return.

He wanted to leave. Now. But he knew too little about the habitat. If he bided his time and used his judgment, his chance of success increased—to a point. Too long here, and he would be discovered. Also, if went back to the house he would have to spend the night with his new owner. Gods only knew what she would want from him. But if he let his aversion to Aristos force his hand, his haste might ruin his chances.

Kelric made his decision.

He was dozing in a pile of cushions when the apparition showed up in his room. Like all Aristos, she had classic features. Rubies studded the shimmering hair pulled up on her head. She had a youthful face, almost a child really, with round cheeks and a small nose. The translucent drapes of her white robe revealed enough to suggest a figure more voluptuous than normal for a Highton.

She stopped in the doorway, hands planted on either side of the frame, and cried, "Oh, surely this couldn't be!" Clasping her hands in front of her curvaceous bosom, she moaned, "I knew it. *I knew it!* Oh, how could I have come to this?"

Still groggy from sleep, Kelric sat up and pushed the curls out of his eyes. It was dark outside, but a lamp in one corner shed muted radiance over the room.

He felt her mind. She created that same mental abyss as a grown Aristo. With her, though, it was chaotic. He had heard Aristos didn't transcend until puberty, but he had never met one this young before. Her mind searched for his with an unformed quality rather than an adult's honed instincts. It shifted and flowed, never giving him anything definite to defend against. If in Tarquine he had seen the end of transcendence, in this girl he saw its emergence.

Aside from her attributes as an Aristo, she had some other rather odd personality traits.

"I *can't* believe it," she exclaimed, throwing her hands wide. "Why? *Why?* What have I ever done to deserve this?"

"Is something wrong?" he asked.

She glowered at him. "How can you act so normal when my world is ending?"

Kelric blinked. "I didn't realize."

"You didn't *realize*?" She came over, standing at her full height, which wasn't much. "Kneel to me, slave," she intoned in a dramatic voice.

"I already am," he pointed out.

"Well, yes, I suppose, in a way." She dropped to her knees and peered at him. "Your face bedevils me."

He pressed his fingers against his temple, trying to subdue his growing headache. "I'm sorry it upsets you."

"Did I say it upset me? I most certainly did not." She sighed. "You providers are *soooo* sensitive. But don't worry. I can read you poetry or something. Would that keep you happy? Or I could punish you. That would make me happy."

I don't believe this, Kelric thought. "I'd rather you didn't."

"Hah!" She clasped her hands in front of her heart. "My life is over and all you can think about is your own comfort."

He wondered if he had stepped into a hallucination. "Why is your life over?"

"You have to ask? There you are, sitting like some vision out of an erotic holovid, and you have to ask? I knew it. The moment I saw you, *I knew it.*"

Kelric tried to think of a way to make her say something coherent. "All I know is that I'm a gift for you."

"Well, of course." She beamed at him. "What more could you ask than to be my provider?" Sitting back, she pouted. "He thinks giving me presents will make everything all right. Well, he's wrong."

It was beginning to make sense. "Do you mean your husband? Admiral Kaliga?"

"Of course." She leaned forward again. "We were married two months ago. He and my parents had an agreement, you see, because *they* wanted our Houses to join. Not that anyone asked *me.* Well, you wouldn't understand, it's all very complicated, this business of marriage. Anyway, you see, when I was born, they betrothed me to him, even though he was already *old* then, over *fifty.*" She paused for breath, then plowed onward. "He's a terrible husband. Do you know, I was talking to him this morning and he—I still can't *believe this*—he told me to *be quiet.* Can you believe it? I can't believe it. I know why he got you for me. He's going to *send me away.* He thinks this will make me agree, you being so beautiful and all, but I *will not* be humiliated." She threw her arms wide, as if to address the universe. "Do you hear me! I WILL NOT be humiliated."

For the first time in his life Kelric felt pity for an Aristo. *Poor man.* Then again, he deserved it, if he was an ESComm admiral.

"Why do you look so dour?" she asked. Glowering, she added, "And why are you wearing clothes?"

"Most people do," he said.

"Take them off."

He flushed. "What?"

She made an exasperated noise. "You're a sex slave, aren't you? So take them off."

"For crying out loud," Kelric said. "You're a married woman. Suppose your husband walks in?"

"So?"

"So? That's it?"

"Why would he care?"

"You're his *wife.*"

"He bought you for me." She waved her hand. "Hightons always buy their spouses slaves. Why should he be different? It isn't like you're a person or anything. If he ever caught me with another Aristo, well, that would be different. He would have me executed."

"Xirene?" The deep voice came from the entrance. "What are you talking about?"

Kelric looked up. The man standing in the doorway had to be Xirad Kaliga. He wore the black uniform of an ESComm officer with an admiral's red braid. Unlike Xirene's chaotic mind, his was razor-sharp, honed to a piercing edge.

"Xiri!" She scrambled to her feet and ran to him. Throwing her hand over her heart, she spoke in an impassioned voice. "Why, Xiri? *Why?* Do I make you so unhappy?"

The admiral rubbed his eyes. "What is it now, Xirene?"

"I won't go away. You can't do this to me."

He lowered his arm. "Do what?"

She paused, apparently nonplussed by his reaction. "Isn't that why you bought me the provider? So I wouldn't complain as much when you sent me away?"

"I'm not sending you away." The admiral took her hands. "Why would I do such a thing?"

I can think of a lot of reasons, Kelric thought. And I've only known her for a few minutes.

Xirene pouted. "You are always upset with me, love."

"I'm not upset with you."

"You ignore me," she stated. With a flourish, she withdrew her hands from his.

Tiredly he said, "Xirene, I don't even remember ordering this provider. I will check with my steward tomorrow. But I've no intention of sending you anywhere."

"Oh." A smile broke out on her face. "I'm so glad to hear that. I don't want to go away. I really do like you, you know."

The admiral drew his wife into his arms and tilted her face up to his. Pointedly ignoring Kelric, he kissed her for a long time, which as far as Kelric was concerned kept her mercifully quiet.

Finally Kaliga raised his head. He glanced at Kelric, then back at

Xirene. "This man isn't a provider. He's a laborer. I ordered several a few days ago. He just came in early."

"But look at him," she protested. "He's too pretty to—"

"Enough!" A muscle jerked in Kaliga's cheek. "It's a mistake. I will have him sent to the dorms."

"But I thought he was a present for me."

Kaliga brushed her hair back from her face. "Go in the central room. I left you something." An image flashed in his mind, a ruby necklace that matched the gems in her hair.

Lucky man, Kelric thought, to have brought her another present.

Xirene glowed, already forgetting Kelric. "You are a most esteemed husband, my love." Then she swept off, in search of wherever Kaliga had left the necklace.

The admiral turned, his focus snapping to Kelric. "Get up." As Kelric rose to his feet, Kaliga said, "Who sent you?"

Kelric knew he couldn't make up a background. He had too little data about Eube to pull it off. "Don't know, sir. I'm sorry."

"You're sorry." Kaliga watched him as if he were a bug on the wall. "Where are you from?"

"I don't know that either, sir."

"Why not?"

"I don't understand those things."

He snorted. "What did they do, take your brain out?"

"No, sir. I don't know. I'm sorry." He felt Kaliga's anger. The admiral thought one of his enemies had sent Kelric as an insult, to suggest the aging warlord couldn't satisfy his pretty young bride better than a brainless provider.

"You will work on the rim crew," Kaliga said. With that, he spun on his bootheel and stalked out of the room.

Only then did Kelric realize he had fallen into a military mode of address with the admiral, in his attempts to sound deferential. He called Kaliga "sir" rather than using the overblown honorifics providers piled on their owners. If Kaliga noticed, though, he gave no sign of it. Kelric suspected he had become so used to military forms, they were transparent to him.

Relieved they were going to leave him alone, Kelric sat in the pillows and mentally sifted through the jumble of data he had picked up from Kaliga and Xirene. The admiral was tired, overworked by some recent political upheaval. A change in government. Something about Eldrin, their stolen Key, but it hadn't been immediate enough in the Aristo's mind for Kelric to extract details.

A maid showed up with a change of clothes for him, a gray jumpsuit with the silver silhouette of a battleship on its shoulder. Kelric recognized the insignia of the Kaliga Line: just as the House of Majda had always produced admirals and generals for ISC, so the Kaliga line did for ESComm.

He thought of Tarquine's revelation about Corey's assassination. Even after so long, it hurt. How would his life have been different if Corey had lived? He would never have ended up on Coba. Probably he would be in Allied custody now, like the rest of his family. At least this way he had the chance to make things better for his people, his family, and Corey's memory. If he could just reach the damn Lock.

After he changed into the jumpsuit, he folded his gold clothes in a neat pile. He had rather liked those garments. So had Tarquine. An unsettling response stirred his thoughts. Gods help him, but a part of him had found Tarquine intriguing. He could no longer pretend drugs caused the emotion. Her designer chemicals no longer saturated his body.

You feel interest too easily, he told himself. He had never really thought about it before, but it did seem he often became very fond of his lovers. Not always. Only if he liked them in the first place. But when he did, he invariably felt affection in a short time.

It wasn't love, though. When he truly loved a woman, it blazed inside him. Was he normal? Not once, but four times, he had fallen in love with great intensity, the type of emotion called "once in a lifetime." He still loved Corey after thirty-five years. He would forever care for Savina, the mother of his daughter. Nor would he forget Shaliece, his first romance, at fourteen. He would love Ixpar until the day of his death.

Hell, he liked being in love. He liked making love. It wasn't only sex, though that played a big part. He could have had plenty of partners if his only interest were the mechanics. It was more than that. As an empath, he thrived on the affection from his partners. The more he gave to them, the more they gave back to him.

It was an odd insight. He didn't normally analyze his moods. But it was true. The better people around him felt, the better he felt. When they desired him, loved him, he experienced those emotions too. The greater their contentment, the greater his. So he sought to make them content. He liked to see his lovers smile, hold them, laugh with them, pleasure them. The more they enjoyed sex, the more he enjoyed it. He often felt his partner's orgasm as well as his own.

That lovely coppery provider Taratus sent him, the two girls and the youth at the banquet, even Tarquine the Finance Minister—they all evoked his affection. Their emotions imprinted on his empath's mind, became part of his neural patterns. Gods help him, but Tarquine fascinated him. It was impossible for him to sleep with a woman the way Cargo Master Zeld had wanted, fast and hard, for lust only. If he had made love to her, he probably would have started to like her too.

He wondered if all telepaths experienced the effect. Although it was known they fell in love more easily than normal people, he had never heard of such extreme reactions. Did some quirk of his mind intensify the process? Fate had given him an appearance people found pleasing, but it didn't seem enough to explain the extreme reactions he inspired, whether it was the queens of Coba going to war over him or Tarquine spending fourteen million credits.

The effect had an ugly flip side: just as his empathic traits enhanced his positive experiences, so they magnified the negative. The auction had been a nightmare. What he had picked up from the Aristos that night had been his own pain. The rape they had committed imprinted on his mind at a level so deep, it had become part of him, like emotional scar tissue.

Combat was even worse. He had experienced the death of every Trader he killed, both taskmakers and Aristos. He felt them die, felt their fear and hatred, felt the Aristos lust for his pain. Over the years it had all become ingrained in his psyche, battle after battle, year after year, scar after scar.

He had liked being a test pilot, though. Alone and isolated, he thrived on the exhilaration of flight, even the danger. It was just him and his craft, sailing the seas of space or the swirling skies of a planet. No hatred, no death, no brutality.

Kelric knew now he would have been happier as a math professor at some university, alone with his equations, married to Corey, able to love her and be loved in return, without the pressure of other minds. Except for lectures. No wonder he hated public appearances. All those minds focused on him were like the pound of waves against a crumbling seawall. It didn't matter whether the sea was beautiful and wild like Skolians, or dark and brooding like Aristos. If the wall broke, he would drown.

"—must come now," the voice said.

He raised his head. The lieutenant who had brought him to the house was standing in the doorway.

"I'm sorry," Kelric answered. "What did you say?"

"You must come now," the lieutenant repeated. "To the dorms."

"Oh. Yes. Of course." He stood up, relieved he was going to spend the night in a dorm rather than sleeping with Xirene, or whatever else she might have decided to do with him.

The magcar waited outside. The lieutenant put him in back, then slid into the front seat. They took off through the starlit parks. He didn't think the officer was actually driving; the car took care of that. The separation had more to do with prestige: an ESComm lieutenant had far more status than a laborer.

The dorms were on the edge of a residential area, where parks gave way to rows of long, airy buildings. The car stopped in front of a pale gold structure. The lieutenant escorted Kelric inside, into a lobby with ivory walls. It had no furniture, only yellow pillows strewn about on a light blue carpet.

A taskmaker met them, an ordinary fellow in a gray jumpsuit with the Kaliga insignia on his shoulder. He carried a holoboard, which he filled out with a light pen as he asked Kelric questions:

name, age, former address, taskmaker class, and so on. The fifth time Kelric said, "I don't know," the man made an exasperated noise, filed the document in memory, and turned off the board.

After the lieutenant left, the other man took Kelric into an airy hall with screen walls. As they walked, the man said, "I'm Melder Xiradson. I'll be your supervisor on the rim crew."

Xiradson? That made him the son of an Aristo named Xirad. It wasn't hard to guess which one. His features were those of Xirad Kaliga. His brown hair showed traces of the Aristo shimmer, and his eyes were more bronze than brown. Kelric also felt an Aristo's mental pressure from this man, though at a lower intensity.

As they walked, Melder watched him. When Kelric raised his eyebrows, the supervisor said, "You're a provider. Why are you here?"

Kelric shrugged. "The admiral didn't want me with his wife."

"Interesting." Wisely, Melder kept his thoughts on Kaliga's wife to himself. "In here." He slid aside a screen in the wall.

Kelric looked down a wide hall lit dimly by a few lamps. Men slept on downy blue pallets marked with the Kaliga insignia. Like the other rooms, this one had no furniture, just a blue carpet and yellow pillows.

Melder indicated several empty pallets. "You can take whichever you like. Breakfast is thirty minutes after dawn."

Kelric nodded. "Thanks."

As he walked into the hall, a few people glanced at him. Most were asleep, though. One man lay under a lamp reading a holobook. The faint chirping of silver-eye crickets came through the parchment walls and the air smelled of night-blooming vines. Kelric chose a pallet in the shadows halfway between two lamps, to cut down on the light so he could sleep. He needed the rest; it would give his hydraulics a break and keep his mind fresh.

But sleep evaded him. He lay in the shadows and brooded. Kaliga was certain to investigate him. The admiral would discover no record existed of the DNA pattern in Kelric's supposed ID. Then what? He couldn't risk drawing attention right now by walking out.

But tomorrow he had to find a way to leave. Otherwise the Aristos would find one for him, on their own terms.

With his hands behind his head, he stared at the ceiling. He understood better now his drive to see his parents and siblings. Rhon. He had always taken his family's close-knit nature for granted. A community of empaths. Through their minds, they shared an unconditional love. He had never understood the concept of "loneliness" until he left home. It was a haven unlike anything else he had known.

He only wished he had it now.

18

Rim-Walker

You mean I just walk?" Kelric asked. "That's it?"

"That's right," Melder said. They were strolling along a blue gravel path among the lawns and willows of the parks. "If anyone needs you, they'll either send a page or call you over." He indicated the palmtop on Kelric's belt. "Pages are usually general. The rim web determines which of you on the crew is closest to the pager and sends that rim-walker."

It sounded straightforward to Kelric, albeit strange. "So we do errands for people?"

Melder nodded. "Within bounds. You've no clearance, so you can't do certain military tasks. If an officer needs a cleared rim-walker, he'll route his request through the page system."

Kelric hid his frustration. The duties most likely to require he visit the hub would be military rather than residential.

Melder stopped at a junction with another path and indicated an amber building to their right, shaded by droop-willows. "My office is in there. If you have questions, come by or contact me on your palmtop."

"All right," Kelric said.

Melder gave him an odd look. "The proper form of address is 'Yes, sir.' Or more."

"Yes, sir." Kelric knew the crew boss wanted him to use the honorifics a provider gave an Aristo. Melder's half-Aristo mind pressed on him, yet another reason to leave as soon as possible. He would take the best opportunity that presented itself today and make the most of it. He tried not to think what would happen if that wasn't enough.

After Melder went to his office, Kelric turned on his pager and continued along the path. The day was like the previous: warm, sunny, and pleasant, with no wind. In the controlled space habitat, they had perfection every day.

Rim-walking seemed a strange job, one with no counterpart in Skolian habitats. Robots and web services could easily do most of the errands. Of course, as far as Aristos were concerned, no real difference existed between robots, primitive EIs, and low-level taskmakers. Apparently even some EIs had higher status than he did as a provider or rim-walker.

"You," a woman called. She was sitting on a nearby lawn with a group of people. "Come over here."

Kelric activated the "in-service" light on his pager and went over to the group, ten men and women sitting in a circle, all with holobooks. Equipment surrounded them, lab boxes, consoles, screens, nets, and various sensors.

The woman patted the lawn. "Here."

He sat next to her on the soft grass. "What can I do for you?"

She showed him her holobook, which had some sort of treatise on bugs. "We're cataloguing the insect population. We need samples."

So he spent the next two hours catching bugs. The ecotechs gave him cans primed with syrups and foliage to attract specimens. Each time he brought back a load, he concentrated on the techs, searching for anything useful in their minds. He caught bits and pieces. One man had an appointment later in the hub, but he had no need for a rim-walker.

Kelric went out to nab more bugs. With his palmtop on-service, no one tried to engage him, but curious taskmakers asked what he was doing. It was a good assignment, one that let him wander far afield, absorbing moods and stray thoughts from many people.

Unfortunately, he found nothing useful. No one wanted a rim-walker for the hub. He did catch a thought from an ESComm corporal on a nearby path. The fellow needed a walker for a heat-exchange facility near the hub. Kelric put himself "off-service" and headed toward the corporal, so he would be available at just the right moment. But then the corporal sent a page to the palmtop system, tagging it with a request for a secured walker.

Kelric almost went to the corporal anyway, hoping to bluff his way into the assignment. But he held back. If it didn't work, he would have played his hand and bought himself a lot of trouble. His freedom was like sand in an hourglass, trickling away second by second. Admiral Kaliga had probably already set about discovering which of his enemies had insulted him. Kelric had to make his move, yet he also had to wait for an opportunity with a reasonable chance of success.

When he returned to the ecotechs, they were packing up their equipment. They took his specimens, then sent him off-service again. So he resumed his walk, following a path shaded by willows.

"You!"

Kelric turned. An Aristo stood by a kiosk a few meters away, in a copse of willows. The man had narrow shoulders and a face of hard planes. He wore civilian clothes, gray trousers and an elegant silver shirt.

Shoring up his mental barriers, Kelric went to him. "Yes, sir?"

"You're a rim-walker," the man said.

"Yes, sir."

"Then why do you have a provider's slave restraints?"

"My owner didn't wish my services as a provider."

"Why not?"

"I don't know, sir." Kelric tried to ignore his sense of slowly falling into nothing. He wanted to probe the Aristo's mind, but his attempt might alert this stranger to his high Kyle rating, drawing more unwanted attention.

The Aristo leaned against the kiosk and crossed his arms. "I've never had a provider rim-walk for me. It might be interesting."

Kelric tried to look bland. "Whatever I can do, sir."

The man focused on him, obviously trying to gauge his empathic responses. "Who is your owner?"

"Admiral Kaliga."

"Indeed." Now he looked intrigued. "Kaliga himself." He straightened up and unhooked a palmtop from his belt. After working on it for a moment, he murmured, "So he is." He entered a few more commands, then snapped the palmtop closed and gave it to Kelric. "Here."

Kelric took the unit uneasily. "What would you like me to do?"

"Deliver it to Admiral Kaliga at Spoke Station Two." A chill smile touched his lips. "Then come back and tell me what happened."

"Yes, sir." Kelric bowed to him.

"And, provider."

He straightened up. "Yes?"

With icy contempt, the Aristo said, "When you come or go, you kneel to me."

Kelric knew he was lousy at acting subservient. It could ruin his cover. Grinding his teeth, he went down on one knee, resting his arm across his other knee while he bent his head, as he had seen other slaves do.

"Very well." The Aristo sounded mollified. "You may go."

Kelric rose and bowed again, with more honorifics. Then he took his leave. He went to a path by the magrail, which ran along an edge of the park under a line of willows. As he walked toward a nearby station, he hooked the Aristo's palmtop on his belt, then put himself on-service and paged a magcar. A check on his own palmtop told him Spoke Station Two was partway around the wheel and halfway up Spoke Two.

He wondered about the bizarre errand. If the Aristo wanted to give Kaliga a message, the web was more reliable. Delivering it by hand might make sense for secured material, but in that case he would have paged someone with clearance. As far as Kelric could see, the Aristo simply wanted to irritate Kaliga, maybe to probe this matter of his putting a provider on the rim crew.

Kelric had no intention of stopping at Station Two. This was his best chance to reach the hub. It would get him past security at the terminal. If anyone checked, they might find he only had permission for a spoke station. However, unless the Aristo had a valid reason for bothering Kaliga, which Kelric doubted, he was unlikely to put specifics of this errand in the web. That might give Kelric some leeway.

A magcar was coming down the rail toward him, a small model suitable for a low-rank slave. An "on-service" light glowed on its front, the same type of light as on Kelric's palmtop, an unsubtle reminder that both he and the car were considered equipment designed to serve.

The car stopped next to him and slid up its door. Climbing inside, he said, "Terminal Two."

Spoke Two terminated in an industrial area that produced parts for the maintenance of SSRB habitats. The spoke rose up from the ground in a great shining column, huge and round, until it pierced the "roof" of the rim. Beyond the rim, it stretched several kilometers through space to the hub. Concentric rings circled the hub at bigger and bigger intervals, like gossamer threads on a gigantic spiderweb. Spoke Station Two was located where a ring intersected the spoke, halfway to the hub.

Kelric rode a stairwalk up to the platform that circled the spoke. Unlike on Tarquine's civilian ship, these elevators required an access code. He didn't have one, but the Aristo should have put one in the palmtop.

No one paid any attention as he crossed the platform. He was just one person in a big crowd. Commuters were changing shifts, either coming off work or just starting.

After hiking all morning, his muscles ached, a good ache, the kind that came from satisfying exercise. His limp had returned, though. Someday biomech surgeons would develop hydraulics that could replace the human skeleton or muscles. But his were for augmentation only. They couldn't provide continual 100 percent function.

At the elevators, he went to a console and clicked the Aristo's palmtop into a slit.

"Stand in front of the screen," an EI voice said.

He moved until he saw his reflection on the screen. A light flashed, making him blink.

"Retinal pattern verified," it said. "Assignment confirmed."

Good. He had made it this far without challenge. Of course, he hadn't yet done anything out of place.

An elevator shimmered open in the spoke and commuters poured out. Kelric joined a number of people boarding the car.

"Please halt," the EI said. "You aren't cleared."

He froze. *Damn. Not already.*

"My clearance is coming," a woman said impatiently. She wore the collar and cuffs of a high-rank taskmaker and her gold jumpsuit bore the black puma of the Qox dynastic line.

"Please accept my apologies," the EI said. "But I cannot let you on until I receive confirmation." Its tone of respect suggested it had made the same judgment as Kelric, that she carried authority. Kelric went into the car, trying to be invisible.

"Your clearance has arrived," the EI said. "Please proceed."

The woman boarded and the elevator closed. A few people input their destination into a panel, but many did nothing, including Kelric. Most commuters probably had their destination filed in their palmtops, which would have already given it to the elevator EI.

Kelric had no idea if the Aristo put a destination into the palmtop. If so, the EI would remind him when he didn't get off at the right time. Either that, or arrest him. However, given that the Aristo had probably sent him to the spoke for no reason other than to harass a powerful admiral, he might have played it safe by keeping the destination private, known only to himself and Kelric. That went against the "well-oiled machine" image of the Aristos, but Kelric had already learned that when it came to plaguing one another, Aristos were at their most creative and least rigid.

The car stopped several times along the spoke and then reached Station Two. Kelric stood quietly while people exited. Then the car resumed its journey. He kept his face bland and hoped the elevator wasn't sophisticated enough to register the rise in his heartbeat.

As they continued, his weight decreased. After a few more stops, they reached the ring that circled the hub. He floated out of the car with three other passengers and propelled himself along a concourse that curved around the hub. The concourse rotated, moving past the stationary hub on his left. Periodically he passed hatchways that opened into the hub. Inside, a regiment of soldiers was practicing exercises to develop their expertise in free fall.

Relaxing his mind, he probed the other people on the concourse. Twice he hit Aristo minds. Each time he withdrew. Fast. Even without empathic ability, Aristos recognized psions simply because they felt better near providers. Although they probably knew he was in the hub, he sensed neither surprise nor interest. Just as the controlled Aristos would never drop their work for an unscheduled meal or nap, so they ignored the unscheduled presence of a provider.

In the past, he had always assumed they were dissembling when they claimed to love their providers. It sounded like a crock to him, a specious attempt to justify their atrocities. He still found it appalling. What stunned him even more was realizing they *did* feel a form of love. Providers gratified them at a level beyond normal human passion. Few Aristos had the emotional capacity to fully comprehend how their own transcendence was hell for their slaves. With no challenges to their authority and no balances on their power other than their own intrigues, they had no referent to understand why Skolians viewed them with such horror.

We're dealing with them wrong, he thought. Skolians and Traders. We put our hatred up front and they put their atrocities up front. They despise us because they can't fathom why we loathe them. If they really understood what they do to us, would they back off? Even a few tendays ago he would have answered with a resounding no. After Tarquine, he wasn't sure. Were there more like her? As Imperator, he could possibly negotiate with such Aristos. He might not like them, but he could deal with them.

An even stranger thought came to him. What would happen if he and Tarquine ever met as equals? An odd idea. His mind glanced over thoughts of the future, many years down the line—and a chill ran down his spine.

Kelric blinked. What did that mean? He almost never experienced precognition. It required a relatively large uncertainty in time to let the human mind sample different possible futures, and rarely happened even to strong psions. He let the thought about Tarquine drop, trying to assure himself it meant nothing.

As he floated along the concourse, he probed nearby taskmakers. None were psions, and he caught only vague impressions. All he figured out was that shuttles arrived and departed on a regular schedule during this shift.

"You." A man was watching him from a decon chamber. "Are you looking for someone?"

Kelric stopped. The taskmaker wore a jumpsuit with a Silicate insignia. The Silicate Aristos were the third Aristos caste, after Hightons and Diamonds. They ran the vast Aristo entertainment industries, which included the production and sale of providers.

Kelric went into terse mode. "Rim-walk."

The man frowned. "Rim-walk what? Why are you up here?"

He tapped the extra palmtop on his belt. "I've a delivery."

The taskmaker extended his hand. "Let me see."

Kelric gritted his teeth. This fellow knew damn well he had no place interfering with a rim-walk, particularly since he belonged to a Silicate Line, far lower in the Aristo hierarchy than the Kaliga Line on Kelric's jumpsuit. But Kelric had a much lower slave rank than this official. A true provider would be incapable of defying authority.

"Well?" the taskmaker said. "What's wrong with you?"

Kelric put a frozen look on his face.

"Give me the palmtop," the man repeated.

"Can't."

"I'm giving you an order."

"Aristo gave me an order."

"You're rim-walking for an Aristo?"

"Yes."

The man's anger sparked. "Then hurry up. Get moving. Get your job done and get out of here."

"Yes, sir." Kelric pushed off again. He felt the taskmaker's outrage at his defiance. The fellow was opening his palmtop, almost certainly to run a check. Kelric knew he had to leave the hub fast, before they caught him.

He went to the next decon chamber and extended his mind. People were inside. He continued along the concourse. Several soldiers were floating out of the next chamber, their bodies at an angle to his.

I am not here, Kelric thought, moving across the concourse.

At the third chamber, he detected only a quiescent EI brain. A data panel by the hatch indicated a shuttle was docked in this berth. This was it. His chance. Probably his only chance.

He activated the chamber's admit cycle. Or he tried. He had forgotten the commands even for a Skolian chamber, and Eubians used a different standard.

Relax, he told himself. Entering decon had to be kept simple, given its importance. The SSRB stations probably shared similar microorganisms, but ships were always coming and going, making decon vital. It wouldn't take long to figure out the procedure, but even a small delay could end in his discovery. This time the people around him weren't distracted by any strange broadcasts.

He tried again, acutely aware of his public location. People would soon notice his abortive attempts. The hub officer was no longer visible around the curve of the concourse, but he had probably warned security to monitor Kelric. If the web tagged him for special attention, that would narrow the range of behaviors it considered acceptable.

On his next try, he made it through most of the sequence. Then a red light lit on the panel. Taking a breath, he tried again, basing his guesses on what had worked so far.

The hatch hissed and retracted.

Kelric almost sagged with relief. Controlling his reaction, he floated inside and closed the hatch. The decon meds began their work, looking for organisms that might bedevil other ecosystems. He schooled his face into the boredom of someone carrying out a dull errand.

This was the point of no return. The record would show his anomalous behavior, and he had drawn enough attention that someone was bound to check. He had no permission to take a shuttle and wouldn't get much farther without tripping an alarm. For that, however, he had a plan. In decon, with nothing else to do, he could work on a palmtop without raising suspicion.

He unhooked the Aristo's palmtop and flipped it open. Small holicons formed above its screen, holographic icons for various functions. An ancient skeleton key gleamed in one corner, indicating the Aristo had locked his palmtop. Only someone who knew the correct security code could access its files.

Kelric had once been a whiz at unraveling codes. They were games to him. But that was for systems almost two decades out of date. Now, when so much depended on his hacking the palmtop, he drew a blank. Where to start? He had to solve the problem fast.

Quis. Of course. He couldn't take out his dice, which still hung in the pouch at his belt, but he could do mental Quis much the way prodigies with perfect pitch could hear and create music in their minds.

He imagined the holicons as dice. Then he played with them much as a mathematician played with equations. Gradually he added more dice, guessing at other functions in the palmtop. He based his guesses on his knowledge of computers, and also on what the evolving Quis patterns suggested about the Aristo's style of organization. The patterns soon fragmented, just as a derivation could go haywire from poor assumptions or a math mistake.

Painfully aware of time passing, he started over with new assumptions. In only moments the patterns disintegrated into a mess.

He started again.

"Decon complete," a voice said.

His concentration shattered.

Kelric took a breath. Then he started over. His tension made it hard to hold the patterns in his thoughts. Clear your mind, he thought. Concentrate on a point of white light. Quiet. Calm.

His mind relaxed, soothed by the exercise. As he prepared to try again, an EI said, "Do you need assistance?"

His hard-earned composure almost cracked. Yet when he said, "No, thank you," he sounded calm.

"Why are you waiting in the chamber?"

"I was told to wait here, to deliver a message."

"Who asked you to deliver the message?"

Kelric glanced at the palmtop. "Jaibriol Raziquon." Many Aristos named their children after the Highton emperors. With a Jaibriol I and more recently a Jaibriol II, Eube would probably soon be drowning in Jaibriols, if it wasn't already.

Silence.

Then: "Rim-walk assignment verified. Proceed."

Kelric hid his relief. The EI must have contacted Raziquon. Apparently whatever it said hadn't warned Raziquon that Kelric was in the wrong place. Spoke stations also had decon chambers, so he could have been in one, waiting for Kaliga.

He brought up the Quis patterns in his mind, honing his choices from the last few tries. This time he reached a viable end to his "derivation"—a possible access code for Raziquon's computer.

He entered the code, tracing glyphs on the screen with his finger. The palmtop would know it wasn't Raziquon's writing. Raziquon gave him permission to carry the unit, though, so that didn't matter. At least he hoped it didn't. This unit had far more functions than Kelric's limited model. If the Aristo thought Kelric might fool with it, he would have protected the palmtop. He doubted a Highton would worry, though. Providers couldn't read and write. Their intellects were suppressed from conception.

The holicons vanished. A prompt appeared: **Attending.**

In silent jubilation, he went to work. A fast search told him the unit had many special features he didn't recognize. However, a solution existed to his lack of knowledge. He pulled a tiny jack off the palmtop and slid it through the hole in his wrist guard, clicking it into his socket. He hid the motion with his hand. The palmtop had no psiber capability, but it might link to his biomech web.

Bolt, he thought. *Can you answer?*

No response.

Hiding his disappointment, he tried again. *Bolt, send permission from Raziquon allowing me to use this shuttle.*

He counted seconds in his mind: *one, two, three, four, five—*

A message formed on the screen: Kelric?

He almost shouted. *Bolt! Can you do it?*

My greetings. I got you access to the shuttle. But you've been denied permission to use it.

The shuttle did him no good if he couldn't go anywhere. *How do I get permission?*

As a provider, you are forbidden to pilot spacecraft.

I'm a rim-walker.

You're listed in the web as a provider.

How can I be? I'm on a rim-walk.

After a pause, the palmtop printed: Permission granted. The nuances in Bolt's glyphs showed a dry humor Kelric had never seen before. He wondered what Bolt had been doing all those years while he was cut off from talking with it.

Smart computer, he thought. Then he went to the air-lock tube. Using his knowledge of the decon panel, he managed this one on the second try. When the hatch opened, he floated into the tube for the shuttle. Just two more meters—

"You have violated security," a voice said. Behind him, the air-lock door thunked closed. "Do not attempt to leave." In front of him, the air took on a distorted quality.

What the hell? He touched the distortion. An invisible wall had formed in front of him, like a solid membrane. Swiveling around in the air, he found another membrane blocking his exit.

The presence of the membranes themselves didn't surprise him. Molecular air locks had been standard even in his time, with mechanical air locks as a backup. Normally he could walk through the membrane. It clung to his body, forming a seal, then resumed its shape after he passed. Its nanomeds stored the memory of its structure. On a normal setting, it was impermeable only to gases. However, applying certain potentials to it activated new enzymes, making it impermeable to other things. Like humans.

Bolt, he thought, floating in the slice of space between the membranes. *What happened?*

More glyphs appeared on the palmtop. I'm checking. The nuances suggested Bolt was confused, in its computerized way.

Kelric strained to hear if anyone had entered the decon chamber. Any moment the hub officials could burst in here. *Bolt, come on.*

A new set of glyphs appeared. This is illogical.

Dryly Kelric thought, *Can you be more specific?*

I'm using this unit's IR capability to check a spy monitor in this tube. The monitor hasn't notified anyone you're trapped. It no longer registers your presence. Every means of communication from this tube has been cut.

Kelric fought down a spike of claustrophobia. The membrane would let nothing pass, neither gas nor human. In such a small space he would soon suffocate. *Did Raziquon's palmtop activate this?*

Checking.

Kelric waited. It seemed forever, though he knew it had only been minutes. He could almost smell the air growing stale.

Bolt? Did you find anything?

No. Then Bolt printed, Yes! Someone sabotaged the palmtop. That person hid a sleeper code on it, one set to wake up if Raziquon entered a docking tube without backup. I estimate 91 percent probability that an Aristo seeking Raziquon's death installed the code.

Kelric stared at the palmtop as if it had sprouted eyestalks. Of all the godforsaken bad luck, he had to be caught in an assassination trap laid by one Aristo for another. It would have been funny if it hadn't been so fatal.

Bolt, this isn't good.

Your assessment is accurate, if not precise.

Who cares if it's precise? if I'm dead, I'm dead.

I'm afraid that's both accurate and precise.

Kelric braced his back against one membrane and pushed against the other with his feet. It gave slightly, then snapped back to its original form when he eased his pressure. *Can we do anything to weaken these membranes?*

With web access, I might be able to hack the membrane generator and turn it off.

Hope washed over Kelric. *All right. Let's work on that.*

I have no web access. This tube has been cut off from the station. Bolt cleared the screen and printed new glyphs. Also, if I enter any web, I will be tracked.

Kelric gave a wan laugh. *So this is an Aristo-proof trap.*

It appears so.

What resources do I have that an Aristo doesn't?

A conscience.

Bolt, are you becoming philosophical in your old age? He pushed again against the membrane behind him. *I've missed you.*

And I you.

Kelric blinked. *You're a military computer. How can you feel lonely for me?*

I don't know, it admitted. Nevertheless it seems to be true. I prefer you not die. As a psion, can you reach others and bring them here? If you're suffocating, they would probably let you out even if they felt compelled to call for backup first.

Kelric considered. *It wouldn't be hard to knock them out. Or they might want to come with me. To escape.*

Hope shaded Bolt's glyphs. For this plan, I calculate a success probability of 4 to 89 percent.

Kelric smiled. *That's terrible precision.*

Bolt's glyphs indicated amusement. We can try.

Closing his eyes, he tried sending *someone needs help* messages to the concourse. With the air lock and decon chamber in the way, he had trouble detecting people. His head began to throb. Even if he did reach someone, he wasn't sure he could alter that person's behavior. It was one thing to have a heightened sense of moods; it was another to transform that awareness into action.

He touched three minds at the same time. Startled, he jerked back. Someone was taking three providers to another shuttle. Although they might have sensed him, they had no means to help.

Again he probed the concourse. After a few minutes a response feathered across his mind. He focused, honing his message: *Help is needed in air-lock tube eighteen.*

Several moments later, the faint hiss of a decon hatch came through the walls of his prison. He relaxed his concentration and the pain in his head receded. He felt tired. Sleepy.

"No," he muttered. He couldn't let lack of oxygen stop him now. He had to be alert.

The hatch opened and a young woman drifted into the tube. A provider. She was silver: collar, cuffs, eyes, even the tint of her skin. Kelric's breath caught. Silver curls floated around her head and shoulders like a halo. Her body undulated in free fall. The filmy drapes she wore swirled around her, giving tantalizing hints of her hourglass figure and a silver chain around her hips.

"Can you let me out?" he asked in Highton.

Her confusion rippled over him. "How did you get in there?" The membrane gave her words a muffled quality.

"I'm not sure." He was growing light-headed. "I'm running out of air. Can you help me?"

"How?"

He looked at his palmtop. *Bolt, quick! What can she do?*

The air-lock controls are on her right. She must enter the codes.

"I'll tell you glyph codes," Kelric said. "Enter them on the panel." Even if she couldn't read, she would know the pictures if he gave enough detail.

"Panel?" she asked.

"On the wall next to you. With the lights and little circles."

She scanned the bulkhead. "Oh. Yes. I can draw on the screen."

He exhaled. "Good."

As Bolt gave him the glyphs, Kelric described them and the girl drew them on the panel. It took so long. His eyes drooped close. Tired. He needed to rest.

Someone was hitting the membrane. He opened his eyes. The girl. She looked distraught. Why didn't she release the air-lock?

He glanced at the palmtop. A final row of glyphs remained. He tried to tell her, but he was too sleepy. As darkness closed around him, the palmtop slid out of his hand and drifted away.

19

Machine Mind

The provider's face came into focus above Kelric. Her worried look shifted like quicksilver into a smile. They were drifting in free fall, still within the tube, he with his head cradled in her lap. Moving slowly, to favor his headache, he found a grip on the bulkhead and pulled himself upright. The membranes had disappeared.

"You'll be all right now," she said. Her lyrical voice made him think of mercury. Her eyes were silver pools. He wondered why Aristos so often modeled their providers after precious metals or gems. Because they saw them as pretty machines? The line between human and machine had become so blurred anyway, it was hard to define.

"How did you open the air lock?" he asked.

"I saw the symbols on your palmtop. When it slid out of your hand."

He exhaled. *Bolt, if you made it slide that way, you have my eternal thanks.* To the girl he said, "I am in your debt."

She blushed and averted her eyes. He inhaled her pheromones, not only those the Aristos had designed into her, but also those that all psions produced. With so many fatal mutations associated with Kyle genes, the Kyle pheromones were a survival mechanism. They drew fertile psions together with an instinct stronger even than that which drove Earth's salmon upstream to reproduce. So natural selection made sure viable Kyle genes propagated themselves.

His voice gentled. "Why are you alone here in the hub?"

"You were also alone," she pointed out.

"I'm a rim-walker."

She tapped his temple. "Provider."

"But I'm on the rim crew now." Before he realized it, he had turned his head and kissed her palm. His response didn't come from desire, but from the recognition of like for like.

She cupped her palm around his cheek. Then she withdrew her hand. "I am to meet Lord Muze in the decon chamber when his yacht arrives."

Kelric had a sudden desire to punch Lord Muze. "I'm sorry."

She regarded him with her liquid gaze. "Why?"

Why indeed? For all he knew, she and Muze were going to have a great time. "Do you like him?"

She averted her gaze. "He is a great Diamond."

"That's not what I asked."

"His greatness exalts those he touches."

"Do you like him?"

"He honors me with his attention."

"You hate him."

The girl undulated away from him. "I have to go."

"Wait." He grabbed the palmtop, which was floating by his arm, its lead still attached to his wrist. On the screen Bolt had printed: You're welcome.

Bolt, is this area still unmonitored? he asked.

Yes.

Good. He looked up at the provider. "Come with me."

"No!" She stiffened. "I must go now."

He caught her hand. "I'll leave you with Shuttle Four. It's designed for interstellar travel. If I don't return, it will take you to Skolia. You'll be free."

"You are crazy." Her fear washed over him. All she could think was that she must be on time for her appointment, to keep Muze happy and minimize his violence.

"You can come with me," he said. He wasn't attracted to her in a sexual sense, not even with the overwhelming pheromones and her great beauty. What he had to offer her was worth far more than a few moments of pleasure. He could give her freedom.

"The monitors will stop you."

"They aren't watching."

"You are forbidden to leave."

"I don't care."

She pulled her hand away from him. "You will make trouble for me." Her voice softened. "Don't do this, sunshine man. If you try to go, they will hurt you even more."

"Not if they can't catch me."

Pressing her palm against the bulkhead, she pushed herself back toward the decon chamber. "You cannot run."

"Why not?"

"They forbid it."

"I don't give a damn what 'they' say."

She held out her hand. "I don't want you hurt. Do what they want and you will be happier."

"They have no right."

"Of course they do." She started to leave. "I must hurry."

"Wait!" He knew he might have to stop her anyway. "You can't tell anyone you saw me."

Puzzlement flowed from her mind. "Why would they ask?"

"Don't say anything about me. No matter what."

"I will not tell. But don't make me go with you. Please."

He flushed, realizing she had caught his thought of stopping her. That worked both ways, though; he could tell she meant what she said. She would guard his secret. No one had reason to suspect she knew anything, so they wouldn't ask. Unless he made her late.

Yet still he hesitated. What if she forgot her promise? "Come with me."

"No." She propelled herself into the decon chamber.

He decided against going after her. Instead he went to the shuttle. When he opened its hatch, a molecular air lock glimmered before him. Here in the bay, they didn't actually need air locks; the membrane formed as a precaution, lest a leak develop. Was it solid? Tensing, he stepped forward. The membrane clung to him like a soap bubble as he entered the ship. Although he had gone through this process with Shuttle Four on Tarquine's ship, he remembered none of it, only his desperation to escape.

The small shuttle only had four seats. He strode to the front and dropped into the pilot's seat. Grids and lights gleamed as panels folded around him, shifting to accommodate his large size.

"Prepare to leave," he said.

"Enter access codes, license, and permissions," its EI said.

He glanced at the palmtop. *Bolt, do I have all that?*

Its glyphs floated on the screen. **I have codes and permissions. I'm still trying to crack the file with Raziquon's license.**

Hurry!

I've opened its outer shell. Plug me into the shuttle and I'll transfer the entire file.

Kelric pulled the jack out of his wrist and clicked it into a socket in the arm of his chair.

"License verified," the shuttle said. "Prepare for departure."

As the engines thrummed, he fastened the safety mesh around his body. "Activate forward holomap."

The screen in front of him glowed with swirls and speckles. A 3-D display formed above it, showing the docking bay outside, as if he were looking out a window. He didn't see much, just the curving wall of the bay. Then its doors opened like a great flower bud. A clang shuddered through the shuttle as the docking clamps retracted. With a surge of power, the ship moved into space.

The SSRB space stations were close in interstellar terms, but in human terms great distances separated them, up to thousands of kilometers. Most of the habitats held millions of people. A slight shift of one meant the displacement of an asteroid-sized object—which carried a lot of oomph. So station managers kept them far apart. The habitats orbited in complex paths that would make air dancers dizzy trying to reproduce. Kelric studied the patterns on his holomap. It was a beautiful problem in orbital mechanics. He would have chosen a simpler solution, but he saw elegance in this method too.

He joined the flow of shuttle traffic. The habitat he had just left loomed large on his holomap. The glinting speck of another station showed to starboard. According to the stats scrolling on his screens, that "speck" was a wheel with a diameter of four kilometers.

He brought up a 3-D schematic showing the entire cluster, all sixteen habitats. His ship made a red blip on the map and other shuttles showed in blue. The Third Lock orbited near the center of the cluster. Bolt's scan of the shuttle EI didn't yield much on the Lock, except that it had more security than the other stations. It was less than Kelric expected, though. Why didn't ESComm keep it bristling with defenses?

Then he realized it *was* bristling. They had secured it in the center of the SSRB, surrounded by fifteen weapons platforms.

He pulled the palmtop's jack out of the shuttle and clicked it into his wrist socket. *Bolt?*

Glyphs appeared on the screen. **Attending.**

Does Jaibriol Raziquon have clearance to enter the Lock?

After a pause, Bolt printed, **He's part of a civilian liaison committee between the emperor's palace and ESComm. He can dock at the Lock, but a security team must escort him anywhere he goes there.**

That's no good.

You need a hidden entrance.

I have its Rhon security codes.

You must be within the Lock to act as a Key.

I don't mean those codes, Kelric thought. *I've also codes for all its entrances, including covert ones keyed to the Rhon.*

That is useful.

Very. It's for emergencies. Like this.

We also need a way for you to approach the station without being detected.

Can you back into its security web?

Not without tripping alarms. Raziquon's clearance isn't high enough.

Any suggestions?

Yes. But it involves danger to you.

Dryly Kelric thought, *All of this involves danger to me.*

This could be permanent.

What is it?

This shuttle delivers cleaning supplies to other stations, Bolt explained. If you look like a machine, the shuttle's approach shouldn't raise an alarm. To dock and make its deliveries, its EI must link to the Lock's web, which will give me access. Once I'm in, it will be easier to hack my way around without getting caught.

Kelric squinted at the palmtop. *How can I look like a machine? Any routine scan will reveal I'm human.*

Not if I turn off your brain.

Say again?

In a sense, your brain is "mechanical" already, Bolt answered. Bio-electrodes and buffers in your neurons control their firing, which lets you "think" to me. If you give me control of those functions, I'll make your firing patterns resemble an EI. Your body is also full of biomech. You're already operating under hydraulic control. It shouldn't be hard for me to convince long-distance sensors you're a machine.

Kelric shifted uneasily. *What's the catch?*

Bolt hesitated. I may not be able to return you to normal, particularly given the brain damage you've already sustained.

If I'm broken when I reach the Lock, I can't do anything.

I really don't know if it would hurt you or not. Bolt paused. Or you could go find Shuttle Four and try to go home.

As much as he wanted to do just that, he couldn't. *I have to see this through. Otherwise, what will I go home to? The Traders will conquer us and capture my whole family.*

Shall I proceed, then?

Yes.

I need your access codes for the Lock.

Puzzled, Kelric thought, *You have them in your secured files.*

I've been unable to access those files for years. Do you remember the codes?

I'm not sure. It's been a long time.

What shall I do?

What? If he gave Bolt the wrong codes, it might alert security when Bolt fumbled with the Lock's web. Even if they didn't set off an alarm, they still wouldn't have covert access to the station. They would have to use a normal docking bay. Bolt might convince long-distance sensors that Kelric was machinery, but the deception would collapse if a human crew or smart robots came to unload him.

He massaged his temples, trying to ease his headache. *I'll give you the codes as best I remember. But if this doesn't work and I'm caught, I want you to do something.*

Yes?

Kelric knew if ESComm caught him trying to break into the Lock, their interrogation would be swift. They would probably discover his identity before Tarquine could reclaim him. *Collapse the fuel bottles for this ship's antimatter. Blow it up with me in it.*

Sorrow shaded Bolt's glyphs. Are you sure?

Yes.

I hope it doesn't come to that.

Kelric exhaled. *I also.* Then he gave Bolt his best guess for the codes.

The universe turned gray and ended.

20

Ruby Legacy

If Not Think, then Think

Insert Conscious

"What?" Kelric asked. *Insert Conscious?* What kind of wacko command was that? And why was he thinking it in his own head?

Dim blue light came from a bar above him. He was standing in a locker with several robots. They had a skeletal framework suited to maintenance work, rather than humanoid form. He still held Raziquon's palmtop in his hand.

Bolt? he thought. *Are you there?*

Yes, it printed on the palmtop. How are you?

All right. He rubbed his eyes. *Why didn't you wake me up when we docked? Who put me in here?* Humans or smart robots would have noticed the "slight" discrepancy in the shuttle's cargo compared to its listed inventory.

I had trouble restoring your neural functions, Bolt printed. So I had the maintenance robots unload you. I told them you were a new model.

He almost laughed. *And they believed you? Everyone knows the human body is a lousy design for a maintenance robot.*

They don't know that. They just clean things.

Oh. Well, good. When it came to robots, apparently Bolt knew more than Kelric about their intelligence level. Or lack thereof.

I have a question, Bolt asked.

Yes?

Why did ISC hide a docking bay here?

A precaution, in case the Rhon ever needed covert access. Like now. He rolled his shoulders, working out the kinks. *Are you inside the station web?*

Yes. I've discovered ESComm knows about this bay.

It didn't surprise Kelric. ESComm was nothing if not efficient. *Have they made it work?*

No. It is protected by a psiberlock only the Rhon can open.

Kelric grinned. *I know.*

They have no idea the psiberlock exists. They've listed the docking bay as "out of order" and slated it for removal.

Without psions, they've no good way to recognize a psiberlock. He stretched his arms. *This sector used to have an access tube for the robots that cleaned the Lock. Is it still here?*

Yes, according to the web. I'm only able to access the web's outer layers, though.

That should be enough. He laid his palms against the locker's door. *Can I go outside?*

Yes. It should be safe.

He touched a circle on the wall. The locker slid open with a quiet hum, revealing a storage room filled with sleeping machines, everything from foot-sized dust sweepers to the lumbering droids that worked the outer hull. For microscopic repairs, nanobots doped the hull. Canisters of the gel that produced the bots lined the walls.

Kelric stepped out of the locker—and fell.

He grabbed a canister by the doorway, one as high as his chest. His legs tingled. When he regained his balance, he tried another step. He nearly fell again, but this time he managed to stay up without grabbing anything. He tried two more steps. He could walk, but with a limp so severe he dragged his foot.

Bolt? he asked. *What's wrong?*

I'm not sure. I am having trouble with your hydraulics.

Why? Turning off my conscious mind shouldn't affect them.

I needed your brain to open the psiberlock on the docking bay.

What does that have to do with my hydraulics?

To "turn off" your brain, I ran your neural processes as a subshell on my system, Bolt explained. I had the subshell mimic my own activity. So you looked like an EI. I was afraid using your mind to open the psiberlock would give you away. So I disguised your subshell mind with a second subshell that I ran in the foreground while your actual mind ran in the background. The foreground subshell distracted the web so I could link your real subshell mind to the psiberlock.

Kelric blinked. *You did all that with my brain?* Amazing.

Well, you see, that's the problem. I didn't have enough memory to hold all those subshells and keep your hydraulics working. So I let the hydraulics go. Bolt paused. I'm sorry. The subshells overwrote some of my software. I'm having trouble linking to your hydraulics.

It felt odd to have his computer apologize. *I understand.* Hanging on to a jointed arm on a droid, he took another dragging step. His legs felt like lead. *Can you get back the links?*

I will do my best.

Bolt's glyph nuances hinted at a doubt that Kelric suspected his node hadn't intended to reveal. So strange. Bolt had become more human while he became more machine. Where did they draw the line that defined humanity? Their self-evolution blurred it, maybe beyond recognition. He didn't feel like a machine, though. He felt like a clumsy man. No matter. Considering the stakes, clumsiness was a small price to pay for his continued freedom.

Do you know anything about the layout here? he asked. *I don't remember where to find the access tube to the Lock.*

I've a map. Bolt's nuances indicated it was pleased to give him some good news. Go to the end of this aisle. Turn right and take ten more steps. That will bring you to the hatch for the tube.

Kelric peered down the dimly lit aisle of droids. They stood over twice his height, robot hulks slumbering in the shadows. Twenty steps to the end of this aisle and ten more to the hatch. Thirty paces. Grasping a retracted claw on a droid, he took a step, dragging his foot with him.

Another step. Stumble. Step again.

Slowly he made his way down the aisle, using droids for support. It didn't help that the station gravity was at 120 percent. Finally he reached the end of the row. Two steps in front of him, a blank wall stretched both right and left. Looking to the right, he saw a hatch in the wall about ten paces away, past two more aisles of equipment. Only ten paces.

It looked like a million.

He took a breath. Then he stepped toward the hatch—and lost his balance. When he grabbed for a droid, his fingers scraped across its convoluted surface. He hit the deck with a great, thudding impact. The droids around him shook as the floor vibrated.

Kelric lay on his stomach, too stunned to move. Then he rolled onto his side and lifted his hand—to see the battered remains of the palmtop. His body had slammed it into the deck when he hit.

Bolt? he asked. No answer appeared on the ripped screen.

"No," he said. He needed Bolt. The responsibility to see this through pressed on him like a great weight. He had an obligation to his family, his people, the Allieds, the Trader slaves; to Ixpar and his children; to all the providers he had failed to help; to all the people who would lose their freedom if the Aristos carried out their dreams of conquest. Could one person be responsible for them all? Without Bolt, he had even less chance of success. He lay on the floor, trying to gather his strength.

"Let's go," he muttered. Grabbing a droid, he struggled back up to his feet. He hung the remains of the palmtop on his belt, giving himself two free hands. Then he limped forward, dragging his foot, using the droids for support.

Ten more steps to the access tube. Only ten. He tried not to think of how far he had to go inside the tube. Cleaning droids trundled that way all the time. He could have ridden one if it had been available. But he didn't dare start machinery here. Who knew what alarms he might trigger? His fall hadn't set off any as far as he knew, but he wasn't sure. He could take no more chances.

So he struggled, one step at a time. Nine. Eight. Seven.

Although he didn't have much sensation in his legs, the rest of his body felt the strain of pulling them along. His hips ached.

Five. Four. Three steps. Two.

One.

With a relieved grunt, he sagged against the hatch. When he had caught his breath, he peered at the control panel. This one he knew. Skolian. It followed a different standard than Eubian systems. He entered the codes easily and the hatch slid open.

Bracing his arms against the sides of the hatchway, he stared down the circular tube that stretched into the distance. Only a dim blue glow lit the walls. Smooth walls. No hand grips. Robots didn't need them, after all.

He limped into the tube and closed the hatch. As he turned around, his legs buckled. This time he was ready for the fall and caught himself on his hands as he hit the ground. He paused, taking a breath. Then he tried to climb to his feet. The glassy walls offered no help. His hands just slid along them. He finally managed using the sheer breadth of his arm span; by stretching out his arms, he could brace his hands against either side of the tunnel. He kept his palms from slipping by pushing outward while he hauled himself to his feet.

So he stood in the tunnel, staring down its blue extent. Like Earth's mythical Atlas holding up the world, he kept his hands braced against the walls, as if he were holding open the Lock itself.

Then he took a step.

Another step. Rest.

Step again. Rest.

Gradually he became aware of an odd effect. His mind felt heavy. It wasn't like what happened with Aristos. This was . . . right. Something within him was responding to a call he felt more than heard.

Far ahead, the tube narrowed to a point. He stopped, trying to focus. The tunnel went on, straight and true, forever, until the effects of perspective narrowed it into a bright white dot. That made no sense. A moment ago it had simply been a tunnel, too dim to see more than a few meters ahead.

He started forward again, moving his hands along the wall. A vibration passed into his body, humming through him. **Come.** It called not in words, but with a sense of meaning below language.

Come to me.

He went another half meter. Another. Step by step...

Suddenly the point of light wasn't far away. It glowed only a few meters in front of him, a circular entrance. No, not a circle. An octagon. That shape had been ubiquitous in the architecture of the Ruby ancients and lay buried in the psyches of humanity now, all of them, Trader and Skolian alike, an echo of the ancient sciences they had lost five millennia ago, before their separate empires existed, when they were all one people.

He took another step, dragging his bad leg. The light blazed around him. One more step and he had reached the entrance. Grabbing its sides, he looked into a small octagonal chamber.

Inside, the Third Lock waited for him.

White radiance glowed everywhere, so luminous he couldn't make out details of the chamber. The air hummed with a vibration he felt rather than heard. As he stepped across the threshold, time slowed.

Now he saw it. A great column of light rose out of an octagonal hole in the center of the floor and vanished overhead in a haze of blurred reality.

The Lock.

A discontinuity in spacetime.

A Kyle singularity.

It offered a portal into another reality. The pillar came out of a universe where space and time had no meaning. Only within this chamber did it exist in his universe. Overhead it pierced the fabric of spacetime and vanished into some other reality.

Created over five thousand years ago, the Lock had survived the millennia, alone and adrift. When humans finally returned to space, they rediscovered the Locks, remnants of an empire that had fallen into ruin and myth. Modern science had yet to decipher the secrets held by these ancient Ruby machines. His people barely knew how to use them. But what little they had learned to create, the Triad and psiberweb, had altered the balance of power among three empires.

Kelric walked in slow motion, his movements torpid in the

anomalous spacetime. He sunk to his knees at the edge of the radiant pillar. His mind responded to its unspoken call with an answering pull. The Lock rumbled in silent power, in his body, his mind, his essence.

I am your Key, he thought.

It gave him welcome. It had waited a long time for him.

Eons.

Kelric rose to his feet and limped to a console by the wall. He lowered himself onto its stool. The console had no jacks or IR ports. He needed none. His distant Ruby ancestors had created Rhon psions for the Locks: his family were the last of its Keys.

Bowing his head, he summoned memories he hadn't known he owned until now, knowledge encoded in his Kyle-mutated DNA. He repeated words from classical Iotic, a language different even from modern Iotic. As the syllables formed in his mind, he sank into a trance. His chant glimmered in the air, hieroglyphs that shifted and flowed in radiant power.

When Kelric finished, the Look's vibration changed, rising into audible range. Without conscious thought, he pressed a square on the controls in front of him. Silent and smooth, a drawer slid open on the right side of the console.

Two ancient gauntlets lay inside the drawer. They were made from a black leather composite that had survived for eons, and a silver material that shone like metal but flexed like skin. Picotech packed the gauntlets: bio-threads, superconducting conduits, web nodes, comms meshes in the leather. He had never seen any other Triad member wear gauntlets, not even his half brother Kurj. But these had a sense of rightness.

He pushed up the sleeve of his jumpsuit and put on one gauntlet. It fit his hand like a black glove, leaving his fingers free, and stretched to his elbow. Although heavy, it flexed with his arm, supple and comfortable, like a second skin. He clenched his fist and his muscles ridged the leather.

At first the gauntlet covered his wrist guard. Then a slit formed at his wrist and widened to expose his guard. The leather fit so snugly about the gold that the gauntlet and guard could have been made from one piece. As he watched, fascinated, glimmering threads stretched out from pores in the gauntlet, reached across his guard, went into the hole drilled in the gold, and entered his socket. When the threads met the biomech in his body, he knew a sense of *joining,* as if the gauntlet had greeted his own system.

Kelric put the second gauntlet on his other arm. It repeated the same process—

And he sensed another presence.

Father? he thought. His mind rumbled.

No answer.

He wasn't sure he felt his father. It was more a blend of two minds. The rest of the Triad? But why two? If his aunt Dehya, the Ruby Pharaoh, had died, only his father remained.

Triad.

Dehya had been the Assembly Key, the liaison between the Ruby Dynasty and Imperial Assembly. His father was the Web Key, focused on maintaining the psiberweb. Kelric was about to become the Military Key. Imperator. But until he joined the Triad, it included only his father. Both Dehya and Soz had died in the Radiance War.

At Kelric's thought of Soz, the Kyle singularity behind him stirred his mind. He rose to his feet and turned to the column. Light shifted within its radiant core. Yes, Soz had been in the Triad. Only echoes of her presence remained. She was gone. He swallowed against the sudden lump in his throat, faced with this final confirmation of his sister's death.

But . . . two other presences remained.

Aunt Dehya? he asked.

No answer.

He walked to the Lock. It swirled before him, full and deep.

Come. Its call formed as neither words nor thoughts, but deep within his mind. **Come.**

He stepped into the singularity.

21

Lord of Otherwhere

Kelric, my son, listen dreaming to the stars.
To the ships, the eons, and the humming cars.
Kelric, my boy, listen softly to the tales,
Of children, of ball games, of blowing sails.
Kelric, my hope, named for endless, dreaming Youth
Come now, little boy, don't pull your sore tooth.

The nursery rhyme murmured in his mind. When he had been a small boy, his father had sung it to him, changing the words to fit the adventures of his son, the boy his parents had named Kelricson, after the Lyshriol spirit of youth, because he was their last child.

Father? His thought rumbled in this place where time and space had no meaning. He had no body. Only thought.

No answer came out of the radiance. He didn't feel his father's mind, exactly, but more a sense of his presence.

A new presence registered, a glimmering mesh that filled space, undulating in an endless ocean of light. If his father was the sea that supported the web, then Dehya Selei, the Ruby Pharaoh, was the web itself.

Aunt Dehya? he asked.

Kelric? Her response came like a distant murmur of waves.

Where are you?

Gone... Her unseen presence swirled in currents of light.

Unlike Kelric or his father, whose thoughts were here but not their bodies, *all* of Dehya was present. Her corporeal being had become part of this universe. Had she died? Was this only an echo of her life?

I exist, she thought.

Come home. Our people need their Pharaoh. He paused. **Your family needs you.**

I will try.

Then her presence vanished.

He waited, letting his mind fill space, but no more wisps of her came to him. Gradually he oriented himself. His mind was here, in this otherplace, but physically he still stood within the Lock. Looking through the luminous column, he saw his image in the reflective walls of the chamber. Tall and erect, he stood within the column of light, his face tilted up, his palms turned outward, his body radiant within that luminous pillar.

He thought of his father: the gentle parent who carried him when he was small; the athlete who taught him to run, throw, and catch; the warrior who trained him with bow and sword, though he knew his son would soon leave home to become a star warrior. Kelric had passed him in physical height when he was barely an adolescent, and as an adult he towered over his father. But he never stopped looking up to this man who had made such an impact on his life.

Father? he thought. **Are you here?**

As if from a distant shore, a thought whispered across him: ***Come home to us, my son.***

Kelric sat on the console stool, staring at the column of light. Although he no longer stood within it, he felt its power coursing through him. His mind had become more. It existed here, but it was also part of that other place now, unbounded by space and time.

So strange. How could Dehya exist *within* that space? No wonder no one knew what had happened to her. Somehow, to escape the Trader commandos who infiltrated the Orbiter, she must have gone *into* the First Lock, mind and body both.

Come back, he thought, hoping the echo would reach her. It made him remember his father's words: *Come home to us, my son.*

His father would be ninety now. He hadn't had access to modern life-extending treatments until he was a grown man. It made a difference even modern medicine couldn't overcome. Eighteen years ago he had already been showing signs of age, silver in his hair, weaker eyesight, a slower walk. Kelric wanted to believe he would always be there, but in that call, he had felt his father's age.

Kelric swallowed. For all that he might command the military of an empire and wield powers beyond spacetime, he couldn't stop his father from getting old.

I will see you again, he thought.

Then he stood and walked to the singularity. Walked. Easily. His hydraulics were operating again. Gazing into the pillar, he said, "I, Kelricson Garlin Valdoria Skolia, accept the title of Imperator."

Blue light still lit the access tube. He could leave the way he had come. But first he had to disable the Lock.

Instead of entering the tube, Kelric left the chamber by another entrance, a curved arch that opened onto a wide corridor. Transparent columns bordered the corridor, each filled with clockwork machinery made from precious metals. Lights spiraled within the columns. The floor extended out from his feet in a diamond-steel composite. The ceiling arched so far overhead, he only glimpsed its distant vaulted spaces.

The architecture evoked Highton cylinder ships. It wasn't pure Aristo: the Ruby designers had used right angles as well as curves and polygons. But the modern Aristo style had its ancestry here. To a lesser extent, that ancestry also showed in the graceful arches and vaults of Skolian architecture. But when the people of Raylicon split into Eubians and Skolians, their ways of defining spaces had also split. It was more than architecture; it affected their fundamental outlook. Over the centuries, the Eubian style had grown ever more complex. For all the cruelty they created, they also achieved a great beauty, a fractal way of thought unlike anything attained, or even imagined, by Skolians.

We all lost when we split, Kelric thought. We became fractions of a people. They lost a part of their basic humanity and we lost a gift of abstract mental creation.

What of Coba? Isolated for thousands of years, the Cobans had retained both the fascinating complexity of Aristo thought and the elegant simplicity of Skolian creation. So their minds gave birth to Quis. Regret rippled over Kelric. Were the universe a different place, he could have become a mathematician at some secluded institute and spent his time using Quis in an attempt to unravel the secrets of the ancients. He would have loved such a life. But he didn't live in that universe. He had too many duties here.

He strode down the corridor as if he were walking through the eons. He had an eerie sense of coming forward from the past, from the time when the Ruby Empire built its inexplicable machines. No wonder neither his people nor the Traders ever unraveled the ancient Ruby sciences. Skolians no longer had the style of abstract thought they needed to comprehend it. The Aristos would never succeed because they had a cavity where their capacity for empathy should have been. By eradicating their Kyle genes, they destroyed their ability to re-create the very Ruby sciences they craved.

To Kelric, it seemed the Traders lost far more than his people. Aristos had become inhuman in their search for the ultimate state of humanity. Yet he couldn't help but wonder: *What if?* What if a way existed to combine the best of Eube and Skolia? What if they melded the Aristo gifts for abstract beauty with a psion's compassion and capacity for love? It hurt for him to imagine the splendor of that joining because he knew it was impossible. Quis was probably the closest humanity would ever come to such a joining. And Quis was only a game. It wasn't human.

The corridor ended at an archway more than twice his height, with lights running around its edges. As he approached, he searched the area with his mind. He detected no one, not the emptiness of an

Aristo, the neutrality of a taskmaker, or the vulnerability of a provider.

He paused at the corridor's end. A large chamber slumbered beyond, shadowed, lit only by the spillover of light from the arch where he stood. On a dais to his right, a giant chair caught glints of light. Its armrests were glimmering silver blocks, half a meter wide and a meter long, packed with webtech. Equipment embedded the massive backrest. The chair's hood contained sensors capable of unsurpassed VR simulations. Silver webbing with psiphon prongs lay on the seat, ready to connect their user to the web. The chair stood like a throne.

His throne.

Had the Lock still been at Onyx and had the web still existed, he would have sat in that chair and linked into the star-flung web that wove his empire together. Instead, he walked past the dais to the consoles on the far wall. He bent over the main unit, scanning its controls. Then he took a psiphon plug and clicked it into his wrist.

The power of the Lock coursed through him. **Attending.**

Suspend, Kelric thought.

Done.

The Lock's subvocal rumble stopped. Just like that. The air dimmed. For all appearances, the Lock had just died.

Sleep well, he thought. He unplugged from the console and returned to the archway. He stared down the long corridor to the Lock chamber. The lights in the arches, in the columns, even the sparkle of the diamond-steel floor—all had dimmed. Far down the corridor, the Kyle singularity had gone dark.

A sense of easing spread through Kelric, as if a weight had lifted from his shoulders. Incredibly, he had succeeded. His chances of escaping Trader space were small, but he had accomplished his most important goal.

He had made peace possible.

Now it only remained for him to leave, as fast as possible. He turned for one last glance at the throne—

And looked straight into the face of the Trader emperor.

22

Rising Sun

Holo.

As his surge of adrenaline eased, Kelric realized he was looking at a holographic image. Jaibriol I had died long before Kelric's birth. Yet there he sat, in the flush of youth. Tall and strong, long-legged and broad in the shoulders, the young man seemed to stare at him. He showed a gentler face than Kelric had seen in other holos of Jaibriol I. In this misleading image, no cruelty marred the classic perfection of his Highton features.

In fact, now that he looked closely, the holo didn't resemble Jaibriol I as much as he first thought. Maybe this was his grandson, the late Jaibriol II, who had sat on the Carnelian Throne during the Radiance War.

"Are you done staring at me?" the emperor inquired.

Kelric froze. Good gods, it wasn't a holo. A living man sat on the throne.

His mind spun with plans: knock out the youth, use him as a hostage, run for the shuttle. None were promising. Any Highton with access to the Third Lock would have ESComm backup. This Aristo could raise an alarm before Kelric even made it a few steps.

Stalling for time, he said, "How did you get in here?"

"I should ask that question of you." The youth gave him an appraising glance. "You were intent on your work. Killing the Lock, I gather." He leaned on his elbow, which rested on the chair's massive arm. It was a classic pose, a study in regal posture.

And yet . . . something else was familiar. Was it only the boy's resemblance to the emperor? This youth had the snowmarble skin, ruby eyes, and glittering hair of an Aristo. But that wasn't what tugged Kelric's memory.

Then it hit him. "You're the one who spoke in the broadcast from the emperor's palace."

The youth was also studying him. "You saw the broadcast?"

"From a distance." Kelric paused, still puzzled. The tug on his memory came from more than the broadcast. What? *What?*

Quietly he said, "I know you."

The Aristo shrugged, an exquisitely Highton gesture that held a world of innuendo: the suggestion of superiority, ingrained Highton arrogance, the assumption of his right to privilege—all contained in one subtle lift of the shoulders. "I should think all settled space knows me by now."

If nothing else, his arrogance gave him away. "You're a Qox," Kelric said.

Although he laughed, it sounded hollow. "Not *a* Qox. *The* Qox."

Kelric stood for a full five seconds absorbing his implication. Then he said, "The emperor's heir?"

In a deceptively soft voice, he said, "I am no heir. I rule Eube. As Jaibriol Three."

Gods. Did they never die out? How many more Jaibriols were lurking around the galaxy? "Jaibriol Two had no heir."

"Or course he did. Me."

Kelric thought his life had surely become surreal, that he stood here conversing with someone who claimed to be emperor of Eube. An undefined sense of recognition still bothered him. "I know you from somewhere."

Jaibriol gave him a well-crafted smile of condescension. "Perhaps you were dazzled by your time in the Lock, Lord Skolia."

Odd, that Qox used his dynastic title. Jaibriol spoke to him as an equal. Yet the Qox Dynasty had long refused to acknowledge the Ruby Dynasty as their counterparts. In diplomatic situations, they used the expected titles. But they made no secret of their disdain.

Here, nothing constrained Jaibriol. Yet for all that his Highton mannerisms were perfect, almost too perfect, his use of the Imperator's title sounded genuine.

Suddenly Kelric knew what bothered him. Jaibriol's mind had no abyss. It wasn't like with Tarquine. Hers felt normal. With Jaibriol, he had a strange sense, as if the young man protected himself with mental barriers so well crafted that even a member of the Rhon could barely detect them. Only a psion could build such shields. Only a psion *needed* them. And Jaibriol III was no psion.

Incredibly, another recognition flared. Quietly he said, "You're Jay Rockworth. The Dawn Corps volunteer on Edgewhirl."

Jaibriol paused, as if considering his answer. Then he moved his hand in dismissal. "This was all in the broadcast."

"That you were with the Allieds?"

"That my parents hid me on Earth. The Allieds discovered it and traded me to Eube."

Gods. No wonder that broadcast had riveted the Aristos. What the blazes had possessed the Allieds to make such a trade? What could Eube possibly offer that was worth giving them a new emperor, especially this vital youth whose presence on the Carnelian Throne would revitalize the war-weary Aristos? Were the Allieds insane?

Softly Jaibriol said, "I had no idea who you were, that day on Edgewhirl."

"Nor I, for you," Kelric said.

Jaibriol hesitated. "Which one are you?"

"Which one?" If Kelric hadn't known better, he would have thought the youth sounded shy.

"In the Ruby Dynasty."

"Kelricson Valdoria."

The emperor froze. He spoke in such a low voice, it was almost a whisper. "Del-Kelric." Grief flowed from his mind, inexplicable, as if he had lost a loved one by that name.

Kelric had no idea how to respond. Where would Jaibriol hear such a name? *Del* was given to Skolian children to honor a beloved relative. Del-Kelric meant *in honor of Kelric.* What could that possibly mean to a Highton lord?

Jaibriol seemed to give himself a mental shake. Once again he became the cool aristocrat. "Where did you come from? You've been dead for years."

Kelric had no intention of answering. "Why were you with the Dawn Corps?" He shook his head. "It makes no sense. You expressed sympathy for the Ruby Dynasty."

Jaibriol shrugged. "Perhaps you remember what you wish."

"No." Kelric wasn't fooled. "And you look familiar. I don't know why. But I *know* you."

The youth stood, rising to his full height, over six feet. He stepped down from the throne and crossed the dais. When he stopped in front of Kelric, only a rail separated them. The dais added enough to his height to bring his eyes level with Kelric's. "Go. Now. While you can."

"You would let me go?"

"Yes."

Kelric didn't believe it. "Why?"

Jaibriol spoke with cool, cultured tones. Yet more underlay his words. Longing? Determination? Hope? In his many-layered voice, he said, "Meet me at the peace table."

"You want me to believe you wish peace," Kelric said, "when you have a Lock and two Keys."

"What Lock?" The youth spread his hands. "It no longer works."

He knew Jaibriol had seen him suspend the singularity. Yet the emperor never even asked if he could bring it alive again.

"We had one Key," Jaibriol said. "We gave him back."

Kelric waited for him to qualify his misleading statement. After several seconds, when the youth remained silent, Kelric said, "Gave who back?"

"Your brother. Eldrin Valdoria."

"Don't lie to me, Highton."

"Why would I lie?"

"It's what you Hightons do. Lie, manipulate, cheat."

That was when it happened. For one instant Jaibriol's mask of cool superiority slipped. In that moment his face revealed a terrified, lonely young man trapped in a situation far beyond his experience. His gaze was so wrenchingly familiar, Kelric's breath caught. Why? Gods, *why?*

Then Jaibriol recovered. Once again the emperor faced him. "I've little interest in your imagined list of Highton ills." His disdain was almost convincing.

Almost.

Kelric tried to fathom him. "Eube would never give its Key to the Allieds. Not when you finally had a Lock. Nothing is worth it."

"Not even me?"

That stopped Kelric. "You, for Eldrin?"

"Yes."

Could it be true? It was the one trade he could imagine the Allieds making with sanity. A young, vibrant emperor on the throne would revitalize Eube. But at the price of their Key? It must have ignited a furious debate.

Jaibriol spoke dryly. "You are right, it wasn't a universally popular decision. But it is done. I am emperor and your brother is an Allied prisoner."

Kelric knew better than to let himself hope. More likely, Jaibriol was toying with him while guards waited outside.

"I am alone," Jaibriol said.

Kelric tensed. "Why did you say that?" It wasn't the first time Jaibriol seemed to know his thoughts. Yet no Aristo could be a psion. It wasn't in the genetic lines they protected with such obsessive fanaticism. For the emperor, they would have verified his DNA down to the last nucleotide.

"You didn't wonder if I had guards?" Jaibriol raised his eyebrows. "I find that hard to believe."

"And you just happened to come in—alone—when I was here."

A smile curved Jaibriol's patrician lips. "Ah, well. It would be a great coincidence, yes? But I knew you were here."

"How?"

"Perhaps you could say I felt it."

"Perhaps. I don't believe it."

"I suppose not." Jaibriol rubbed his chin. "I detected your entrance in the station web."

Kelric knew the boy was lying. But why? What did he have to gain? And why did Jaibriol look so hauntingly familiar?

"Imperator Skolia." Jaibriol took a breath. "Meet me when we can discuss peace."

"Why should I believe you want this?"

"Ask for something I can grant as proof of my intent."

It was a fair, if unexpected, question. Kelric considered. "There is a man. A Skolian. Jafe Maccar. Captain of the *Corona.* After a battle at the space station *Chrysalis,* Maccar was sentenced to ten years in an ESComm prison. Unjustly." He regarded Jaibriol. "Pardon him."

The emperor paused. "I will consider it."

His lukewarm response didn't surprise Kelric. He doubted Maccar would see his freedom. If Jaibriol pardoned him, it would undermine ESComm's claim that Maccar instigated the incident.

Jaibriol motioned upward, a gesture that seemed to include all Eube. "It's like a great thundering machine I hold by the barest thread. If I am to find a road to peace, I need your help."

Then, finally, it hit Kelric, what he had known at a subliminal level throughout this surreal conversation, an awareness that grew until it became conscious in his mind. It was impossible. Utterly impossible.

Jaibriol III was a psion.

He felt the youth's mind. Jaibriol did have barriers. They had been dissolving as he and Kelric talked, probably without Jaibriol realizing it. His luminous Kyle strength glowed.

In a low voice, Kelric said, "You're a telepath."

"No." Pain layered Jaibriol's denial. He became pure Highton. Polished. Smooth. Cold. Unreal. "I am what you see. Qox."

"At what price?" Kelric asked softly. "What must you suffer to hide the truth?"

Jaibriol met his gaze. "Was anyone here when I came into the Lock? I never saw him."

What hells did this young man live, ruling from the Carnelian Throne, surrounded by Aristos every day of his life, never knowing surcease? How had it happened? Watching Jaibriol, he knew he would learn no more answers here.

He spoke gently. "Gods help you, son."

Jaibriol swallowed. "Go. Now. While you can."

Kelric stepped back into the arched entrance of the corridor. When Jaibriol said nothing, Kelric turned and started the long walk down the Lock corridor. His back itched as he waited for the gunshot, maybe a neural blocker to disable him, or an EM pulse rifle that would shred his body.

"Lord Skolia," Jaibriol said.

He froze. Turning, he faced the emperor. Would the game end now? "Yes?"

"If you make it to Earth—" Jaibriol lifted his hand, as if to reach toward Kelric. He stood poised, his posture showing the strain of longing balanced with denial. Then he lowered his arm. "Go see Admiral William Seth Rockworth."

So. Jaibriol did have a link to Seth. "I will go." He wanted to ask more, but he dared remain no longer. Turning, he resumed his walk. As he strode down that avenue of the ages, he had a strange sense, as if Jaibriol spoke in his mind:

Gods speed, my uncle.

Kelric ran down the access tube, his soft-soled boots thudding on the deck. He reached the maintenance hold and ran past the droids, remembering how he had dragged himself through here such a short time ago. The shuttle was where he expected, hidden in a dimly lit bay behind the storage holds.

As he fastened himself into the pilot's seat, he thought: *Bolt, if you receive this, make my right leg move.*

His right foot shifted on the deck.

Bolt, listen. He snapped the safety web around his body. *If you put my mind in a subshell again, will you lose my hydraulics? If the answer is yes, move my right leg. If no, move my left leg. If you're unsure, move my right arm.*

His right leg shifted. Yes.

Will you be able to get them back?

His left leg moved this time. No.

It was the Lock, wasn't it? Kelric asked. *You recovered because I entered the Lock.*

His right leg moved. Yes.

So now what? He couldn't risk being detected when they left the station, but he didn't want to lose his mobility again. Of course, if Qox revealed him, it would make little difference how he protected himself. He had no idea what was going on with the emperor. He even wondered if he had hallucinated the meeting, an eerie side effect of joining the Triad or turning off the Lock. But he thought it was genuine.

Meet me at the peace table.

"All right," Kelric said. "If I get out of this, you have a deal, Emperor. If you really mean to follow through."

Before he could meet anyone, however, he had to escape. Which meant this shuttle had better look like a drone leaving the station after a routine delivery.

Bolt, he thought. *Put me in the subshell. Get us out of here.*

23

Jeejon

...goto Restart: insert Conscious for NotConscious. P=P+1

If P>30, goto Emergency Restart.

If NotConscious, goto Restart: insert Conscious for NotConscious. P=P+1

If P>30, goto Emergency Restart

Emergency Restart: Set Neurons (1:M:N)=1

Fire Neurons—

Kelric groaned as he came out of the convulsion. His body ached where he had thrashed against the safety webbing. Darkness surrounded him. Alarms clamored.

"—*fired* on us," the insistent voice was saying. "Please. What should I do?"

"What?" He tried to orient himself.

"A buoy on the SSRB perimeter defenses very rudely fired on us," the shuttle EI told him. "It ruined the finish on my hull."

Kelric tried to see in the dark. Even the warning lights on his console had gone dark. "What is the situation?"

"I was trying to locate this Shuttle Four of yours," the EI said in a vexed tone. "That's what you told me to do, if you remember. A space buoy on the perimeter surface told us to stop. It refused my security codes. When I took up a holding pattern, this ill-mannered Bolt of yours interfered. It made my thrusters fire, accelerating me right into the perimeter, precisely where the buoy told us not to go. The buoy fired on us. It damaged my hull in a most unattractive way. This is all very upsetting. ESComm security shuttles are coming. I am in a holding pattern until they arrive."

For crying out loud. What kind of EI was this? Apparently he no longer had the option of sneaking through the perimeter. He probably could have guided the shuttle out himself, using a stealth pattern, but apparently Bolt had run into trouble restarting him.

"Get us out of here," Kelric told the EI. "Invert."

"I am not designed for interstellar travel," it said primly.

"You have inversion engines. So invert."

"My inversion capability is confined to small distances. The volume of the SSRB, to be precise."

"I don't give a flaming damn about precision. Invert!"

"You don't have to use foul language."

"If you don't get us out of here before ESComm arrives," he growled, "I'll wipe out your processors with my language."

Its voice quavered. "If I attempt to accelerate, the buoy will fire again."

"Accelerate fast."

"It will still fire. I do not wish to be destroyed."

"Don't you have mods for stealth and evasion tactics?"

"No," the EI sniffed. "I am a cleaning shuttle."

"Use a random pattern of accelerations and decelerations. Bolt will give you an algorithm. You probably can't dodge the buoy for more than a few seconds. So you have to reach inversion speed fast. In one second. But you're small. You can manage."

"That requires hundreds of thousands of g-forces." It sounded appalled. "Your body wouldn't survive. It would make a mess."

Exasperated, he said, "Put me in quasis."

"It is inadvisable in your condition—"

"Do it, damn it. *Now.*"

"You needn't yell. Quasis activated—"

When Kelric came out of quasis, he threw up. He heard palm-sized robots whir and felt them skitter over his body, cleaning him up. He didn't try to move. He couldn't see worth a damn.

Oddly enough, his right arm kept twitching. *Bolt,* he thought, glad that thinking required no motion. *Are you making my arm move?*

His right leg jerked.

What had that meant? *Yes.* That was it. Right leg meant yes. With relief, he thought, *You have control of my biomech.*

His right arm moved. Maybe.

How can you not be sure? When his right arm moved again, he realized his question didn't have a yes-no-maybe answer. *You have some control?*

His right leg jerked. Yes.

More than last time?

His left leg moved. No.

You couldn't help my legs before, he pointed out.

His right leg moved this time. Yes.

You have control of my legs, but lost something else?

His right leg moved again.

Kelric swallowed. *My optical nerve. I'm blind.*

Again his right leg moved. Yes.

Disheartened, he laid his head back on the seat. He needed to plan, but he felt sick from being too long in quasis. It was hard to concentrate. He was blind. *Blind...*

A voice pulled him alert again. "—sorry if I hurt your feelings back there," the shuttle EI was saying. "I was afraid I was about to be destroyed."

He gave a wan smile. "That's all right. I'm sorry I cussed at you."

"Would you like me to find Shuttle Four?"

"No. We can't risk dropping out of inversion again."

"Where shall I take you?"

Tiredly he said, "Home."

"Where is home?"

"Skolian space."

"I don't have enough fuel to go that far."

"Do what you can," he said.

A blaring alarm roused Kelric. Groggy and confused, he rubbed his eyes. "Shuttle? What's going on?"

"I am no longer space-worthy," it informed him.

He blinked. "We still seem quite worthily in space."

"I took us out of inversion. If I make it to the outpost, I will let you off there." Awkwardly it added, "Otherwise I will disintegrate with you onboard."

"Uh, shuttle, I would rather you didn't do that."

"I will do my best to avoid it."

"Do you know where we are?"

"This volume of space is on the Eubian side of the Eube-Allied border surface."

So they hadn't made it to Skolian space. His fading dream of home receded again. "You said an outpost was here?"

"My files say we are within one point four light-days of Spikedown, an asteroid with a border outpost. I had hoped to bring us out there. Or where I estimate it should be now. I don't know how current my data is. My purpose is to carry cleaning supplies. As far as I know, this outpost has nothing to do with cleaning supplies. So I have almost no data on it."

Cleaning supplies. Kelric sighed. "How fast are we going?"

"About forty percent light speed."

At that rate, it would take three and a half days to reach the outpost. "Can you go faster?"

"I advise against it. My condition is fragile. I may survive the final deceleration at Spikedown, but only if I don't accelerate and decelerate any more than absolutely necessary."

He winced. "I'm sorry."

"We're not dead yet," it said with attempted cheer.

He managed a smile. "Do you have enough food to keep me alive for three and a half days?"

"My stores will last four." It paused. "For someone your size, they may only last three."

If this outpost was anything like other frontier posts he knew, they wouldn't give him squat unless he paid for it. Nor were they likely to have facilities for a blind man. If he couldn't survive on his own, tough.

Even worse, right now a border station might have refugees pouring into it, like Edgewhirl. He doubted they had facilities for dealing with such a deluge. Gods only knew what they would do with everyone. They might shoot him if he couldn't pay his landing debt.

Bolt, he thought, tired. *Will I ever see again?*

His right arm moved. Bolt didn't know.

"Human?" the shuttle said.

"Yes?" Kelric asked.

"Good luck."

He exhaled. "Thanks."

"You got a stolen shuttle," the woman from the Port Authority said. She was speaking in Eubic, the Trader equivalent of Skolian Flag. "Why should we let you land?"

Kelric rubbed his unseeing eyes. "Because if you don't, this ship will fall apart and I'll die."

"Should've thought of that before you stole it. Your ship is sending us its codes, thief. They say it's ESComm issue, SSRB."

"They wanted me to be a slave. I disagreed." Quietly he said, "Please let me land."

Although she still sounded wary, for some reason the hostility left her voice. "Can you pay for a berth?"

"Didn't the shuttle send you a credit line?"

"It's got no credit line. Just detergent."

"I'll work off the debt."

She gave a tired, bitter laugh. "You and how many others? You know how many refugees we got here? Crammed with 'em. You people keep coming in. No one can get out again. We got two hundred passengers for every berth, and can't none of them pay. Your ship is falling apart? It'd cost you more than I make in ten years to buy out on another ship. If you don't got enough to dock, I can't let you land." The edge left her voice. "I'm sorry."

Kelric laid his head back in his seat. Had he been a normal human, with normal endurance and no augmentation, he would have been long dead by now. Even he had almost reached his limit. His problems getting in and out of the lock had drastically accelerated the failure of his health. Either he would die now or he would die on Spikedown, his sight gone, his body crippled, his brain exhausted.

Cut it out, he told himself. He couldn't give up. If nothing else, he hated the thought of dying alone.

He spoke over the comm again. "Maybe I have something I can pay you." But what? He had no money or goods. He had finished the food a day ago.

"What?" She sounded skeptical.

He ran his finger over the ridge of an armband under his shirt. *Ixpar,* he thought. *I'm sorry.* Aloud he said, "I've gold. And gemstones. Real gems. Almost flawless."

"We can't eat rocks and metal. You got food?"

"No food." He raked his hand through his hair. "If you let me land, I'll sell my goods in port. Then I can pay you."

She snorted. "Isn't no one will buy what you got. You want gems? We can make thousands of 'em. This used to be a mining outpost. Asteroid is part of a planet that broke up. Chock-full of minerals. They're not worth spit. No one wants Spikedown rocks. Hell, my quarters are full of gold. Dishes. Goblets. Boxes. Worthless. Market's glutted."

"Not with what I have." Even knowing they wouldn't want it, he still tried. "My wrist guards are over a thousand years old. The armbands are almost as old. To an archaeologist, they're priceless."

She made an incredulous noise. "You think we got professors? Metal is metal. Rocks are rocks. You got food, something like that, we can trade. Or currency you can back. We'll take Highton or Allied credit vouchers." In a kinder voice she said, "I'm sorry. I really am. But we're dying down here. You people are killing us."

Gods. What else did he have? Nothing. Just himself.

Himself.

He forced out the words. "I've something you might like."

"I doubt it."

"Find out first."

"What?"

"I'm a provider."

A long silence followed his words. He wondered if he was about to be arrested for trying to bribe a port official. Or maybe *solicit* was a better word.

Then she said, "Send me a holo."

He switched to his private channel and spoke to the shuttle EI. "Send her a holo of me. Make it look good."

"Shall I change your features or physique?" it asked.

"No. She'll know as soon as she sees me if I tried to cheat her. Just add fixes I can do here. Brush my hair, get rid of wrinkles in my clothes, that sort of thing."

"Done. Image sent."

After a moment, the woman spoke again. Her voice had a different tone now, tentative and self-conscious. "Maybe we can work something out. Got a docking code for you after all." She took a breath. "I'll meet you at the gate."

The engine rumble ceased as docking clamps secured the ship. Kelric released the breath he had been holding. So. Spikedown. He had made it, at least to the port.

He pushed out of his seat and took a step. With relief, he found that his hydraulics did indeed work. He still had a limp, but he walked reasonably well. Too bad he couldn't see.

He felt his way to the back of the shuttle, moving his hands along the seats. It helped that the asteroid's gravity was only about one quarter the human standard. Without visual cues, it was hard to orient himself, though.

Just as he reached the gap between the last seat and the air lock, a deep male voice said, "Kelric?"

He froze. "Who is that?"

"Kelric?" the man repeated. "Can you hear me?"

He swung around. "Where are you?"

"From your behavior, I gather you can." The voice was still right next to him. It moved when he moved. In fact, it sounded like it came from his gauntlet.

"Are you on my comm?" Kelric asked.

"If you can hear me, think your response," the man answered.

Think my response? Why? Who is this?

"It's Bolt."

Bolt! He grinned. *How are you talking?*

"Your gauntlets have been extending bio-optic threads throughout your body. They're using your reactor to drive chemical reactions they need to grow. That's why you've been so hungry and tired. I linked up with the new network and contacted your gauntlets."

The idea of ancient gauntlets threading his body with who-knew-what startled Kelric. What would he be by the time they finished? Human? Or something else?

Human. The answer came at a level deeper than surface thought, almost subconscious. **Human and more.**

What are you? he asked.

The answer again came without words: **Yourself.**

"Kelric?" Bolt asked.

Relief washed over him. Whatever the gauntlets made him, he still had Bolt. "It's good to hear you."

"Kelric, think your answers," Bolt said. "My link is to your brain. I do also have a link to your vestibulocochlear nerves, but right now I'm using those resources in my attempts to solve the problem with your optical nerves."

What the blazes are my vesti-whatevers?

Bolt's voice had the sound of a smile. "Vestibulocochlear. The nerves that carry impulses from your ears to your brain."

Oh. He paused. *It's better this way anyway. If I walk around talking to a disembodied voice, people will think I'm crazy.*

Bolt actually laughed, a deep rumbling. Then it—he—said, "Hold up the gauntlet and put the comm next to your ear."

He raised his arm, bringing a mesh on his inner arm to his ear. *Try it now.*

"How is this?" Bolt asked in a low voice.

Perfect. Kelric smiled. *Smart computer.*

"I haven't had much to do for the past eighteen years," Bolt admitted. "I occupied myself by developing my EI."

You sound human.

"Thank you."

It intrigued him that Bolt considered it a compliment to sound human. He doubted all EIs would give that response.

"Can you see at all?" Bolt asked.

Nothing. Any luck with my optic nerve?

"Not yet. I will continue trying."

Someone is waiting for me. Kelric lowered his arm. *You better not talk too much if we're around people.*

"All right. Good luck."

Thanks.

Moving his hands in front of him, he stepped forward. His palms brushed a bulkhead, then the air-lock panel. He fumbled in the exit sequence and was rewarded by the hiss of a hatch retracting. As he stepped into the docking tube, he moved his hands around, to make sure he didn't hit anything. His fingers brushed the tube on either side.

He wished he had a robot to lead him or a sensory net linked to his biomech web. Walking along the tube, he felt unprotected. He had never realized before how much he took his sight for granted.

At the end of the tube, he cycled through the air lock and entered decon. This was easy. He just stood while the chamber went through its paces. When it finished, he went forward until he touched a wall. He felt along the curved surface to the exit. Taking a breath, he opened the hatch.

Voices assaulted his ears. People filled the area. Their moods washed over him, concentrated and agitated. Despair. Many had no tickets, yet desperately wanted a berth on an outgoing ship. Others had just arrived, refugees, exhausted, confused, and hungry. The babble of voices, languages, and emotions surged over him. Officials were calling out directions. The clamor beat against his ears.

He froze in the hatchway, caught in his darkness. Now what?

"Kelric Garlin?" a woman asked.

He knew that gravelly voice. It was the woman from the PA. She sounded different from anyone he had heard recently, with neither the too smooth tones of an Aristo nor the designed sensuality of a provider. She spoke with a unique, refreshingly natural quality. It appealed to him.

Kelric turned in her direction. "I'm Garlin."

Her appreciation flowed over him. He captivated her. His size startled her, though. She would have felt more comfortable with a man closer to her own height. She had a warm personality, far more so than she had let show during their interchange on the comm. Shy and unassuming, she would never have expected her work shift to end with her meeting such a man. She had a deep curiosity about providers, a wonder that bordered on awe.

Despite his attempt to barrier his mind, it responded to her warmth and gave it back to her, magnified by his Kyle strength. He tried to clamp a lid on his empathic reaction, but it did no good. His neurons fired, creating fields associated with his feelings; his Kyle organs magnified and modulated those fields; the fields affected her brain. With so few mental defenses, he couldn't stop his mood from flooding her. His rock-headed brain had a mind of its own, regardless of what he wanted it to do—which was, when he considered it, a bizarre thing to think.

She wasn't a psion. She had no idea what he was doing. It affected her anyway, softening her even more toward him. Having never before met a provider, she had an unrealistic idea of what it meant to be one of those rare, legendary favorites of the Aristos.

Her thoughts about herself were far less kind. She pretended she didn't care that people considered her ugly, but it bothered her far more than she let anyone know. She was nowhere near as tough as she acted. She also assumed that under normal circumstances a man like Kelric would never deign to notice her.

You're wrong, he thought. How could he help but notice that warmth? "I'm Garlin," he said.

"You look like your holo." Pleased surprise trickled from her mind. "I figured you'd cheat it."

"I wouldn't," he said.

That evoked cynicism, and also a flicker of hope she suppressed. After years on Spikedown, she trusted no one.

"So." For some reason her voice suddenly had a guarded sound. Wary. "You coming?"

"Yes." What had he done to put her off? He found the answer in her mind: she had held out her hand and he had ignored the gesture.

Awkward now, unsure where she stood, he reached out. After a pause, she took his hand. As his fingers closed around hers, some of her wariness eased. He squeezed her hand, wondering if she had any idea how much he needed that touch.

She gave a tug, trying to draw him forward. With a surge of panic, he realized he either had to admit he couldn't see or else walk blind into a strange place where he had no idea what he faced.

Taking a breath, he stepped forward. The low gravity felt like molasses. His foot drifted through the air and settled on the ground. The woman was on his right, so he moved his left hand in front of him, just slightly, trying to be discreet so she wouldn't notice.

They took more long, languid steps. Then a man said, "Name?"

The woman drew Kelric to a stop. "He's with me," she said.

"Heya, Jeejon," the man answered. "Who is this?"

Kelric turned toward his voice. Was Jeejon the woman's name, a word from another language, or part of the slang greeting "Heya"?

"Kryx, I already cleared him," she said.

Kryx? Kelric stiffened. It was a common Aristo name. And this official projected a trace of the Aristo mind. He had one somewhere in his lineage, maybe a grandparent.

"Don't worry," the man said. "I'm not going to claim rights to that collar of yours."

Kelric hid his confusion. Was Kryx talking to him? Had his alarm shown? He should have covered his collar. Not that it mattered; if the woman hadn't cleared him, the Spikedown officials would check anyway. After they traced his identity, they would return him to Tarquine. Gods only knew how the Minister had reacted when she learned her fourteen-million-credit property had up and walked off. Knowing Tarquine, though, she would recoup more than her losses, by making an insurance claim and then suing the blazes out of Taratus.

"It's all right," the woman said, her voice offering comfort. "Come on. We can go through."

Kelric was fairly certain she was talking to him. He took a step—and his foot hit a barrier. Disconcerted, he moved his hand in front of him. A counter blocked his way. Sliding his palm to the right, he found its end. Then his hand bumped the arm of the woman at his side.

"Skolia be damned," Kryx said. "He's *blind.*"

"Leave him alone," the woman said. She guided Kelric to the side. In a lower voice she said, "Through here."

From the beat of minds against his, he knew people were watching them. Acutely uncomfortable, he moved his hand in front of his body, feeling his way, while he clenched the woman's fingers in his other hand. She walked slowly, shock emanating from her mind. The last thing she had expected was for him to be blind.

His vulnerability evoked her protective instincts. His mind picked up her reaction and his neural firings slipped into resonance with hers, building the positive sensations, making her want to care for him. The more she wished to help, the more it strengthened the link and created a feedback loop. His response to her was unusually fast. He almost never had this great a resonance with anyone.

Bolt, I've got to control this empath business. He raised his arm as if to scratch his ear. *It's getting out of hand. What's wrong with me?*

Softly Bolt said, "Why should anything be wrong? You *are* an empath. So you make people like you and then you like them. Is that so terrible? You seem especially compatible with this one. You need her, Kelric. If you enjoy being with each other in the process, what is wrong with that?"

"You all right?" the woman asked.

He lowered his arm. "Yes."

After that they fell silent. Kelric had no idea what to say. He felt as if he should apologize for his misbehaving neurons.

Voices flowed around them and the crowd jostled their elbows. As far as he could tell, they were moving down a concourse. It disquieted him, walking in the dark. She took the pace slow, though, which helped. It made him feel more in control.

"Is your name Jeejon?" he asked.

"That's right." She hesitated. "You didn't say you were blind."

"You didn't ask."

"You always been this way?"

"No. Only a few days. I was hurt when I escaped."

"Well, I'll tell you, no more Aristos here." She spoke with a blend of satisfaction and disbelief, as if she still hardly believed her own words. "Allieds moved in with their dreadnoughts and ran ESComm out."

Well, saints almighty, how about that? Something had finally gone his way. The shift in boundaries wouldn't solve most of his difficulties, such as where he would get his next meal and how the hell could he take command of ISC when he was stuck on this asteroid. But it helped. He was no longer in Trader space.

"That's good to know," he said.

"I'm sorry about you being a provider. I won't hurt you. I promise."

Startled, he stopped and turned to her. Her curt manner hid depths he was just beginning to plumb, as his mind aligned with hers. He lifted his hand to her face. He missed and touched her hair instead. He found her cheek, then her lips. Bending his head, he kissed her, in thanks as much as desire, because he thought she might like it.

At first she stiffened. It was a moment before she relaxed and kissed him back, her lips softening against his. Then she pulled his head down and spoke against his ear, the sound of a laugh in her voice. "Not here. Later, yes?"

"All right." He smiled. More than his neurons were misbehaving.

They resumed their walk. Although they fell silent again, this time it had a companionable quality. He felt her surprise; she never softened this fast toward a stranger and wasn't sure why he evoked such a response. She attributed it to his beauty. He had the urge to ask her what was wrong with everyone. He was huge, with metallic skin. That didn't strike him as "beautiful." At times he wondered if people underwent some sort of selective insanity when they looked at him.

He understood, in an abstract sense, why his mother awed people. Her glorious, statuesque splendor outdid any provider. To him, her beauty lay in her mother's love rather than her appearance. Even so, he saw why she evoked such adoration. People told him he was a masculine version of her, muscular and handsome where she was curved and feminine. He didn't see it. He was just Kelric.

"Here," Jeejon said. She tugged him to the side, then waited as he reoriented on the new direction. They went several steps and stopped. He heard the creak of an old portal opening. She led him into a quiet area, then closed the portal. As they started walking again, he tried to fathom this new place. It felt enclosed.

"It's about two klicks to my quarters," Jeejon said. "We can reach it using these tunnels. Won't have to go in the spikelands."

"Spikelands?"

"Outside the port."

He stretched out his arm and brushed his fingers along the tunnel wall. "What's out there?"

"Was a domed city. Surrounded the spaceport."

"Was?"

"Nothing but gangs now. Last I heard, they were tearing down the city and burning the rubble. If you hadn't, uh . . ." She cleared her throat. "Hadn't paid your landing fees, police would've dumped you out there too."

He felt her mood in all its nuances and details. As he lost his other senses, his Kyle awareness was becoming more sensitized. She disliked seeing herself take advantage of someone whose vulnerability had forced him into this situation. The more she thought about it, the worse she felt. It had the reverse effect on him; the worse she felt about it, the more he respected her integrity.

Jeejon pulled him to a stop. Turning, he raised his hand and searched for her face. "What is it?"

"I'm sorry." She took a breath. "You can stay in my quarters until you find a place. You don't have to—to do anything . . . you don't want to do."

He bent his head and brushed his lips across hers. "I won't do anything I don't want." Then he kissed her.

Her surprise washed over him. She genuinely didn't believe he would want her, given a choice. What kind of life had she lived, that she thought such a thing? She must have been a taskmaker, one low in rank, judging from this nowhere asteroid. Given the way Traders treated such taskmakers, it was no wonder she had a poor opinion of herself.

Putting his arms around her waist, he drew her closer. She slid her hands up his back in a tentative embrace that made him suspect she had little experience with men. So he gentled his kiss. Her enjoyment suffused his mind. He gave the emotion back to her, blending it with his own desire. Yes, this was good. Maybe Bolt was right, that he should enjoy his empathic responses and quit worrying. If it made them both happy and hurt no one, what did it matter if it was a weird way for humans to interact?

As Kelric raised his head, Jeejon gave a self-conscious laugh. She took his hand. "We should get going, before someone finds us."

He smiled. "All right."

She moved forward and he went with her, through the dark. He had never considered himself a conversationalist, and now was no exception. But she was content with the silence. Small talk didn't interest her either.

Although he tried to remember the path they took, the turns blurred in his mind. They walked for about half an hour, drifting in the low gravity.

Finally she drew him to a stop. "This is it." She brushed his hand across a metal portal. "My quarters."

He was picking up even more from her now, details of memory and mood, all in greater depth than he experienced even with most psions. Although she wasn't a virgin, her few encounters had been long ago, with high-ranked taskmakers who used her for their own pleasure. As with most low-ranked slaves, Eubian law forbade her to marry. Nor did the Aristos consider her good breeding stock. She had released Kelric from his promise because the trade made her feel as if she were turning into one of the very people she resented, the Traders who had ruled her life for so long, until she had gained her treasured freedom.

Jeejon had no intrigues. No cruelty. She simply wanted to survive. Given the chance to spend the night with a provider, she had taken what was, for her, an extraordinary step. She had paid his landing fees in exchange for his time. Such a trade was unthinkable for the conditioned slaves of Eube. That she had done it anyway told him a great deal about her drive to fight conditioning that had formed her since birth, possibly even before.

With dismay, he realized she had put herself into debt for years to pay his fees. He had no way to pay her back. Incredibly, she had expected no more than one night with him, and even then she thought she had the better part of the deal. In her limited view of the universe, he was simultaneously among the Trader elite and at the bottom of their hierarchy; elite because providers lived in a luxury beyond what most taskmakers could imagine, and at the bottom because they had no power at all. They were the best that humanity had to offer the Aristos, whom she considered godlike. A slave fit for an Aristo was far too good for her.

She knew in theory what Aristos inflicted on their providers. But being incapable of brutality herself, she didn't understand. She believed the Aristo propaganda, that it elevated a provider when an Aristo transcended. She expected to repulse Kelric. She assumed her lack of perfection would offend his refined taste.

"Ah, Jeejon," he murmured. "You're so, so wrong."

"Wrong?" she asked. "About what?"

"You're better than any Aristo. You deserve the stars."

"You think so, eh?" Baffled, but pleased, she gave a laugh. "I'd be happy just with bigger quarters."

He listened as she opened the door. The portal hissed, its pitch changing as the door slid into the wall. Jeejon tugged him forward. Just inside, his hand hit a table, then a vase. He barely managed to grab the vase before it fell to the floor.

"Sorry," he muttered. Damn, he wished he could see. He was lucky to have a place to stay. What would he have done, blind, in a ruined city overrun with gangs? The more he learned about Spikedown, the worse it looked for his getting off the asteroid. And he was tired, a bone-deep fatigue that sleep no longer cured.

"It's all right," Jeejon soothed. The door hummed shut. "Don't worry about breaking anything. There's nothing worth much."

He sighed. "I just wish I could see you."

"Ah, Kelric. It's better you don't."

"Don't say that." He moved closer to her and felt her face. His fingers slid over her cheeks. Her bone structure reminded him of Corey. The planes of her face were rougher, but she had similar angular cheekbones and strong features. Where Corey had a thoroughly aristocratic nose, though, Jeejon's was crooked.

"Someone broke your nose," he said.

"Got mugged seventeen years ago. On my fortieth birthday."

"Hey. You're my age."

She snorted. "Sure."

"You are." He tapped the lines at the corners of his eyes. "Can't you tell?"

"You wear the years far, far better." Her gruff tone would have hid how much she liked him, except her mind projected it straight into his.

"How did you get mugged?" he asked.

"Went to a bar in the city. Gang jumped us. We had 'em back then too, though nowhere near as bad as now. Lot less people in Spikedown then." Pride came into her voice. "I took out three of those spikerats. Knocked 'em clear to the med shack." She rubbed her nose, her knuckles scraping Kelric's hand. "Got me the beak to prove it, eh?"

"It's beautiful."

"It's ugly as hell."

He slid his hands into her hair. Short and curly, it had the wiry texture of gray hair that had never been tattooed or treated with dyes. "Beautiful."

"Now I know you're blind."

"You're like my first wife."

She stiffened. "You're married? Didn't tell me that."

"She's dead."

Mortified sympathy replaced her tension. "I'm sorry."

Softly he said, "It's been thirty-three years."

Her relief washed over him. To cover her chagrin, she said, "Man who looks like you wouldn't marry a woman looks like me." She hesitated. "I thought you were a provider. Can't marry."

"I'm Skolian." He moved his hand over her chin, feeling its strength. It was true, she wasn't soft, young, or smooth. She didn't have classic looks or perfect features. Jeejon had her own beauty, strong and spare. He liked it, better in fact than biosculpted "perfection."

"Skolian?" She took his hands into hers. "Pirates raid your ship?"

He nodded. "I was serving on a merchanter. We went into Trader space to meet a client. There was trouble and ESComm caught us."

"Bastards. They aren't supposed to sell prisoners."

"I was the only one they sold." Dryly Kelric said, "When I protested, they suggested I 'file a complaint.'"

She brought up his hands and kissed his knuckles. "Hope you don't mind me saying this, but I can see why they wanted you."

He shook his head. "I *can't* see why everyone does."

"That's all right." She slipped her hand into his hair with a tentative motion, as if she couldn't believe she had him to herself. "It's better that way."

"What way?"

"Not important."

He picked up what she meant, anyway; she thought he was modest about his looks, which made her like him more. She did, very much, want to sleep with him. It was pleasant. She didn't want to hurt him, like an Aristo, or use him, like Zeld. For some absurd reason, she saw him as some sort of treasure.

"Jeejon, you're nuts," he said.

"Why?"

"For the things you think about me." He felt like an eavesdropper. It wasn't right that she didn't know. He tapped his temple. "Psion."

"Oh." Her unease washed over him. "Of course. I forgot. Providers feel moods."

"I like your moods."

"You do?"

"Yes."

"Can you tell what I think?"

"A little." He stroked her hair. "You think you're taking advantage of me. But you're not. I thank you for letting me stay here."

Her voice softened. "You're a nice man."

He spoke quietly. "I'm not. I've killed more people in my life than you've probably known. I used to be a Jagernaut."

"That's a high-rank position among Skolians, yes?"

"Yes."

"Ah." Sympathy flowed from her mind. She thought his claim to high rank was a fantasy he created to make his life more bearable. "I like you just the way you are."

He smiled. "Thank you. And, Jeejon."

"Yes?"

"I'm not deluded about being a Jagernaut."

She patted his cheek. "I know." Hesitating, she added, "You tired? Would you, uh, like to lie down?"

"Yes. If you'll come with me."

"Ah. Well. I could do that." Holding his hand, she drew him forward. After one step, he hit a table. As she guided him to the side, he ran into several chairs clustered around the table, then a desk. They went through a narrow archway with no door. In the room beyond, his knees bumped a bed frame. Feeling to the side, he found a metal pole that anchored the bed to both floor and ceiling.

"I know you're used to a lot better," she apologized.

"This is fine." He sat on the bed and held out his hand.

She curled her fingers around his and settled next to him, shy and self-conscious. Putting his arm around her waist, he drew her close. With his other hand he searched for her face until his fingers brushed her lips. Then he bent his head and kissed her, taking up where they had left off in the tunnel. She did remind him of Corey, and of Ixpar too. As much as those memories hurt, they also softened his feelings. Maybe that was one reason he responded so well to her. She had shades of the strength and integrity that had always attracted him in a woman. Gods help him, he had seen hints of it in Tarquine too.

She pulled back her head. "Why are you so sad?"

"Sad?" He tried to laugh. "What makes you think I'm sad?"

"The kiss. The way you look now."

Unable to answer, he pulled her close again, putting her cheek next to his so he wouldn't have to face her questions. He didn't want to talk about how much he had lost in his life.

She didn't pry. So he stretched out on the bed with her, holding her in his arms. For a while they just lay together. It was good to relax. He felt so tired after his time in the Lock. Next to him, Jeejon settled into her own quietude. She lay still, breathing deeply. Very deeply.

For crying out loud. She had gone to *sleep.* Miffed, Kelric scowled. Apparently he wasn't such a great lover after all, if he put women to sleep before he even made love to them.

Then he winced at himself. *Getting an ego, aren't you?* he thought. He turned on his back and pillowed her head against his chest. He lay with one arm around her, stroking her hair while she slept.

Jeejon stirred. What—? A man in bed with her? Someone broke in—

No. Wait. The provider. Skolia be damned, it was true. A provider lay in her bed, holding her in his arms.

Maybe "Skolia be damned" wasn't the most tactful oath here. He was Skolian, after all. And she wasn't Eubian anymore. Wasn't sure where she stood with the Allieds. Not a citizen. Allied officials gave her papers for "political asylum." Whatever that meant. They said a lot. She listened. Then she cut to the grist. Was she a slave? Answer was no. NO! Free...

Pushing up on her elbow, she treated herself to the sight of the sleeping provider. She hadn't turned off the lights when they came in her bedroom, so she had her fill of seeing him now. Lashes lay long, thick, and golden on his cheeks. Fine lines around his eyes. That surprised her. Thought Aristos always made their providers look young. His face wasn't aged, exactly, but more mature. Such a handsome man. She liked the gray in his hair...

Turning on his side, Kelric murmured, "More gray now."

She lay down next to him. "You know what I was thinking?"

"A little." He opened his eyes into darkness and shifted her in his arms. "You didn't know who I was at first. You were thinking about being an Allied citizen. Or not being one."

She made an impressed noise. "You must have a high Kyle rating."

"Taratus's people put me as ten." He felt along her body and the bed, trying to get a sense of his location. "But it's higher."

She gave a sleepy laugh. "Hey, you could be Rhon."

He knew she was humoring him. Smiling, he said, "You know, Jeejon, I'm the Imperator. You're lying here with the ruler of an interstellar empire."

"I'm dazzled."

He laughed softly. Then his smile faded. Would anyone ever know he had become Imperator? He would have liked to be a peacemaker. However, until the universe changed, ISC needed a warlord, not a mathematician. He wasn't ideally suited to the position, but he believed he could make a good Imperator, maybe better than if he had craved war for its own sake.

He had to face reality, though. His chances of leaving Spikedown were slim to none. He would try, of course. But it didn't take a Quis genius to see the patterns of his situation. It was far more likely he would die here than become any kind of leader.

Perhaps someday another Rhon psion would detect traces of him in the Lock, as he had felt Soz. He wanted history to remember Kelric Valdoria as more than a Jagernaut who vanished in battle before he accomplished anything in his life.

Still, he felt an odd contentment, even as his body prepared to shut down. He had achieved his most important goal and now he had someone he liked to share his last hours.

"Kelric?" Jeejon asked. "You look sad."

He folded his arms around her. "Hold me. Don't let me die alone."

She gave an uneasy laugh. "Don't make jokes like that. My ugly old bones don't think it's funny."

"Stop calling yourself ugly. You're beautiful." He moved his hand over her abdomen and hips, feeling her lean shape, angular rather than round, but well toned. And real. He slid his palms up her body. She had the large, softer breasts of an older woman. No angles there. Exploring her jumpsuit, he tried to open its front. "Why do so many people think they have to biosculpt themselves to so-called perfection for someone to want them?"

She touched his cheek. "Strange man. But kind."

Kelric gave up trying to open her jumpsuit and nuzzled her hair. He let his head rest next to hers on the pillow. Her mind blended with his, patient, gentle, warm. He could rest now. So tired. He was so tired . . .

"—all right?" Jeejon sounded alarmed. "What's wrong?"

"Tired," he mumbled. He would sleep a long time now.

"Oh, hell. You weren't joking." She shook him. "Come back!"

"I'm tired."

"Thirty damn years I spend alone here. Now you come. Then you die in my bed? You can't do that."

She was right. It would be unforgivably rude to die in her bed. He grinned. "I guess I'm not that sleepy."

"Saints almighty, Kelric! That wasn't funny."

"Come here." He pulled her into his arms again. "Bring me back to life."

"Ah. Well." She nestled against him, her relief almost tangible. "I can do that."

He finally found the fastener on her jumpsuit. Opening the front, he slid his hand inside. Her breasts felt even better without cloth in the way. Large, soft pillows. Very nice.

When he tried to pull the jumpsuit off her shoulders, she nudged him down on the bed. Then she took her turn, unfastening his clothes. When he started to help, she murmured, "Let me. You just enjoy."

So he lay back while she undressed him. She dropped his clothes somewhere, on the floor probably. Her pleasure in his body suffused his mind. He liked feeling her desire him. Hell, it turned him on knowing she wanted him that much.

When she started to unfasten his Triad gauntlets, he tensed. The threads they had grown into his sockets were webbed all through his body now. They were also attached to his wrist guards, which didn't come off. He didn't know if he would ever be able to remove the gauntlets.

Jeejon clicked open the clasps inside his elbow that held the gauntlets closed. Just as he was about to stop her, a *question* came into his mind: **Is she allowed this privilege?**

Kelric blinked, Privilege? What privilege? Of course it was all right for her to remove them. He just didn't think it was possible.

As soon as he formed that thought, a sense of *release* entered his mind. Unaware of his silent communion with his gauntlets, Jeejon blithely continued to undo them. Then she removed the right one. Somehow it separated cleanly from both his wrist guard and the new webs it had created in his body.

"Amazing," he murmured.

"Hmmm?" She removed his other gauntlet.

"Don't put them far away." Even without them on his arms, he felt as if they were part of him.

"I won't." She reached across him and set them on the bed. Then she kissed his chest, running her fingers through the curling hair. "You've strands of both gray and gold."

"Gold?" Was the tattoo job wearing off?

"Like metal." She played with his chest hair as she caressed him.

Her touch had the innocence that came from an utter lack of pretension or guile. She still found it hard to believe he was here with her. Sliding down her hand, she splayed her fingers across his torso. He was glad now for all the exercises he had done. It gave him a flat stomach. Vanity, he supposed. Still, it pleased him that she liked what she felt.

Then she moved her hand lower, to his erection. As she curled her fingers around him, he exhaled and closed his eyes.

When he tried to pull her into his arms, she laughed softly and pushed him back down. "Your turn now, Kelric. They always made you please them, hmmm? Not anymore. Let me do the work."

He thought of Tarquine, cool and absorbed in her own pleasure. Relaxing back, he let Jeejon explore. With her simple caresses, she was making him more crazy than all the skilled providers.

Kelric couldn't stay put for long. He had always been an active lover. Pulling her into his arms, he pressed her against the length of his body. He undressed her far more deftly than she had him, moving his hands on her body as much to arouse her as to separate her from her clothes. She had a jumpsuit much like his. In fact, it felt like what he had seen every low-level taskmaker wear. The uniform of slavery. He hoped she realized she could dress as she pleased now.

When he finished taking off her clothes, he rolled her onto her back. So they came together, bare skin to bare skin. They took their time. She made no secret of her amazement in him, both for what he considered positive attributes, such as his well-toned muscles and strong build, and negative ones, like the old combat scar on his shoulder. Her mind was wide open. She liked his imperfections. He discovered that mattered to him. After only a short time with the Aristos, he had begun to see himself as flawed because he didn't match their impossible ideals of perfection.

She liked the dusting of gray at his temples, the lines around his eyes, the maturity of his face. It didn't occur to her to think of them as flaws. She worried he would find her lacking because she had so little experience. In truth, it charmed him. Everything he wanted to try intrigued her, although he also made her shy. She thought of herself as clumsy, but she delighted him, so refreshing in her curiosity and innocent desire.

So he showed her all he knew, at first gently, then letting himself go as her passion rose with his. They made love, rested, and loved again as the hours slipped by. Spikedown continued its tumble through space. The Traders, Skolians, and Allieds continued their dance of politics and war. Here in the protective cocoon of a bunk under a blasted city, he and Jeejon ignored it all.

Finally they slept, their limbs tangled together, two aging, formerly lonely people curled under a scratchy blanket, more content than all the beautiful, perfect, ageless Traders alive.

24

Spikedown

Darkness. Kelric stood with his hands braced in the doorway of Jeejon's bedroom and stared at nothing. Her living room was in front of him. He had also found a tiny kitchen and a bath cubicle. That was it. A small place. Easy to memorize.

And dark.

He clenched the doorframe. He wanted to see, damn it. *Bolt, can't you do anything?*

"I'm working on it." Bolt was using his gauntlet comm again. When Kelric had put the gauntlets back on, they integrated seamlessly back into his biomech web.

Do you know what's wrong yet? he asked.

"Your optical nerve is damaged," Bolt said. "Threads from your enhanced optics wrapped around the nerve and cut it."

It shouldn't do that, he protested. *Those threads are engineered not to interfere with my vital organs.*

"Yes. But the entire system has degraded. Mutated nanomeds are weaving the threads around your optic nerve." Bolt sounded apologetic. "It's a mess."

Kelric grimaced. *Can you fix it?*

"It depends. If a fiber in your peripheral nerve system is only partially cut, and if the cell body and segments of its damaged myelin sheath remain continuous, it may slowly regenerate. However, injured nerves within your brain and spinal cord can't naturally regenerate."

What the blazes does that mean?

"The situation is this," Bolt explained. "If the damage is only to your optic nerve, and isn't severe, you may regain a portion of your sight. If the damage extends to your brain, it is unlikely you will see again without immediate help. The damaged neurons will develop scar tissue, if they haven't already, which makes it much more difficult to artificially spur any form of regeneration."

He wanted to hit the wall. They both knew his brain had damage. A lot. His condition had gone far beyond the danger points that had worried Tarquine's doctors, Taratus's people, Mareea Gonzales on the *Corona,* Doctor Tarjan on Edgewhirl, and all his doctors on Coba. He was paying the price now of the risks he had taken to break into the Lock and escape again. He had pushed his failing biomech web and his damaged health too far.

Bluntly he asked, *How long do I have to live?*

"I'm really not sure any useful purpose in esti—"

Bolt, answer the question.

A long silence filled the room. Then Bolt spoke quietly. "You have between one and four days."

One to four. Gods. He was almost as good as dead.

"Kelric?" Jeejon spoke from the door. "Why are you talking to yourself?"

He turned toward her. "When did you come in?" He hadn't heard the door open or close.

"Minute ago." She was walking toward him. Her footfalls sounded muffled. "How do you make your voice like that?"

"That was Bolt."

"Who?"

"Bolt. My spinal node."

"Oh." Now she was a few paces away, probably by her desk. He read her mood easily. She thought he was a bit unbalanced. It didn't bother her as long as he wasn't violent, which she assumed was impossible for a provider. If he wanted to talk to the air, that was fine. She was just glad he hadn't left after she went to work. Finding him still here, in her quarters, gave her a sense of wonder. So he had strange ideas? He was a kind man, far better than the brusque taskmaker bosses she had served as a slave and now worked for; far better than the Aristo owner she had only seen twice in her life, who looked through her as if she didn't exist; and far better than the gangs that roamed the spikelands. If Kelric was eccentric, so what? It added to his charm.

"I'm not crazy," he grumbled. He was flattered by her vision of him, for the most part. But he didn't want her to think he was a nut. "I really am a Jagernaut."

"Really?" Her voice had the sound of a smile. "A Jagernaut."

He glowered in her direction. "Yes, really." *Bolt,* he thought. *Talk to her.*

"My greetings, Jeejon," Bolt said.

"Hey!" She jumped. "How did you do that?"

He let go of the archway and felt along his gauntlet until he touched the mesh. Tapping it, he said, "This is a comm. It's how Bolt spoke to you. I lost the internal links that let him 'think' to me, but then he linked to the gauntlets." Kelric started to lose his balance and grabbed the doorframe again. "I still think to him, so that's why you hear his voice and not mine."

Gently she said, "That's interesting."

He scowled. "I may be blind, crippled, and almost dead, but I am *not* crazy."

Alarm brushed her thoughts. "Why do you keep talking like that? You aren't going to die."

His annoyance faded. "Jeejon, I'm sorry. I wasn't joking last night." Quietly he said, "If I'm lucky, I've a few days left."

"Don't say that! Why would you die?"

"I'm sick inside."

Her thoughts took on a frantic edge. "Could a nurse help? We maybe still got one in port."

A nurse. He didn't know whether to laugh or cry. "I need an ISC hospital that can treat Jagernauts, transplant or regenerate organs, perform brain surgery, rebuild biomech systems, and reseed nanomeds. At least some of those procedures will require blood transfusions. I'm a Rhon gamma humanoid with engineered alterations to my phenotype. Almost no one alive has my blood type. I'll need a transfusion from a family member or one of the secured medical banks that stores Ruby Dynasty blood. If any of those even exists anymore. Can you find me all that?"

"Kelric, maybe if you lie down—"

"Answer the question." He knew he sounded crazy, but it was too important she understand. He didn't have time to gentle his words.

She spoke softly, giving the answer he already knew. "Just to buy you passage off Spikedown would take more wealth than I could make in years."

Frustration edged his voice. "I've more wealth than everyone on this asteroid combined, a thousand times over. It does me no good if I can't touch it. Do you know what I did while you were gone? Talked to your console." He clenched the doorframe. "I couldn't find one doctor on Spikedown. Not *one.* This asteroid hasn't a single link to anywhere else. Ships won't even take messages offworld unless you pay them a ridiculous price."

"We never had offworld links even when a psiberweb existed." Tiredly she said, "The doctor left. *Everyone* who could get out is gone. Most ships that come here are in trouble. Like yours. Have to turn them away now. Allied dreadnoughts patrol the region, but they almost never land here. We got a few traders in dock, but pretty soon we'll have to turn them away too. The port is falling apart and we got no resources to fix it." In an aching voice she added, "I'm sorry. I checked every ship today trying to find you passage. There's nothing."

"I'm sorry too." He swallowed. "But thank you for trying."

She came over and laid her hand on his arm. "Would you like to lie down? You look tired."

"I want to live, damn it." He let go of the doorframe, then lost his balance and tripped. Flailing for a handhold, he stumbled into the living room and hit the table. As he hung on to it, vertigo swept over him.

"That's the other thing," he muttered. "My blasted vesti-whatever is going. Pretty soon I'll be deaf and unable to balance."

She offered her arm. "I'll help you back to bed."

"I don't want to go to bed. I want to go—" Where? "To an ISC base."

"Can't do that," she said in a matter-of-fact voice.

"A big ISC base."

"We only got Eubian and Allied ships in port. Doubt you'll find anyone going into Skolian space."

"I can't go to the Allieds." What, then, *could* he do? "We can go to an Allied starport that has Skolian flights. From there we'll find passage to a Skolian world with a central ISC base."

"The closest Skolian outposts are small," Jeejon said. It was hard to tell whether she was humoring him or giving serious answers. Her mind suggested a bit of both. "They won't have ships cleared for any ISC base, let alone a central one."

She was right, of course. Getting clearance for what he needed would take longer than he had to live. If he convinced ISC he might possibly be who he claimed, it would expedite matters, but he still might walk into an assassination. And Naaj Majda was in charge. Although he knew her well as an officer, on a personal level she had always been a cipher. She might not want a long dead heir coming back as Imperator, particularly given he could also claim substantial Majda assets.

What if he went to the Allieds? They had even less reason to believe his story. If he did convince them, they would take him into custody. A major Allied medical facility could help him, but they didn't have the know-how to treat Jagernauts. They would have to bring in biomech experts, which only ISC could provide. It would all take time, energy, and political maneuvers.

But did an advantage exist in going to the Allieds? If he was in their custody, it would protect him from assassination. In fact, they would do their utmost to keep him away from ISC, so he couldn't work at rebuilding the Skolian forces. With ISC, he had one chance: if he approached the right people, in time, he lived; if he guessed wrong, he died. With the Allieds he had more time to gather strength, to plan for the day when his family escaped and once again rose to power.

Of course, that was exactly what the Allieds wanted to avoid. For all he knew, they might assassinate him themselves. They certainly wouldn't be overjoyed if he showed up. From what he had seen, though, they engaged in far fewer intrigues than Skolians, who in turn tolerated far fewer than the Traders. He had long suspected that the Allieds had a hard time comprehending the full threat posed by the Aristos because they simply couldn't conceive of a people that odious.

Sometimes he thought this *niceness* of the Allieds made them weak. Other times he wondered if they had achieved a higher state of civilization than Skolia or Eube. Then again, they might turn the galaxy into one big shopping mall, which hardly seemed a heightened state of anything. He supposed it was better than interstellar wars that slagged empires, though.

What to do? He had to choose right the first time: he wouldn't live long enough to make a second try.

What finally tilted the balance was his memory of his father's words: *Come home to us, my son.*

He turned toward Jeejon. "Is there an Allied representative on Spikedown?"

"Major Montgomery," she said.

"Who is she?"

"He. Some kind of Earth army officer. Allieds set him up here after they kicked out ESComm."

"Good," Kelric said. "Let's go visit Montgomery."

"A lot of people wish to see him, ma'am," the lieutenant said. She spoke Eubic with an accent. "There aren't enough hours to hold that many appointments."

Jeejon exhaled. Kelric shifted in his chair, aware of her sitting next to him and the lieutenant at the desk in front of them. They were in an enclosed place, an office, he assumed. He felt the lieutenant's weariness. She comprised the major's entire staff.

"I'm sorry." Jeejon sounded uncertain. "We don't want to make any trouble."

He could tell Jeejon never dealt with authority figures, other than to follow their directions. It astonished him that she was making herself speak up. She had been taught from birth never to argue, question, disobey, or push. It made him appreciate her support all the more. But he knew the lieutenant was about to put her off. It wasn't hard to guess what would happen then: Jeejon would struggle to hold her ground, the lieutenant would get impatient, and they would soon be out the door.

Kelric spoke. Instead of Eubic, he used Highton, putting a cultured snap into his voice. "Lieutenant, we must see the major as soon as possible."

Startled, she shifted her focus to him. Her thoughts brushed his mind: she wondered where Jeejon had found herself a man like Kelric. It irritated him. Why didn't anyone wonder how he had found a woman like Jeejon? It was just as valid a question.

The lieutenant answered in Highton. "He's not on Spikedown right now, sir." She spoke the language reasonably well, though with a heavier accent than Eubic. She wasn't sure what to make of him. Obviously he wasn't an Aristo. He wore a gold slave collar. A provider, then. He didn't have a provider's diffidence, however. "Are you Skolian, Mr. . . . ?" She let the sentence hang, waiting for a name.

He knew if he claimed his Ruby Dynasty heritage, she would throw them out of her office for wasting her time. So he just said, "Valdoria. And yes, I'm Skolian." He switched languages. "Do you speak Iotic? I'm more comfortable with it."

The lieutenant paused. From her mind, he picked up that she was accessing a translator. At first he thought she had a node in her spine. Then he heard the tap of fingers on a panel and realized she was using a desk console.

"Iotic." She whistled. "You've an impressive linguistic background, Mr. Valdoria. I thought no one spoke that anymore." She tapped some more. "It says here only the upper Skolian noble Houses use Iotic."

"Yes," he said.

Jeejon stiffened. She had understood enough to fear he was going to tell another wacko story and ruin their chances of seeing the major.

Jeejon, I'm all right, he thought, focusing on her. He wasn't sure if she received his words or only an impression, but she held back whatever she had been about to say.

"Are you claiming to be Skolian nobility?" the lieutenant asked. Although she didn't believe him, his command of both Highton and Iotic kept her from dismissing him out of hand.

"Through marriage," Kelric said. "The House of Majda." He still used Iotic: not only did it give him advantage, it also supported his claim better than any argument he might make. He had no accent in Iotic, a fact her console would note if it had a worthwhile translator. His facility with the language wasn't proof of his link to the Houses; he could have had a node implanted that helped him speak perfect Iotic. But if he could afford the exorbitant cost of such a selective upgrade, that at least implied he came from wealth and could eventually pay for his offworld passage.

"You're wearing a provider's collar," she said in Iotic, her words slow enough to suggest she was using her console to translate. It didn't surprise him that she spoke Highton better; the army would have chosen her for this post according to her expertise in Eubian culture.

"My ship was attacked by Traders," he said. "I was taken prisoner."

"I'm sorry." She had the wary regard of someone who thought she might be hearing a story, but wasn't sure. In a courteous voice she said, "Sir, do you mind if we speak Eubic? I'm afraid my Iotic is terrible."

"That's fine," he said in Eubic. Without his sight, he was even more attuned to emotions. Although it was true she had trouble with Iotic, she also wanted to switch languages out of simple courtesy, so Jeejon could understand them. He had no objection: he had already made his point.

More taps came from her console. "I can give you an appointment with Major Montgomery at third shift, sixteen hundred hours." She stopped, momentarily disoriented. She usually thought in terms of days, but that made no sense on an asteroid tumbling through space. A memory came to her, one vivid enough for him to catch. In her briefing about Spikedown, she learned that this asteroid had been part of a barren planet. An ESComm training exercise had torn the planet out of its orbit and sent its shattered remains hurtling into space. The lengths ESComm went to in their drills didn't surprise Kelric, but it had stunned the Allieds.

She mentally shook herself. "In Spikedown time, that's one hundred twenty-five hours from now. Shall I put your names in for that slot?"

"No!" Jeejon protested. "Kelric might be dead by then."

"Dead?" The lieutenant shifted her focus to him. "Does she mean you, Mr. Valdoria?"

"I've a medical condition that can't be treated here," he said. "If I don't get help, I'll die within the next few days."

A long silence came from the lieutenant. She wasn't sure what to believe. She could see his exhaustion. He looked drained. But dying? Was it a play for sympathy? Had he created the Majda story in the mistaken belief it would get him off Spikedown without a ticket? Desperation drove people to far worse than telling stories. But what if he told the truth?

"We have a doctor who can look at you," she said. "He's an excellent medic. He'll be coming into port on the *Explorer* in forty-three hours."

"That's too long," Jeejon said. "Kelric might not have that much time."

The lieutenant spoke gently. "Ma'am, we have thousands of cases with just as compelling circumstances. Two Trader star systems in this region recently become Allied territory. Both have populated planets. Also four space stations, including one with over a thousand people. Not to mention outposts like this. For all that, we've only limited personnel and equipment to deal with protection, assimilation, and refugees. Myself and Major Montgomery are the entire staff for this and two other outposts combined. Do you have any idea what that means?"

In a subdued voice Jeejon said, "No, ma'am."

"I wish I could help everyone." Frustration made her voice more curt than she intended. "It's just not possible." Her attention shifted to Kelric. "I can promise you will see the doctor. Tell me what you need and I'll have him notified when the *Explorer* docks."

Kelric pulled back his sleeve, revealing his gauntlets. "I'm a Jagernaut. My biomech web is failing."

"A Jagernaut?" Irritation snapped in her voice. "Mr. Valdoria, half the gangs out in the spikelands wear gauntlets like that. I'm sure they would all like to be Jagernauts."

"What would you consider proof?" he asked.

"Identification."

"ID?" He heard the sarcasm in his voice. "I've been a Trader slave, Lieutenant."

She exhaled, her irritation fading. "If you were a provider, that does mean you're a psion," she admitted.

"That's right!" Jeejon said. "A strong one."

Kelric smiled, startled that she would jump to his defense even when she thought he was crazy.

"Do you have psiphon sockets?" the lieutenant asked.

"My neck, wrist, and ankle sockets are covered. I can show you the one in my lower back." It meant he would have to take off his jumpsuit.

Embarrassment flooded her mind. Awkwardly she said, "That won't be necessary." She came to a decision. "I'll talk to the *Explorer*'s captain. I can't make any promises. We've already scheduled too many passengers. But maybe they can manage one extra. If we do, they'll take you to Lockman Army Base after the doctor finishes his rounds of the outposts. From Lockman you can arrange passage to a more central location. In the meantime, I'll need your retinal scan and samples of your DNA, to see if we can verify your ID."

Kelric swallowed. He didn't know if he would survive long enough to reach the army base. "Is there any way to get me a berth on a ship leaving sooner?"

Softly Jeejon said, "Ma'am, he might not live forty-three hours."

"We only have civilian ships in port right now." In a flat voice the lieutenant added, "To get you an unpaid berth, I would have to commandeer the ship."

"Can you do that?" Jeejon asked.

She made an incredulous sound. "With what troops to back it up? We're barely hanging on as it is. I've trouble keeping enough police here to maintain order in the port. We gave up on the spikelands. If things get much worse, the major and I will be pulled out as well. Besides, if I tried to commandeer ships for everyone who claimed he was important, I'd have daily riots on my hands. Hell, we already *have* daily riots." She blew out a gust of air. "If you can arrange a paid ticket on a ship that leaves sooner, we'll help you board. That's all I can promise."

Kelric felt what her anger hid. She ached with frustration over her inability to help people. She was exhausted from trying to carry an impossible workload and troubled by what she had learned here about the Traders. He and Jeejon had pushed her as far as she could go.

In the end, they arranged for him to see the doctor and agreed to check with the lieutenant when the *Explorer* docked.

He just hoped he would be alive then.

Jeejon and Kelric strolled along one of the port's quieter concourses. He kept his hand on her arm and let her choose the path. Since leaving the lieutenant's office, they had walked aimlessly, with no destination.

"I don't think she believed us," Jeejon said.

"She's not sure, though," he said. "At least she's willing to help."

"You're good at talking to people like that." She drew him to the side, into an area with a more isolated feel. The voices on the concourse faded. "Come on."

Intrigued, he said, "Where are we going?"

She guided him to a staircase. As they climbed, she said, "There's an observation deck. Nice one. Looks out at space."

"I can't see space."

She spoke gently. "I'll tell you how it looks. And we'll have privacy."

At the top of the stairs, she took him across an open area.Then she stopped and set his hands on a rail at chest height. Reaching forward, he touched a smooth expanse of dichromesh glass. Beyond that glass, vistas of space were surely glittering in their cold beauty.

Pulling Jeejon close, he put his arm around her shoulders. Her head only came to his chest. Warmth flowed from her mind. Since he had lost his sight, his Kyle senses had become so sensitized that he felt her moods almost as much as his own. Or maybe it was that he could relax with her, as if they had known each other for years. He wished he had met her sooner, when he was in better shape to offer a relationship. Then again, such a meeting may have done no good. Back then, politics, heredity, and duty constrained his existence. Ironically, he had more freedom now than ever before in his life.

"Tell me how it looks out there," he said.

She sighed. "It's right good. Stark beauty, if you know what I mean."

"Yes. I do."

"You can see the asteroid. Spikelands is behind us, across the port. Nothing here but rock and craters. Horizon is close. Real close. We go out there, we could sail off the cliffs like flying."

He grinned. "Without air?"

Jeejon laughed. "We'll breathe space." She put her arms around his waist. "You can see forever stars."

"Forever stars?"

"They go on forever. Trillions of 'em. Gold, blue, red, orange, white."

He could imagine them in his mind, the glorious radiance of a trillion stars shedding their gem-light on Spikedown.

"Kelric?"

"Hmmm?"

"Tell me a story," she murmured. "One to make sadness go away."

"Ah, Jeejon." He rubbed his cheek on the top of her head. He didn't know any stories. So he told her about his recent life, pretending it was a fable. He changed his name, calling himself Rikson, a mythical bumbling prince for her to chuckle over.

Except she didn't laugh. When he finished, she was silent. Her mood spread like a deep, still pool with an unreadable surface. When he stroked his finger across her face, he found her cheeks wet.

Mortified, he said, "What's wrong? What did I say?"

She nuzzled her head against his chest. "They're good tears. It was a fine story. Very heroic. I always cry when people tell good stories."

He gave an incredulous snort. "Heroic? The hero was an idiot."

"Why do you say that?" She sighed. "I've always liked folk tales like that. A valiant and intrepid prince takes on the entire Trader Empire. And *wins.* It is a very fine story, Kelric. You mustn't call the hero an idiot."

He couldn't believe it. Valiant prince indeed. She had been stuck on Spikedown too long.

For some absurd reason moisture gathered in his eye. A tear ran down his cheek. Fortunately she was looking out at space, so she didn't see.

They stood arm in arm, watching the starscape he couldn't see. It didn't matter. He would savor the forever stars through her appreciation of their beauty, and because of the gift she gave him just by being herself.

25

The Last Day

Jeejon helped him into the bedroom. It was a relief to lie on her bed. He stretched out on his back, wondering what his last hours would be like. It could have been a lot worse. He could have been alone.

The bed creaked as she sat next to him. "Are you comfortable?"

"Yes." He was too tired to say more. The trips to the army office and observation deck had taken the last of his energy. He reached for her hand. When she folded her fingers around his, he said, "I'm glad you're here."

"Kelric—" Her voice caught. "Tell me you'll make it."

"Of course I will." He managed a smile. "I'm a stubborn old mule." He felt so tired, though. It would be good to sleep.

"You can stay here as long as . . . as you need."

Her voice had a sound of tears. Reaching up, he wiped the moisture off her cheek. "Don't cry."

"I should tell you . . ." She ran her fingers over the ridges made by the armbands he wore under his jumpsuit, as he had done since he reclaimed them from Tarquine.

"Tell me what?" he asked.

"I went to the port after my last shift. Tried to buy you passage offworld with your armbands. No one wanted gold. It's worthless."

He could tell she feared he would be angry she had offered his bands. He squeezed her hand. "Thank you for trying."

She sighed. "It's frustrating. My living room is packed full of those metals and I can't do anything. Gold, silver, bronze, platinum, copper—all worthless."

Kelric froze. "What did you say?"

"My sorry. I don't mean to dwell on it." She took a breath. "Are you hungry? I can make dinner."

He hardly heard her. Pulling himself into a sitting position, he said, "You have platinum in your living room?"

"Everything there is metal. Can't get wood here. One tree's worth more than all them platters and dishes I got."

He took hold of her arms. "Platinum? *Platinum?*"

Her puzzlement washed over him. "The vase you knocked over last night is platinum. Got two others like it. Fifteen years ago there was a glut and people were dumping platinum." Bitterly she said, "I thought someday it'd be worth something. So I stocked up, dolt that I am. You see all the good it did me."

"Jeejon!" He wanted to laugh. Shout. "You were right!"

"Right?"

"Do you know whose provider I was? Tarquine Iquar. The Highton Finance Minister." He grinned. "All they talked about was *platinum.* Eube has a shortage, a bad one, but they're trying to hide it, to keep down prices. Those vases of yours are worth a fortune. More than enough to buy passage off this spikeball."

"No. It can't be." She hesitated. "Do you mean it?"

"I mean it."

"But—no, I can't believe it." Hope flushed her voice. "A fortune? Are you sure?"

Laughing, he said, "I'm sure." His smile faded. "If they're really platinum."

"Solid." Her mood blended disbelief and hope. Given what was at stake, literally his life, she feared to believe him. "Do you think? Maybe it could work?"

Kelric struggled with his own hope. He had so little time and they had so far to go. "We have to try."

"If I can sell them, what ticket do I buy for you?"

He took both her hands in his. "Not me. Us."

"You want me to come with you?"

"Yes." He wished he could see her face. "Very much." Awkwardly he added, "If you would like to."

She made a soft noise. "Yes. I would." Then she straightened up. "But to where? Surely not Eube."

He had no time to be tentative in his approach. They had to go all the way. "To the Allieds, Jeejon." He squeezed her hands. "We're going to Earth."

Shouts beat against Kelric's ears in waves of desperation. They had an eerie muffled sound, as if they came through water. Words echoed and faded.

He walked along the main concourse with Jeejon, holding her arm, trying to fight his sense of falling. His limp had grown worse and their drifting steps heightened his vertigo.

The noise grew louder. Now he could distinguish voices in the rumble. Gripping Jeejon's arm, he slowed down. "What is it?"

"People outside the boarding gate for our flight." She swallowed. "We got to go through them."

"Why are they at the gate?"

"They want off Spikedown. Threatening to storm the ship." She put her other hand on his, where it lay on her arm. "Happens all the time. That's why we got riot squads."

"Will they let us through?"

"The lieutenant said yes. Gave the police our tickets..." Her voice faded.

"Jeejon? I can't hear you."

"Is this better?"

Relief washed over him. She still sounded muffled, but he could make out words. "Yes."

"My sorry, Kelric. I turned my head while I was talking. Where did you lose the words?"

"Something about our tickets."

"The official checking this flight has 'em in his computer." She sighed. "We just got tickets. I'm not good at bargaining. Even after selling all three vases, I barely had anything left over."

He squeezed her arm. "You did fine." It astounded him that she had gone on her own, while he slept, and bought them passage, even with a few funds left to spare. He doubted he could have done much better. She had wanted him to rest, to conserve his last resources. And she was right. They were racing a deadline, with his life in the balance.

"We won't have much left when we reach Earth," she said. "You sure you want to go to this Scandinavia place?"

"My parents are there."

If she answered, he didn't hear. The noise from the gate was swelling as they approached. He could decipher only a few words from the crowd, people demanding, pleading, cajoling for passage on the ship. Other voices, police, he thought, were telling them to disperse.

Jeejon's steps slowed. She guided him to the right. Minds pressed in on him. Too many people. So close. He and Jeejon were on the outskirts of a ragged throng.

Jeejon was speaking, but he had trouble catching her words. Then he heard her say, "Let us pass."

His arm rubbed someone. Another person jostled him from behind. People moved all around them, flooding his senses with distress and anger. More people blocked their way. Someone at his side shouted something about having credit from an obscure bank. Someone else shoved past Kelric. Another person tried to follow. Unable to keep his balance, Kelric stumbled to the side and almost knocked over Jeejon.

"—let us through!" Jeejon's voice rose, adding to the noise. She slid her arm around his waist and he leaned on her, regaining his balance before he toppled like a giant tree into the throng.

They managed another step forward. Then people blocked their way. The crowd surged, its agitation increasing as the shuttle's departure time neared. Bodies penned him on all sides, jostling him back and forth as the crowd churned. Voices echoed in his ears. The edge of hysteria in the mob threatened to erupt. With a growing dismay, Kelric realized he and Jeejon might not make the flight.

"Let us through!" Jeejon shouted.

"No. Not you!" Someone shoved her, tearing her away from Kelric.

"Jeejon!" He grabbed for her, but his hands closed on empty air. Without her support, he swayed, his equilibrium eroding. People kept pushing him, their voices a cacophony of noise. He put his gauntleted forearms to his head, pressing against his ears to block out the echoing shouts. Without his hands for balance, he lurched to the side and nearly fell. Had to *get out*—

"Combat mode toggled," Bolt said against his ear.

Kelric lashed out with his arm. His hydraulics took control, toggled by library routines in Bolt designed for hand-to-hand combat. He kicked his leg up to the side, high in the air. At the same time, he punched out with one hand, *fast,* while he used the other to protect his face. Both his foot and his fist connected with solid flesh and he felt rather than heard the gasps.

Losing his balance, he spun in what felt like slow motion. In the low gravity, his feet easily left the ground. Yet compared to everyone else, he was moving fast, his hydraulics boosted to enhanced speed. His body had reverted to its engineered purpose: fighting.

As he landed, he struck out again, even as he swayed for balance. His fist hit flesh. His heel impacted a body. His kick lifted the person and they sailed off his foot, undoubtedly arching through the air in a slow trajectory. He spun around, lashing out with one arm while he kept the other in front of his face, kicking his leg in a dance of deadly grace. It was why he operated so well in free fall: he had trained in a martial art so sophisticated it was as much an art form as a method of self-defense.

As if from a far distance he heard screams. The smell of singed hair and burnt skin assaulted his nose. A crackling surrounded him, like lightning.

Finally catching his balance, he came to a stop, his feet planted wide, his hands held at his sides. He was alone now, without even one person touching him. A loud snapping cracked around him, as if his body were making electricity. Breathing deeply, he stood poised, ready to fight again.

The crackling faded. The crowd had gone utterly silent.

"God," someone finally said. Others spoke then too, their voices too low for him to hear.

"Leave him alone," Jeejon said.

Someone put a hand on his arm and Kelric reflexively punched out with his fist. He meant to hit the person in the stomach. Had he been able to see, he would have broken ribs. His foe was smaller than he had expected, though, and he caught him—her?—on the shoulder instead, knocking her away from him.

"Kelric." Her voice was calming. Soothing. No hostility. No threat? "It's me. Jeejon."

He took a breath. *Bolt, toggle me out of combat mode.*

Jeejon spoke again. "I'm going to give you my arm. You won't hit me again, will you?"

He exhaled. "No."

Her fingers touched his elbow. She took his hand and carefully laid his palm on her arm, giving him an anchor. Then she spoke to the crowd, raising her voice. "He's a Jagernaut. He could have killed any of you. Don't push him. He can't see. If you startle him, he'll fight again. You might not be as lucky next time."

Although Kelric knew she was guessing, making it up as she went along, she had hit the truth.

Another voice spoke, giving directions, it sounded like. Jeejon said, "Yes, sir," and drew Kelric forward.

No one touched them. No one spoke loud enough for him to hear more than a muted murmur. He wasn't even sure the murmur was real, rather than an effect of his damaged hearing.

They walked a few steps. Then Jeejon stopped him. A man said, "Names?"

"Jeejon and Kelric Garlin," she said.

The man paused. "I don't have you listed here."

"I already paid for the tickets," Jeejon said. "Our names got to be there. Major Montgomery's office verified it."

"I'm sorry." Tension edged the man's voice. "I can't let you through. You'll have to step back."

"No !" Jeejon cried. "I *paid.* It's all set up."

Kelric heard a gun slide out of its holster. "Step back," the man repeated. *"Now."*

"Wait," Kelric said. What name had he given the lieutenant? "Try Valdoria."

Another pause. Then the man exhaled. "Jeejon and Kelric Valdoria. We have it." A rustling came from his direction, as if he were gesturing with his arm. "Stand here for the retinal scan."

Wary relief trickled from Jeejon. She tugged Kelric to the side. A retinal scanner clicked, followed by a mechanical voice. "Verified."

"You're cleared to pass," the man said.

Kelric felt the officer's tension, even the ache in his hand where he was gripping his pulse revolver. Nor was it only this gate official. Everyone around them was watching Kelric as if he were some wild, beautiful animal that might go berserk again if anyone made the wrong move.

Jeejon nudged him forward. "Boarding is over here." She guided him to the right.

After they took several steps, the quality of the space around them changed. "Where are we?" he asked.

"Decon." A moment later she asked, "Kelric? Can you hear me?"

"What? Yes. Did you say something?"

"Decon is finished." She drew him forward. "Step up—yes, right here."

Putting out his hand, he felt the edge of a hatchway. "Is this the docking tube?"

"Yes." She led him forward, walking slowly so he could keep his balance. Her tension stretched all around him, interwoven with his own. He couldn't relax until they were on the shuttle, which would take them to the Allied ship in orbit around the asteroid.

They stepped through another hatchway. Another step and his hands brushed the back of a seat.

Softly Jeejon said, "Here." She guided him into a seat.

He felt other passengers watching them. This shuttle apparently followed a design favored by Allied commercial ships, with seats arranged around the perimeter of the cabin, facing inward on a table so people could socialize if they wished. Trader and Skolian shuttles were less friendly, with rows of seats facing forward.

After he sat down, Jeejon tried to fasten his safety webbing. He pushed her hands away. "I can do it," he growled. He wasn't an invalid yet.

She withdrew. Then her voice came from the seat next to him. "We made it."

Kelric exhaled, his tension finally easing. In a low voice, to keep their conversation private, he said, "Did I hurt anyone?"

"Only some bruises. Singed hair and clothes too."

"Singed? How?"

"Your gauntlets were jumping arcs of electricity." She sounded disconcerted. "It was wild. Looked like you were some avenging god with lightning. Scared the blazes out of those people trying to trample you."

He rubbed his hand along the gauntlet. "Being Imperator has advantages I didn't know about."

Her voice gentled. "If you want me to call you that, I will. Whatever you like."

He bent his head and spoke by her ear. "I'm not crazy."

"You're..."

After waiting for her to finish, he said, "Jeejon?"

Acceleration pushed him back in his seat. They were taking off, and he hadn't even heard the engines start.

"—hear me!" Her voice was right in his ear now.

"Ah, don't." He pulled his head away. "That's too loud."

"Is this better?" she asked.

"Yes." He touched her hair, orienting himself. They were seated together with their heads tilted toward each other. "What were you saying?"

"You're turning gold. I wasn't sure earlier, but it's easier to see in this light."

"You mean my skin?"

"Skin. Eyes. Hair. Got a lot of gray in your hair too."

He smiled. "It's Tarquine's chemical cocktails."

"Cocktails?"

"I bought a genetic tattoo to hide my coloring. Tarquine had it reversed." He regretted having to give up the medical cycles in his body. They might have lengthened the time he had left now. "Jeejon, if I don't survive this trip—"

"Don't!" She closed her hand around his arm. "You'll make it."

He put his hand over hers. "Listen, please. We both know I might not. If I don't, you have to promise me something. Even if you think it's crazy."

"What is it?"

"My parents are in custody at the Allied United Centre north of Stockholm in Sweden. Go to them. Tell them what happened and how they can recover my body. My mother's name is Roca Skolia. My father is Eldrinson Valdoria. You must tell them about me."

"Skolia? Valdoria? You mean Ruby Dynasty?"

"Yes."

With great gentleness she said, "Whatever you like."

He sighed. "I'm not crazy."

She patted his arm. "You're a good man. That's what matters."

"Promise you will do this for me, even if you're certain no one will believe you."

She pressed her lips against his cheek. "I'll do it."

He felt the truth of her answer. She would do it even though she thought his mind had cracked. Her loyalty went all the way. No conditions. Stunned, he realized she would have faced down Aristos for him if necessary. He wondered if the Traders had any idea what a gem they had with Jeejon. He doubted it. Idiots, to waste her on Spikedown. No matter. Their loss was his gain.

With a grin, he tapped his cheek where she had put her lips. "Nice kiss."

Her laugh was so soft, he felt more than heard it. "Are you angling for another one?" she asked.

"Could be." He brushed his lips over her hair.

"Eh. Behave yourself. What will people think, us two oldsters necking here?"

He smiled against her soft curls. "They will envy me."

She snorted, but he could tell she was pleased. So was he.

A comforting sense of release settled over him. Even if he didn't make it to his family, they would know what happened. The record of all he had done was in his biomech web. Bolt would survive.

With his fingers curled around Jeejon's hand, he closed his eyes, knowing he could finally rest.

26

Green Hills

Silence.

It encompassed the world. Kelric turned slowly in a circle, trying to keep his balance. The silence and darkness that had become his life enveloped him.

He stopped turning. "Jeejon?" His mouth formed the word, but he heard nothing. He was fairly sure he hadn't whispered or shouted, but as to the exact tone, he had no idea.

She had left several hours ago. Too long. How would he know when she returned? He had barely heard her when she told him she was going out. As soon as he was alone, he turned on the holovid to its loudest setting. It was like a whisper. He turned it off, afraid of disturbing the hotel's other patrons.

He had refused Jeejon's help this morning and waited until she left before he dressed. He easily found his clothes on the armchair. He never did locate his boots, though, despite a search of the room. Maybe Jeejon had put them on a shelf he didn't know about.

Was she all right? Where was she?

He knew she thought he had gone nuts, insisting they use most of their remaining funds to buy airfare from Sydney, Australia, where they had landed, to Sweden. They had converted their last few Trader credits to Swedish kronor at the Stockholm starport. It left them enough to pay for a day at this hotel.

Her loyalty stunned him. She believed he would die here and

wanted to ease his last hours. She had no idea what she would do after his death. She would be alone on a world where she knew none of the languages. She had no permission to stay after her tourist visa expired, no funds to buy a ticket for anywhere else, and no idea how to deal with the culture. Simply walking under an open sky left her numb with shock. She struggled with Earth's heavy gravity. On Spikedown she had exercised regularly and lifted weights, as required by her owners to maintain her "prime operating condition." But it would take more than regular exercise to make her comfortable here.

Jeejon had been born a slave. Bred to it. She had never questioned authority nor turned from her duty. Yet, incredibly, she had come with him. Despite all the conditioning, breeding, brainwashing, coercion, genetics, and manipulation, the Aristos had failed to mold her into a machine. Given a chance for freedom, she had jumped at it. She made a dramatic contrast to the silver provider who hadn't even understood his offer of freedom.

What caused such differences in people? He didn't know. He was just glad she had come. So odd, to find so bright a gem at such a low point of his life. Except he didn't feel low. He ought to be devastated by his condition. But he felt oddly content. Free.

He just hoped Jeejon was all right. They had arrived in Stockholm this morning, though apparently at this time of year, this far north, it was still dark well into the "day." As soon as she came back, they would go even farther north, to the Allied United Centre. He hoped.

During the twenty-second century, Earth had developed a world government. Born of the United Nations, the government established the Allied United Centres throughout the world, huge complexes in some of Earth's most beautiful regions. Jointly supported by the political, military, academic, industrial, and financial communities of the world's nations, which still existed, the Centres were dedicated to studying the ramifications of combining Earth's many diverse cultures and governments under one umbrella. Given the military and political aspects of the work, admittance to an AUE complex required a high-level security clearance.

It didn't surprise Kelric that his parents were in custody here. Although Sweden's AUC was associated with Stockholm, its was located farther north, in countryside where no one lived now except Centre employees. Deep within the forested AUC, his parents would have the freedom to live on open land while being kept under guard.

A nudge pushed his mind. Kelric stiffened. Then he drew in a breath, calming his adrenaline surge before Bolt took the notion to throw him into combat mode. Reaching out with his mind, he caught the gentle brush of Jeejon's thoughts. He smelled her too, a pleasing fragrance from the soap they had used earlier when they took a bath together. Remembering the bath, he smiled.

"You can come over," he said. "I won't attack."

He stayed still, unsure which way to face. A hand settled on his arm. Even expecting her to touch him, he still almost struck out in reflex. He laid his hand on hers, curling his fingers around her hand. Leaning toward the bed, he searched with his other hand until his palm brushed the quilt. Then he drew her down onto the mattress.

They lay together, holding each other. She squeezed his arm and her breath tickled his ear. He gave a wan smile. "As much as I like it when you blow in my ear, I'm afraid I can't hear anything."

She stroked his hair, her hand trembling. He wished she were a psion. With his family, he could pick up verbal thoughts. Jeejon's thoughts came through as words only if they were unusually vivid in her mind, spurred by surprise, shock, or joy.

"Ah, well," he whispered. "Hearing isn't so important." Touching her face, he brushed tears from her cheek. "Don't cry. Please don't cry."

She hugged him, burying her head against his shoulder. He worked the covers down under their bodies and then pulled the sheets and quilt over them both. It made him feel closer to her, a connection he needed now, as he lost his other links to the world. He smelled her fragrance, felt her arms, knew her moods. Her mind suffused his with the warmth he had come to know so well these past few days.

For a while he simply absorbed her presence. It relieved him to have her back. A few hours alone, in a strange city, on a strange world, in the silent dark, had been enough.

"Don't go out again without me," he said. She nodded, her head on his shoulder, her arm across his chest.

"Did you find out about the visitors' center?" he asked.

She nodded again. Sliding up along his body, she brought her lips to his ear. Again her breath tickled the sensitive ridges of his ear. It felt good, but he had no idea whether she was trying to talk to him or initiate love-play. When they were close like this, he always felt her sensual haze of desire. Right now, though, that haze was distant.

Her breath stopped. She paused, then slid back into his arms.

"If you just told me something," he said, "nod your head."

Jeejon nodded.

"I didn't hear." Gods. He really was deaf. "We need a code."

Again she nodded.

"How about this?" he suggested. "Use your thumb. One tap means yes. Two means no, three means you don't know, and four means you can't answer just using taps."

Jeejon tapped her thumb once against his chest.

"Did you find out about the AUC?"

She tapped once. Yes.

"Does it have an information office?"

One tap. Yes.

"Can we go today?"

Two taps. No.

"Why not?" When she tapped four times, he asked, "Is it because we don't have enough money?"

After a pause, she tapped twice. No.

He wondered about the pause. "We do have enough money?"

Another pause, followed by one tap. Yes.

Kelric shook his head. Their tap code wasn't enough. "Do you know any sign language?"

Two taps. No.

"We need to make up some."

One tap. Yes.

Although they couldn't do much in such a short time, over the next hour they managed to work out signs for a few Eubic glyphs. With that and their tap code, Jeejon communicated what she had learned. The AUC had a visitors' center for tourists. At this time of year, in winter, it had no scheduled tours, but the center stayed open. They had too little money to rent a hovercar, but they could buy two tickets and ride the magrail north to Ockelbo. From there they could catch an airbus to the AUC. At the visitors' center, she would find someone in charge and tell them Kelric's story.

They both knew she would face disbelief. After her life as a slave, she feared both she and Kelric would be punished for bothering the authorities, then deported or imprisoned. Yet still she agreed to help, because she believed it would make his dying easier. And deep inside a part of her wondered—as he turned more gold each day, as she touched his gauntlets, as his mind brushed hers—if maybe, just maybe, some small part of what he told her was true.

When they finished making plans, she arranged to have the hotel EI wake them early the next morning. As they settled in to sleep, Kelric winced, his joints and muscles aching. The strain of using his deteriorating hydraulics was taking its toll on his body, particularly in this heavy gravity.

Jeejon nudged him onto his stomach. She undressed him, working his clothes out from under his body. Then, unasked, she gave him a slow, thorough massage, easing his pain. When he tried to offer her the same, knowing how the gravity exhausted her, she refused. From her mind, he picked up that she simply liked to feel him, that it relaxed her almost as much as him. After the massage, she touched him in ways he liked, brushing her fingers down his spine or over his arms. He sighed, settling into the nest of covers with relief.

Later she offered more sensual comforts, loving him with an untutored eroticism. And he loved her back, appreciating the gifts that life granted in the most unexpected ways.

* * *

The vibration under Kelric's seat stopped. Jeejon drew him to his feet. He pulled up the hood of his new parka, enjoying the soft synth-fur against his skin. It wasn't real fur, of course; on this ancient homeworld of humanity it had long been illegal to kill animals, those few species that remained.

Cold air hit his face as they stepped down from the bus. It was a "Tuesday" morning, whatever that meant. He moved in silence, aware of icy wind blowing across his face. He smelled trees and felt Jeejon's arm under his hand. They were walking up an incline. The ground was solid, maybe plastiflex or cement. He detected no other people, at least not nearby.

They walked slowly, both fatigued just by this short trip. How had humanity survived on this cold, heavy planet? Then again, Earth's humans didn't normally grow as big as Kelric or his ancestors, who had engineered themselves for a hot, low-gravity world. It wasn't his height so much as his musculature. At six foot seven, broad-shouldered and massive, he felt too heavy for the home of his own species.

"Jeejon?" he said.

She tapped her thumb on his knuckles.

"Are you all right?" he asked.

Puzzlement came from her mind. She tapped once. Yes.

"Your bones? Have you broken any?"

She projected the sense of a laugh and tapped twice. No.

He smiled, relieved she found the question funny. It suggested she wasn't in as much difficulty as he feared. "I'm sorry about the gravity."

She squeezed his arm.

"Is it far to the visitors' center?" he asked.

She tapped twice. No.

"Less than a hundred meters?"

Two taps. No.

He felt too tired to guess. It took all his concentration to keep limping up the hill. "Think the distance. As loud as you can."

Her thoughts brushed his, vague and distant.

"Again?" he asked.

Two hun . . .

"Two hundred meters?"

She tapped his knuckles. Yes.

Two hundred meters. Hardly any distance at all. The prospect loomed as if it were a light-year.

They continued on, slow and steady. His concentration drifted, but his body kept moving, directed by his worn-out hydraulics.

Jeejon tightened her grip, stopping him. Then she nudged him forward. He took a step and his foot hit a solid object. Raising his leg, he felt the barrier with the toe of his boot. A step.

They went up three stairs and walked forward again. The sweet scent of fresh wood wafted in the air. Stretching out his arm, he touched a wall made from planks. Real wood.

Jeejon took him inside the building. They went a short way, then stopped. He felt her attention on someone. Her hand clutched his so tight it made his fingers ache. Then she tapped her thumb five times on his knuckle, the signal for Kelric to talk.

He spoke in stumbling English. "Hello? Have you a person here who speaks Eubic? My friend speaks Eubic. I hear not."

He waited, in silence. Then Jeejon nudged him again. They went somewhere and sat in chairs.

As they waited, Kelric felt a curious sensation in his mind. A lightening? No. Anticipation? No. Something else. It came at a level below conscious thought, like a deep, deep drumbeat.

So deep.

What?

Jeejon drew him to his feet. They went to another part of the building. From changes in the air, he thought they walked through an open area, maybe a lobby. Then they entered a closed-in space. He stretched out his arms, but felt nothing. Understanding what he wanted, Jeejon nudged him to the side until his hand brushed a wall.

Eventually they sat down again, in an office maybe, though he wasn't sure. In the chair at his side, Jeejon moved as if she were speaking, gesturing with her hands. She stopped, spoke again, stopped. He picked up vague impressions from the others in the room, more than one person, at least two, maybe three. Their minds bathed his with a blurred mix of puzzlement, curiosity, and incredulity.

He also felt Jeejon's unease. She had no real idea what she was doing and little facility with words. Yet she kept on, doggedly, never giving up. Why this remarkable woman had given him such loyalty, he had no idea. He wished he had a way to repay her.

Throughout it all, the drumbeat in his mind continued, deep and full. It spread through him, filling his mental niches.

Puzzled.

Searching.

Where?

Kelric tilted his head, trying to understand the sensation. Then Jeejon drew him to his feet. Again they went for a long walk. He didn't think they were in the visitors' center anymore.

The next room smelled of antiseptic. At least four people were with them now. He stopped just inside the door, put off by what he sensed. A trap? Whoever he faced here, in this office, bore him neither ill will nor hostility. If anything, they seemed genuinely concerned for his health.

Mental health. Pah. They had brought him to a psychiatrist.

When Jeejon tugged his arm, he jerked away from her. "I'm not crazy," he said in Eubic.

The attention of everyone in the room focused on him. Distrust. Wariness. How did he know their location? Was he really deaf? Assurance from Jeejon. More questions from the others. He thought Jeejon was telling them he was an empath. They didn't believe her.

Suddenly she started to unfasten his parka. He caught her hand, clenching his fingers around hers. Gently she pried open his fist. Then she continued to undo his coat. He stood in a rigid posture, fighting the urge to knock away her hand. Finally she opened up his parka. A vibration transmitted to his neck as she tapped his collar. He understood then. Provider. It proved he was a psion.

Puzzlement. The Allied authorities had no idea what to make of his story. All the while the drum beat within him.

Stronger now.

A growing sense of... of what?

Recognition?

Something was happening now, Kelric didn't know what. Alarm tinged the thoughts of the AUC personnel. Why? It wasn't him, or not him exactly. Something else? Jeejon was puzzled too. What was happening?

The drum continued to beat.

Warmer.

Jeejon's hold on his arm tightened. Whatever was going on, she didn't understand. The other people in the room were bewildered. Their agitation became so strong, he picked up brief images from their minds. He glimpsed himself, standing tall and silent by the door, his hand clenched on Jeejon's arm, his gaze directed at no one, his hair shimmering gold, streaked with gray, his unseeing eyes pure gold, his skin gleaming gold in the light. No trace of the tattoo job remained.

The drum in his mind kept up its beat. It filled him like a sun. Filled him until he glowed. *Glowed.*

And then recognition came.

He understood. It wasn't a drum.

It was a heartbeat.

The heart of the sun.

Kelric had already turned to the door before he even realized what he was doing. He stepped out of the office, holding on to the doorframe for balance. Jeejon came with him, but she didn't try to stop him. The others also followed. They seemed unsure what to do. Stunned. Why? *Why?*

As the intensity of their focus increased, he glimpsed what one of them saw. Himself. He had just entered a short hallway. The entrance to a lobby stood only a few paces ahead, its door open, revealing the big room beyond. He could see across the lobby to a huge set of double doors that looked as if they might open to the outside, possibly onto the grounds of the AUC itself. The view was too blurred for him to pick up much, but he saw those doors.

The image faded, but Kelric kept moving. Gripping the wall for support, he limped toward the lobby. When he reached the entrance, he hung on to the doorframe, staring sightlessly toward the double doors. He wanted to go farther, but if he let go of his support, he feared he would fall.

The sun in his mind blazed.

He knew when the doors opened. Even if the image hadn't burst with vivid clarity into the minds of everyone around him, he still would have known.

Yes, he would have known.

Reflected from the minds of every person with him, he saw the doors across the lobby swing open. It was dark outside, but lamps glowed on the wooden porch. A woman stood silhouetted against their light.

A hip-length mane of spectacular gold hair blew back from her body in the wind. She was wearing an ankle-length night robe and beneath that a nightdress that fell in classical ivory drapes to her ankles. Her eyes, skin, hair, even her eyelashes—all shimmered gold. Tall and statuesque, like the realization of an ancient goddess in human form, or an angel come to Earth, she stood framed in the doorway, impossibly beautiful.

AUC soldiers surrounded her. Light glinted off their EM pulse rifles. They held the weapons awkwardly, as if unsure what to do with them while they escorted this glorious apparition. The woman held the doors wide open with both hands, gazing across the lobby at Kelric.

He took a step into the lobby, losing his grip on the doorframe. That was when the woman let go of the doors. She ran across the lobby, tears streaming down her golden face. The soldiers came as well, but no one tried to stop her. She called out, her lips forming Kelric's name. Her heartbeat filled him, steady and strong, thrumming with life, heritage, blood. Her sunlight filled his mind.

They met in the center of the lobby. He took her into his arms, as astonished as always to find himself so much taller than she. She held him tight, her head against his shoulder, her tears soaking into his shirt. He was crying too, but he didn't care. The tears rolled down his cheeks, free and clear.

Hoshma, he thought. *I've come home.*

His mother's stunned, astonished, overjoyed welcome filled his mind.

27

Heritage

Darkness.
Silence.

System End

Restart

"Imperator Skolia?" The woman's craggy voice came again, in Iotic, quietly insistent. Kelric absorbed the words.

Words?

Yes, words.

"He still isn't responding," a man said.

"Wait." That came from another man. "I'm getting a spike in his brain activity."

"Lord Skolia," the woman said. "Can you hear us?"

Yes, Kelric thought. He wanted to shout the words from every mountain on the planet. Barring hallelujahs, a whisper would have sufficed. He couldn't seem to manage even that, though.

He was lying on a bed. His eyelids felt heavy. He had on soft trousers, probably pajamas. Oddly enough, he still wore his gauntlets.

Bolt? he thought. *Can you talk?*

"Yes," Bolt said.

The woman made an exultant sound. "He spoke!"

One of the men said, "It came from his arm."

There was a silence. Then the other man said, "His arm?"

"The comm in the apparatus he's wearing."

Another silence. The woman said, "Imperator Skolia, can you hear me?"

Bolt, tell them I can hear. He felt like grinning, but his smile muscles weren't responding either.

"Yes, he can hear you," Bolt said.

"He?" one of the men asked.

Identify yourself, Kelric thought.

"I'm Bolt," the node said. "The node implanted in his body. I've linked to the comm in his gauntlets."

"Good Lord," one of the men said.

"Why can't we get the gauntlets off him?" the woman asked.

Good question, Kelric thought.

"We don't know," Bolt said.

"We?" she asked.

"Imperator Skolia and me."

"Ah." She paused. "Lord Skolia, we're going to remove the gel from your eyes."

Ask what that means. Kelric thought.

"What does that mean?" Bolt asked.

"We worked on your optic nerves," one of the men said. "The gel packs protected your eyes while you healed."

"Will he be able to see?" Bolt asked, anticipating Kelric's question.

"We don't know," the other man said.

Fingertips brushed Kelric temples. He lay still while one of the doctors loosened something on his face. The pressure on his eyelids eased, then went away. He tried opening his eyes, but his lids remained closed.

"Can't see," he whispered.

"*That* was him," one of the men said.

The woman spoke gently. "It needs time."

Kelric wet his lips. "My parents..."

"They've been here almost continuously," she said.

"Here?"

"In the AUC hospital."

"How long?"

In the same gentle voice she said, "Three weeks."

Three weeks? If he remembered his Allied time measures right, that meant twenty-one days. So long.

She massaged the corner of his eye with her fingertip. "We've done a great deal of work. That's why you were down for three weeks. We also arranged with your government for a team of biomech specialists to come here."

Softly he said, "Thank you."

"You're welcome." She massaged his other eyelid.

For a while he simply lay, enjoying the fact that he was alive. Then he said, "Where... Jeejon?"

"With your parents." The woman checked his eyes again. "Can you open them now?"

Slowly he raised his eyelids. The blackness around him lightened a bit.

"How is it?" a man asked from the other side of the bed.

"Gray," Kelric answered.

"That's good," he said. "It means you're detecting light."

"More... than light." The outline of a head was becoming visible. It was a doctor standing by his bed. She had weathered features and a cap of snowy hair.

This time Kelric did manage a smile. "Doctor... you're a vision."

She gave a good-natured snort. "I'm an old workhorse." Then she added, "You're going to make it, Imperator Skolia.

Momentarily left alone by his stream of doctors, Kelric reclined in his hospital bed, sitting up comfortably. Half asleep, warm, and without pain, he was content.

Apparently during the past three weeks, the doctors had kept him "turned off" while they made repairs. Today they turned him back on. Now his body had to reintegrate its new systems. With so much new biomech, he expected to feel like a machine. He didn't, though. He felt more human than he had in a long time.

He became aware of a change. Blinking, he opened his eyes.

His new optical systems focused. A man was standing by his bed. Wine-red hair brushed his shoulders. He wore gold-rimmed spectacles, a choice he made because he had never been comfortable with the glittering medical technology of his wife's universe. His eyes were the same dark violet as those of Kelric's Coban son. At five foot ten, this man was shorter than most of his towering sons. Freckles dusted his nose. More silver showed in his hair than Kelric remembered, and more lines around his eyes.

The man smiled. "My greetings."

Kelric's voice caught. "It's good to see you, Hoshpa."

Moisture glimmered in his father's eyes. "And you, Kellie." He reddened. "Kelric, I mean."

Kelric smiled at the boyhood name. He doubted his parents would ever really lose the habit of using it. He and his father reached for each other at the same time. Closing his eyes, Kelric embraced the aging bard. This AUC might not be any place he had known before, but with his family here, it was home.

Eldrinson gave an odd, strangled gasp. Mortified, Kelric let him go. Just what his father needed, to be crushed by his long lost son.

Eldrinson laughed. "You always were the strong one." His smile faded. "After your Jag was lost—your mother and I, we always hoped. But there seemed no chance you were alive." He slid his hand across his cheek, under his spectacles, wiping away a tear. "Yet here you are."

Something inside Kelric released, like ice melting. For all that Eldrinson Althor Valdoria, the Key to the Web, presented a reserved demeanor to the rest of humanity, with his family he had never hidden his feelings. Both his parents were that way, and many of his siblings. The balm of their warmth healed his loneliness.

Sometime, somewhere, he and his parents had switched roles. He had become the protector, the Jagernaut, the warrior. Now, as Imperator, that shift was complete. But though he might be the bulwark, he would always treasure the haven of their love.

"You've a nephew now," his father said. "Ami's son."

"Ami?"

"Kurj's widow."

"Kurj married?" That surprised him. Although his half brother had taken many lovers, he had never shown interest in marriage. Kelric spoke carefully, knowing his room had to be monitored by the hospital staff, Allied military intelligence, and probably ISC spies as well. "And Majda?"

In a reserved voice his father said, "General Majda sends her salutations and joy at your return."

But? Kelric thought.

Eldrinson jerked as if he had been shoved by a great, ragged power.

Gods, Kelric thought. Had he done that?

It is all right. His father's thought flowed like a serene river, deep and sure, power without undue force. ***Is Naaj Majda truly pleased at your return? I can't say. The ties between the Ruby Dynasty and Majda have always been strong. But still. I am glad you are here, rather than there. Better you face ISC with all your strength.***

So. He had made the right decision. He smiled, wondering what Jeejon thought now about his tale of the bumbling Ruby prince.

His father winced, then rubbed his temple. Kelric's good humor faded. Would he damage the Triad? His mind was full of jagged, injured edges. Already his father was fatiguing under the onslaught.

I'm fine, Eldrinson thought.

I don't want to hurt you or Dehya, Kelric answered.

You won't. Your mind is much like Kurj's and he fit well in the Triad. You just need time to heal. Then he stopped, puzzled. ***You said Dehya?***

I reached her in the Lock. She's in there somehow.

I, too, have thought she lives. How and where, I can't say.

Nor I.

I've said nothing to the Allieds. Better they don't know another of us may be free.

Kelric nodded. **Yes.**

Eldrinson glanced at Kelric's neck. "I'm sorry your doctors haven't been able to remove the collar yet."

Kelric touched the gold band. "Do you know why?"

"Its systems are too intertwined with your biomech. It would injure you if they just pulled it out. They have to operate, to unravel its picotech from yours."

It didn't surprise him. He brushed his fingers over one of his gauntlets. "And these?"

Dryly his father said, "Those apparently don't wish to come off. They shock anyone who tries to touch them."

Kelric blinked. "They almost seem alive."

His father nodded. "They have some kind of ancient AI." Then he asked, "How did you get them?"

"In the Lock. The drawer in the console. Didn't you know?"

His father shook his head. "I never saw a drawer."

Kelric wasn't sure how he had known it existed. No sign of it showed in the console. He suspected the gauntlets had their own mind, an ancient EI unlike any they used now, one that may have lain quiescent for millennia.

"I've taken them off," he said. "So has Jeejon." They had wanted his permission before they let her remove them, though.

"Jeejon? You mean your friend from Spikedown?"

"Yes." Kelric leaned forward. "Is she here?"

His father watched him with that gaze of his that had always seen more than Kelric intended to reveal. Gently he said, "She and your mother are outside. The doctors would only let one of us see you at a time."

So Jeejon was all right. He exhaled, settling back in bed.

"She told us how you met," Eldrinson said. "Gods know how you survived all those years."

At first Kelric didn't know what he meant. Then he realized they all must have assumed he had been a Trader slave these past eighteen years. If he told him it wasn't true, he would have to explain, which would jeopardize Ixpar and his children. He couldn't lie, though, not to his father.

He hesitated, wanting a private communication but fearing to injure Eldrinson's mind.

Son, I'm fine.

Kelric reddened. His father had been in the Triad for decades. He was well able to judge what his mind could handle.

She didn't transcend, he thought.

She? his father asked.

Tarquine Iquar. The Aristo who bought me.

Eldrinson stiffened. ***No one "owns" my son.***

Well, yes. Dryly Kelric thought, **I felt that way too.**

I didn't know it was possible for them to stop transcending.

She had part of her brain taken out.

His father stared at him. ***What?***

Her KAB. She had it removed. So she wouldn't be tempted.

I'm surprised the other Aristos haven't destroyed her. Don't they consider that an aberration?

They don't know. Regarding his father steadily, Kelric added, **I don't want them to know, either. Or anyone.**

Eldrinson gave him a long, appraising look. Kelric met his gaze. He wasn't sure how he felt about Tarquine, but he knew his father would see past any smoke screen he tried to create. So he said nothing.

Finally Eldrinson thought, ***Why don't you want anyone to know?***

I can negotiate with her. Kelric rubbed his chin. **We've been dealing with them all wrong. There are better ways. I need to think on it more. I believe we might find our way to a treaty, especially now that the Lock is dead.**

Deactivated.

Kelric raised his eyebrows.

A slight smile quirked Eldrinson's mouth. **Yes, I know that trick.** He gave Kelric another of his looks. **I do believe you can do it.**

It?

Deal with the Hightons.

Kelric swallowed, gratified by such an expression of confidence from one of the people whose opinion he most valued.

He wondered what the various spies monitoring his room thought about this silence. He and his father were watching each other, running through a gamut of facial expressions and gestures. It was obvious they were having a conversation. How did one monitor telepaths? With other telepaths, of course. However, none was as powerful as the Ruby Dynasty. So none could penetrate the barriers he and his father raised around their psilink. No way to eavesdrop. *Tough luck,* he thought to the unseen spies.

Eldrinson smiled. **Tough indeed.** Watching Kelric, he added, **That is astounding about the Finance Minister.**

Yes. Kelric still found it hard to believe.

Are more of them like that?

I wondered about Emperor Qox.

Eldrinson went very still. **Why?**

I met him. He was in the Lock when I joined the Triad. A way existed to verify at least part of what Jaibriol had told him. **He claims the Allieds traded him for Eldrin.**

It's true.

Kelric stared at him. **Eldrin is free?**

Yes. Or not free, but in Allied custody on the planet Delos. They will bring him here.

That's good. Incredible.

Yes. It is. Eldrinson's simple words, so calmly given, held a world of emotion. In a matter of days, he had regained two children he had thought lost to war. Quietly he thought, **It is very good.**

Kelric felt his eyes grow hot. Better to change the subject, or he might embarrass himself by shedding tears.

What else happened? his father asked.

Qox let me go.

Why?

He claims he wants to meet at the peace table.

But you doubt him.

He is Qox.

Maybe this one is different.

Kelric wondered about his father. What did he see? **I did have an odd sense of him.**

Odd how?

Kelric wasn't sure yet he wanted to reveal his suspicion that Jaibriol III was a psion. Instead he thought, **He told me to talk to Seth Rockworth.**

Eldrinson exhaled. *I'm afraid you will have trouble doing that. Admiral Rockworth has been in military custody since Jaibriol III ascended his throne. The boy had been living in Rockworth's home as a refugee.*

It didn't surprise Kelric that Seth was in custody. He doubted the Allieds had been happy to learn one of their war heroes sheltered the heir apparent to the Carnelian Throne. **What does Rockworth say?**

He didn't know Qox's identity. Eldrinson rubbed his chin. *Seth also took in three other refugee children. Apparently none was pure Aristo, though all showed signs of Aristo heritage.*

Jaibriol III looks pure Highton. Almost too perfect. **Where are the other three?**

Apparently they ran off. So far no trace of them has shown up. All we have are the names Seth gave them. Jay, Lisa, Peter, and Kelly Rockworth.

Jay. It was obviously short for Jaibriol. **Peter is the English version of the Aristo name Vitar. I don't know about Lisa.** Then he scowled. **You said Kelly?**

His father smiled. *You don't have sole rights to the name, you know.*

Who were they?

We may never know. Eldrinson adjusted his spectacles. ***I do wish we could find them.***

Why?

I should like to meet them. To better understand this new emperor. They spent over a year with him in Rockworth's home. Eldrinson shook his head. ***During the Radiance War, Jaibriol III was going to high school in the Appalachian Mountains on Earth. Apparently he was a good student, shy and reserved, but well liked. We know nothing of his background.***

So strange, Kelric thought. Maybe they would never know the full truth.

Quietly Eldrinson thought, ***Sometimes the truth does more harm than good. The children are probably safer wherever they went.***

Safer for whom? Us or them? Kelric leaned forward. **This is a truth, Father. Someday I will see that all our family is safe and free. I swear it to you.**

Eldrinson's face gentled. ***Then I can rest content, my son.***

It was his first sight of Jeejon.

She came in while he was dozing in his raised bed. He opened his eyes to see her reading a chart by his bed. Her face was as he had imagined: strong, with clean lines, high cheekbones, and a firm chin. She had brown eyes. Gray curls drifted around her face, looking as soft as they had felt. However her nose had once appeared, it had a crook now. Lines showed around her eyes and mouth, as if she smiled a lot.

"I knew it," he said. "You *are* beautiful."

Startled, she looked up at him. "You're supposed to be asleep." Then she crossed her arms and averted her gaze. "Sorry to wake you, Your Esteemed Imperatorness."

"Jeejon, come on." He pulled himself up straight. "Look at me."

She glowered at him. "Haven't the right."

"You liked looking at me fine what I was a provider."

"That was before you turned out to be king of the universe."

Kelric laughed. "I just command ISC." He moved to the side of the bed. "Come up here with me."

This time she seemed genuinely puzzled. "Why?"

Exasperated, he said, "Because I want to hold you."

"Why?"

"Why?" He blinked. "I don't know. I just do. I like to." He supposed it wasn't the most romantic declaration. But it was true.

She lowered the rail and climbed up next to him. Pulling her into his arms, he nuzzled her hair. So they sat, she with her head resting against his chest.

"What happens now?" she asked.

"The Allieds will keep me here. Beyond that, I'm not sure."

"I understand."

He didn't like the sound of that. "Understand what? I hope you aren't planning to walk out on me."

"Don't make fun of me."

"I'm not."

"We both know the reality."

"What reality?"

She shrugged. "I'm a former slave. No position, no wealth, no nothing. Old. Ugly. Imperator needs a better arrangement."

"One part of that is true. You are a former slave. Like me."

"Oh, Kelric."

"'Oh, Kelric'? What does that mean? You're right, you have no wealth. So what? I have more than anyone needs. As for arranged marriages, I've already done that. More than you know. This time I choose my own woman. And I like the way you look. I don't want you to change. So you're not a vacuum-headed trophy bimbo. Neither am I."

A smile tugged her mouth. "You certainly aren't."

"Will you stay with me?"

"You really want?"

"I really want. I'll put it in writing."

"You don't have to do that."

"I don't want any question about your status." Without the protection of his title, Jeejon would have a rough time, surrounded by the intrigues of the Imperial court. If he wanted to keep her with him, he needed to make sure no doubt existed as to her position.

Still, that decision left him with a sense of loss. With Jeejon as his consort, he couldn't return to Ixpar, at least not while Jeejon lived. Although he had already known, at a basic level, that such a return was unrealistic, this made it final.

He feared he wouldn't have Jeejon long either. She had neither his genetics nor the benefit of life-extension treatments started from birth. The Traders worked their low-rank taskmakers hard and threw them away after they used them up. Jeejon was near the end of her supposedly useful years. But she could still start the treatments. She didn't have to die just because the Traders decreed it. She wouldn't have a life span anywhere near as long as his, but they could still have a few good years together.

Jeejon sighed. "It's crazy, Kelric."

"I really wish you would quit calling me crazy," he grumbled. "Say yes instead."

"You'll dump me for a pretty provider."

"We don't have providers."

"You know what I mean."

"Marriages among the nobility don't work that way. I can't 'dump' you. Adultery is punishable by execution."

"So why get stuck with me?"

"It's not 'stuck.' I want to be with you."

"Why?"

"I don't know. Because we have a good neural resonance, better than I've had with most people. Hell, Jeejon, it started the moment I met you."

At first, when he felt her shaking, he thought she was crying. Smugly he realized he had moved her to tears. That was more like it. Then it dawned on him that she was laughing.

"What's so funny?" he growled.

"'We have a good neural resonance'? Very romantic proposal."

He gave a rueful smile. "Well, you know."

"I suppose it would be good to be queen of the universe."

"You *suppose?*"

Softly she said, "I suppose I am deeply honored, Kelric. It is hard for me to say romantic things too."

He settled her more comfortably in his arms. It was the first time, as an adult, that he had proposed to a woman. He had been married six times, but in every case either he had no choice or else the woman had done the asking.

Kelric bent his head and spoke against her ear. "Too bad we have no privacy in here."

"We could turn out the lights."

"They would watch on IR." In truth, he never wanted to be in darkness again. He would sleep with all the lights on.

"It's all right," Jeejon said. "You can see whenever you want."

He brushed his lips across her hair. "You see too much." She might as well be an empath, for how well she was learning to read him.

She laughed softly. So they sat together, each giving the other something they had never known before, she the choice to be free and he the freedom to choose.

Epilogue

A holostage filled the front of the small, elegantly paneled auditorium. Kelric stood back from the stage, with his mother on one side and Jeejon on the other. A few paces away, always discreet but always present, soldiers in the AUC peacekeeping force kept guard on them. Tiller Smith, the Allied liaison to the Ruby Dynasty, stood next to Kelric's mother.

Today Jeejon showed less strain. Apparently the treatments to help her deal with the gravity were working. Kelric shifted his feet, leaning his weight on his burnished cane. It was a beautiful piece, carved from pine wood, with vines engraved along its length and the head of a lion for its top. His doctors had wanted him to use a hover chair, but he refused. Until he had full control of his new hydraulics, he needed support in this gravity, but he wanted to be on his own feet. Especially today.

The holostage formed an ellipse. His father sat at one focus, facing a screen that curved around the other focus. Eldrinson's chair had an ornate back worked with gold and rubies. Kelric doubted it was coincidence that it resembled a throne. Great care had been taken in choreographing this event.

Console banks curved around the back of the holostage, each staffed by three operators. A hum of words passed among them and also over the comms on the consoles, as the many people across Earth involved in the planning for today tried to make sure nothing went wrong. More officials stood near Kelric and his family, all waiting. Harold Cohen, the president of the Allied Worlds of Earth, waited with them. A dignified man with curly brown hair sprinkled by gray, he stood near the holostage watching Kelric's father.

An operator spoke from one of the consoles. "We're ready here, Mr. President," she said.

Cohen nodded and turned to Eldrinson. "At your wish, Your Highness."

"You may begin," Eldrinson said.

The president glanced at the operator. "Activate."

She took a deep breath. Then she spoke into the comm, in Swedish, her voice clear and well modulated. "His Royal Highness Eldrinson Althor Valdoria, Web Key to the Triad and King of Skyfall."

Kelric blinked. It always disconcerted him when he heard his father called the King of Starfall. True, "Skyfall" was a Skolian translation for the word Lyshriol, the name of his home world. But "king"? Eldrinson's title was Dalvador Bard, a hereditary position that involved recording the history of the Dalvador Plains in ballads, commanding the Dalvador army, and serving as the judiciary system for the Plains area. He was hardly "king" of an entire planet. For that matter, since he no longer lived on Lyshriol, the acting role of Bard had gone to one of Kelric's older brothers. Even if the title lacked accuracy, though, the image of the handsome, rustic king with his gold queen and beautiful children had a great deal of appeal in the media.

A deep voice with a Highton accent came over another console: "His Esteemed Highness, Jaibriol the Third, descended from the Line of Qox, son of Jaibriol the Second, grandson of Ur, great-grandson of Jaibriol the First, and great-great-grandson of Eube, Sublime Founder of the Concord."

Kelric's mother snorted. "Give them another few generations and it will take so long to introduce their emperor, they won't have time to send warships against us."

Kelric smiled. "A novel method for attaining peace."

On the stage opposite Eldrinson, a holographic image appeared, a young man sitting in a chair inlaid with carnelian gems. Kelric recognized him: this was the Highton he had met on the Third Lock.

Jaibriol and Eldrinson regarded each other. A tense silence followed, as everyone waited to see who would speak first. Skolian and Eubian protocols, both derived from ancient Ruby formalities, required the person requesting the communication to begin. In cases such as this, which had been a carefully orchestrated proposal from both sides, the lesser power went first. If the powers were matched or disputed, the newest leader went first. If experience was matched, the youngest spoke.

Today, whoever spoke first lost an edge. That leader would be implying either that his counterpart won the Radiance War or else that no one could claim victory. Most agreed the war had no winner, but neither side had made a formal statement. If they accepted an equal balance, then Eldrinson's greater age and experience required Jaibriol speak first. But if Jaibriol spoke, it implied the Highton emperor considered the Ruby Dynasty deserving of protocols reserved only for those that Aristos considered human—which meant Aristos. If Eldrinson went first, it implied he accepted that definition. It would also weaken his position by relinquishing his rank to a younger ruler.

Kelric didn't see how they could break the deadlock. Regardless of what people such as Tarquine and Taratus said in private, the Qox Dynasty would never formally acknowledge the Ruby Dynasty as an equal. And Eldrinson would never acknowledge a denial of his rank.

As the two leaders watched each other, the silence became strained. Kelric had an odd sense, almost as if both wished they could speak. It was subtle, an effect he noticed only from a lifetime as an empath who could match body language with what he picked up from people's minds.

Then Jaibriol spoke in Highton. "The Line of Qox acknowledges the Ruby Dynasty."

In the resonant voice that had made his spectacular baritone legendary, Eldrinson answered in Highton. "The Imperial Dynasty acknowledges the ascension of Jaibriol the Third to the Carnelian Throne."

A clever solution, Kelric thought. Jaibriol acknowledged Eldrinson's seniority, but dictated they use his language, which the Hightons considered the tongue of true humans. Usually Skolian-Eube discussions were carried out in a neutral Allied tongue.

So began the negotiations between Ruby and Qox to arrange peace talks, which would take place on Earth. The Skolian representatives would be First Assembly Councilor Barcala Tikal, Eldrinson, Kelric, Roca, General Majda, and a number of ISC officers and Assembly councilors. The Hightons would include Jaibriol, Corbal Xir, Calope Muze, Admiral Kaliga, and several ESComm officers and Ministers. Kelric wondered what it would be like to see Tarquine again, or what Kaliga would think when his truant rimwalker showed up as Imperator. They would all attend as holographic simulacra. The Allieds had no intention of letting the Ruby Dynasty appear in person, lest they find a way to escape. Also, the risk of putting so many interstellar leaders in one place was far too great. However, everyone benefited from the symbolism of Earth as a neutral site.

After Eldrinson and Jaibriol had spoken for a while, the Allied president beckoned to Kelric. So Kelric limped forward, using his cane. He climbed the dais alone, under his own power, and walked to his father. He stood behind Eldrinson's chair, tall and strong, like a protective wall. Imperator.

Jaibriol III nodded to him. "Imperator Skolia."

Kelric nodded. "Emperor Qox." Would Jaibriol reveal they had met? He doubted it; Qox had nothing to gain and everything to lose if the truth became known.

Jaibriol spoke the formal words. "The Line of Qox acknowledges the ascension of Kelricson Garlin Valdoria to the Imperial Triad."

Kelric wondered how the emperor felt, having to acknowledge a man who still wore the slave collar of a provider. Strange, how the universe worked.

Standing behind his father's chair, he listened as his father and Jaibriol resumed their negotiations. After various convoluted exchanges meant to establish goodwill, the emperor said, "As proof of our good intent in this endeavor, I have pardoned Jafe Maccar, the Skolian merchant arrested and imprisoned by ESComm."

Kelric felt his father's surprise. "A magnanimous gesture, Your Highness," Eldrinson said.

Jaibriol glanced at Kelric. His eyebrows quirked. Kelric nodded, astonished, but managing to keep his reaction modulated to a more appropriate reserve.

A channel was opening. Perhaps Qox and Skolia could find a way to navigate its currents. Kelric knew now how to approach the Aristos: more than that, he knew at least two who might be willing to talk. Maybe more.

Hope gusted through his thoughts. He saw a future he valued, one where he might make a useful contribution. Instead of a warlord, perhaps he could truly become a maker of peace.

Time Line

circa 4000 B.C.	Group of humans moved from Earth to Raylicon
circa 3600 B.C.	Ruby Dynasty begins
circa 3100 B.C.	Raylicans launch first interstellar flights; rise of Ruby Empire
circa 2900 B.C.	Ruby Empire begins decline
circa 2800 B.C.	Last interstellar flights; Ruby Empire collapses . . .
circa 1300 A.D.	Raylicans begin attempts to regain lost knowledge and colonies
1843	Raylicans regain interstellar flight
1866	Rhon genetic project begins
1871	Aristos found Eubian Concord (aka Trader Empire)
1881	Lahaylia Selei born
1904	Lahaylia Selei founds Skolian Imperialate
2005	Jarac born
2111	Lahaylia Selei marries Jarac
2119	Dyhianna Selei born
2122	Earth achieves interstellar flight
2132	Earth founds Allied Worlds
2144	Roca born
2169	Kurj born
2203	Roca marries Eldrinson Althor Valdoria

2204	Eldrin Valdoria born; Jarac dies; Kurj becomes Imperator; Lahaylia dies
2206	Althor Izam-Na Valdoria born
2209	Havyrl (Vyrl) Torcellei Valdoria born
2210	Sauscony (Soz) Lahaylia Valdoria born
2219	Kelricson (Kelric) Garlin Valdoria born
2237	Jaibriol II born
2240	Soz meets Jato Stormson ("Aurora in Four Voices")
2241	Kelric marries Admiral Corey Majda
2243	Corey is assassinated ("Light and Shadow")
2258	Kelric crashes on Coba (*The Last Hawk*)
early 2259	Soz meets Jaibriol (*Primary Inversion*)
late 2259	Soz and Jaibriol go into exile *(The Radiant Seas)*
2260	Jaibriol III born (aka Jaibriol Qox Skolia)
2263	Rocalisa Qox Skolia born
2268	Vitar Qox Skolia born
2273	del-Kelric Qox Skolia born
2274	Radiance War begins (also called Domino War)
2276	Traders capture Eldrin; Radiance War ends
2277	Kelric returns home *(Ascendant Sun);* Dehya coalesces *(Spherical Harmonic)*
2278	Kamoj Argali meets Vyrl *(The Quantum Rose*)
2279	Althor Vyan Selei born
2328	Althor Vyan Selei meets Tina Santis Pulivok (*Catch the Lightning)*

Family Tree: RUBY DYNASTY

Boldface names refer to members of the Rhon. The Selei name denotes the direct line of the Ruby Pharaoh. All children of Roca and Eldrinson take Valdoria as their third name. All members of the Rhon within the Ruby Dynasty have the right to use Skolia as their last name. "Del" in front of a name means "in honor of."

= marriage

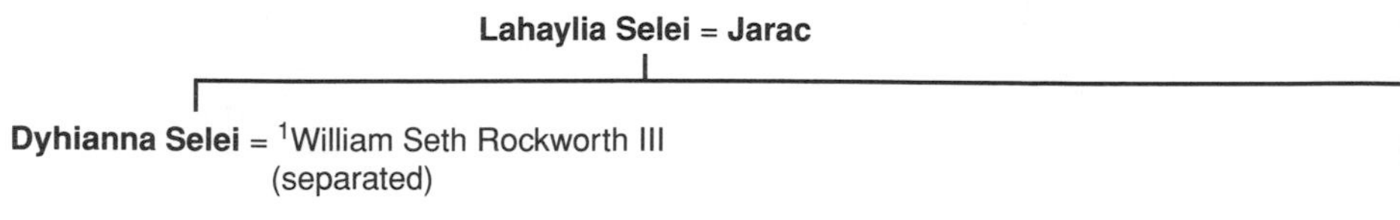

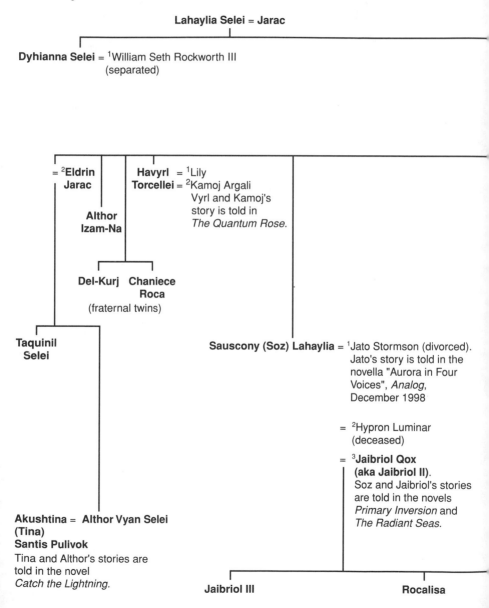

Lahaylia Selei = **Jarac**

Dyhianna Selei = [1]William Seth Rockworth III (separated)

= [2]**Eldrin Jarac**

Althor Izam-Na

Havyrl Torcellei = [1]Lily
= [2]Kamoj Argali
Vyrl and Kamoj's story is told in *The Quantum Rose.*

Del-Kurj **Chaniece Roca**
(fraternal twins)

Taquinil Selei

Sauscony (Soz) Lahaylia = [1]Jato Stormson (divorced). Jato's story is told in the novella "Aurora in Four Voices", *Analog*, December 1998

= [2]Hypron Luminar (deceased)

= [3]**Jaibriol Qox (aka Jaibriol II)**. Soz and Jaibriol's stories are told in the novels *Primary Inversion* and *The Radiant Seas.*

Akushtina (Tina) Santis Pulivok = **Althor Vyan Selei**
Tina and Althor's stories are told in the novel *Catch the Lightning.*

Jaibriol III

Rocalisa

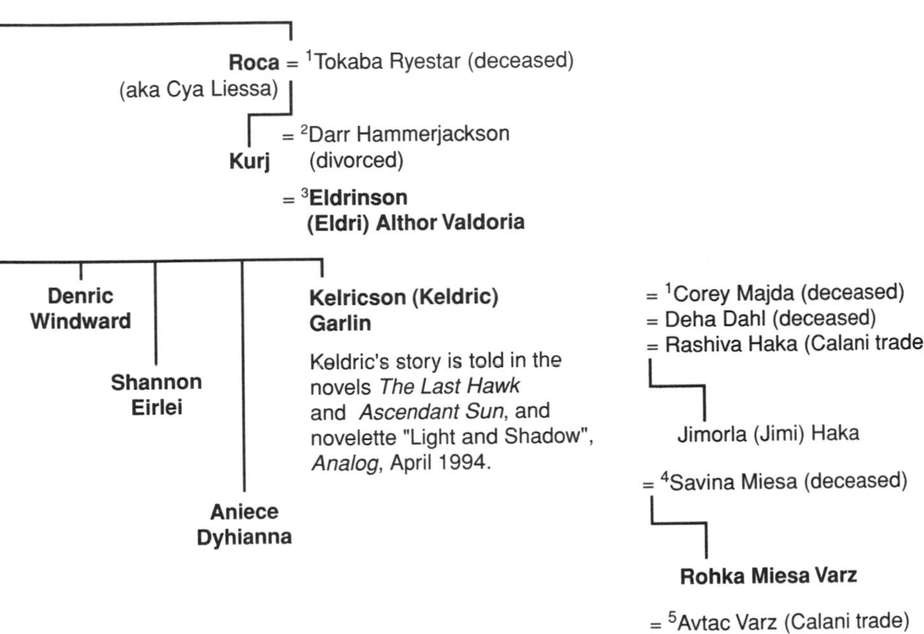
Roca = [1]Tokaba Ryestar (deceased)
(aka Cya Liessa)
= [2]Darr Hammerjackson (divorced)
Kurj
= [3]Eldrinson (Eldri) Althor Valdoria
Denric Windward
Shannon Eirlei
Aniece Dyhianna
Kelricson (Keldric) Garlin
Keldric's story is told in the novels The Last Hawk and Ascendant Sun, and novelette "Light and Shadow", Analog, April 1994.
= [1]Corey Majda (deceased)
= Deha Dahl (deceased)
= Rashiva Haka (Calani trade)
Jimorla (Jimi) Haka
= [4]Savina Miesa (deceased)
Rohka Miesa Varz
= [5]Avtac Varz (Calani trade)
= [6]Ixpar Karn

Vitar **del-Kelric**

Family Tree: Qox Dynasty

Boldface names refer to members of the Rhon.

● female ■ male = marriage + children by

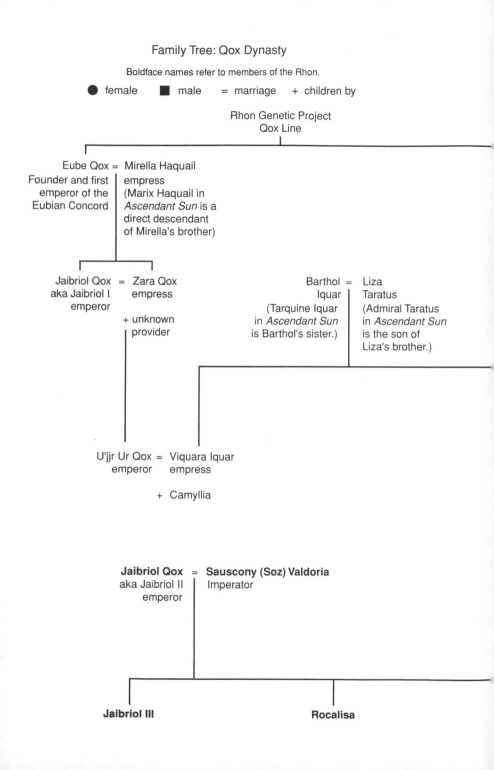

Rhon Genetic Project
Qox Line

Eube Qox = Mirella Haquail
Founder and first emperor of the Eubian Concord
empress
(Marix Haquail in *Ascendant Sun* is a direct descendant of Mirella's brother)

Jaibriol Qox = Zara Qox
aka Jaibriol I
emperor
empress

+ unknown provider

Barthol Iquar = Liza Taratus
(Tarquine Iquar in *Ascendant Sun* is Barthol's sister.)
(Admiral Taratus in *Ascendant Sun* is the son of Liza's brother.)

U'jjr Ur Qox = Viquara Iquar
emperor
empress

+ Camyllia

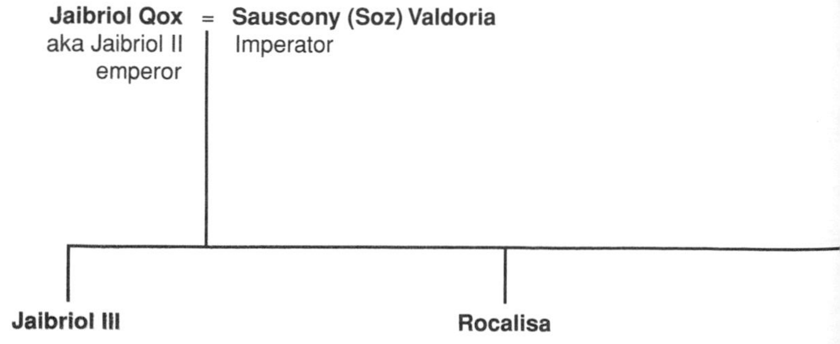

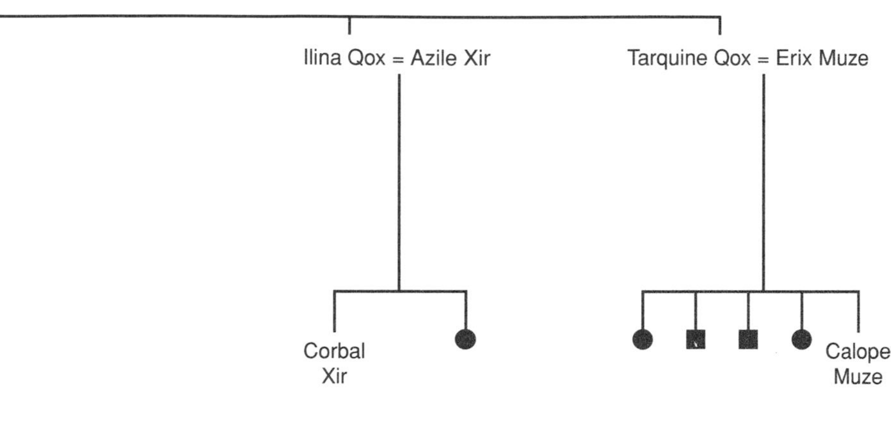

Barthol II

The great-grandson of Barthol II is Kryx Iquar, the Eubian Trade Minister in *Catch the Lightning.*

Vitar

del-Kelric

About the Author

Catherine Asaro grew up near Berkeley, California. She earned her Ph.D. in chemical physics and her A.M. in physics, both from Harvard, and a B.S. with highest honors in chemistry from UCLA. Among the places she has done research are the University of Toronto, the Max Planck Institut in Germany, and Harvard. She currently runs Molecudyne Research and lives in Maryland with her husband and daughter. A former dancer, she founded the Mainly Jazz Dance program at Harvard and now teaches at the Caryl Maxwell Classical Ballet, home to the Ellicott City Ballet Guild.

She has also written *Primary Inversion, Catch the Lightning, The Last Hawk, The Radiant Seas,* and *The Quantum Rose,* all set in the Skolian Empire/Ruby Dynasty universe and *The Veiled Web,* a near-future suspense novel. *Catch the Lightning* won the 1997 UTC Reader's Choice Award for best science fiction novel and the 1997 Sapphire Award for best science fiction romance. *The Last Hawk* was on the final ballot for the Nebula Award. Her Ruby Dynasty novella, "Aurora in Four Voices," the cover story of the December 1998 *Analog,* won the Analog Readers poll, the CompuServe Homer Award, was on both the Nebula and Hugo Award final ballots, and was listed on the *Locus* and *Tangent* Recommended Reading lists.

Catherine can be reached by E-mail at asaro@sff.net and on the Web at http://www.sff.net/people/asaro/. To be put on Catherine's E-mail list for notices about upcoming books, please send E-mail to the above address.